CONSERVATORY OF MUSIC

CENTRAL PERFORMING STAGE

P9-ELG-083

RUIN OF THE ORIGINAL CONSERVATORY OF MUSIC

TEMPLE OF HEROES OF SUPERLATIVE CHARACTER

HALL OF THE EIGHT PRECIOUS VIRTUES

HALL OF LILTING RADIANCE

BOYS' AND GIRLS' DORMITORIES

COURTYARD OF SUPREME PLACIDNESS

BRIDGE OF SERENE HARMONY

TEMPLE OF SAGACIOUS MONK GOOM AND CHINGU

GALLERY OF PARAGONS OF HONOR

EASTERN HEAVEN DINING HALL

GREAT GATE OF COMPLETE CENTRALITY AND PERFECT UPRIGHTNESS

PEARL FAMOUS ACADEMY of SKATE AND SWORD

RAIL-GONDOLA TOWERS

PEASPROUT CHEN

BATTLE OF CHAMPIONS

HENRY LIEN

HENRY HOLT AND COMPANY
NEW YORK

Henry Holt and Company, *Publishers since 1866*
Henry Holt® is a registered trademark of Macmillan Publishing Group, LLC
175 Fifth Avenue, New York, New York 10010 • mackids.com

Library of Congress Cataloging-in-Publication Data

Names: Lien, Henry, author.
Title: Peasprout Chen: battle of champions / Henry Lien.
Description: First edition. | New York : Henry Holt and Company, 2019. |
    Series: Peasprout Chen ; [2] | Summary: "Second book in a Taiwanese-inspired
    middle-grade fantasy series about a young girl's quest to become a champion of wu liu,
    an art form that blends figure skating with martial arts"—Provided by publisher.
Identifiers: LCCN 2018021022 | ISBN 9781250165756 (hardcover) |
    ISBN 9781250165763 (ebook)
Subjects: CYAC: Martial arts—Fiction. | Ice skating—Fiction. |
    Schools—Fiction. | Asia—Fiction.
Classification: LCC PZ7.1.L536 Pe 2017 | DDC [Fic]—dc23
LC record available at https://lccn.loc.gov/2018021022

Our books may be purchased in bulk for promotional, educational, or business use. Please contact
your local bookseller or the Macmillan Corporate and Premium Sales Department at
(800) 221-7945 ext. 5442 or by email at MacmillanSpecialMarkets@macmillan.com.

First edition, 2019 / Designed by Carol Ly
Printed in the United States of America by LSC Communications, Harrisonburg, Virginia
1 3 5 . 7 9 10 8 6 4 2

Sisters of the skate,
Brothers of the blade,
Come and lend your hands
and stand up for your motherland.
Answer the command,
"Come and join our band!"

—"THE PEARLIAN BATTLESONG"

CHAPTER
ONE

He says his familial name is Niu.

And his personal name is Hisashi.

He has dimples, like the boy that I knew.

We stand before the Great Gate of Complete Centrality and Perfect Uprightness at the entrance to Pearl Famous Academy of Skate and Sword. I know we should stop obstructing the stream of other students with their belongings as they leave the campus for the New Year's month, but my skates feel as if they're frozen into the pearl beneath them.

The twin seahorses that form the Great Gate rise behind me, touching snout to snout. This boy Hisashi and his twin sister, Doi, stand before me, both looking like the boy that I befriended last year.

But the truth is, that boy doesn't exist. Instead, it was Doi—all of it. For an entire school year, she impersonated Hisashi and posed as both twins while her brother was in Shin rescuing hostages from the Empress Dowager.

When at last I get enough air in my lungs to speak, I say to this boy, this new, familiar Hisashi, "I am called familial name Chen, personal name—"

In a single glide, Doi is beside me. "This is my friend Chen Peasprout," she says, facing her brother. She's standing close enough that her sleeve brushes mine.

Hisashi's face lights up like a lantern. The dimples appear again on his cheeks and press little aching mirrors of themselves into my heart.

"You're Chen Peasprout?" he says. "My sister has told me so much about you. The Empress Dowager got your letter orb."

He bows to me. I bow back.

He straightens, and suddenly, his arms are around me in an embrace. "Thank you for your assistance in the mission," he says, his chin tucked behind my shoulder. "Thank you for your courage."

His voice, his warmth, even his scent, like plains sweetgrass, are all so familiar. I embrace him back and never want to let him go. I know I'm being foolish, but when Doi revealed that she had been pretending to be Hisashi, I thought the boy who captured my heart was gone forever. Here he is, the same. Or is he?

"Wah!" Hisashi says. "You give the best hugs! And you smell pretty, too."

Doi skates in a rustle behind me, and Hisashi and I disentangle.

She looks like a dog that has been kicked but won't unclamp its teeth from a pant leg.

Doi faces Hisashi and says, "And this is Chen Cricket. He's also my friend." She has one arm wrapped firmly around Cricket's shoulder.

"I like your friends, Wing Girl." He must call her that because they are dragon and phoenix twins, boy and girl. I can't tell how Doi feels about the nickname.

"Where's Father?" Hisashi asks. "They said at the New Deitsu Pearlworks Company compound that he's on campus."

"Yes, he's overseeing preparations for the maintenance of Pearl Famous Academy. Why do you want to see him?" asks Doi.

"I have something really important to share with him!" Hisashi pats the great round container on a sledge behind him.

Doi looks around at the bustle of students skating by us to line up at the rail-gondolas exiting the campus. She whispers, "Is the hostage Zan Aki inside?"

Heavenly August Personage of Jade! We got the New Deitsu skater back before the Empress Dowager bound his feet and—

"No," says Hisashi. "Poor boy's still in Shin."

Doi hisses, "The plan was for you to trap the Empress Dowager in it and then demand release of Father's hostage in exchange."

"Please, just trust me. I need to get to Father without anyone else seeing. Father's going to be very pleased." He halts and adds gently, "With *both* of us."

Doi's face shows no pain at the mention of the Chairman. The last time she saw her father, he promised to end her wu liu studies and then struck her so hard, he sent her sliding across the room. I reach my hand to hers. She weaves her fingers into mine, then closes them so our hands form one fist.

"It's all right," she whispers to me. "I have you."

Hisashi looks from Doi to me, then back. "What did I miss?"

A boom sounds from the northeastern corner of campus. All of us and the other students lining up to leave the campus turn to look.

"What was that?" asks Hisashi.

Cricket says, "The team from New Deitsu Pearlworks Company is starting their architectural repair and maintenance work for Red Cloud Feasting on School."

"Red what?" asks Hisashi.

Cricket replies, "Red Cloud Feasting on School. That's what the booms are announcing. It's when the entire campus is submerged for—"

I jump in and say, "No, you're telling it to him all wrong. It's when the entire campus is flooded during the New Year's month. The senseis said that little phosphorescent red krill in the water crawl all over the campus and eat off all the pollution left by the students."

"But that's not the real reason, Peasprout," says Cricket.

"Of course not," I say. "The real reason is that they need to give the campus a thorough soak so the pearl won't shrink, and they can keep it expanded with just targeted watering throughout the year. And they don't want the students seeing it."

"Oh. You know about that," says Hisashi. "You have very informed friends, Wing Girl."

I smile at his words. Doi frowns at my smile.

Hisashi says, "We need to move this conversation somewhere else. I can't let anyone see me before I speak to Father." We skate toward the front of the Hall of Six Excellences, with Hisashi pulling the pavilion along on a tether while scanning behind him.

"I'll take you to your father," I say. "I know the fastest path between any two points on the campus." He'll get to see how capable I am, how helpful, how kindhearted, how I am more knowledgeable than anyone about every—

"I'll go by myself," says Hisashi. "I don't want to involve you. This is a . . . delicate matter."

"You'll never be able to get this pavilion there by yourself," I say.

"It's got blades under it," he says. He motions in the air as if pushing a toy cart back and forth. "And, anyway, it's not the pavilion itself that actually mat—"

"No, no, no, you don't understand," I say. "Because you don't know about the ropes."

"What ropes?"

"Because of Bite the Sea Cucumber," says Cricket.

"Because of Bite the Sea Cucumber," I repeat loudly. Why does Cricket have to hoard all the attention? "They empty all the furnishings and equipment and artworks out of the structures and put them all on wooden planks so they'll float when the campus is flooded. And they tie all the planks together so they don't drift out to sea. You'll never get that pavilion over the ropes without my help."

Maybe now he'll understand how much he needs my help. When he sees how I'm the most capable, the most informed, the most—

"Why do they call it Bite the Sea Cucumber?" he asks.

"Ah," I say as I struggle to think of an answer, since I have no idea, "just because."

Cricket says, "Because a sea cucumber empties itself of its internal organs as soon as something attacks—"

I say, "That's what I was going to tell you before I was interrupted. Anyway, you're going to need my help in getting this sledge over all the ropes. We can perform two-footed iron grasshopper leaps down around the pavilion to jump it over each rope. My rope-jumping skills are legendary. I was champion of rope jumping for all of Shui Shan Province three times by the age of six."

"How did I ever manage without you, Chen Peasprout?"

His words warm my heart and my Chi surges. Then I see Doi's face. She looks like she just skated through a pile of monkey droppings.

"What?" I ask her.

"Nothing," she says. "I've just never heard you giggle."

"I wasn't giggling."

"Right."

Make me drink sand to death.

Another boom resounds, and we turn toward its source on the northeastern corner of the campus.

Cricket says, "Peasprout, you'd be able to jump the pavilion over the ropes better if you had some help."

Doi adds softly, "If you wanted help."

The image flashes in my mind of Hisashi smiling in gratitude as I alone help him get the pavilion across campus. I shove it out of my thoughts and say, "Of course I want your help. Both of you. I need you there."

Was that the right thing to say?

I say to Doi, "That doesn't mean I don't want you there. Just because I—"

She gives me one of her rare smiles.

"I understand you, Peasprout," she says.

"Thank you. You're better at this than I am."

"Better at what?" she asks.

How should I answer that? *Understanding? Being a friend?*

"Everything," I say.

Hisashi asks, "How are we going to get this thing across the whole campus without being seen? I can't let anyone learn that I'm back before I talk to Father."

"Why?" I ask.

"Please just trust me."

I reply, "Most of the students here never notice anything unless it involves them."

"What about the senseis?" asks Doi.

I say, "We'll just say we forgot something back at the dormitories."

"The senseis know I spent the last year pretending to be both

Hisashi and myself," Doi says with a firm shake of her head. "As soon as they see us together, they'll know he's back and that something important is inside the pavilion."

"That's a problem," says Hisashi. "Father needs to be the first one to learn about this."

"Wait!" I say, holding my palm up. "Something's coming to me." I skate back and forth around the pavilion. Doi is on one side, with her short-cropped hair, the high collar of the *gakuran* jacket, and the sweeping cloak of the academy robe. Hisashi is on the other side, identical except he's wearing pants instead of the pleated skirt that Doi is—

"I have an idea," I say. I reach into my sack of belongings, pull out my extra skirt, and thrust it at Hisashi. "Change into this. If any senseis see you, they'll think you're Doi."

"But they'll still know as soon as they see the two of us together," says Doi.

"So make sure they never see the two of you together. Stay on the opposite side of the pavilion from each other so that one of you is hidden at all times from any sensei we meet."

"Hah!" says Hisashi. "Keep this friend, Wing Girl. She's good under pressure. All right. Time for a fashion show." He slips off the pants and tucks them into the kit strapped on the side of the pavilion while standing there in his undergarments. He steps into the skirt with no embarrassment.

He stops and looks toward the southeastern corner of the Hall of Six Excellences. I turn and catch sight of someone ducking out of view.

"Someone's watching us!" I say. "It's Suki!"

Doi asks, "Are you sure?"

"Yes, I saw her elbow."

Cricket says, "But, Peasprout, that doesn't make any—"

"Suki spent all year trying to destroy Doi and me. You think she's going to see us sneaking around and not shriek like a monkey on fire being chopped to pieces?"

Hisashi asks, "So we don't like this Suki?"

"No!" scream Doi and I.

"If she finds out, she'll squeal to the senseis immediately," I say, taking Hisashi's hand. "We have to get out of here! Now!"

Hisashi, Doi, Cricket, and I push the pavilion across the southern quadrangle. Streams of students skate past, parting for us but seeming to pay no attention to the object that we're escorting. They seem more distracted by their irritation with us for skating in the wrong direction.

We encounter the first cluster of ropes in front of the Gallery of Paragons of Honor. The scroll portraits of honored past students of Pearl Famous are strung on a forest of poles crowding the area in front of the gallery. Shinian servant girls are hoisting them onto planks of wood tied together with ropes lying across the pearl.

Another boom splits the air and the students around us pick up the pace of their skating toward the gondola towers. Hisashi, Doi, Cricket, and I take advantage of the cover from the echoing sound to execute simultaneous two-footed iron grasshopper leaps. We impact the pearl at the same time. Hisashi beams at me when the force sends the pavilion bouncing over the first knot of ropes in front of us, just as I predicted.

We round the corner of the Gallery of Paragons of Honor and cross the Bridge of Serene Harmony over the Central Canal. The front of the Palace of the Eighteen Outstanding Pieties is piled with training equipment, weapons, and shields, interlaced with one another into filigree towers of metal atop wooden planks. A storm of screeching and the beating of wings sweep over us. It's Sensei Madame Phoenix's green birds, and right under them, skating around the southeastern corner of the Palace of the Eighteen Outstanding Pieties, comes Sensei Madame Phoenix, hauling a trunk of pearlplate and kelp wick on blades.

"Stop following me!" she shouts at the birds circling above her. "I'm not writing the *Pearl Shining Sun News* headlines anymore!"

She passes us on the bridge, squeezing by Doi, with Hisashi hidden on the far side of the pavilion. She doesn't seem to recognize, or care about, any of us. She laughs and says, "And I don't have to teach you those boring books anymore! If you thought last year was boring, wait until you see the books in the second-year literature curriculum! *Teach Yourself Committee Procedure*! But you know what? None of that is my problem anymore, thank the Enlightened One! Wah!"

As she skates away from us, a voice behind us says, "Ahihahaha!" I turn to see, coming out from the great entrance of the Palace of the Eighteen Outstanding Pieties, Supreme Sensei Master Jio, clutching an armload of little white sculptures. "You must forgive Sensei Madame Phoenix. She just received a contract from Houtu Famous

House of Literature and has resigned from teaching to pursue her lifelong dream of being a novelist. Why aren't you headed to the gondola towers, sweet embryos?"

I say, "We are. But we saw some students leave this pavilion here blocking the bridge, so we decided we'd move it onto one of the planks with the other treasures."

I check to make sure that only Hisashi is visible and Doi is staying out of view on the other side of the pavilion.

"Your selfless natures honor Pearl Famous. For as you shall learn when you attain sagehood, 'It takes ten thousand drops of sweat to build a temple, and one drop of saliva to spit on it.'

"Now, if you'll excuse me, I must dispose of these." He holds up the handfuls of sculptures. "Some students left behind these commemorative figurines of last year's lead skaters of the New Deitsu Opera Company. They look like the official collectible merchandise, but they're cheap imitations carved out of soap! They become extremely poisonous if they get wet. Imagine if fish or turtles swallowed them? More shoddy imports from Shin— That is, ah, thank you for pitching in."

He squeezes past Hisashi on the western side of the pavilion, and I see Doi pivot around to keep Supreme Sensei Master Jio as far from her as possible. Hisashi bows low to obscure his face, accidentally rubbing his robe against one of the soap figurines in Supreme Sensei's hands. It leaves a white streak.

"Ah, forgive me, little embryo!"

Hisashi tries to wipe it off but only smears it wider.

"Oh, you can't wipe it off," Supreme Sensei tells him. "These cheap imitations use dolphin dung as the binding agent. Very oily, due to their diets. You'll need to bake your robe in direct sunlight for a day to get it off. It'll be as good as new by the beginning of the school year!"

As soon as Supreme Sensei is gone, we execute two-footed iron grasshopper leaps and send the pavilion popping over another knot of ropes. We edge our cargo along the path fronting the Palace of the Eighteen Outstanding Pieties. Hisashi keeps looking behind us, but I see no sign of Suki.

We push the pavilion across the bridge leading to the dormitory compound. The central courtyards of both the girls' and boys' quarters are filled with fat, clear tubes. Within these glistening, gelatinous casings are enveloped rolls of futons, blankets, desks, and chairs. It looks like some giant sea creature ate the entire contents of the dormitories and passed out anything that wasn't a girl or a boy in a clear skin.

From the girls' dormitories on the left, Sensei Madame Yao comes skating out toward Hisashi. Instantly, I shift into defensive stance. When she sees him, she gasps with shock. "Gah? Why are you still on campus, Niu Doi? Answer me, scheming, treacherous girl!"

Hisashi bows to her and clears his throat. I forgot about his voice. He might look like Doi, but his voice has already changed. He begins to say in a timid tone, "We were—"

"That's a filthy, disgusting lie, Niu Doi! You're all trying to get to the Conservatory of Music to steal my gongs. Thieves!" she shouts, looking around for other senseis. "Shameless, unwhipped thieves!"

On the right, Sensei Madame Liao comes skating out from the boys' dormitories toward the real Doi. I quickly shift to make sure she can't see Hisashi on the other side. She calls out, "What is it now, Sensei Madame Yao!"

"Niu Doi and her accomplices are trying to take advantage of Bite the Sea Cucumber to steal my gongs!"

Sensei Madame Liao looks at Doi and calls over, "What makes you think that, Sensei Madame Yao?"

"Niu Doi has gong-polishing powder smeared all over the front of her robe!"

Sensei Madame Liao looks at Doi and her unsullied robe.

"What are you talking about, Sensei Madame Yao?"

Doi and I look at each other and sweat immediately beads on my forehead. I have to make sure Sensei Madame Liao doesn't skate around to the other side and find out our scheme.

"Come over here and look!"

Sense Madame Liao gazes in bafflement at Doi, then skates around to the other side of the pavilion, to Sensei Madame Yao. I quickly skate toward the other side as well. What am I going to do?

When Sensei Madame Liao sees Hisashi, with his identical cropped hair and features, wearing my skirt under his academy robe, she stops short.

She skates back to Doi's side, then back to Hisashi's.

She looks past Hisashi, past Sensei Madame Yao, and at me.

I mouth silently to her, "*Please*." I touch my palm to the pavilion we are transporting.

Sensei Madame Liao looks at me, looks at Hisashi, and says, "There's been a misunderstanding, Sensei Madame Yao. I asked Niu Doi and her friends to . . . help me move my new . . . meditation pavilion. It's been flaking powder and needs refreshing."

"No, they're up to something! I know it!"

"Are you challenging the truth of what I said, Sensei Madame Yao?"

"I'm going to tell Supreme Sensei Master Jio!"

Sensei Madame Yao skates off in the direction of the Palace of the Eighteen Outstanding Pieties.

Sensei Madame Liao turns to me.

"I can explain, Sensei Madame—"

"Oh, yes, you are going to explain everything to me, Chen Peasprout. But at present, it looks like you need to go."

I bow to her and say, "Thank you for trusting me, Sensei."

Another boom sounds just north of us, from the direction of the Hall of the Eight Precious Virtues. We push the pavilion toward the hall. Beside me, Hisashi is looking over his shoulder. A figure slips behind a wing of the girls' dormitory just as I catch sight of it.

"Hurry," I say. "Suki's still following us."

He begins to say, "Peasprout, we don't have to worry about this Suki follow—"

"You have no idea what Suki is like. Trust me, Hisashi."

We execute three consecutive sets of leaps and hop the pavilion over the knots of ropes tying the casings filled with dormitory furnishings.

We push the pavilion with us across the bridge leading to the Hall of the Eight Precious Virtues at the far northeastern corner of the campus.

The Chairman and the New Deitsu Pearlworks Company maintenance team are nowhere within view. We push the pavilion across the bridge to the left, onto the great square of Divinity's Lap spreading across the north side of the campus. Nothing there, either.

"Wait here. I'll get a better view." I skate back to the Hall of the Eight Precious Virtues and execute a string of side flips up its ten tiers. From here, atop the highest level of the tallest structure at Pearl Famous, I see the New Deitsu team hidden behind Eastern Heaven Dining Hall on its seaward side, on the southern part of the campus, where we just came from. Ten thousand years of stomach gas.

Behind the Hall of Lilting Radiance, a barge is parked along the north shore of the Principal Island. It's masted with great scallop-shaped pearlsilk sails and oared with ribbed flippers. A plump tail of silver fur trails on the surface of the water behind it. A cluster of girls is gathered on the shore near it, readying to embark.

The girls of the House of Flowering Blossoms. And in their midst is Gang Suki, pointing straight up at me.

"Who's that atop the Hall of the Eight Precious Virtues?" she shouts.

I begin scrambling down the tiers of the hall, but I have to proceed carefully because they're slick from the spray of the waterfall cascading down its western face.

Suki and her girls reach the pavilion before I can. They're pointing at Doi and Hisashi and screeching like a monkey being struck by lightning.

"Seize that pavilion!" screams Suki.

I leap into the waterfall and ride the rest of the tiers down its plume. I execute a triple screaming squall jump and leap onto the pavilion. I ride it as it shoots into the canal dividing Divinity's Lap and the Palace of the Eighteen Outstanding Pieties.

"Get on!" I shout at Hisashi, Doi, and Cricket. They skate alongside the pavilion as it bobs down the canal, sling themselves into the air, and land atop its steeply pitched roof. The energy from all of us making speeding leaps onto the pavilion sends it shooting even faster down the canal.

We approach the first bridge and leap over it together, as the pavilion passes under. We come down together and regain our balance.

Suki and the House of Flowering Blossoms girls streak alongside us on Divinity's Lap. They spring at us with uncurbed skate blades, one after another, shooting like flurries of flashing knives. Hisashi pants, "I think I see what you mean about this Suki, Wing Girl!"

However, we have the advantage because we present a moving target. We easily block all the skates flying at us and send the girls bouncing back onto the pearl beside us.

We leap over the next bridge in the canal and prepare for the hard turn around the northwestern corner of the Palace of the Eighteen Outstanding Pieties. "Southwest diagonal backflips!" I command. Our moves send the pavilion rotating at a velocity that will help it negotiate the hard curve without jumping the canal.

The pavilion bumps as it takes the corner of the canal, but the rotation makes its ornamental exterior flourishes grip the turn so that it actually comes whipping around even faster. The lucky of us pedal and hop to compensate for the spin and jolts as it bumps southward down the canal.

We leap the next bridge with ease and approach the southwestern juncture. However, this time, instead of keeping the pavilion from jumping the turn, we actually need it to pop up and pivot toward the southeast so that it can continue eastward in the Central Canal. As we approach the hard curve, I call out, "Iron hammer throw with north-to-east rotation!"

We sling ourselves to flip and strike down in the form of spinning hammers. The impact plunges the pavilion down into the water and then its buoyancy makes it come popping back up. The pavilion splashes down in the Central Canal with us atop it, headed east on our final approach toward Eastern Heaven Dining Hall.

We ride the currents of the Central Canal and pass under the Bridge of Serene Harmony. We don't need to leap over it since it's so high, but Hisashi does a pear blossom forward somersault anyway, stepping over the bridge lightly with a little flip like a petal skipping in the wind. He meets us on the other side.

"That was for you, Chen Peasprout!" he says with a flash of dimples.

I swallow down the disturbance in my Chi as we ready for the final leap. When we approach the last curve, I spot Suki and the House of Flowering Blossoms girls pouring toward us along the path on the east side of the Palace of the Eighteen Outstanding Pieties. It's no use, though—they're too far. They'll never make it to us before we reach Doi and Hisashi's father, and Suki wouldn't dare challenge an adult, especially not someone that powerful. I can just hear her screaming, "Infuriate—"

A great force slams into the pavilion beneath our skates, sending us flying off its roof, onto the pearl.

The point of a great bronze arrowhead as large as a person is buried in the wall of the pavilion, but the pearl is too thick for it to penetrate to the interior. The arrowhead is attached to a chain that leads out to the nose of Suki's private barge that she had been about to embark. It rowed down here to intercept us! Ten thousand years of stomach gas.

The flipper oars of the ship begin to stroke in reverse, hauling the harpooned pavilion out of the canal and onto the pearl on its side. Suki and her vile girls swarm it. "Roll it into the Courtyard of Supreme Placidness and cut it open!" orders Suki. The girls roll the pavilion through the archway of the courtyard, encircle it, and begin taking one leaping slash after another at it.

"Let's go," whispers Hisashi to me, skating away quietly.

"What do you mean 'let's go'? What about whatever was inside the pavilion?"

"She was never inside the pavilion."

"What do you mean 'she'?"

"The pavilion was just a distraction in case we got stopped. She was following behind us all along."

I whip my head around and catch a glimpse of the figure I thought was Suki. So Hisashi kept looking back to make sure she was still following us, not to get away from her.

"Who's this girl that was following us?" I ask.

"I'll tell you everything, but first, I have to speak to my father."

Ahead of us, dressed in a spreading robe of shimmering gold pearlsilk embroidered with a frenzy of intertwined eels, stands Chairman Niu Kazuhiro. The man whom I made a bargain with to betray the Empress Dowager. The man who could still destroy me by shipping me back to Shin. He stares at Hisashi, then Doi, then Hisashi's skirt.

Hisashi skates to him, ending in a slide onto his knees that finishes at his father's feet. He says, "Venerable and esteemed Father. I humbly beg you to listen to my worthless entreaty—"

"What are you doing here?" spits the Chairman, glancing at the riot of girls trying to slice open the pavilion behind Hisashi. "You're supposed to be in Shin. Did you obtain the hostage Zan Aki?"

"Father, we need to go somewhere private. There is someone you need to meet."

Hisashi looks back over his shoulder and beckons. For a moment, we see nothing except a sculpture rising out of the little pool. Then from behind the sculpture comes a girl in a swirl of yellow robes. She doesn't wear skates but instead pushes forward on a board using snow poles like the ones I saw the elderly tourists using when I first arrived here.

She's also the most beautiful girl I've ever seen, luminous and tragic like a lost moon.

The Chairman's gaze bounces back between the girl and Hisashi. At last he says, "Come with me."

We all proceed toward him.

"I don't mean all of you," he sneers. "Just this girl. And my son."

CHAPTER
THREE

I **lie awake half the night in the dormitory chamber at** 8,888 Cups, the boardinghouse in the city that Sensei Madame Liao arranged for Cricket and me to stay in during the New Year's holiday month. I want to go over to see Doi in the dormitory chamber she rented for the night with the last of her money, but I should let her rest. When birds start singing outside, I give up trying to sleep and go to take a bath. Outside the dormitory box is a letter orb. I twist it open.

From the orb, Hisashi's voice says, "You're finally awake! I'm downstairs in the saloon!"

I wake Cricket and Doi and we rush downstairs.

Hisashi's in the saloon, balancing five eating sticks standing upright on his fingertips.

"Good morning!" he says, snapping his fingers closed and snatching the sticks into a bundle.

"So what happened with your father?" I ask.

"I'm sorry, but I can't tell you. Father forbade me from discussing it before the hearing."

"What hearing? You owe me a lot of explanations!"

"I'm sorry, but I can't risk displeasing Father. Not after all that Doi and I have sacrificed."

I look to Doi. She looks at Hisashi, sighs, and nods. Why is she concerned about pleasing their father after the way he treated her?

"Fine. Is there anything that you *can* tell us?" I ask Hisashi.

"Well, first of all, Wing Girl, you're not going down to Auntie's house in Tao-Ka as planned. I used most of our money to rent us dormitory chambers here at 8,888 Cups for the New Year's month. I know I can get Father to talk with you and reconsider his decision to take you out of Pearl Famous. I'll convince him not to commit you as a novice nun at Pearl Rehabilitative Colony for Ungrateful Daughters."

I look to Doi, but her face shows no reaction to this.

"Who is this girl that you brought back from Shin?" I ask.

"I can't tell you that. But it'll all be public after the sanctuary sponsorship hearing."

"The what? Where is she now?"

"She's staying with Father at our family compound atop Thousand Catbear Peak until the hearing. I can't say anything more before the hearing or it could jeopardize her status."

"You tricked us into helping you help this girl."

"Peasprout, I'm sorry I didn't try harder to explain that what I brought back was a girl and that she was important. But the truth is that I just got a little overwhelmed by you."

"Oh, so this is my fault. So you're saying that I was too aggressive, that I intimidated you, that the force of my personality trampled you into silence?" No answer. An infuriating little grin appears on his face.

"Hello? Anyone home? I asked you a question," I say.

"Peasprout!" cry Doi and Cricket together.

"What?"

"Hah!" laughs Hisashi.

I turn to him and say, "What are you laughing at?"

He answers, "It's just that even though I only met you yesterday, I already know that I'm never going to forget you."

With these words, I feel the anger drain from me. I feel the Chi vibrating from all three of them still. I've made everyone around me uncomfortable. I don't want to do that.

"All right," I say. "I'm done being angry. I know you must have your reasons for withholding information. Hisashi, was there an 'I'm sorry' somewhere in what you said? Wait, don't answer that. I know that's what you meant. Accepted. Now, can we get something to eat?"

We ask the cook what the offerings are today here at 8,888 Cups. She decided to use up some ground pork that was about to turn bad by sprinkling a little of it into all the dishes offered today. Thus, we leave and skate down Midmount Road, the largest boulevard in the Aroma Bay quarter of the city of Pearl to get something to eat.

Around us, youngsters speed like minnows everywhere, unattended by adults. They leap from handrail to handrail and call out challenges to one another of simple wu liu jumps and spins.

What would my wu liu be like now if I had had a childhood as theirs, here in a city such as this?

Elders in white robes peacefully do their morning liu chi exercises together in lines across a low bridge, slowly dipping, lifting, and turning together as one.

Will I be one of them someday, living out my destiny here in Pearl?

Although it's still technically the Season of Drifts, the Season of Spouts has already begun to make itself felt. Small rudimentary spouts of water rise from the canals over the banks and stroll up the streets of the city before spinning themselves into mist. Everywhere around us, plumes of spray from the little water cyclones gently stroke the sides of halls and temples.

A little water cyclone rears up out of the canal that runs down the median of Midmount Road. It keeps up with us as we skate, sucking its way along swiftly and effortlessly. It runs over a vein of kelp that drifted into the canal. For a moment, the little water cyclone frenzies with streaks of vegetation, then it appears to choke on the kelp flippers and flotation orbs, threatening to topple and splash into us.

The lucky of us duck into the doorway of a small teahouse overhanging the canal to avoid the spray. The doorway leads into a teahouse formed of two lotus-shaped caps cupping a windowed gazebo from above and below.

"Let's look inside," says Hisashi.

We skate in, and I can tell immediately that this teahouse is like one of those shops that are so refined, normal people can't even tell what it is that they're selling.

"This place looks really expensive," I say to Hisashi. "We only have enough money to cover our meals until the new school year."

"Just a minute," he says, counting coins from his purse. "We have enough for a little treat if we share. Miss, table for lucky, please."

A teahouse girl skates over, dressed like a princess in a high-collared, sleeveless *qipao* of embroidered black and silver pearlsilk. She looks up and down our academy uniforms and says, "Ah, Pearl Famous students?"

"Yes," answers Doi.

"Welcome, welcome," she says, bowing low. She leads us to a table by a moon-shaped window open to the canal below us.

Hisashi says, "Just one pot of simple green, please."

"With the discount for Pearl Famous students, you can upgrade to a pot of triple-fantasy jasmine green tea fresh from Eda."

"Sold!" says Hisashi, beaming like he just won a palace on the moon. It's hard to stay annoyed with him.

From our table overlooking the canal, I see a group of young dolphins sporting in the water below us. Back in Shui Shan Province, I learned some river porpoise language from a trader and I'm tempted to try the few clicks and whistles that I remember. However, I decide not to because I can't do them very loudly, and I'm sure these Pearlian dolphins don't speak the same dialect as Shinian river porpoises.

I also don't want Doi to think I was doing it strictly to show off for Hisashi.

Which I would be.

Our tea arrives, and Hisashi pours for us. The sunlight shafting through the window turns the steam into ribbons of rising luminescence between us. We sip the tea.

"Do you like it?" asks Hisashi.

"Yes, thank you," I say. "It'll be my birthday soon, and this is like an early celebration."

Hisashi says, "You were born in the New Year's month, too?"

"Yes, and Cricket, as well. I was born in the year of the sea otter, in the Pearlian zodiacal system, so I'm about to turn fifteen, same as you and Doi. Cricket was born in the year of the sea turtle, so he's about to turn luckyteen."

"So we're all New Year's–month babies!" cries Hisashi. He shouts at the teahouse girls, "It's our birthdays! Do you have any birthday specials?"

One of the teahouse girls skates over and says, "Please excuse me. Did I accidentally overhear that we have a birthday?"

"Yes!" says Hisashi proudly.

"Ah! We offer Pearl Famous students a complimentary infinity noodle on their birthdays!"

"Sold!" says Hisashi.

"Does the infinity noodle or broth have any animal parts in it?" asks Doi.

"Of course not! This teahouse is completely New Year's Spiritual-Enlightenment-Cleansing-Regimen-Compliant all year round. See." She points to a little shrine in the corner with a statue of the Enlightened One, covered in adoring animals, including two little birds perched on her smoked spectacles. "I shall bring you one infinity noodle."

Hisashi says, "Can we have three more orders? It's all of our birthdays!"

The teahouse girl laughs behind her hand. "You only need one. It's an infinity noodle!"

After the teahouse girl leaves, Cricket asks him, "What's an infinity noodle?"

"I have no idea," says Hisashi. "But I liked the price. Anyway, Doi, Peasprout, and I are all year of the sea otter! So that means we're going to grow up to be very confident and curious. Cricket's year of the sea turtle, so he's going to be wise and long-lived."

"Illogical superstition," scoffs Doi.

"But, Wing Girl, isn't every year-of-the-sea-otter person you know very confident and curious?"

"Yes, but only because they've been told their whole lives that they're going to grow up to be confident and curious since they're year of the sea otter."

"Hah," says Hisashi to Cricket and me. "My sister. She always sees what no one else does."

"In Shin, only infants and the elderly have their birthdays celebrated," I say.

"What about in Pearl?" asks Cricket.

"We celebrate every birthday in Pearl," answers Hisashi. "Shall we celebrate our birthdays together in the traditional Pearlian fashion?"

"We would love that," I say. "Thank you. What are your birthday customs?"

Hisashi grows wistful and says, "Every year, you spend your entire birthday on your knees bowed in front of portraits of your ancestors, thanking them for the gift of your existence and begging them to forgive you for turning out such an unfilial and undeserving disappointment. Unless you don't have ancestral portraits because you're poor or an orphan. Then you have to spend your entire birth month on your knees, praying to the memory of your ancestors and begging them forgiveness for allowing family decline to occur on your watch or allowing your parents to die. Our traditions are so beautiful." He wipes his eyes. "We can start tonight."

Cricket and I look at each other.

"He's joking," says Doi.

Hisashi roars with laughter, tipping back his chair and balancing it on two legs.

I watch him laughing and teetering at the other side of the table, as comfortable with Cricket and me as if he's known us his whole life. He's like the boy I knew last year—the one who didn't exist—except louder, wilder, and more openhearted.

The boy I knew, that I thought I lost, has not only come back; he's even more himself than he ever—

Peasprout, stop it. Don't forget that the boy you thought you knew last year withheld things from you because he thought he had a good reason to. He told you the greatest lie you've ever been told and hurt you more than anyone ever has. And everything that he was turned out to be an illusion. This boy appears to be everything that the boy was, except more of it. All of it. Proceed with caution.

The teahouse girl skates out with two other girls. Together, they hoist a massive black porcelain bowl onto the table. It's large enough to bathe in if you really squeezed. In it is a steaming ball of noodles soaking in a broth of shaved ginger, plump shiitake mushroom caps, and slices of bamboo shoot, carrot, and burdock root, sprinkled with sesame seeds.

"Please slowly enjoy your infinity noodle," they say together with a bow.

"Oh, it's like longevity noodles," says Hisashi.

"It's nothing like common longevity noodles!" exclaims one of the teahouse girls.

"It's far longer," says another of the teahouse girls. "This is one unbroken noodle that is so long, it would take a fifth of an hour to skate its length!"

"It's a new *hatsubai*!" says the third girl. This is Edaian for "new product."

"From Eda," the three of them say with reverence.

The first girl instructs us, "You must eat the entire noodle without cutting or breaking it in two, or you will have bad luck all year. Further, if your birthday is in the New Year's month, then before you take the first bite, you must tell of one thing you learned that was a revelation about a friend you kept in the past year."

The words of "The Pearlian New Year's Song" rise in my head.

The teahouse girl grasps the noodle, which is as thick as a finger, with long silver eating sticks and hands it to Cricket. "Here's the beginning of the noodle, little one."

When she skates away, Cricket says, "This past year, I learned that someone who is my family is also my friend." He bites the noodle, takes a sip of broth from a ladle as large as a normal rice bowl, and passes the eating sticks and ladle to Doi.

Doi says, "This past year, I learned that someone who couldn't give me what I thought I wanted most gave me what I needed most." As she takes a bite of the noodle, I wave at the steaming broth between us, blinking hard to keep my eyes dry.

Hisashi takes the eating sticks and ladle. He says, "This past year, I met the most extraordinary girl I have ever met." He takes a bite and a sip and politely offers me the handles of both eating sticks and ladle.

I swallow nervously. I know he can't be referring to me since we just met. However, he did say he already knows that he'll never forget me.

I look at him.

He's not looking at me. He's tilted back in his chair, his palms on the table, his eyes closed as if he is savoring the taste of the noodle. Or of some memory.

I realize he wasn't referring to me. He was talking about this girl that he brought back from Shin. I quickly stamp down the toss in my Chi.

At that moment, a boy skates through the entrance of the teahouse. The sash strapped across his robe reads NEW DEITSU PEARL-WORKS COMPANY.

He sees Hisashi and says, "There you are!" He skates over, bows, and says, "Disciple Niu Hisashi. I have a letter orb for you from Chairman Niu Kazuhiro."

Hisashi takes the letter orb from the courier, who bows again and skates out of the teahouse. He twists it open. We hear the voice of the Chairman say, "The sanctuary sponsorship hearing date has been moved up. Come to the statue of the Enlightened One on Divinity's Lap on campus tomorrow at White Hour."

Doi looks at me with as much dread on her face as I feel in my chest.

"Do not bring that sister of yours or that Chen Peasprout," the voice from the orb continues. "Wu Yinmei and I will be waiting for you."

Wu Yinmei.

So that's her name.

The most extraordinary person he has ever met.

My grip on the slick silver eating sticks slips. They drop into the soup.

When I reach in to pick them out, I see that they have scissored off part of the infinity noodle.

The severed length floats in the broth, as adrift and alone as a memory unshared.

"**W**hat is this sanctuary sponsorship hearing? Is it for this girl?" I ask Hisashi as we follow him out of the teahouse.

"I don't know if I'm allowed to—"

"We have a right to be at this hearing," Doi interrupts. "We all helped you get her to Father. Otherwise, she would have been deported. You made us break the law for her."

"We helped you smuggle a Shinian citizen to Pearl," I jump in. "I want to meet this extraordinary girl from Shin."

The last part doesn't come out the way that I want.

Hisashi shows us his open palms and says, "Peasprout, much as I would—"

"Don't you start finding—"

"—like to honor Father's command, I completely agree with you."

CHAPTER
LUCKY

The statue of the Enlightened One rises six stories above us here in the great square of Divinity's Lap on the north side of the Principal Island. She towers so high that we can't see her face through the dense drifts rising from the pearl.

None of the senseis or the Chairman are here yet.

However, standing there on a swiftboard at the base of the statue of the Enlightened One, in a robe of cherry blossoms on white, is the girl.

Hisashi says, "Doi, Peasprout, Cricket, I present to you Princess Wu Yinmei, great-great-granddaughter of the Empress Dowager."

The girl gazes back at us, bright, unblinking, still.

Doi says to her brother, "You were supposed to trap the *Empress Dowager* in the pavilion and demand that she release Father's hostage. Not her powerless heir!"

"That was a good plan, Wing Girl," he says, clapping Doi on the shoulder. "Elegant. Tight. Bold. Like your wu liu. It completely failed, but wah, what a story it would have made!"

"What happened?" I ask.

"The Empress Dowager got the letter orb that Chen Peasprout sent, but she still wouldn't step inside the pavilion. She didn't believe the story that if she slept inside it, it would produce an oracle that would tell her the secret of the pearl."

"Are you sure?" I demand. "I've met the Empress Dowager. She's curious about everything."

"Well, of course I'm sure!" Why is he getting irritated?

I look at this girl standing there, trying so hard to appear innocent. However, her feet give her away. "She can't be a member of the imperial court. Look at her feet. All court ladies have their feet bound at the age of five. And why is she using a swiftboard and poles if she has unbroken feet?"

Hisashi replies, "That's her story to tell, in time."

I insist, "The Empress Dowager doesn't have a great-great-granddaughter."

"The Empress Dowager had to keep her a secret until she could inherit the throne."

"She can't inherit; she's a girl. That's why the Great Council of Holy Men has been conducting a search for the reincarnated Emperor."

"Ah, well," Hisashi clears his throat. "The Empress Dowager has been trying to change the law to allow for female succession."

"I've never heard anything like that. I think I know a little more about laws in Shin than you do."

"I spent the last year in the imperial court. The Great Council doesn't want to allow the Empress Dowager to change the law of succession so they said she can only do so if she brings Shin an unprecedented treasure because they want her to fail. However, she came up with the idea of learning the mystery of the pearl. She wants to build Shin a pearl city of its own."

Doi barks at Hisashi, "So why did you bring her here?"

This Wu Yinmei speaks, and it jolts me like a statue coming to life. "Because the Empress Dowager poisoned the rest of our family. I was afraid I would be next."

"But that doesn't make sense," reasons Doi. "If the Empress Dowager's trying to change the law so that you could inherit, she wouldn't harm the next in line."

"That didn't stop her from poisoning every other heir in line," says this Wu Yinmei. "She wants someone young that she can control. A puppet empress."

I cry out, "And what will the Empress Dowager think when she finds that Pearl has her heir? What have you done, Hisashi? She'll be furious if her heir fled and found sanctuary from her in Pearl. You've flung salt in the Empress Dowager's eyes!"

As I fight back the panic, one thought becomes clear: This girl's presence here is deadly to me.

"We can't let this girl get sanctuary here," I say. "The Empress Dowager will order an invasion. She already wants our pearl."

We.

Our pearl.

I guess this is my home now.

I continue, "If you've spent time with the Empress, then you've seen how vicious she is when she feels insulted. I helped you trick her. If she gains control of Pearl, you and I will both be executed. Why are you helping this girl?"

It makes no sense, unless it's not coming from Hisashi's head but his heart. Who is this girl to him? They spent a year together, then made a harrowing escape. He risked his life for her. A ludicrous lump of jealousy rises in my chest.

Don't be a fool, Peasprout! You don't know him. All you know is that he's put you in danger.

"Chen Peasprout," he says. "The Empress Dowager wouldn't do that. You'll have to trust me on this."

"She could be a spy," Doi says. "The Empress Dowager could have set all of this up to find out the secret of the pearl. She could have commanded this girl to take advantage of your kindness and beg you to smuggle her back to Pearl."

"I can't believe what I'm hearing!" Hisashi says, and shakes his head. "Wing Girl, what's happened to you?"

"What's happened to *you*?" Doi asks him. "I'm not going to let you put Peasprout in danger!"

The two of them with their short, soldier's haircuts and beautiful, unhappy faces stare each other down like reflections.

And in between them stands the cause of all this trouble, staring back at me like a ghostly mirror sent from Shin.

The girl's gaze moves from me to Doi.

Then from Doi to Hisashi.

Then from Doi to me.

Then from me to Hisashi.

I feel as if she's run her hands over my face. And Doi's. And Hisashi's.

She looks at Hisashi.

She says, "One should never have to choose between a sister and a friend."

She looks at Doi.

"Or between a friend and a brother."

She looks at me.

"Or between a friend and . . . a hope."

She means Hisashi. She thinks I have hopes regarding Hisashi.

Doi's eyes flash at the girl, and I can feel her Chi rippling with emotion.

The girl fixes her gaze back to Doi. They stare at each other, Doi's face chiseled in anger, the girl's face flowing in shades from intensity to neutrality, then back to serene, glowing beauty.

She says, still staring at Doi and smiling, "Or between a friend and . . . a hope."

It's the same words, but I know she intends a different meaning for Doi. I look at Doi, but her face is locked down in a mask of stone.

A voice behind us hisses, "What are they doing here? I told you not to bring anyone else."

I turn to see the Chairman, stately like an emperor in a robe of kingfisher blue with silver mandalas. Glaring with fury, he comes flanked by the twelve senseis, all of them as somber as crows.

I'm relieved to see Sensei Madame Liao, although her expression remains stern. "Sensei, New Deitsu Pearlworks Company cannot sponsor this girl for sanctuary status."

The Chairman seethes, "How dare you tell me what I can and cannot do?"

Cricket whispers to me. I nod and say, "My brother and I had to study the statutes last year when we crossed into Pearlian territory. A private Pearlian company cannot sponsor a Shinian for sanctuary status if her presence here will endanger the security of Pearl."

Doi leaps in and adds, "This girl claims to be the heir of the Empress Dowager. The Empress Dowager will order an invasion if we harbor her runaway heir!"

The Chairman shouts, "Hisashi! I told you not to bring them!"

I say, "Sensei, this girl's presence here endangers us all!"

"You have no rights," responds the Chairman. "You're not even a permanent citizen of Pearl."

Doi skates to her father and calls out in a firm voice, "Senseis. I invoke my legal right as a citizen of Pearl to oppose New Deitsu Pearlworks Company's sponsorship of this girl for sanctuary status, and I call Chen Peasprout and Chen Cricket as my witnesses."

Cricket says, "Wait, I didn't—"

Doi announces at the top of her voice, "I hereby formally accuse Chairman Niu Kazuhiro of treason against Pearl."

CHAPTER
FIVE

Heavenly August Personage of Jade. What will the Chairman do to Doi to punish her for accusing him, if he's not convicted? She's risking this for me. We have to prevail at this hearing. Supreme Sensei Master Jio announces, "We need someone to bring down the hands to litigate on. Sensei Madame Liao, will you please—"

"I volunteer!" Sensei Madame Yao shoves past Sensei Madame Liao toward the statue. She rips away her robe to reveal an undershirt that clings to her bulging muscles.

She crouches down, then explodes toward the statue of the Enlightened One. She bounds off the statue's knee, then the shoulder. She executes a forward somersault followed by a two-footed lightning hammer move, pounding down on one of the open palms stretched heavenward. The impact slams the palm down onto the pearl before us, triggering a complex of creaking levers in the mechanical fulcrum of the arms and sending the other palm shooting up into the sky.

Sensei Madame Yao motions for Doi, Cricket, and me to step onto the open palm before us. It's so vast that a third of the second-year class could stand on it and not touch one another. When I step off this palm, I'm either going to be safe or in even more danger than before. Sensei Madame Yao ascends the diagonal fulcrum of the arms. In three leaps, she is at the other hand. She lands on that open palm with a thundering slam. As that hand plummets, the palm beneath Doi and me rises so quickly that we have to throw our arms around the statue's fingers to avoid being flung upward and tossed into the sea.

Up here, the face of the statue is as large as half the girls' dormitory compound. Far below, through the rising drifts, Hisashi and the Chairman skate onto the other palm. The two of them lift the girl off her swiftboard to stand on the palm.

When Sensei Madame Yao skates off the palm, the weight on the two hands balances and our palm begins to fall. Doi, Cricket, and I crouch for balance until the hands are level and we face, far across on the other palm, Hisashi, the Chairman, and this Wu Yinmei.

Below us, Supreme Sensei Master Jio skates forward from the crescent of other senseis and calls up to us, "Petitioners, commence your first argument!"

The Chairman bows slightly to the senseis below on the pearl and says, "I present to you, Princess Wu Yinmei, the great-great-granddaughter of the Empress Dowager." A great rustle of startled discussion rises from the senseis below. "New Deitsu Pearlworks

Company seeks to sponsor her for sanctuary status, which shall not endanger the security of Pearl but shall instead give us a strategic advantage."

This girl says in a voice as sweet and bright as a brook, "Sage and venerable Senseis, this worthless one humbly begs you to pity a girl who has fled in fear for her life from the ruthlessness of the Empress Dowager of Shin, who poisoned all the rest of her family."

A rustle and hum spread among the senseis.

"Respondents, reply!"

"Senseis," says Doi. She points at this Wu Yinmei but why does she refuse to look at her? "If this girl that Niu Hisashi has brought back from Shin is the Empress Dowager's great-great-granddaughter as she claims to be, then granting her sanctuary here will be viewed by the Empress Dowager as an insult and a hostile gesture. Send her back. My fath— Chairman Niu's harboring her here endangers all of Pearl and constitutes an act of treason."

Sensei Madame Liao asks, "Do you understand that if this council rules in favor of your accusation, the accused persons will be referred to Pearlian authorities? Do you understand the consequences of your accusation of treason, Niu Doi?"

"Yes. Traitors of Pearl are unskated and serve life sentences at the penal quarry on Headlouse Island, like all the traitors during the Bamboo Invasion."

"Does your accusation of treason extend to Niu Hisashi?"

Without hesitating, Doi says, "No. My brother has a tender heart that is too easy to manipulate."

I steady my voice as I remember that the last time these senseis heard me make my case, it was after Doi and I nearly destroyed the entire campus with illegal balls of salt. We don't have a lot of credibility. I say firmly, "I can attest that the girl's words cannot be trusted. The Empress Dowager has no great-great-granddaughter. The newspapers report on all members of the Empress Dowager's bloodline, to the third degree of remove. And everyone knows that all females of noble birth have their feet bound at the age of five. Her feet are unbroken. This girl cannot be who she says she is. She is probably a spy sent by the Empress Dowager to learn the secret of the pearl. You must not allow her sanctuary."

Sensei Madame Yao looks like she's about to say something about how *I* was the one suspected to be a Shinian spy last year, but Sensei Madame Liao cuts her off and says, "Tally, please."

Supreme Sensei Master Jio states, "Arbiters, to which arguments do you give more weight?"

The senseis reach behind them. I hear the sounds of metal snaking over metal. Then the air is filled with whipping chains flying at us. Each of the arbiters has flung a length of chain twice as long as a person at one of the arms of the statue. Six chains catch and wrap themselves around the arm near Doi, Cricket, and me, six on the other near Hisashi, the Chairman, and this girl. The two palms of the statue remain balanced at the same level.

The girl replies, "The Empress Dowager kept me a secret while she decided whether to select me as the heir to the throne."

"That can't be true," I say, trying to keep the exasperation out of my voice. "Females can't inherit in Shin." How good a spy can she be if she hides behind such an obvious lie?

She replies, "The Empress Dowager's mission has been to change that. That is why, for the eighty-eight years since the Emperor's death, she has not selected any male in the bloodline to be the heir.

"The Great Council of Holy Men says that someone can change the laws only if that person brings to Shin an unprecedented treasure. The Empress Dowager has promised to build for Shin a pearl city of its own to fulfill this quest."

"See!" I cry. "She just admitted that the Empress Dowager is trying to steal the secret of the pearl. She's here to spy for the Empress Dowager."

"I am here to flee from the Empress Dowager. Only a fool would not fear her ruthlessness," this Wu Yinmei says, peering at me. "Any whose path has crossed with hers never forgets that."

She looks hard at me and before I can stop myself, I glance away. My parents certainly must remember the Empress Dowager's ruthlessness. If they're still alive. The picture comes into my mind again in a rush. Cricket and me, left at the door of the wu liu temple as our parents fled from the brutality that the Empress Dowager called justice. We held hands until the dawn came up, waiting for them to return.

At least I had Cricket.

This Wu Yinmei had no one left.

Did she have a little brother once? Did she watch the Empress Dowager poison him? I know that whatever I've been through, her life has been harder. But I also know that this is what she wants me, and everyone else, to feel. I look her straight in the eye and say,

"And you are bringing all of us straight into the Empress Dowager's path."

The senseis murmur and consult.

The chains sling through the air.

Five more chains wrap themselves around the arm near us, seven on the other. We total eleven weights now, they thirteen. The fulcrum moans as the hand holding Hisashi, the Chairman, and this girl dips down toward the pearl below us.

Doi cries, "If she's truly the heir, then allowing her sanctuary here will draw the Empress Dowager's wrath on us."

Hisashi replies, "Returning her now would not buy us safety. She's already been insulted. It's too late."

Doi retorts, "Because of your rash decision. You were supposed to do something to help get Father's hostages back. You've put all of us in danger."

Hisashi's face flips through emotions, like a fan folding closed, facet by facet, until it snaps shut.

He says calmly, "Sometimes it's easy and in one's own interest to stand up for others. Often it's not. I hope that I can always make that decision whether it's easy or not. I would be very . . . disappointed in myself for doing any less."

Doi shoots back, "And I would be very disappointed in myself for being tricked by such obvious lies."

Five chains fly up to our side, seven to theirs. Sixteen weights on our side, twenty on theirs. They're only one story above the pearl below us. Doi looks at me, and I can see my own panic reflected in her face. We are higher in the sky than when we did aerial combat last year. We crouch down low on the palm beneath us, Doi and I huddling around Cricket to keep him secure. Below us, the Chairman, Hisashi, and this Wu Yinmei stand straight, as if readying to step off their palm to the pearl just below them.

"Final argument!" announces Supreme Sensei.

The Chairman says, "The Empress Dowager seeks to conquer Pearl. If this girl is granted sanctuary here, she can serve as a figurehead, as a rival to challenge the rule of the Empress Dowager."

The girl nods and adds, "I am her only remaining blood heir. I am the only one with the claim of the imperial line. If you take me, you hold the future throne of Shin in your palm."

I see, far below, twelve heads nodding at her logic. I'm no match for her. But I know I'm right.

"She is not who she says she is!" I shout below. "She's seeking sanctuary behind our gates, but she's here to open them for the Shinian army."

The girl speaks, in a voice directed at the senseis, but with a gaze directed at me far above. "I seek sanctuary here because the people of Pearl are known for their fairness. Pearlians understand that we should not leap to conclusions about what is inside a person's heart simply because that person is different."

Her round face is like a mirror burning its light into me. She says, slowly, firmly, "We should not hate someone just because she is not from here."

Her words hit like a fist in my center of Chi.

I remember Suki's attacks toward me last year, accusing me of being a Shinian spy. Am I becoming Suki?

"Chen Cricket," asks Sensei Madame Liao. "Do you have anything to add?"

I say, "Cricket fully supports our posi—"

"Let him speak!" commands Sensei Madame Liao. "What is your position?"

"Uh," says Cricket, "may I ask Princess Wu Yinmei why she uses a swiftboard and poles if she doesn't have bound feet?"

This Wu Yinmei says, "My great-great-grandmother fed me ivory yang salts." The opposite of the ivory yin salts that Cricket took to keep his body small enough to learn girls' wu liu moves. "The Empress Dowager was not afraid of me revealing her plans since I was implicated in them. But she wanted to ensure that I would not run away. My feet are unbroken, but now if I take five steps within one day, my heart and lungs will grow as much as they would in a year. If I do not rest, they will burst."

Just like the Dian Mai performed on me last year that turned my own body into a prison. I clutch my heart at the thought of it bursting if I took more than five steps.

She concludes, "So you see, I cannot flee from Pearl without help."

I blurt, "She doesn't have to flee. She could send messages back—"

"Silence!" orders Sensei Madame Liao.

Why won't she let me speak? I thought she was my friend.

The senseis chatter below us. The final twelve chains flip through the air. Two fly to our side, the other ten wrap themselves around the far arm. The palm on which Hisashi, the Chairman, and the girl stand comes slamming down onto the pearl. The sound echoes across the campus.

We've lost. And now we're in greater danger than we've ever been in.

The senseis gather around this girl as Hisashi and the Chairman help her back onto her swiftboard.

Sensei Madame Liao removes the chains strung on the far arm to lower the palm that Doi, Cricket, and I are on. We step off.

Doi and Cricket look at me. Doi reaches her hand to me. I want to embrace her. I want to cry into her shoulder. I want to grab them both by the hand and flee. But that's not what I need to do now. I need to focus on how I'm going to keep us safe.

I wave away Doi's hand gently and say, "I think I want to be alone."

Doi and Cricket skate to depart Divinity's Lap with everyone else. They all begin to move across the plaza, leaving me at the base of the towering statue, this Enlightened One who has just decided Pearl's fate, one way or another, and mine with it.

And then, in the middle of the sea of backs, this girl at the center of that fate, this Wu Yinmei, a girl from Shin who defeated this girl from Shin, looks back at me over her shoulder. The placid expression she has worn is gone.

With a lift of only one side of her mouth, she smiles at me.

CHAPTER
SIX

In the morning, I wake to find two letter orbs and a parcel addressed to Cricket, Doi, and me in the mail trough at 8,888 Cups. The three of us squeeze in the dormitory chamber that Cricket and I share, because whatever the packages contain, it seems best that we open them together. When I twist the rings of the outer shell of the letter orb to solve the postal rebus, the sending address reads, PEARL FAMOUS ACADEMY OF SKATE AND SWORD, BUREAU OF FINANCIAL PITY.

I open it and a voice whispers, "Chen Peasprout and Chen Cricket, we are pleased to inform you that the application submitted on your behalf by Sensei Madame Liao for renewal of the diplomatic waiver of your tuition for this coming year at Pearl Famous has been approved."

I open the parcel. It's two new pairs of skates for Cricket and me. How am I supposed to know how to feel about Sensei Madame

Liao? Is she my friend or not? Doi twists open her letter orb. "Wing Girl! Wanted to ___ you that I talked with Father." Words keep dropping out whenever Hisashi forgot to whisper. "___ all taken care of. You're not going ___ that nasty ___ colony. I got him to pay your tuition and Wu Yinmei's. ___ you at the ___ of Welcoming! ___ are both ___ you ___ friends ___ ___!" By the end of it, he's completely forgotten to keep his voice a whisper. Half the words escaped out of the orb before we unsealed it. All enthusiasm. No delicacy. All boy.

Doi slowly screws the halves of the orb back together. There's no celebration in her expression at the news that she'll be returning to Pearl Famous.

Instead, her lips are pressed firmly against each other.

She looks at this orb sent by her brother who changed what she could not change. Her brother who, with one swift sweep, successfully requested from their father what she spent the entire last year trying to get and failing. And their father is paying for this Wu Yinmei, whom Hisashi met mere weeks ago, to attend Pearl Famous.

Doi shoves the paper shoji panes of the window open.

She flings the orb out the window with such force that it whistles as it cuts through the air.

When we skate into Eastern Heaven Dining Hall for the Feast of Welcoming, I see Sensei Madame Liao watching me from the senseis' table. I can feel her Chi all the way across the hall. There's no ease in it, only tension, concern, fear. The Chairman is seated next to her at the senseis' table. Why is he at the senseis' table? Why is he wearing a sensei's robe?

Suki and the House of Flowering Blossoms girls enter the hall. They all skate assisted by poles topped by ornately carved handles. Suki must have heard the whisperings that a real princess has joined the students at Pearl Famous and that she uses a swiftboard and poles.

Then this Wu Yinmei arrives. She pushes on her poles with effort as her bladechair crests the end of the ramp leading into Eastern Heaven Dining Hall. Hisashi, who's beside her, doesn't assist. She doesn't look like the type to want assistance. She rises from the bladechair at the entrance to the hall. She parks it to the side, slides a swiftboard from a slot in the back of it, and slips her feet into the straps on the board. She stands and pushes herself on the swiftboard into the hall using her poles to propel and balance. Nothing on her face, nothing in her demeanor. As solemn as a pillar. Silence sweeps over the hall, but it's soon filled with a cloud of twitters as everyone watches her. Everyone except for myself.

I'm looking instead at Hisashi, this boy who smiles like a friend but who has endangered me like an enemy.

Doi, Cricket, and I seat ourselves at a table. At the far end of the hall is a great round metal cage. Something's visible through the bars, under a sheet of oiled white cotton. I look closer and recoil when I see that forms poke through the cloth, suggesting figures with smothered faces. The whole structure and whatever is in it resemble the round head of a metal dragon holding a great, deformed pearl in its teeth. I glance around to see if anyone has taken notice. The other students seem to share my confusion.

When Supreme Sensei Master Jio ascends the lecture dais and cries, "Ahihahaha," his laughter sings with falsehood. He's nervous. Which makes me nervous.

"Before we commence the Feast of Welcoming to receive the sweet new first-year embryos to Pearl Famous Academy of Skate and Sword, I have important news to share. However, I assure you that there is no reason to be alarmed."

As soon as he says that, I'm alarmed.

He continues, "There has been an infestation of coiling water dragons. They have made a sweet nest where they are nurturing their own little embryos in the waters beyond the Conservatory of Architecture. Rest assured that Pearl Famous has negotiated with the coiling water dragons. The creatures can be fearsome when protecting their eggs. However, because they are wise and rational beings, they have agreed to a contract not to harm us as long as none of us goes into the sea, especially beyond the Conservatory of Architecture near their nest. Heed, my dear, sweet, little ones. For, as you shall learn when you attain sagehood, those who miss to seek fortune seek to miss misfortune."

A confused rumble rises in the hall. Dragons aren't real. Does he think we're babies? Why's he telling us this? Immediately, I suspect that the dragons are a distraction rather than a threat. What are the senseis trying to cover up?

Sensei Madame Liao is the only sensei not tensely smiling. Her angry expression tells me all I need to know. I don't believe it's dragons, but there's still reason to be alarmed.

"These are generally benevolent creatures," Supreme Sensei

Master Jio continues, "but they can be very, very dangerous. If you hear a coiling water dragon approaching, you must close your eyes, for seeing a coiling water dragon will turn you into a statue of salt."

How can they possibly believe that the students would believe this ludicrous—

Then Sensei Madame Yao skates to the metal cage at the far end of the hall. She reaches in carefully, tugs down the cloth, and skates backward. She shakes the cloth as she pulls it, as if dislodging grains of sand.

As the cloth is whisked away, it exposes the figures of soldiers carved in white.

Dozens of silent, still soldiers.

All of them made of salt.

My Chi trembles. I can tell from Doi's expression and the quiver in her Chi that she feels the same. None of the other students know that just one of these salt figures could melt all of Eastern Heaven Dining Hall and bring the structure collapsing down around us.

The metal cage keeps the figures of salt from touching the pearl beneath them.

Sensei Madame Yao was shaking the oiled cloth so that any loose grains of salt wouldn't be dragged out of the cage and onto the pearl floor.

I force myself to look at the salt soldiers' faces, bracing myself for their terror, but I'm surprised to see they all look the same, as if they were all conscripted from one family. Something's not right.

The great doors of the hall burst open. Three students skate in. From the embroidered blue filigree trim on the seams of their robes,

I know that they're the three new third-year students invited to devote to the Conservatory of Architecture.

They're dripping with water.

"Supreme Sensei!" cries one girl. "We beg your forgiveness!"

"What has befallen these three sweet embryos of the Conservatory of Architecture?" answers Supreme Sensei with a sweep of his arm.

"We were skating to the Feast of Welcoming from the Conservatory of Architecture when a little water cyclone blew us off the rail."

"Blew you off the rail? Yet surely you did not enter the sea and violate the contract with the usually benevolent but now vicious coiling water dragons, did you, little ones?" Supreme Sensei says it not to the three wet students but to all of us, as if he were broadcasting his voice to the back of an opera hall. I try and catch Doi or Cricket's attention. What is going on here?

"Yes! We fell in the sea. A dragon's coming to punish us for breaking the contract! It's flying here now!"

Everyone stands up from their seats. The hall resounds with students fervently debating what is happening, whether this is real.

It can't be real. There aren't any dragons except in stories. This must all be some sort of drill or experimental opera production. I know when I'm in the middle of someone's plot. I don't know what the plot is or who's behind it, but one thing I do know is that dragons aren't real.

What is happening here?

Fingers dig into my arm. I turn and see Sensei Madame Liao's face, fury fighting with fear.

"Peasprout, protect Cricket," she says. "This is real."

Around us, the students are beginning to panic. "Students," she announces to them. "This is not a drill."

"Where's Cricket?" I say to Doi beside me, searching frantically. "He was just here!"

"Senseis and prefects," barks Sensei Madame Liao, "lock down all window slats and doors."

The senseis and prefects race down the hall, sweeping the tall window slats shut with leaping third- and luckieth-gate spins, followed by one fan chop after another to secure the latches. However, Eastern Heaven Dining Hall was designed with so many windows because it was intended to be airy and open to the view of the sea over the cliff edge, like a temple floating on a cloud. The entire long back wall facing the sea is filled with slender window slats reaching three stories high. I don't know how we're going to securely lock everything down before the dragons attack.

"Now," commands Sensei Madame Liao, "all students, gather in the center of the hall. Stay away from windows. First-year students in the innermost center. Second-year students around them. Third-year students around them. Senseis form a perimeter."

I find Cricket in the center of the hall, Doi's arms wrapped around him. I join them and throw myself around Cricket so that Doi and I form a basket of arms around him.

"Put out all lanterns, sweet ones!" commands Supreme Sensei.

The lanterns wink out around us and the hall grows as dark as the night outside. Students stifle their whimpers in sleeves and behind fans as we huddle in a mass of quivers in the center of the hall.

I see the Chairman. He's huddled under the senseis' vast dining table. He has undone the sash of his New Deitsu officer's robe under his sensei's robe and is using it to tie himself to the leg of the table. He urgently motions to Hisashi and this Wu Yinmei to get under the table and circles his fist to indicate tying.

Then the air begins to ring with a high metallic hum. The quality of the atmosphere changes. Friction sparks leap from my robe as the cloth rubs against the robes of the students crouched next to me.

A sound pierces the air. It starts as a high keening, then becomes a shriek buried inside a roar, as if a tiger opened its mouth to bellow while out of its throat flew one screeching eagle after another. The windows and doors of the hall rattle furiously in their frames as the winds whip and buffet us.

Under it all, the metallic hum rings with such force that my teeth ache. I look over to Cricket. His eyes are squeezed shut in a wince of pain.

"Cricket!" I cry, but he can't hear me over the thundering noise around us.

His hands are cupped not to his ears but to his nose.

Red seeps out between his fingers as he tries to stanch the blood flowing from his nose.

"It's going to strike!" screams Supreme Sensei. "Hold on to one another, little ones—the coiling water dragon is going to strike!"

CHAPTER
SEVEN

The impact of the coiling water dragon rocks the hall and sends our huddle of students and senseis scattering on hands and knees in a fan shape across the floor.

What appears to be a dark, watery claw half as high as the hall rakes viciously across the entire back wall, sending the window slats clattering open as tendrils of black water lash toward us.

"We have to stop it!" cries Sensei Madame Liao at Supreme Sensei Master Jio.

"It is not possible to stop it," he shouts back. "Don't look at it, students!"

"Senseis, secure the windows!" orders Sensei Madame Liao. The twelve senseis leave the students and launch themselves at the slats. The Chairman stays lashed to the leg of the table under which he's hiding. Doi and I crouch with Cricket wrapped in our arms, but I can't see where Hisashi and Wu Yinmei are in this pile of students.

The senseis launch themselves in snapping lotus kicks at the seaward wall, their skate blades scissoring together to slam the window slats shut in their frames, but there are only twelve senseis and eighty-seven window slats. As soon as they kick one set of windows shut, the coiling water dragon rips open more, and the simple latches and hooks can't hold against its force.

"There aren't enough senseis!" says Doi.

"We have to help them!" I say.

We both rise.

"It's coming again!" hollers Cricket through his hands cupped over his bloodied nose.

Everyone turns toward the window slats flapping open and revealing the sea beyond.

"No, the other side!" cries Cricket.

At that, a force punches open the two great doors of the main entrance behind us. A whipping frenzy of cold black tendrils bursts through the entrance, lashing us with their wet fury.

"Doi!" I command. "Take it from the left." I search out Hisashi in the crush of panicked students. "Hisashi, take it from the right."

Doi, with her short hair and black academy robe swirling like a dark orchid, turns into a blaze of movement on the left. On the right, Hisashi, identically shorn and dressed, turns into a matching flurry, whipping through the same motions.

The two of them turn and bound in perfect mirror synchrony with each other, weaving across the hall like a fine embroidered design rendered in black cloth and silver blade, to meet in the middle at the two main doors to the hall.

"Hit it now!" I shout at them.

They explode at the doors with the power of twin fireworks cannons in some complex pairs move that I've never seen before.

Doi's and Hisashi's kicks slam the doors shut, severing the lashing tentacles and tails protruding through. The dragon's amputated appendages drop to the floor and appear to turn into splashes of water.

"Secure the doors!" I say, throwing two chairs toward them.

Doi and Hisashi each stab the leg of a chair through the handles of the great doors, barring them. The two of them press against each other, back-to-back, fists lifted in preparation for the next attack.

"It's coming from the north, along the seaward wall!" yells Cricket.

I skate to the north end of the hall. The rumbling grows and grows as the coiling water dragon speeds toward us. I call to Cricket, "Tell me when it's going to strike us!"

"Seven beats! Six beats! Five! Fo—lucky!"

I burst down the hall toward the south end. At the last moment, I turn and give up one of my lifetime's riven crane split jumps and leap over the cage of salt soldiers.

"Three!" shouts Cricket.

I channel the Chi force from the riven crane split jump off the south wall, toward the front wall. I skate along its unbroken surface, veering over the main doorway, with Doi and Hisashi peering up at me from below.

"Two!"

I sling myself midair into a reverse flying halberd triple jump, flipping and bounding off the north wall.

"One!"

I kick off the end of the triple jump and fling myself toward the window slats of the seaward wall, just as the coiling water dragon flies past the hall outside, like a thundering train of rattling iron carriages. The force of my leap sends me flying alongside it.

As the coiling water dragon blasts each window slat open with its passing, I sweep along the seaward wall beside it, my skate extended in front of me, slamming each window shut as soon as it opens.

The roar and scream of the creature diminish as it flies over the sea, then rise as it circles back for another attack.

I shout at Cricket, crowded with the other students in the middle of the hall. "Cricket! How many beats until it—"

Every window slat swings open at once, and the coiling water dragon vomits torrents of water, pummeling us and threatening to drown us in the hall. The coiling water dragon then hurtles out toward the sea. I exhale in relief, then realize that the dragon is moving away from us so quickly that it leaves a void of pressure in the hall. It begins violently sucking the water out the slats in streams.

"Hold on to something!" commands Sensei Madame Liao.

I dive under the table nearest to me as the other students scramble to do the same. We all wrap our arms around the table legs and one another as the water around our skates forms a tide rushing out the slats. Although the tables are carved into the floor of the hall itself, the water tries to pull us out and take us with it, spilling over the cliffside and into the sea.

"You have to stop this!" bellows Sensei Madame Liao at Supreme Sensei Master Jio again. I can barely hear her over the roar of water and the screams of the students.

"It's too late!" he cries back.

The ringing and thunder in the air begin to rise again, and we brace ourselves for another attack.

"We all have to help!" announces Sensei Madame Liao. "Second- and third-years, form lines in front of each window slat! Take turns leaping at it. We must not let the coiling water dragon reach inside again."

Doi, Hisashi, and I take our positions in front of the window slats. Most of the students, however, remain huddled in the center of the hall, too afraid to move.

"Students!" cries Sensei Madame Liao again. Still, only a few students move to join us.

A beat begins to pound in the hall. We all turn toward the sound.

Standing on her swiftboard at the dais is this Wu Yinmei. She's pounding on the lectern with her poles, as if beating on a great drum. She opens her mouth, and a voice as piercing and serene as a pearlflute sings out.

" 'Sisters of the skate!

" 'Brothers of the blade!' "

She pounds out the rhythm of "The Pearlian Battlesong" with her poles like a calm and steady heartbeat.

" 'Come and lend your hands and stand up for your motherland!

" 'Answer the command!

" ' "Come and join our band!" ' "

The sight of this girl with her immobile feet, unable to flee, unafraid and standing in the face of this crisis, causes a few students to collect themselves out of their panic. They join us at the lines in front of the window slats.

"'Come and join, come and join our band!'" she sings out. Several more students remember themselves, as if called out of a dream, and add themselves to the students lined up to protect the hall.

"'Come and join, come and join our band!'"

Several more students join the line and sing along, "'Come and join, come and join our band!'"

"'"Come and join our band!"'" she cries, pounding out each beat like a command to our better selves while the coiling water dragon flies toward us over the dark water. The hall shudders and quakes with its approach.

"Don't look at it!" orders Sensei Madame Yao.

The creature rams into us.

We launch ourselves in volley after volley at the window slats, slamming them shut each time they threaten to flip open.

The air in the hall is filled with a high whistling as the coiling water dragon blasts its watery breath through the window slats trying to pry its way to us, but it can't get in.

"It's working!" I cry as the creature retreats from the seaward side. "It's flying away."

"No, it's coming from the other side!" shouts Cricket. His nose is streaming blood again, but he doesn't seem to notice.

The coiling water dragon plows into us from the other side with such devastating force that it tears the entire hall off the foundation of pearl beneath it, flipping the structure onto its side so that the window slats are now below us and the wall with the main entry doors is above us. Chairs bounce over our heads, but the tables, which were carved into the structure itself, hold to the floor, which is now the wall beside us. Doi comes sliding into me, but we shoot out our arms to cushion the crash. Cricket is hurtling toward us from the floor flipping beneath us. Doi and I catch him in a lucky-fisted palanquin position, absorbing his fall.

The coiling water dragon collides into us again, sending the hall sliding toward the sea. When the structure finally comes to a stop, one-third of the length of Eastern Heaven Dining Hall hangs over the cliff edge of the Principal Island. The window slats over on that end of the hall now swing open, revealing churning black water far below.

The students caught on that end of the hall scream with panic as they leap from window frame to window frame over gaping chasms, toward the safety of our side of the hall. I catch sight of Suki, her face twisting with panic as she nearly loses her balance launching off a narrow window frame, but she quickly rights herself. It's the first time I've seen her look shaken.

The cage filled with salt soldiers is crammed at an angle in one window slat. The slender frame holding the cage from falling suddenly snaps. The entire cage plummets into the sea with the salt soldiers trapped within.

All the senseis fling themselves in hammer-throw moves toward the wall that used to be the floor, in an effort to flip the hall upright with their pounding impact. The Chairman dangles high above us on the wall, still lashed to the table leg. Rows of students join the senseis in leaping at the wall, but they can't generate enough force to flip it. Their efforts only nudge the hall away from the cliff edge.

Doi and I look at each other. We see the solution at the same time.

"No!" we exclaim together.

"Sensei Madame Liao, don't flip the hall upright!" I say.

"The window slats are facing down now!" says Doi.

"We just need to move the hall away from the cliff edge. The windows are blocked closed!" I cry.

Sensei Madame Liao nods at us and barks, "Everyone, stop trying to flip the hall upright! Leap instead at the north end of the hall!"

Phalanxes of students and senseis turn and leap at the north wall in wave after wave like grasshoppers. The metallic scream begins to rise in the air outside as the coiling water dragon makes its approach again.

Each strike against the north end of the hall pulls us a little closer inland, but are we moving fast enough?

The structure shudders violently as the coiling water dragon flies toward us.

We leap in desperate strike after strike at the north end of the hall until it's pitted like the head of a lotus.

We barely manage to shift the entire length of the hall safely onto dry pearl when the coiling water dragon strikes. Its screeches are muffled this time, now that all windows into the hall are sealed shut beneath us. The metallic hum doesn't reach my teeth now. We can feel it trying to find a way in. It wraps around the ends of the hall like a dog mauling a bone too big to bite.

Everyone is tucked down with their hands over their heads, as taught in earthquake drills. But I can't help looking up.

Above us, the great doors to Eastern Heaven Dining Hall shake furiously in their frame. I can see that Doi and Hisashi cleverly stabbed the chair legs into the handles in an arch formation, which is only strengthened with the more pressure that is put on it.

The main doors above us hold.

The window slats below us hold.

It can't reach us.

We've foiled it.

The coiling water dragon screams in frustration with one last outburst of air from its lungs.

The two main doors above us are ripped out of their frame like paper shoji screens, and I'm staring straight up at the coiling water dragon.

I whip my head away in horror, but it's too late. I saw it.

The whipping tendrils of water, like tentacles.

The furious black waves of its coils and tails coursing past, like a dark river in the sky.

I pat my limbs, shaking.

I saw it, but I haven't been turned to salt.

Is it because I didn't see its face?

Its sound is retreating. The roar has stopped. The screaming wind is dying down. We've defeated it.

It's leaving us.

Don't look up again, Peasprout. Don't risk it.

But I can't help it.

Through the doorway above me, I see, in the dark sky, the silver of a spiraling tail. The coiling water dragon disappears, like a serpent of mist and rain, softly whistling, into a sea of stars.

CHAPTER
EIGHT

Afterward, the Hall of Benevolent Healing is filled with students cradling sprained arms, scratches, swollen lips, and other minor injuries.

I spot Doi and Hisashi together, talking excitedly.

"That final third-gate forever symmetry pangolin roll was an ingenious choice, Wing Girl!" beams Hisashi, clapping his sister on the shoulder.

"You set us up for it," says Doi. Something like a smile flutters on her lips.

I don't approach them. Whatever my feelings are about Hisashi, he's the only family that Doi really has anymore. I want them to make their peace.

A ring of students crowds around Wu Yinmei, clapping and chanting "Captain! Captain!" She turns her head toward me, but I skate away. So what if she played some part in defeating the coiling water dragon? She's probably overjoyed at the opportunity to appear as if she's loyal to Pearl.

Now that the threat is gone, all the other students are acting like this is a party. Comparing stories of what they saw and did in the battle against the coiling water dragon. It's long past the hour for sleep, but everyone is staying up, sharing blankets while drinking bowls of warm soy milk and chewing fried crullers, chattering about our adventure. I want to join them and celebrate that we fought, we won, and we are safe, at least for now.

But I can't. I know something is wrong.

I skate over to where the weird healer Doctor Dio is examining all the injured students. When she gets to Cricket, she says, "His nosebleed was just due to atmospheric change. He has a severe sensitivity in his sinus bone. Nothing to worry about." She adds slowly, "Although . . . I can't be certain it's not something more serious unless I remove his nose for study. It's always safest for the patient's health to remove the nose for study."

I ignore her. If I learned one thing last year, it's that I can't trust anything she says. Cricket shrugs and skates over to a group of students. I should follow.

But I can't. A creature that I believed wasn't real showed itself to be devastatingly real in the most unforgettable way possible, as if punishing me for my doubt.

And this thing's mere approach made my brother bleed.

I can't join the other students in celebrating because I was wrong about the coiling water dragon. What else could I be wrong about?

All I know is that I can't be wrong like this again if I want to keep Cricket and myself safe.

When we gather for the assembly the first morning of classes, the presence of the dragon can still be felt. Most of the students are so terrified of falling in the water now that everyone stands far from the seaward edge of Divinity's Lap.

However, some second-year boy with delicate features and hair powdered shimmering silver is peering over the lip of the edge toward the water. "I just saw some scales flashing down there!" he shouts.

Another second-year boy with bleached bangs swats the powder from the other boy's hair and says, "What are you talking about? It was just your hair glitter!" Everyone laughs, and, seeing that they have an audience, the two start wrestling like puppies near the edge of the water, trying to thump each other on the hair. With a shout, the bleached-bangs boy slips, and his skate shoots out from under him. He teeters on the edge overhanging the water.

My stomach and everyone else's stomachs plummet as we watch him spiral his arms to keep from falling into the sea. The silver-haired boy shoots out his hand and grabs a fistful of robe, hauling his friend away from the cliff edge.

We all exhale in relief.

My relief is swiftly replaced with anger. One careless student falling into the water could bring those creatures down on us again.

We could be anywhere when it happens. Like here, out on this open, uncovered square.

It seems like all the students are looking out at the water beyond and below, teeming with lethal creatures, thinking the same thing: *We are trapped on an island, and we are surrounded.*

No one's laughing now.

The senseis, which now include the Chairman, arrive and array themselves in the form of an arrowhead.

Supreme Sensei Master Jio skates forth to address us. "Sweet ones, as we all learned so unforgettably yesterday, everything has changed this year. Due to the increasing level of threat from the Imperium of Shin, the essential mission of Pearl Famous has also changed. To explain the alterations, we have the legendary and healthful Sensei Master General Moon Tzu. Welcome him with ten thousand bows of veneration and awe."

An old man pushes forth on a bladechair. He rises and stands before us in a robe like a swirl of cloud, trailing a snowy white mustache that's so long, he's followed by two pages acting as mustache-bearers.

Sensei Madame Yao and the Chairman skate forward and flank him on either side.

Sensei Master General Moon Tzu lifts one of his poles and mumbles a few words. Sensei Madame Yao places her fist across her heart and intones, "Sensei Master General Moon Tzu says, 'Soft and depraved students of Pearl Famous Academy of Skate and Sword. Opera is frivolous in a time of impending invasion.

Pearl Famous is no longer an arts school. It is now a military academy.'"

We're all stunned into silence by this. Then the students erupt into whispers of disbelief and outrage. Around me, students murmur, "How can they do this?" and "We didn't sign up to be soldiers. We're artists!"

Next to me, Cricket whispers, "Does this mean we're going to have to hurt people?"

What is going on here? I look to Sensei Madame Liao. She looks like she's been forced to take a mouthful of poison and is deciding whether to swallow it or spit it out.

Sensei Master General Moon Tzu murmurs a couple more syllables.

The Chairman places his fist across his heart and states, "Sensei Master General Moon Tzu says, 'Thus, we resurrect the Thousand Flowers Campaign. During the Bamboo Invasion decades ago, New Deitsu Pearlworks Company sponsored an effort to harness the young minds of Pearl. Our students were tasked with inventing new applications of wu liu to save us from the Shinian invaders. So now once again, we call on the youth to save our homeland. Let a thousand flowers bloom and a thousand schools of wu liu thought contend!'"

Wait—the general can't possibly have said all of that. He only uttered a couple words.

I raise my hand and ask, "But venerable Sensei Master General Moon Tzu, how would Shinian ships even cross the water to get to us if it's infested with coiling water dragons? It seems like they're our best possible defense against invasion."

The Chairman smiles and says, "This is not the time for questions, little—"

"I thought you wanted to harness the power of young minds," says Sensei Madame Liao. The Chairman shoots a look at her and fumes. She continues, "Chen Peasprout asks a valid question. You should answer it." She pauses and adds, "If you can."

Thank you, Sensei Madame Liao.

The Chairman looks at all the faces staring at him and slips on his sugar face. "Clever little bird. An excellent question. But coiling water dragons do not attack ships. Anyway, as Sensei Master General was saying—"

"How do you know that?" I ask.

The Chairman glares at me. His hatred rolls off his Chi in waves, but he swallows it down. He smiles and says, "Because I said so."

"That's not logical or even grammatically correct."

The Chairman is so filled with bottled rage toward me that he can't blink his eyes in unison. Still, he contains himself. He says, "So admirable! Students, please observe Chen Peasprout as an example of confidence in your own abilities, no matter how low your ranking. What place did you take last year, Chen Peasprout? Sixteenth?"

I feel everyone watching me. Including Hisashi. I open my mouth for a sharp retort, but Doi beside me whispers, "Not here, Peasprout. We'll learn more from my father if we don't set him on guard."

"That's enough," Sensei Madame Yao leaps in. She continues, "Sensei Master General Moon Tzu says, 'You shall be taught—'"

She stops when she realizes that the general hasn't spoken yet. He whispers five more syllables. Sensei Madame Yao continues, "Sensei Master General Moon Tzu says, 'You shall be taught wu liu, plus wu liu combined with each of the other three disciplines. First-year students shall be taught wu liu by Sensei Madame Liao; wu-liu-combined-with-architecture by Supreme Sensei Master Jio . . .'"

So they're mapping wu liu onto everything. To turn everything into a weapon. Doi looks as stricken as I feel.

"'. . . Second-year students shall be taught wu liu by Sensei Master General Moon Tzu, assisted by myself, Sensei Madame Yao . . .'"

Her face does something strange. Parts of it move and others don't.

Oh. She's trying not to smile. Because she at last gets to teach wu liu in some way.

"'. . . wu-liu-combined-with-architecture by Chairman Niu Kazuhiro . . .'"

This is outrageous! I turn to Doi when I hear this. I can feel the fear and fury pulsing off her Chi. She doesn't return my gaze. She and Hisashi are looking at each other.

"'. . . wu-liu-combined-with-literature by Sensei Master Ram; and wu-liu-combined-with-music by Sensei Madame Chingu. Third-year . . .'"

"Wait," I say to Doi. "*Chingu?* What was that she said?"

However, Doi and her brother are still locked in a silent argument, emotions flowing through their Chi.

The Chairman waits for Sensei Master General Moon Tzu to mumble, then says, "Sensei Master General Moon Tzu says, 'Students shall not compete individually but shall instead form into bands to battle together as a team, as the heroic students who fought in the Bamboo Invasion did.

"Your battleband will take what you learn in class and apply it in three competitions, entitled Annexations. Students are again encouraged to devise unique ways to defend Pearl's perimeter and protect Pearl's capital city.'"

Sensei Master General Moon Tzu lifts both canes in the air and says at the top of his voice, "Every battle is fought before it is won."

Sensei Madame Yao frowns and says, "Won before it is fought. Sensei Master General Moon Tzu meant, 'Every battle is won before it is fought.' You must choose your battleband mates before the First Annexation. Your choice shall be critical in your success. We shall now demonstrate the importance in the Thousand Flowers Campaign."

Sensei Master General Moon Tzu produces three peonies from his sleeve, then with a groan of effort, flings them as hard as he can. They drop to the pearl a few steps in front of him. Sensei Madame Yao skates forth, picks them up, and tosses them deep into the crowd of students.

With a streak of movement to the right, Suki claws one of the flowers out of the air. Etsuko flings herself into a triple cicada spin, flies into the air like an insect, and catches the second peony between her ankles.

The third flower flies in a high arc above us. A forest of hands rises up to catch it. I have to get that flower. After the Chairman's comment about my sixteenth-place ranking, I have to save face. I crouch down in a diagonal crab claw formation and shoot to the side, up toward the flower. Right as I'm about to grab it, I slam directly into another student.

"Ahh, my nose!" Gou Gee-Hong, whom I called Mole Girl all last year, is clutching her nose.

"I'm sorry!" I crouch down to her. "Oh, your nose is bleeding."

She touches her fingers to her nose, looks at the red, and begins to scream as if she just discovered all her limbs were cut off.

"I'm so sorry, Mole G—I mean, Gee-Hong!"

Another student escorts her to the Hall of Benevolent Healing. Doctor Dio is going to be delighted to receive another nose injury. I hear whispers around me of "She always has to be the center of attention" and "She'll shove anyone aside" and "She gave her own brother a nosebleed."

I'm too ashamed of myself to turn around and see who's saying these things. Did Hisashi hear them? Where is he? With Wu Yinmei? *Peasprout, why should you care what he thinks or whether he's with that girl?* To my right, everyone's crowded around the student who caught the third flower. Heavenly August Personage of Jade, it's Cricket! He's smiling at everyone as if he just won the lead in the Drift Season Pageant.

The Chairman motions for the three of them to come to the front of the assembly. "To demonstrate the importance of choosing battleband mates carefully, these three shall constitute a battleband for this exercise."

Suki and Etsuko look at Cricket and step away from him, as if he were covered in whale dung. Shinian servant girls holding baskets of pink and white flowers skate to Suki, Etsuko, and Cricket and begin pasting blossom heads all over the robes of the three of them.

"Only the pink ones," spits Suki at the servant girls. "What is this glue? If this stains my robe, my father will have you deported!"

When the servant girls are done, Suki and Etsuko look like a pair of princess goddesses risen from a lake of pink petals. Cricket, off to the far side and wrapped in the remaining white petals, looks like a fly cocooned by a spider.

The Chairman says, "Now, all the students are to attack these three and rip the flowers off their robes. The three of them will be scored based on how long they can together fight you off, and have at least one flower left among them."

The students look at one another, then proceed to surround the three of them like a pool of black pearlsilk and metal.

Suki and Etsuko are stranded in the middle of most of the students, while a thinner crowd tries to encircle Cricket. Doi and I push toward Cricket through the crush of students.

Suki and Etsuko look at each other. Their paths of escape out of the courtyard of Divinity's Lap are all cut off.

Suki shoves Etsuko into the crowd. The students descend on Etsuko and begin plucking the blossoms off her. As petals toss and fly into the air, Suki slices through the throng and races in the direction of one of the bridges leading toward the Palace of the Eighteen Outstanding Pieties.

The students surrounding Cricket turn to watch the mayhem. "Cricket, go now!" I shout.

Cricket does a series of deft two-heeled pivots and dodges the students who lunge at him. He skates over one of the bridges leading south from Divinity's Lap.

I elbow past other students to keep up with him. I hear whispers around me of "Can you believe her?" and "She's dying because she's not the center of the activity" and "So pathetic." I follow Suki and Cricket around to the front of the Palace of the Eighteen Outstanding Pieties. At its main entrance, Suki is fending off twelve attackers by stringing together fifth- and sixth-gate moves in all the zodiacal schools. However, even her talent is no match for the sheer number of students surrounding her, and patches are beginning to form on her robe where flowers have been pulled off.

South of this battle, Cricket has stationed himself at the crest of the Bridge of Serene Harmony spanning the Central Canal. A cluster of students attacks him from the south end of the bridge— far too many for him to take on at once. I want to help him, but Cricket would probably be disqualified for it.

Then I see why he chose this spot. The bridge is narrow, so only one attacker can come at him from the south at a time. Cricket has chosen terrain that makes their greater number irrelevant!

"Suki! Join me!" cries Cricket.

Suki sneers when she hears Cricket, but then she sees his stratagem as he faces a column of attackers lined up on the bridge, one by one.

Suki races to the crest of the bridge. She turns and faces the line of attackers pursuing her from the north.

Then I watch as the person I love the most and the person I hate the most battle together, back-to-back, defending their hill. My brother, Cricket, holding his own with the top-ranked skater in our class, each of them managing their half of the task, each of them standing down their half of an army. I'm filled with a stir of emotions as riotous as a thousand flowers.

Eventually, the numbers overwhelm them, and Cricket's robe is plucked free of its last flower. Suki's robe is also stripped of all its flowers. As the crowd parts from her, Suki's hair is in a wild tangle, her face paint streaming down in tears.

"Why me!" she wails. "Why always, always me!"

I skate over to Cricket and hug him.

"Cricket, are you all right?"

When we disentangle, I'm surprised at the expression on his face.

"Why are you smiling?" I ask.

"Because that was fun!"

He meets the world with such cheerfulness. He gives me hope that perhaps this year, with all its uncertainty and change, won't be so bad.

As we skate back toward Divinity's Lap to divide up for our first classes of the morning, several students clasp Cricket's hands. A couple of boys say to him, "If you ever need a battleband to join . . ."

Whatever my new concerns are this year, I think that Cricket's not going to be one of them. He's going to do all right. He's finding his own way, not just in archi—

A screech cuts through the air. We turn our gazes heavenward.

The *Pearl Shining Sun News* birds are looping in the sky. They failed to bring a single grain of good news for me last year. I take off my smoked spectacles to read the headline they're writing.

"Empress. Dowager. Demands. Return. Of. Traitor. Chen. Peasprout. Threatens. Invasion. If. Pearl. Refuses. Buy. Pearl. Shining. Sun. News. To. Get. Whole. Story."

Everyone has arrived back in Divinity's Lap. All eyes are looking up at the birds.

Supreme Sensei Master Jio calls out, "Does anybody have a newspaper?"

"I subscribe to the morning letter orb edition," says Sensei Master Bao. "I haven't unsealed it yet." The senseis pass the orb hand to hand along their rank until it reaches Supreme Sensei Master Jio. He twists open the two halves and cups them to his ears.

"It says," he shouts at us, "that the Empress Dowager demands that Pearl send back the degenerate traitor and enemy of the Imperium, Chen Peasprout, whose ancestors must have all been low prisoners and criminals." Supreme Sensei looks at me and says, "That's not very nice, I don't agree with that at all, sweet embryo. Oh, and now it's saying that if Pearl refuses to send back the degenerate trait—well, send back Peasprout, Shin will prepare to invade. The Empress Dowager orders every one of her subjects to abduct Peasprout if given the chance and return her to Shin to receive punishment. If abduction is not possible, then the Empress Dowager orders every one of her subjects to seize any opportunity to kill Peasprout and anyone who harbors her."

All gazes turn from Supreme Sensei to me, then Cricket, and then this Wu Yinmei.

"Do I have to comply with that, too?" asks Cricket. "Am I still one of her subjects?"

"No, Cricket," says Doi.

"Because I won't do it!" yells Cricket, stamping his skate. "I tell you, I won't do it!"

"You don't have to, Cricket. You don't have to," Doi tells him, rubbing his back.

"She's behind this," I announce, and spin around to point at this Wu Yinmei. Instead of the mask of serenity that she usually wears, there is confusion and alarm on her face. She looks to Hisashi beside her. Instead of the confidence that usually radiates from him, he also looks thrown by this news.

"This girl," I continue, "is sending secret messages back to her great-great-grandmother. She probably told the Empress Dowager to do this because she wants to get rid of me!"

The Chairman says, "While we applaud imagination in our students, the idea of someone sending back secret messages to the Empress Dowager is rather ludicrous."

"No, it's not," I shoot back at him. "I did it for *you* last year!"

A wave of murmurs passes through the audience. Doi stiffens, but it doesn't matter anymore who knows about my deal with the Chairman. Not when he's prepared to sacrifice my life.

I continue, "I'm the only one who suspects this Wu Yinmei's real reason for coming here, so she's trying to get rid of me. She's dangerous!"

"You're the one who's dangerous." I pivot to find Suki flanking me on the right. "Shin is going to invade unless we give you up, Chen Peasprout. Senseis, send her back where she came from!"

"That's not going to achieve anything!" I exhort the senseis. "The Empress Dowager is looking for an excuse to invade. She'll just find another reason!"

"No one is sending Peasprout back to Shin," says Sensei Madame Liao. *Thank you, Sensei.*

"You don't get to decide that!" says Suki.

"How dare you say that to a sensei!" I say.

"Because she can't," snarls Suki. "She can't decide by herself to put the whole city in danger because of her favorite little darling."

"That is correct, Disciple Gang Suki," says Sensei Madame Liao calmly. "I cannot. Relations with Shin are matters for the Pearlian government. However, Pearl Famous is a sanctuary school. If we choose to grant sanctuary to someone, Pearlian authorities cannot touch her as long as she stays within the campus."

"My father's going to hear about this! Do you know who my father is?"

"Your father is not a sensei," says Sensei Madame Liao, as cool as jade. "And only the senseis get to decide this matter."

"Yes, the senseis decide this," says the Chairman behind me. I spin away from Suki and face him. "But sanctuary is granted to a person only if all the senseis agree to it." He looks at me and says, "And I'm afraid to tell you, little bird, that not all the senseis agree to it."

Doi skates forward to my side, looking like she's about to challenge her father publicly again, but Hisashi grabs her arm. He whispers, "Don't. It'll make it worse for Peasprout."

I helped this snake of a man deceive the Empress Dowager in order to help him get back his hostages, keep from losing his position as Chairman of New Deitsu, and fend off the calls for his imprisonment. He doesn't need me anymore. He has this Wu Yinmei as his Shinian puppet now. I knew last year that I was making a deal with a scorpion. I knew that he would refrain from stinging me only as long as I was carrying him on my back across the water.

I guess I didn't realize that we'd reached the riverbank.

But he doesn't realize that I can sting, too.

I can sting like salt.

"Chairman, we all want to avoid what is dangerous to Pearl," I say with a polite smile. "We all know that the Empress Dowager wants the secret of the pearl. We all understand that the only information as valuable as how to make a thing is how to destroy it. And that the most dangerous thing we could do is to send back to the Empress Dowager a little bird that knows how to sing a song she wants to learn. That would be as stupid as pouring *salt* in your own eye."

The Chairman's expression burns with fury. Then he smiles and fingers the bump at his breast under the front of his robe. I know that bump. It's a pendant with one of those shrinking trinkets in which he imprisons criminals. Is he threatening me?

He says smoothly, "A bird learns to keep quiet if singing would lure a tiger to its little chick."

The Chairman looks at Cricket.

He's threatening Cricket! If I tell the Empress Dowager that salt eats through the pearl, he'll find some reason to imprison Cricket and crush him into a trinket.

"I call a vote," says the Chairman. "Who is in favor of Pearl Famous granting Chen Peasprout sanctuary from the Empress Dowager's demand?"

I spin to the left and see at once the row of twelve senseis raise their hands. Even, to my great surprise, Sensei Madame Yao, but I can tell from the glint in her eye that she probably just relishes the idea of Shinian invasion because it would mean she would get to use violence.

The only sensei who doesn't raise his hand is the Chairman.

"Wait," I say.

What can I say? What does he want?

He wants to stop Shin from invading. He's petty; he's nasty. But what he wants is what I want. What we all want. That's why they've changed the curriculum. That's why we're a military academy now rather than an arts school.

So I'll give him what he wants.

"Sensei Chairman Niu. Grant me sanctuary status and I'll come up with weapons for Pearl to use against Shin."

"Why should I trust that you, a girl who took sixteenth place last year, have the talent to create anything useful for Pearl?"

"You don't have to trust me," I say. "If my efforts don't earn me first place at every Annexation, you can revoke my sanctuary status at any time."

"No," he says calmly.

"Father," Hisashi says, skating forward. "Give Chen Peasprout a chance to show she's valuable to Pearl."

"No."

"Why not?" Doi cries. Hisashi again tries to restrain her but she shakes his hand off her arm. "We have nothing to lose. What are you afraid of?"

"And I have everything to lose," I say, raising my chin. "I'm going to be developing weapons for Pearl to use against my own homeland. Every one of my efforts is going to just infuriate the Empress Dowager further. And if I don't deliver like I promised at every Annexation, then I get sent back, right into her rage. But I'm not afraid of taking a chance for Pearl. Are you?"

"I repeat Chairman Niu's call," says Sensei Madame Liao. "Who is in favor of Pearl Famous granting Chen Peasprout sanctuary from the Empress Dowager's demand?"

All the senseis except for the Chairman raise their hands. I see him making calculations in his mind. He is vile but not emotional. He is weighing my offer.

He says at last, "*Provisional* sanctuary status. Dependent on her performance at each Annexation." He raises his hand.

"Infuriate me to death!" says Suki.

As soon as the Chairman turns away, Cricket, Doi, and Hisashi throw their arms around me.

We're safe.

But only for now.

Only as long as I keep winning first place.

Last year, other things ended up being more important than taking first place.

This year, nothing will be more important.

As we prepare to leave Divinity's Lap, I see this Wu Yinmei. She's pushing away on her swiftboard, but she's turned to look at me over her shoulder.

Once again, her mask of placidness has slipped and she smiles at me—only at me.

I watch her as we board the train of gondolas that they've installed on all the rails connecting the islets of the various conservatories with the Principal Island. I don't see the point of her going to class this first week, since it's devoted entirely to pure wu liu. She can't do wu liu; she can't even take five steps without her heart and lungs threatening to burst. So she's just coming to observe.

But observe for whom?

The senseis make us take the gondolas to classes on the conservatory islets because they don't want any students skating on the rails, falling into the water, and angering the coiling water dragons again. They've adapted the gondolas so that they're clamped on top of the rail instead of suspended below them like at the entrance to the campus. The gondolas are strung together end to end, like a giant necklace of opals. We all look over the sides, trying to see if there are coiling water dragons churning under the surface of the black water below us.

We each take an oar handle. We row the gondolas forward along the rail and through the air with the giant scallop-shaped pearlsilk oarfans. This Wu Yinmei does her part to row, as well.

The train of gondolas enters a dip. We come out of it speeding toward a sharp curve on the rail leading to the Conservatory of Wu Liu. As we whip around the curve, some students scream in fear of flying off and into the water, into the jaws of the coiling water dragon. There is fear or tension on all our faces.

All except this Wu Yinmei.

What has this girl seen in her life that makes her unafraid of even coiling water dragons?

When we arrive at the Conservatory of Wu Liu, the second-year students gather in the central training court.

Sensei Master General Moon Tzu is there in the middle of a magnificent coughing fit. When he at last finishes coughing, he sways on his swiftboard, balancing on two trembling poles.

Sensei Madame Yao stands beside him like a warden escorting a prisoner. She announces, "Due to the reputation of your class as being unteachable, shameless, and prone to explosions of senseless violence, I have been begged by Sensei Master General Moon Tzu to serve as Assistant Wu Liu Sensei and Enforcer of Order. The First Annexation shall test tactics pertaining to perimeter defense. The Empire of Shin"—she stops to shoot a sneering, lingering look at me, then Wu Yinmei, then Cricket—"is unlikely to capture the city of Pearl because wu liu practitioners are undefeatable on the pearl. However, the rest of the island is not covered in the pearl. Only a small wall along the perimeter of the entire island protects against invasion. The First Annexation shall test your battleband's strategies for perimeter defense. You shall choose your battleband mates and the captain, who has final say on all matters."

Doi and I turn to each other. We knew all along that we would form a team. We knew this on some level even last year. But to my surprise, the ritual of formally declaring our partnership squeezes my heart. I look at this girl, who is not only the most brilliant practitioner of wu liu I have ever met but also the truest, most selfless friend I have ever had. This girl with whom I have been through so much. This girl whom I would be honored to have in my battleband.

We say to each other at the same time, "Will you join my ba—"

Oh.

She wants me to join *her* battleband. Meaning that she must want to be the captain.

Well, she did rank fifteenth last year, and I ranked sixteenth. So perhaps she does have a greater claim to be the captain.

But I only ranked sixteenth because I stopped her rampage to destroy Pearl Famous. And I was the Peony-Level Brightstar. And I was Champion of Wu Liu for all of—

Stop it, Peasprout. She protected you again and again. She risked and nearly lost everything for you. She deserves to be the captain of the battleband more than you do.

I smile at her and, with an ache in my chest that only those who have known great sacrifice can understand, I decide to allow her to be the captain of our battleband.

We say to each other at the same time, "You should be the captain."

Oh, thank the Enlightened One.

I say, "Oh, are you sure, all right then, thank you, that's so generous of you, you're the best friend anyone could ever have, I'm so glad that's settled."

She smiles at me and says, "It doesn't really matter, as long as we get to work together. To keep you safe. We're going to win every one of these Annexations. I'm not going to let anything happen to you."

And then the guilt seeps in. I still have so much to learn. I begin to protest again that she should be captain, this time in earnest, but she says, "No, really, Peasprout. It's not important. We have . . . more important things to worry about."

When I look in the direction of her gaze, my Chi freezes.

On the far side of the court, Wu Yinmei is smiling and bowing, surrounded by a circle of girls.

And at the head of this band of girls is their leader.

Suki.

Suki's inserting herself next to Wu Yinmei every chance she gets. Helping her stow her swiftboard when we ride the gondolas to wu liu class. Shoving a chair out of the way when Wu Yinmei uses her bladechair at meals. Not that I think Wu Yinmei is the type to want such help.

I don't know if she's formally joined Suki's battleband, but so many are already forming.

The Battle-Kite Sparkle-Pilots: This battleband's made up of all the best-looking boys in our class. Their skills are probably all terrible.

Beast Band: These girls are good. I've seen them training together, but they're always fighting and throwing things at one another. They're going to destroy everyone if they don't destroy one another first.

Ten Thousand Secret Deadly: They wear black veils, black

assassin's skull caps, and smoked spectacles that are so dark, they can barely see. And they never take any of it off, because they're just that secret. It's fun to watch them try to eat.

Wu Wu Wu Liu Liu Liu: It's made up of boys and girls who everyone knows are pathetic at wu liu and who seemed to form for the sole purpose of having a name that makes a good call and response cheer.

Forever Action Beauty Girls: These girls (and three boys!) are seemingly distinguished solely by their ludicrous practice of braiding their hair *into one another's* and always traveling in a ring. How are they going to fight like that? We're facing invasion by Shin, and they're braiding their hair together.

Forever Action Beauty Girls aren't the only ones who like braids. One night in the girls' dormitory courtyard after evenmeal, Suki and her gang of girls are seated in a circle facing the same direction, each braiding the hair of the girl in front of her. In the middle of the ring is Wu Yinmei, showing them the steps to do the braid. Now that we have an actual princess from Shin among us, braids are considered pretty, I guess. They weren't considered pretty last year, when the only girls with braided hair were the Shinian servant girls and myself.

This Wu Yinmei catches my gaze and smiles as if she's got something on me.

"Why is she always grinning at me?" I hiss to Doi. "It infuriates me to death."

"Peasprout, that's Suki's favorite thing to say."

"So what are you saying? That I'm becoming like Suki now?"

I immediately regret snapping at her. "I'm sorry. I'm just worried about fulfilling my promise to you—taking first place at the Annexations."

"Don't worry," Doi says, and squeezes my arm. "Let Suki have Yinmei. We're going to build the best battleband in Pearl Famous history."

"That's right. And we're going to wipe our skates on Suki's robe as she's sprawled flat on the pearl!"

"We need to talk about who else to invite into our battleband."

"I know Cricket's not the best wu liu practitioner, but he's really good at—"

"Of course we're going to invite Cricket." Doi laughs. "I was talking about Hisashi."

"What about him?"

"We could use him, Peasprout. He and I are more powerful together. We always have been."

"What makes you think he'll even want to be in my battleband? Maybe I'm not *extraordinary* enough for him. Maybe he'll join this Wu Yinmei."

"He'll join us if we ask. Peasprout, please, your safety depends on this. It's important to put aside jealousy."

"Who says I'm jealous?"

She says softly, "Who says I'm talking about you?"

Ah, I'm so dense and self-involved. She still has misplaced feelings for me from last year. And I still have misplaced feelings for Hisashi from last year. But the difference is that she's willing to control her feelings to keep me safe.

"Doi, what did I do to deserve a friend like you?" I lean over and embrace her tightly.

"Just keep an open mind about Hisashi." Doi smiles as she embraces me back.

At the end of our week of wu liu class, we board the train of gondolas to travel to the Conservatory of Literature for our class with our new teacher, Sensei Master Ram. For some reason, Sensei Madame Yao is on the train with us.

We arrive at the grand lecture hall within the Skybrary on the Conservatory of Literature. Sensei Master Ram stands before the rows of desks, leaning on a stack of scrolls. He has the hard, handsome features of a hero from legend. Strong jaw, noble nose, thick beard, and intelligent, wise eyebrows. I can tell from how he stands in his sensei robe that he's even more powerfully muscled than Sensei Madame Yao.

When he sees the students disembark, he sweeps his arm as if pulling all one hundred of us into a welcoming embrace. He says in a voice full of warmth and charisma, "Well, come along. I'm sure you're all eager to get as far away from Yao as you—"

He stops when he sees Sensei Madame Yao emerge from the last gondola. "Uhhhhhhk," he groans as he expels all the air out of his lungs. "Why are *you* here?"

"I have been appointed Enforcer of Order."

"Come no closer, Madame."

"Someone needs to keep your class in order."

"Come no closer, or I . . . or I shall scream!" he says, clutching the front of his sensei robe. I'm biting my lip to keep from grinning but I'm failing badly.

Sensei Madame Yao skates toward him, saying, "If you're not going to keep your class—"

"Ahhhhhhhhh!" Sensei Master Ram's shriek pierces the air. He skates around the lecture hall wringing his hands and screaming at a pitch so high that our eyes nearly water. All the students are laughing. Even Doi. I think this is the first time I've ever seen her show her teeth. Sensei Madame Yao skates after him, hands outstretched like eagle claws to subdue him.

He grabs the nearest student, who happens to be Gou Gee-Hong, who instinctively covers her nose to protect it. I must have traumatized her about the safety of her nose. Sensei Master Ram whips Gee-Hong around to face Sensei Madame Yao, cowering behind the girl and wielding her as a human shield from Yao's grasp.

He mewls at Sensei Madame Yao, "Get away from me! I can't stand the nightmares anymore!" He flings one scroll after another at Sensei Madame Yao's fuming face, as we all shriek with laughter.

Sensei Madame Yao grunts in fury and says, "I'm going to tell Supreme Sensei Master Jio!" She boards the gondola train leading back to the Principal Island and leaves.

"She hates it when I do things like that. Works every time," says Sensei Master Ram. "Thanks," he says to Gee-Hong. "We did it!" He's as charming as a grown-up Hisashi. He clasps Gee-Hong's forearm in that way that pilots of battle-kites do, and she clasps his in return. Everyone claps, and Gee-Hong smiles. I don't think she's ever had anyone clap for her before.

I think this sensei is my new favorite person.

Doi, Cricket, and I take seats in the front row of desks. Hisashi skates to the spot next to Doi. He looks at Doi and me and asks, "Is it all right if I sit here?"

Doi looks at me. I say nothing. Cricket says, "Of course, Hisashi!"

"Now," continues Sensei Master Ram, "this year's curriculum will have you learning wu liu combined with the other three disciplines. So in wu-liu-and-literature class, we will study how war is like theater, in that it is all about creating an illusion in order to control your audience.

"In Pearlian opera, you use all the tools of literature to manipulate the emotions of the viewers, from fear to fury, from calm to chaos, and position them where you want them. *The same is true in war.* For example, that ploy to get rid of Yao. Who can tell me which of the stratagems of the Pearlian Analects of Martial Strategy, Cunning, and Unorthodoxy that I employed?"

Doi's and Hisashi's hands shoot up.

Sensei Master Ram nods at them.

They look at each other, stand, and answer in unison, "The Defiler Defends Against the Devourer."

"Correct!" sings out Sensei Master Ram. "Expand. What does that stratagem teach?"

"To use revulsion to deflect an attacker," says Hisashi.

"Correct! Expand. What passage from Pearlian opera most famously illustrates this?"

"The escape of the rabbit from the mouth of the tiger by passing gas," says Doi.

"From the Tale of the Tiger and the Gassy Rabbit," adds Hisashi.

"Correct! Expand. How did I use revulsion to deflect Yao?"

Doi says, "Sensei Madame Yao detests weakness or anything she perceives as weakness. Especially in someone she thinks should be a paragon of strength."

Hisashi grabs a nearby scroll. Swinging it like a flyswatter, he says, "And you used humor against her. Those who look down on humor panic when faced with it. Especially when someone's able to get a whole room laughing."

"Outstanding analysis!" says Sensei Master Ram.

Doi and Hisashi really are more powerful together.

Sensei Master Ram beams at the two of them. "This is what I'm talking about, students. Wu liu and literature. Really the same thing. And these two are truly exceptional students. See? This is why I regret not having children."

I look at the two of them, who tried so hard to win over their father, standing in front of this warm man who appreciates them for the courage and talents they have developed on their own.

Courage and talents that I need in my battleband.

I turn to Doi and nod. She nods back.

After class, I say to Hisashi, "Niu Hisashi. It would be my joyful fortune and profound honor if you would join my battleband."

He beams at me. Ten thousand years of stomach gas, his dimples make me ache a little. Hisashi says, "I am so deeply honored. However, I'm sorry, Peasprout. I just joined Suki's battleband."

The blood drains from my face and my heart plummets into my intestines as I think of him—

"Peasprout, he's joking," says Doi.

"Hahahah!" He grabs a writing brush from the desk as if it were a sword and mock-lances me in the heart. He claps his heavy hand on my shoulder, then Doi's. He's like a giant baby catbear, or a smaller Sensei Master Ram.

When he sees my face, he says, "Oh, I'm sorry. That wasn't very funny, was it?"

"No," says Doi. "It wasn't."

"I'm sorry. But it was a little funny, right?"

His constant laughter is sort of irritating. But I have to admit that it's also sort of charming.

At evenmeal, Doi, Cricket, Hisashi, and I all eat together for the first time. As we line up to spoon dishes from the serving table, Doi helps me select things that don't have animal parts in them that, once we are seated, she is going to assemble together into a curry crunchy roll with carrot-ginger dipping gravy, with iced lychee pudding for dessert.

Ahead in the line, Hisashi is scooping sliced pork onto his plate.

Hisashi eats meat.

But he . . . how could . . . I thought . . .

"Pigs are as intelligent and affectionate as dogs," I blurt out. "And don't you know what kind of lives they lead on most farms?"

Hisashi looks at me in bafflement. As if he has no idea what I'm talking about.

"Peasprout . . ." says Doi.

I continue loudly, "And do you know what they do to octopuses during the Festival of Lanterns? Can you imagine what it's like to be burned alive?"

How can he forget, when he was the one who taught me to see the cruelty of the octopus lanterns and the kindness of his heart? No, not him. It was Doi.

I say to Hisashi, "I thought . . . I was hoping you were . . . I just thought you were . . . different."

"He *is* different!" says Doi.

I turn to her. Why is she angry? She should be just as hurt as I am.

Then I see.

She is.

As hurt as I am.

But for a different reason.

Hisashi laughs a bit uneasily. "Ah . . . I'm not sure where that came from." He gestures with the spoon at the dish. "But anyway, this is sliced simmered tofu pocket, not pork. It's terrific." He spoons some on my plate. "Don't worry. I'm with you and Wing Girl on this. I don't eat animals, either, because I love them. I've got a phoenix for a sister, after all."

I can sense from the ripples in the Chi coming from Doi that she's trying to collect her emotions. She was right. Hisashi is different. An entirely different person. I can't just transfer what I experienced last year with Doi to this boy. Every time I do that, I hurt myself and I hurt my best friend.

Doi skates around me in the line. As she passes, she whispers to me, "This isn't last year."

We're all nervous when we begin our first week of wu-liu-combined-with-architecture. We still have thirty-nine days before the First Annexation, but the lucky of us are anxious because of having to be near the Chairman. Especially Doi. We arrive at the courtyard of Divinity's Lap to find the Chairman standing on a dais in front of rows of desks, on top of which are set cups and bowls.

I look to Doi as she regards the cold, ruthless man she got as a father. Whom she went to such extraordinary efforts to try to please. Who struck her and was ready to take wu liu away from her and send her to a penal colony. And whom she tried, and failed, to have charged with treason on my behalf.

I reach out to touch Doi's arm.

So much rage and fear in her unsettled Chi. She looks at me.

I whisper, "Doi, he's not worth it. You broke two records last year. You skated unarmored at the Iron Fan Dance Motivation. You did two hundred rotations at Beautymarch. You made Pearl Famous history. Twice. That's why Sensei Madame Liao called you 'captain.' Because it means, the best, the bravest, the highest. And you did all of that without *him*. You don't need him. You never did. The people who really matter see you for what you are."

I feel the tumult in her Chi begin to disperse. She nods and gives me a small smile.

Doi, Hisashi, and I move to take seats in the back row. I motion Cricket over, but he says, "I want to sit in the front row."

"Cricket, come here," I call. He skates on. "Eh, Cricket. I'm talking to you. Oh, when did you learn to ignore your sister? That's nice."

The Chairman has slipped on his sugary-charm mask. I don't pay much attention to his lecture about combining wu liu with architecture. My most important goal in this class is to make sure that Doi gets through it all right.

"So, little birds," the Chairman continues droning, "that is but one example of how to combine wu liu with architecture. Today, we are going to explore others. In front of you, you will find a cup of water and a cup of a specially treated pearlstarch. Who can tell me what the pearlstarch resembles?"

A hand at the front of the class goes up.

"Yes, Chen Cricket."

"It's like cornstarch," he replies. "In texture, consistency, grip, and grain."

"Excellent, little bird. Yes, it is like cornstarch. And it shares another property with cornstarch. I'd like you all to mix the cup of water and the cup of powder in the bowl in front of you and stir everything together with the spoon."

We all do so. The mixture turns into a porridge-like liquid.

"Like a mixture of equal parts cornstarch and water, this

material is liquid when stirred slowly, but try striking it with the spoon. Go on. I promise it won't splash your robes."

We all strike the mixture, Hisashi giving it an extra-loud whack as if to prove how hard he can whack. To my surprise, it turns solid when struck. The hardness quickly disappears, and the spoon sinks back into the mixture.

"Now, your task, little birds, is to spend this class devising ways that this material can be used in combat against an enemy. Can you do that for me?"

All I can think of is that if you were to throw a dollop of this at your enemy, it would turn as solid as a rock as soon as it hit—

Aiyah, something just hit my head! I turn around and see Suki smirking and holding the spoon with which she just whipped the dollop at me.

I scoop a spoonful from my bowl and ready to throw it at her, but at that moment the Chairman looks straight at me, and I put my spoon back down.

The Chairman skates down the rows of desks, examining each of us on our proposed application of the fluid.

Next to me, Gou Gee-Hong whispers, "I wonder what it tastes like."

"Don't eat it," I say.

"But cornstarch and water make a delicious porridge when you add rock sugar!" she says.

At the end of the class, the Chairman says, "Well, little birds, who would like to present their invention?"

To my surprise, Cricket immediately rises from his desk, ascends the sensei's dais, and faces us. Heavenly August Personage of Jade, he's wearing just his underclothes! Cricket, what under heaven are you doing?

Through the laughter, Cricket says in little more than a squeak, "I propose two applications for this fluid. One is for defense, the other offense. For defense, you could dip clothing into the fluid." He holds up his academy robe. It doesn't look any different. "Unlike metal or pearlplate armor, it would be as flexible as cloth, since it is liquid, and would not hinder fighting ability like traditional armor. However, if anything were to strike it, it would turn solid immediately, protecting the wearer."

He strikes it, and the entire robe instantly stiffens into a suit of stone before relaxing back to its flowing state. The laughter dies out as the students appreciate the cleverness of Cricket's solution.

He continues, "Purely hypothetically, for offense, you could secretly feed it to your enemy by mixing it into rice porridge. Then, when it is inside your enemy's stomach or intestines, you could strike your enemy at those points. The fluid would turn solid as a brick, and the walls of those organs would be crushed between the force of your strike and the solid inside. This would cause the organs to burst. Although, that is not very nice and would be an abuse of pearlstarch."

The class is silent.

Next to me, Gou Gee-Hong raises her hand and whimpers, "But you'd have to eat a lot of it, right?" She wipes something white from the corner of her mouth.

"Well done, Chen Cricket," the Chairman says. "There's no need for any other students to present. Cricket is the clear winner for presenting not one but two applications."

I don't know who this new person is, standing at the front of the class and wearing my brother's face. All I know is that I'm glad he's going to be in my battleband.

I see Wu Yinmei watching Cricket with shining, unblinking eyes as he explains his inventions. And sitting beside her is Suki.

I stand up and announce, "No one else gets to use that." Everyone turns to me. "Or if anyone else uses it, my battleband must get extra points at the Annexations."

The Chairman smiles at me and says, "You did not develop that. Chen Cricket did."

"But he's in my battleband."

Upon hearing that, Cricket puts a hand on his chest and says, "*Me?*" With as much shock as if I'd just asked a mouse to be Emperor of Shin. My heart breaks a little at his surprise.

"Yes, you. Of course you're in my battleband."

I skate toward Cricket. Doi and Hisashi follow. We ascend the dais and stand beside him.

I glare at the Chairman and say, "This is just the first of the weapons that my battleband is going to develop. We are going to prove our value to Pearl. And we are going to take first place at the Annexations."

I cross my arms and lock gazes with the Chairman.

Doi crosses her arms and looks her father in the eyes.

Hisashi nods at his sister, turns to their father, and also crosses his arms.

Together, we stare down the Chairman, as strong as steel, as fierce as fire, as—

"Thank you, Peasprout," whimpers Cricket. And then he buries his face in my shoulder and bursts into tears in front of the whole class.

Make me drink sand to death.

CHAPTER
ELEVEN

The next day, we begin our final introductory course of instruction before the First Annexation. My Chi is becalmed knowing that Cricket has been hard at work developing ideas for our battleband. As our gondola train approaches the Conservatory of Music, the entire second-year class is unusually subdued. We're riding the rails as they unnecessarily circle us around the whole conservatory, high above the water on columns that now seem so slender. Everyone is carefully peering down to see if they can catch a flash of scales or a whip of tails under the water's surface.

Further, all the students are terrified of Chingu, and they didn't even have to sit locked in a tiny box with her as she had fits and hacked about with her cleaver like I did. And now she's our sensei for wu-liu-combined-with-music.

When we arrive at the conservatory, we find Sagacious Monk

Goom in the center of the great circular stage area. Chingu is nowhere to be seen.

As we skate toward him, I see that he's cradling in the folds of his robes some pink, wrinkled baby. The baby turns to face me, and I gasp.

I would know those amber eyes anywhere. It's Chingu, except she's completely hairless, and her bare pink skin is covered all over with a complex of scars that look like the fronds of beautiful ferns.

And for the first time in twenty years, she's not holding her cleaver.

Chingu's sucking her thumb. Her eyes are darting from one student to another timidly.

"What happened to her?" I cry.

"Ah, you've noticed the change in Sensei Madame Chingu's appearance. A group of applicants for the first-year class was visiting the campus. Chingu was being very not nice to them. She forced them up the Pagoda of Filial Sacrifice, trapping them on the top tier, chasing them around with her metal cleaver raised high above her head. It was during a storm. There was lightning.

"So one moment, it was all 'Screech! Chop! Screech! Chop!' The next moment, 'Zzzzzappp!!!'"

"Poor Chingu," I murmur.

"It burned off all her hair and the lightning left scars."

"Where is her cleaver?"

"She renounced violence after this second lightning strike. She's really quite harmless now. Frightened of everything, actually. My poor baby nice nice." He coos at her as she clutches him, looking through shining, wet eyes at all of us.

"So it's probably less dangerous to get oracles from her now," I say.

"She no longer gives oracles," answers Sagacious Monk Goom. "She refuses red sorghum wine now. She's quite cleaned up her style of living. And when you take her hand and try to ask her for an oracle, she just hums a song."

"So she's lost her oracular abilities?"

"Apparently so, but she's gained outstanding musical ability. That's why she's your sensei for wu-liu-combined-with-music this year. Show them, my very nice nice."

He sets Chingu—I mean Sensei Madame Chingu, it's going to be hard to remember that—down in front of a row of instruments. She grabs a bow and *erhu* fiddle and begins sawing on it. As she plays, she squats in front of a twenty-five-stringed *guqin zither* and begins plucking at it with her feet. At the same time, she curls her tail around a thick drumstick and begins striking the beat on a small *taiko* drum behind her.

Then she opens her mouth and emits a piercing vocalization over the music. It sounds as shrill as a stray cat reincarnated as a Meijing opera singer imitating a ghost while having all her teeth pulled out. Everyone clamps their hands over their ears.

When Chingu at last finishes, Sagacious Monk Goom applauds. "Very nice, very nice. Since you liked Sensei Madame Chingu's music so much, how about a little contribution?" When he sees none of the students offer even one coin, he says, "No appreciation for music."

"That wasn't music," I whisper to Doi.

"And what does it have to do with wu liu?" she whispers back.

Hisashi overhears and smiles. "It's a weapon," he says, grabbing a nearby *erhu* bow. "Stick her in front of a charge of attackers and make her sing at them. Think of the damage." He sweeps the bow as if lopping the heads off an army.

He says, "Let's just thank the Enlightened One that it doesn't have a smell! Hahahah!" He stabs the *erhu* bow into a nearby bladder horn, which burps out a rude flapping noise.

There is something about how he laughs at his own jokes that is confident without being boastful. As if laughter were just a happy thing that happens, something to be shared that no one can take credit for, like the shining of the sun.

It's charming.

"Now," says Sagacious Monk Goom, cradling an enormous *taiko* drum on one shoulder. "All drums used for music in the city of Pearl are closed on the bottom. Why?"

A hand goes up at the front of the class, wrapped in a black fingerless glove and shimmering with silver rings.

"You," says Sagacious Monk Goom. "Fancy boy with yellow hair."

He points at Dappled Lion Dao, the captain of the Battle-Kite Sparkle-Pilots. Dappled Lion Dao tosses his head to sweep aside his long forelocks frosted gold through bleaching with kelp-vinegar solution.

He says, "Drums started out as martial instruments to communicate with during war. A closed drum creates a darker, more resonant sound. A boom, not a bang. A boom travels farther and is better for communication purposes."

Another of the Sparkle-Pilots, a boy with a nest of spiked hair powdered silver with moon-orchid pollen, says, "*Bwei bai, bwei bai.*" This is the standard understated "not bad" that Pearlians prefer. The two of them engage in a swift sequence of complex hand clasps and pats.

"That is incorrect!" yells Sagacious Monk Goom. "Worthless answer!"

He skates close to Dappled Lion Dao and bangs the drum with thundering force. The boy winces and covers his ear.

"Who can give a worthy answer?" demands Sagacious Monk Goom.

Another hand goes up.

"You," says Sagacious Monk Goom. "Mysterious and faintly eerie girl from Shin."

Yinmei replies, "Venerable holy Sagacious Monk Goom. I noticed something as I drummed on the lectern with my poles during the coiling water dragon attack. The lectern was hollow, and it seemed to bounce up in reaction to each strike of my poles. Is it that the pearl reacts to the sound of drums with force?"

"Worthy answer!" says Sagacious Monk Goom. "The pearl responds to certain sound vibrations as force that it greatly amplifies and shoots back at the source, particularly the sound of drums."

Look at this girl, who seems to never blink, who sees everything. Just like a spider. Observing everything she can about the pearl.

"That is why drums used in music all have covered bottoms. If they didn't, they would go shooting off as soon as you struck them," Sagacious Monk Goom continues. "Show them, very nice nice!"

Sensei Madame Chingu crawls over to the drum. She begins chewing on the kelp-leather skin covering one end of the drum. When she has eaten the whole skin, she tips the drum upright so that its uncovered end is on the pearl. The drum is twice as high as she is, but she clambers up the side like a monkey and sits on top.

Sensei Madame Chingu clenches her hands and feet and brings all lucky fists down hard on the skin of the drum.

The impact produces a great *bang*, and the drum goes blasting into the air, with our sensei riding atop it!

They go up as high as the statue of the Enlightened One, seven stories up, then arc back down. Sagacious Monk Goom staggers back and forth, arms outstretched to catch her.

Sensei Madame Chingu comes plopping down into Sagacious Monk Goom's embrace.

The *taiko* drum, from which Sensei Madame Chingu ejected while in flight, comes down right on Gou Gee-Hong, trapping her so that the only thing visible are two skates sticking out the bottom. Cricket and Hisashi race over to help her.

Over Gee-Hong's muffled cries, Sagacious Monk Goom coos at Sensei Madame Chingu, "There's my nice nice." He looks up at Wu Yinmei, who nods humbly. "And you. Very, very nice, so very nice!" He sets Chingu down to applaud.

Cricket whispers to me, "You could bang on a drum during combat and shoot away from an attacker. Yinmei's clever to draw the connection between music and pearl."

Hisashi says, "Cricket's right. We could use her in our battleband."

I snap at Hisashi, "We're doing just fine without her."

Doi looks at me. She says nothing, but her words come back to me. *Peasprout, your safety depends on this. It's important to put aside jealousy.*

Doi says softly, "Do we want Suki to have her?"

I know that they're all correct. However, I also know that she's not who she claims she is and that she's using us somehow. But perhaps we can use her as well.

Sagacious Monk Goom says, "Now, students. I need a volunteer to serve as apprentice wave organist."

Wu Yinmei raises her hand and asks, "What is a wave organ?"

"The temple through which your gondola passed on its circuit around the Conservatory of Music is actually a massive instrument. It makes sound by creating waves through water rather than air—a delightful instrument. We use it to sound the hours, play assembly call, announce meal times, and warn of imminent comet strikes."

I raise my hand and say, "We didn't hear anything like that last year."

"Ah, well, the senseis couldn't find a student to volunteer to learn it. The last student quit."

Wu Yinmei asks, "What was the student's reason for quitting?"

"Ah, well, she griped that playing the wave organ was cold, wet, cramped, broadcast every one of her playing mistakes for the whole campus to hear, and placed her in constant danger of drowning. She also complained that any surge in tide caused the keys to slice uncontrollably at her hands, and she wanted to preserve her remaining fingers. But really, it's a delightful instrument and so easy to play. She was difficult—very difficult. So who would like to volunteer as apprentice wave organist?"

When he sees not a single student raise a hand, his sighs could blow all the hair off a monkey.

Sagacious Monk Goom proceeds to interrogate each student one by one about volunteering. While the students are busy preparing their excuses to decline the offer, I see Chingu, huddled by herself, sucking her thumb.

I don't believe that her oracular powers could be entirely gone. I crouch down and gently reach my open palm to her. She flinches but then looks at my palm as if remembering it from last year.

I fold my hands over her hand.

The hairless skin on the back of her hand, covered in fern-shaped scars, is warm and soft, like a newborn mouse.

I say to her in my mind, *What will be discovered to be the secret to winning the Annexations?*

She gazes up at me with round, shining eyes. She whimpers.

Are they just random sounds, or is Chingu trying to answer me?

I try with a different question. *What will be discovered to be the secret to stopping the Shinian invasion?*

Again, she hums the same little song back to me.

I sigh. It's not a message. It's just a whimper of fear.

I stand up and turn from Chingu to find that Wu Yinmei has been watching us. Listening to us. Then, in a burst of motion behind me, Chingu springs away and leaps off the Conservatory of Architecture toward the ocean.

We all gasp at the sight of her flying over the water, in which the coiling water dragons lurk. She plops onto the gondola rail and scrambles toward the wave organ pavilion. We hold our breath as she bounces from one part of the roof to another, high above the water, until she finally disappears inside the wave organ.

"Don't worry," says Sagacious Monk Goom, waving us away in irritation. "She'd never fall in the water. She's as agile as a monkey! You students worry too much."

The sound of levers clicks within the pavilion of the wave organ. There is a wash like tides surging through a comb. Then tones rumble out of the water below, as mournful as the lowing of whales.

"Oh!" says Sagacious Monk Goom. "Why didn't I think of that? Of course she likes it in there. No danger of being struck by lightning."

Chingu keeps playing the same short sequence of notes. I realize that it's the sequence of notes she hummed to me.

I watch Wu Yinmei angling her head to drink in the sound. Her brow furrows. She stows her swiftboard poles under her arm.

She traces a finger on her palm, as if she were writing logograms or making notations. She silently mouths words. Then she looks up at me, her face wavering between stun and something like . . . delight.

She pushes on her swiftboard to me and says, "What under heaven did you ask her?"

"It doesn't matter," I say. "Her oracular abilities are gone."

"No," she says, smiling. "They are not."

"Did you hear something in the wave organ?" I ask Wu Yinmei.

"What did you ask Sensei Madame Chingu?" she asks again.

"I'm not telling you anything," I say.

"Then I shall not, either."

Ten thousand years of stomach gas.

As I skate away from Wu Yinmei, she calls out, "You are the lock, Chen Peasprout, but I am the key."

CHAPTER
TWELVE

We are given a night to ourselves without any homework exercises in anticipation of the Annexation. That evening in Eastern Heaven Dining Hall, they're serving spicy sesame peanut butter noodles with sliced cucumbers, scallions, and bean sprouts, which all the students love, so everyone is in a happy mood.

During evenmeal, whispers float among the tables of students that the senseis are all going to have a staff meeting that evening, leaving the campus unmonitored.

I catch the words "All the All" twittering around us in hushed tones.

"What's everyone talking about?" I ask.

Doi says, "It's a sort of secret shadow market where students can buy or sell all sorts of things that can't be bought anywhere else, using special All the All credits."

Hisashi claps his hands together and says, "Now that sounds like fun!"

After evenmeal, when the senseis have convened in the Conservatory of Architecture, we skate to the dormitories. In the middle of the path between the girls' and boys' dormitories, the All the All Tree is erected. It's a big false tree from an opera stage set, strung with wooden placards.

I read one dangling placard. It says, DIVE: A STUDENT AGREES TO DELIBERATELY FAIL AT AN EXERCISE IN CLASS. AVAILABLE FOR BUY OR SELL. FIRST-YEARS ONLY.

Cricket points at a placard and says, "Oh, look! There's a wood-carving competition! It says, 'Enter to carve a sculpture of a campus structure'!"

My chest fills with a great weight as I remember the exquisite sculpture he carved of the temple last year. My mind's ear sounds with the sickening *snick* that my skate blades made as I sliced his sculpture into pieces. With emotion in my throat, I say, "You should enter, Cricket. What's the prize?"

Cricket pulls down the placard and reads. "It says, 'No entry fee. First one to finish gets to choose a servant for a day from the other entrants. Last one to finish has to eat everyone else's carvings.'" Cricket quietly hangs the placard back on the tree.

Some people have weird ideas of fun.

There's a whole section of branches advertising merchandise for use in the Annexations.

Hisashi says, "Look! They're selling coiling water dragon protection!" He unhooks a wooden box dangling from the tree. "It says, 'Guaranteed to prevent user from being drowned by a coiling water dragon!'" He opens the lid of the box and finds inside a dagger with a tag tied to its handle. He reads the tag. "'In the event of an impending coiling water dragon attack, insert dagger into own throat.' Hahahah! I almost want to buy it, just because it's got so much personality!"

Doi fingers another placard and says, "Suki will ask if she can buy these in bulk."

I skate over to read the placard. It says, ASSASSIN: HIRE A STUDENT TO SABOTAGE YOUR RIVAL'S PERFORMANCE AT AN ANNEXATION. AVAILABLE FOR BUY OR SELL. SECOND- AND THIRD-YEARS ONLY.

"This is shameful!" I say.

"It's only shameful when it's used against you," says someone.

We turn to see a tall girl skate out from behind the All the All Tree. She's wearing aquamarine and orange ribbons in her hair.

"Be careful of her," whispers Cricket to me. "That's Lao Biling. She was a second-year student who managed to finish last in every discipline last year. She wasn't among the fifty students invited to come back for the third year, so she probably didn't get into an opera company after leaving. She's not supposed to be here."

Doi says to her, "You're not supposed to be on campus."

"Just trying to make a living here. And what are they going to do, kick me out? Anyway, I think you want to see what's in my book."

She holds a book bound with what looks like baby sea dog fur.

She says, "You're going to be making important decisions soon about forming your battleband. You need as much information about each student as you can get to make your decisions. *The Book of Qualities* can help you."

She pets the book and continues in a showy stage whisper, "It has profiles of each student at Pearl Famous, including a complete performance log as well as confidential sensei evaluations. This is what you really need to decide your battleband lineup."

"Doi, Cricket, Hisashi, and I are a battleband," I say to her.

"And that is all? You need to consult *The Book of Qualities* to make good choices about your battleband teammates, now more than ever. Especially if your ranking last year was . . . a disappointment." Lao Biling smiles and I see a smear of lip rouge on her teeth. "Do I skate too close? I can see from your expression that I skate too close. Really, your sixteenth-place ranking last year is nothing to be ashamed of . . . if that's what you want from your second year."

"Peasprout, we should go," whispers Cricket.

"It costs ten All the All credits to view each profile. If you do not have All the All credits, other currencies are also accepted, including . . . information."

"Peasprout, she's a fraud," says Doi.

"The information is real," Lao Biling cuts in. "If you don't believe me, you may view your own profile for free and see for yourself."

"Peasprout, you don't need that," says Hisashi. "We know your qualities."

I needed to hear that from him. I say, "I know. But . . . just give me a moment."

He's right. I don't need some book to tell me what I am. I don't need to see some observer's log of my performances or confidential sensei evaluations, revealing what they really think about me to . . . Ah, make me drink sand to death, I really want to see it. I turn back to Lao Biling. "All right, show me my profile."

She flips through the pages, finds my profile, and spreads the book toward me on her open palms as if declaring her sincerity.

It reads: *Chen Peasprout.*

Origin: Serenity Cliff Village, Shui Shan Province, Shin

Lineage: Insignificant

First-Year Ranking: Sixteenth

Performances: First Motivation, first ranking, successfully completed twenty moves; significant moves included single-footed grasshopper, hammer throw spin, two-heeled sesame-seed pestle jump, single-footed forward flip, one-footed final landing; significant errors included additional two-footed landing on hammer throw spin, additional step taken on landing of triple scissor heel backflip.

How does she know all this? I scan down to the confidential sensei evaluations portion. It reads: *Chen Peasprout is courageous, with tremendous talent and a huge heart. She is, in her own way, a genius, a true original, and impossible to forget. She is also boastful, sometimes strange, often extreme, and intensely lonely with a pronounced difficulty in forming lasting, meaningful connections.*

It's signed Sensei Madame Liao.

I close the book.

Lao Biling says, "Do I skate too close? I skate too close."

I turn my back on her and skate to the far side of the All the All Tree.

Cricket and Hisashi begin to follow me, but I hear Doi whisper to them, "Give her some privacy."

I try to calm my Chi, but I end up just clenching it. I don't want to cry here, in front of everyone.

Strange.

Extreme.

Lonely.

I place my hand on the great trunk of the All the All Tree to steady myself. I don't know if it hurts because I think her words are unfair or because I think they're fair.

I thought Sensei Madame Liao was my friend. I'm facing so much danger. A part of me hoped that if I couldn't save myself, Sensei Madame Liao would help me. I thought if I couldn't figure out all the answers that I—

I notice the words on the placard dangling from the All the All Tree in front of me.

It says, AVAILABLE: THE ANSWERS TO YOUR QUESTIONS. FOR SALE TO: ONLY MISS LOCK.

Wu Yinmei's words ring in my mind. *You are the lock, Chen Peasprout, but I am the key.*

She put up this placard. Offering me what she knows I most want. She's literally dangling it in my—

Behind me, a voice hollers.

"It's a raid! Yao's coming! Everyone get in your dormitories!"

We all scramble out of the courtyard and race to our dormitory chambers. We slam the shoji doors shut. All the students pretend to be asleep and make no sound as we hear Sensei Madame Yao outside screaming, "Who did this?! Vile, devious students!"

As Sensei Madame Yao proceeds to batter and chop the All the All Tree to splinters, I think of Wu Yinmei's placard. She's offering to sell me the answer to how I can prevail at the Annexations. And the answer to how I can stop the Shinian invasion.

But the one thing her placard failed to say is this: What price does Miss Key want?

So I have to decide what to do about this Wu Yinmei.
Quickly. Because the deadline to declare the lineups of our battlebands has arrived.

Two days before the First Annexation, we are assembled at the
principal training court at the Conservatory of Wu Liu for the official declaring of battleband lineups. The students who have already
formed battlebands are gathered in clusters.

Sensei Master General Moon Tzu and his mustache-bearers look
down at us from a dais, but Sensei Madame Yao does all the talking.
She announces, "Sensei Master General Moon Tzu says that today
you shall finalize the lineup of your battlebands." She gestures to a
great urn filled with poles on which are suspended long scrolls of
red pearlsilk.

"You shall write the name of your battleband on the front of
your banner, as well as the names of the captain and each member

on the back." She gestures with her open palm to a table of bowls filled with shimmering liquid and brushes. "The ink is resin made from the soil of the abalone burial ground, so it will dry within one hour. Choose your battleband name, captain, and members before it dries."

Across the water from the east, the tones of Chingu playing the wave organ moo at us. Is there really an oracle hidden in it? Does Wu Yinmei really know how to interpret it? Is the answer to my questions about how to win the Annexations and how to stop the Shinian invasion really being broadcast for everyone to hear, if they only had the key to understand?

I announce to Doi, Cricket, and Hisashi, "We need to talk about Wu Yinmei."

Hisashi says, "Well, she told me she hasn't accepted Suki's offer to join her battleband."

So he's still talking to her.

Cricket says, "She figured out that the pearl responds to the sound of drums. She sees things that others don't."

Hisashi says, "There are a lot of things about her that are extr—"

I bark at him, "I don't want to hear about how *extraord*—"

"—emely complicated, but we can use her."

Oh.

He looks at the expression on my face with puzzlement. He says carefully, "I'm not that smart, but I'm smart enough to respect the most extraordinary girl I have ever met."

The words all rush out of my mouth in a torrent. "What's so *extraordinary* about her? What has she done besides be good at music? Chingu's good at music. I don't see anyone melting into a puddle about her. Why are braids suddenly so beautiful now? Just because she's a princess? I thought Pearl didn't believe in royalty. And she's Shinian. Do you know how much hatred I got last year for being Shinian? How much hatred I'm still getting? From your father? And he's sponsored her sanctuary status while trying to get me sent back to get chopped into a thousand pieces by *her* great-great-grandmother? What does she have that everyone loves so much? What does she have that I don't? What's so *extraordinary* about her?"

I pant with the force of my words. Hisashi mashes his brows together again. It makes his expression look soft. Almost tender.

He says quietly, "Peasprout. When I said over the infinity noodle that this past year, I met the most extraordinary girl I have ever met . . . I was talking about you."

It takes a moment for this to sink in.

Me.

He was talking about me.

Even if the world is threatening to crumble on top of me, he sees me. And for some reason, that makes me feel as if I can face my world caving in. But he doesn't need to know that yet.

"Oh," I say, avoiding his gaze. "I knew that. So. About this Wu Yinmei. It's clear that she has talents. She even said that she figured out how to interpret Chingu's oracles. But I don't trust her."

Hisashi says, "I'm not defending her. But you need to be a good battleband leader if you want to win. She's been groomed for leadership her whole life. Learn from her."

Cricket adds, "You might not like her, Peasprout. But sometimes we have to learn to work with people we don't like. And maybe when we work with them, we learn to like them more."

Cricket might have a point. Not the part about learning to like her, but the other part. For as ancient Pearlian wisdom teaches:

Embrace your enemies so close to you that they cannot draw bows.

Clasp your enemies' hands, for held hands can hold no daggers.

Actually, I'm not sure these count as ancient Pearlian wisdom. I read them on the wrappers of the eating sticks at the vegetarian dumpling house where we usually ate while staying in the city during the New Year's month. However, they did sound very wise, and it was a very old dumpling house.

"All right, we'll invite her," I say. "Plus it'll burn Suki like lava when she learns that we have a real princess in our battleband."

"That's not very nice, Peasprout," says Cricket. "Let's be nice this year."

We find Wu Yinmei in the crowd of students and skate to her. I bow low and say, "Wu Yinmei. It would be my joyful fortune and profound honor if you would join my battleband."

She bows back moderately, balancing on her swiftboard poles to keep from tipping too far. "I would be honored to join your battleband." She adds with a serene smile, "For now."

"What do you mean 'for now'?" I say.

"You will want to see if the alliance is suitable. As will I. Not every key fits every lock."

So she's not going to tell me how to interpret the oracle yet. She's going to see if it suits her purposes before she gives up that leverage.

Ten thousand years of stomach gas. What do I do? Rescind my offer? If I do, she'll never tell me how to understand the oracle. But if I let her in, she'll have power over me. I wish I could ask Sensei Madame Liao for advice. But she'll just say I'm being extreme and strange and unable to form meaningful connections.

"Fine," I say. I skate to the urn and lift one of the banners of red pearlsilk out. I grab a bowl of resin ink. I write on the back of the banner CHEN PEASPROUT, CAPTAIN followed by NIU DOI, CHEN CRICKET, NIU HISASHI, WU YINMEI. I turn the banner around, dip the brush in the bowl, and write THE TAMERS OF THE PEARL on the front side.

"The Tamers of the Pearl?" asks Hisashi.

"Yes," I say. "That's the name of our battleband."

"Bit serious, isn't it?" he says. "Don't we want something with a bit more style?"

"We're a serious battleband. I'm serious about winning." I hesitate and know I shouldn't say it, but out it comes: "Aren't you?"

"Peasprout," says Doi gently, "I agree with Hisashi but for different reasons. I think it's a little too boastful."

Boastful. Just like Sensei Madame Liao said about me in *The Book of Qualities*.

"It is the sort of name that Gang Suki would choose," adds Yinmei. "Pretentious and conceited."

Make me drink sand to death.

"This is the name of our battleband," I say firmly.

"Peasprout," says Cricket. "Perhaps we should hear some other suggestions before deciding?"

"Yes, why don't we hear your wonderful suggestions," I say, crossing my arms.

Hisashi speaks first. "Well, I like the name Emperor Stardust and the Eunuchs of the Forbidden City."

"That's ridiculous!" I snap at him.

"Ridiculous isn't necessarily bad," he replies.

"Yes, it is," I sputter. "I mean, that name is so ludicrously unsuitable for so many reasons that I don't even know where to begin."

"What's wrong with a little humor?" he says. Those dimples are starting to become very annoying very quickly.

"We're talking about *our name*," I stress. "You want to make a joke of it?"

"Peasprout," says Doi, "nobody would choose a name that would—"

"Oh, so now I'm nobody. That's what all of you, clucking like a gaggle of fire-chickens, have concluded. Fine. Then why don't we just call ourselves Nobody and the Fire-Chickens?"

I lay the banner on the pearl, scrape the logograms for the Tamers of the Pearl off with my skate blade, and smear the resin ink back into the bowl. It's gotten harder already, so I stir it vigorously with the brush, then write NOBODY AND THE FIRE-CHICKENS on the banner in jagged logograms.

"Peasprout . . ." says Doi, reaching for the banner, but I snatch it away.

Behind me a voice says, "So what name did you choose?" I turn to see Suki bearing a banner on which is written RADIANT THOUSAND-STORY VERY TALL GODDESS followed by the House of

Flowering Blossoms girls. I see that they've added about twelve new recruits. Suki continues, "Stealthiest Skaters from Shin? Unstoppable Secret Weapons of Shin?"

I'm in a bad mood already. I don't need Suki putting ideas in people's heads. One thing Suki taught me last year is that if someone says something enough times and with enough volume, a line of believers starts snaking behind her. So I need to separate the head from the rest of the snake.

I shout at her, "I am so sick of your stinking, sour face. And you know what? I'm not the only one. Etsuko, why are you following her? She's just going to shove you into a vicious crowd again as soon as it serves her. She kept you hanging on as her second choice last year at the Fifth Motivation. Until she was turned down by her first choice: me."

Suki seethes and says, "How dare you speak to my first lieu—"

I talk over Suki, "And you know why I turned Suki down? Because she's a thousand-tailed scorpion. Etsuko, you placed second last year. You could have placed first if she didn't stop it. She's keeping you down." I turn to the rest of Suki's girls. "She's keeping all of you down. Etsuko should be the captain of your battleband. Not Suki. Suki's only strong if you make her strong. She's nothing without followers. She's nothing without you. And she knows it."

Suki hisses, "You filthy, low-quality, Shinian— What are you doing?!" She turns to see that Etsuko has snatched their banner from her. "How dare you! Give that back to me, or I'll have you whipped for insubordination!"

Etsuko steps one skate back behind the other in a defensive combat position. Then one girl after another places her skate in the same position, facing down Suki.

I can't believe this.

I broke their battleband.

I started a palace coup.

I dethroned their Empress Dowager.

Only two inconsequential girls skate over to join Suki. Suki says to Etsuko and the rest of the girls, "You are going to pay for this. I will live to hear you scream for mercy as I wreak my revenge on you." She spins to face me. "And I'm going to enjoy watching you beg for help as you're being torn in two."

As Etsuko scrapes off the resin ink spelling out the names of the expelled members from their banner, Suki and her two remaining followers skate to the urn and take out a fresh banner. Suki brushes the name RADIANT THOUSAND-STORY VERY TALL GODDESS on the banner.

"Etsuko, look," I say.

"You can't use that name," says Etsuko.

"I thought of it!" cries Suki.

"Sensei Madame Yao!" calls Etsuko.

Sensei Madame Yao skates over.

"Think of a new name, Gang Suki," she says. "And hurry up. Any battleband without an acceptable name by the end of the hour will be called Last-Place Losers on Skates."

"Infuriate me to death!" says Suki, but she scrapes the hardening resin ink from the banner. She writes RADIANT TEN-THOUSAND-STORY MOST TALL GODDESS MADE OF GOLD AND RUBIES.

"No names that are too close to other names or are misleading," says Sensei Madame Yao. "Think of a new name quickly. Time's almost up."

Cricket tugs at my sleeve and says, "Peasprout . . ."

"Not now, Cricket!" I'm enjoying watching Suki's humiliation.

She looks like she's about to burst into flames with fury, but she scrapes off the name and begins to write in gummy letters PRINCESS SUKI AND—

"She can't use that name," I say to Sensei Madame Yao. "It violates the rule against misleading names, because there's a real princess at Pearl Famous now."

Sensei Madame Yao nods in agreement.

"Peasprout . . ." says Cricket more urgently.

"Not now!" I say.

Suki hurriedly begins scraping the name off when we hear a *bwong* resound in the air. Sensei Master General Moon Tzu and his mustache-bearers have struck the gong.

"Time's up! Brushes down!" calls Sensei Madame Yao.

Suki's battleband is now committed to the name Last-Place Losers on Skates.

I turn to gloat over Suki's reaction. Her mouth looks like a jellyfish trying to turn itself inside out.

But then she starts to smile. She's looking above and behind me.

I turn around.

I see all of my battleband mates.

Doi is furious. Cricket is shaking his head with sadness. Yinmei peers at me in disbelief. Hisashi is laughing.

I look up and see what Suki was smiling at.

It's the banner displaying the new name of our battleband.

Nobody and the Fire-Chickens.

Make me drink sand to death for ten thousand years.

CHAPTER
LUCKYTEEN

So our battleband is now called Nobody and the Fire-Chickens. And the whole school is talking about it. I hear whispers all around me as I pass other students. "What kind of captain would choose a name like that?" and "Maybe she doesn't speak Pearlian very well," and "Someone who finished sixteenth is pretty much nobody," and "If I had a captain like that, I'd feed myself to a coiling water dragon in shame."

The day following the naming disaster, Sensei Madame Liao approaches me after the morning assembly. It's the first time I've seen her since reading her comments in *The Book of Qualities*. I can hear those words as if spoken in her voice. *Boastful, sometimes strange, often extreme, and intensely lonely with a pronounced difficulty in forming lasting, meaningful connections.*

"Peasprout," she says. "Please meet me in the Humbleness

Chamber at the Conservatory of Wu Liu. I have selected you to participate in a special class on leadership."

All that morning, my Chi hums because my heart is full. A special class on leadership. So Sensei Madame Liao does appreciate me. I'm ashamed that I doubted her belief in me. *The Book of Qualities* probably mixed in false sensei evaluations with accurate performance logs.

When I arrive at the Humbleness Chamber at the beginning of White Hour, Sensei Madame Liao is already there. I bow deeply to her. "I am humbled by the honor of being selected to participate in this special class."

"Please take a seat, Peasprout."

There are only two desks. This must truly be an advanced class for there to be only two—

A girl comes skating in frantically. "Oh, I'm so sorry, am I late?"

It's Gou Gee-Hong.

"Oh, hi, Peasprout. Congratulations! I heard you're captain of your own battleband, too!"

She's also the captain of a battleband? Who would want her as a captain? And why is she in an advanced class with me on leadership? I mean, I like Gou Gee-Hong, but I wouldn't call her leader material.

Before I can ask Sensei Madame Liao if there's been a mistake, she begins reading to us wisdoms from the Pearlian Analects of Sage Leadership and Benevolent Rule:

" 'A leader makes decisions that no one wants to make.

" 'A leader doesn't just make decisions between two unbearable choices. A leader finds a new third way.' "

On and on she drones, running through maxims that seem as empty as they are basic. Why are we wasting time on this? Then, over the course of the hour, as we hear one rudimentary military leadership aphorism after another, I begin to realize something with horror.

This isn't an advanced class on leadership. It's a remedial class.

So she really does think that little of me. It should infuriate me to death, but instead, it just takes everything out of me. It hurts.

At the end of the hour, Sensei Madame Liao says, "And Peasprout. There is one maxim from the analects that I would like you to contemplate especially: 'The true leader leads by exhibiting honesty in the face of a mistake and humility in admitting responsibility for it.'"

I bow my head, my face burning with shame. I want to be a true leader. I want to exhibit honesty if I have made a mistake. I want to learn humility in admitting my responsibility for mistakes.

Except that it wasn't my fault that we got stuck with the name Nobody and the Fire-Chickens. If my battleband mates hadn't been so unreasonable about the beautiful name I chose for us, we wouldn't be in this situation now. Stubbornness is a devastating character flaw, and it would be wrong for me to shield them from responsibility for their own flaws.

After evenmeal the night before the First Annexation, all the second-year students disperse across the campus in their battlebands.

We have two hours before curfew to finalize strategy for the next morning.

I lead my battleband to the Courtyard of Supreme Placidness. The sound-insulating properties of the courtyard will help protect us from being overheard.

I say to them, "Cricket, is the pearlstarch solution ready?"

Cricket says, "I have all the ingredients, but I can't mix them until right before we're ready to dip our robes into the mixture."

I turn to Yinmei and say, "And what about the forcedrums?"

Yinmei says, "We shall each have one strapped to the waist to punch if we need to make a quick escape."

"Good. Now Sensei Madame Yao said that the First Annexation will test strategies for perimeter defense. What do we know about the perimeter of the island of Pearl?"

Cricket raises his hand. I say to him, "You don't have to raise your hand. Just speak."

"According to my research, the city of Pearl is made out of the pearl, but the rest of the island is solid earth and protected only by a low wall made of the pearl. The wall runs the entire perimeter of the island, but there's not enough of the pearl to make it very high. As long as the invaders remain on the pearl, a wu liu practitioner can defeat them. But it becomes much more difficult if an invader reaches solid earth, where skates can't go."

"Then what good is it?" I ask.

"Such a wall serves two purposes. It slows down invaders, who have to climb over the wall from the sea. Further, as soon as a guard spots an invader, she can use the wall as a road to skate across to get quickly to the invader or to an alarm to call all guard towers nearby. But there aren't enough wu liu practitioners to staff the wall very heavily."

I say, "So we shouldn't stand in the middle and wait for the invaders to come over the wall. We should be stationed on the wall itself so that we can skate to them quickly."

At that moment, Etsuko enters the Courtyard of Supreme Placidness with her battleband, Radiant Thousand-Story Very Tall Goddess.

"Etsuko," I say, "if you don't mind, we're using this space."

"Oh," she says. "I'm sorry. I didn't see *Property of Nobody and the Fire-Chickens* painted over the archway. Or is your name Stealthiest Spies from Shin?"

Ten thousand years of stomach gas. I've created another Suki.

"Let's go," says Hisashi. "Not worth it. I know someplace better."

Hisashi leads us to the northeastern edge of the Principal Island. My Chi clenches when I see where he's brought us. The Temple of Heroes of Superlative Character. Where we went last year instead of attending the Festival of Lanterns.

Not we! Get that through your head, Peasprout! It was Doi, not him.

We row the gondola train to the islet on which the temple sits. None of us likes being over water that could be filled with coiling water dragons obscured by the dark of night.

Inside the temple, before the towering statutes of the heroic boy Lim Tian-Tai and the noble eunuch Mu Haichen, Hisashi grabs a fistful of lit incense sticks. He gestures at the round atrium rising high around us. "The First Annexation is going to take place in here.

Because it's on an islet by itself, just like Pearl. Who wants to bet on it? Loser has to skate up the ramp and go shooting out of the archway at the top. Wing Girl, do you have the dragon-phoenix boat on you?"

Doi answers, "No." I feel her looking at me, but I don't meet her gaze. I don't want to talk about it.

"What did you do with it?"

"I gave it to Peasprout."

Hisashi turns his big brown eyes on me. Then he looks at Doi. Then he looks back at me. Like he's suddenly putting something together. I feel as if I'm skating unarmored during the Iron Fan Dance Motivation.

Thanks, Doi.

Cricket interjects, "It can't be held here. There's no perimeter wall."

Yinmei says, "Please excuse me, but there is somebody here inside the temple."

We turn to where she is looking. A chill shivers through my Chi as I see the silhouette of a cloaked figure in the archway, looking down on us.

"It's probably one of Etsuko's spies," says Doi.

"Let's get out of here," suggests Cricket.

I'm happy for an excuse to leave this temple. It's not the temple I experienced those memories in, since it was rebuilt after it was destroyed last year. But it looks exactly like it, and things that look exactly like something they're not are causing me distractions I don't need right now.

We leave the islet of the temple. We cross Divinity's Lap to see Forever Action Beauty Girls in silent battle meditation under the statue of the Enlightened One, seated in a ring, of course, with their hair braided into a lantern that hangs in their center. I'm looking forward to seeing them try to fight like that.

Cricket looks at the ring they form and says, "Ah! I know where the First Annexation's going to be held!"

We follow him across the campus until we are facing the Radial of Mighty Tranquility.

"There," says Cricket.

Doi says, "He's right."

Cricket smiles at Doi's words like he just placed first at a Motivation.

"Oh, I see," says Hisashi. "A structure, on an islet of its own, surrounded by water, yet with a perimeter wall formed by the covered stadium seating. Like the island of Pearl itself. Well done!" He gives Cricket's forearm the battle-kite pilot clasp.

Doi says, "So we'll be in the center, and invaders will come over the wall."

"And we have to protect the core," says Hisashi. "What do you think, Wing Girl? Double tsunami flying fist and all the twin iron butterfly quadruple leaps, as well as the hasty eagle mirror flurry formations?"

"Yes, definitely," answers Doi, "but also double-headed flying snake enduring through ease and danger, as well as herons meeting under two branches of pine, shuddering in a late-autumn gust."

"Exactly what I was thinking, Wing Girl."

I say, "What about larger battle strategy?"

Hisashi replies, "Sensei Master Ram had me read the opera *Farewell, My Porcupine*. Do you know it? Emperor afraid of assassination builds a great wall; chief eunuch advises emperor that a strong kingdom doesn't build walls but instead engages with all those around it."

"How does that apply to our battle strategy?" I ask.

"I see," says Doi. "We shouldn't spend energy keeping the invaders off the wall."

"Yes," says Hisashi. "We allow them onto the parapet made of the pearl at the top of the wall, on which we have the advantage."

"And we engage them on our own terms," Doi finishes.

"Also remember," says Yinmei, "that battle strategy need not involve battle. It may also be wholly strategy."

"Please expand, Yinmei." I nod. She may not be able to skate in the First Annexation, but she's proven herself to be a shrewd strategist.

She doesn't continue, though. Instead, she looks behind me.

I turn and see, peering around the corner of the Hall of Six Excellences, the hooded spy sent by Etsuko.

"Go away!" I look around for something to throw at her.

Yinmei says, "I know a better place where we can talk."

She pushes her poles and slides away on her swiftboard. When I see where she's leading us, I clench my Chi and make sure not to look at either Doi or Hisashi.

We're at the entrance of the Garden of Whispering Arches.

Far ahead, the massive Arch of the Sixteenth Whisper looms above us, where Doi once whispered to me, "I knew you could do it."

This isn't last year, Peasprout. This place is just full of echoes.

We follow Yinmei to a strange arching bridge that is crossed perpendicularly by another arching bridge, so that the two form the skeleton of a dome. The plaque on it reads, THE ARCH OF CROSSED DESTINIES.

She indicates for me to stand in the center, under the point where the two arches meet. The rest of us each stand near the foot of an arch. Yinmei whispers into an arch, "There is a Shinian battle strategy called Besiege the Cloister of Xie to Rescue the Kingdom of Wo." Her words are as clear as if they were whispered into my ear. "Do not fight the enemy; seize the thing that is most precious to the enemy. When the Shinian army invades a city, the first things it seizes are the schools."

"Why?" I ask. I sense that the answer's going to make me ashamed to be Shinian.

"To take the children hostage if the enemies do not lay down their weapons," she says calmly.

I swallow my revulsion. "That's *not* the kind of strategy we use here," I say firmly.

"I raise it as metaphor."

"We're not going to use a dirty strategy."

"It is a winning strategy. It is a Shinian strategy."

"*I* am Shinian," I say.

"Are you sure?" she says, as if striking an instrument to see how it's tuned.

"If that kind of contribution is the extent of what you have to offer my battleband, we have a problem. Do you have any other ideas?"

"Very well." Yinmei looks at me as if measuring the weight of my words. She speaks, "If we are protecting a space within a radial, we need bells. Please station Cricket and me tomorrow in the center of the radial. We shall stand back-to-back. Between the two of us, we shall be able to see in all eight directions. When we see invaders come, we shall strike bells, each of the eight notes of the scale corresponding with one of the eight directions."

"Why bells?" I ask. "Why not just shout commands?"

"Because we can strike multiple tones at the same time to indicate simultaneous attacks from different directions. The tones can harmonize, disharmonize, and create chords, yet still be distinguished. Words shouted simultaneously would be gibberish."

My anger toward her softens. Once again, she has found battle applications for music that would never in ten thousand years have occurred to—

We hear the scramble of skate blades overhead.

Someone's on the crossed bridges above us.

Doi, Hisashi, Cricket, and I race to the ends of the bridges to entrap the person there.

It's that spy that Etsuko sent. She clutches her hood, hiding her face.

"Tell Etsuko that she's not going to learn anything spying on us," I say.

"Etsuko didn't send me," she says, pushing her hood back.

Suki.

"Why are you spying on us?" I ask her.

"I'm not spying on you," she says. As vile as she is, she's a terrible liar. "I came to . . ."

"What? To sabotage us? To plant something so we'll be blamed for something we didn't . . ."

I trail off when I see her face. Heavenly August Personage of Jade, she's crying!

She says, "I came to . . . I came to . . ."

I realize what she can't bring herself to say. Make me die of shock.

I say with disbelief, "You came to ask to join our battleband."

Pain stings Suki's face like she's being branded with a white-hot iron.

Doi and I look at each other and immediately say, "No way under heaven."

"Wait," says Cricket. "Let's hear what she has to say."

"Cricket! She tried to get us both expelled last year!"

"But, Peasprout, this isn't last year."

Suki says, "You need the best wu liu practitioners in your battleband."

"We have them!" Doi and I say together.

"Yes," says Suki. "You two are the best. You should have taken the first two spots last year. I only won because you were disqualified." She looks like she's swallowing one mouthful of dirt after another. "I know you have no reason to forgive me for last year. But maybe you can find a place for me. I'd like to be useful to you."

"Why?" ask Doi and I.

"Because," she says, struggling for words, "because . . . now I know . . . how much I took away from you."

I ask her, "What about the other two girls in Last-Place Losers on Skates who stood by you when Etsuko threw you out? You're just going to abandon them?"

Suki stretches empty palms and says, "Who cares about them? Do you?"

"So you just discard people when you don't have any more use for them?" I ask.

"Yes," says Suki. "It motivates them to keep trying to prove their worth."

Yinmei pushes over on her poles and says, "Let us do the same to her. Let her join our battleband. We shall use her skills and discard her when she's of no use."

I turn to Yinmei. "How would you like it if I did that to you?"

"But you are doing it to me," she says, smiling. "And I am doing it to you." She adds in a whisper, "Miss Lock."

"This is not how I choose to lead my battleband. If you disagree, it makes me wonder whether you can work with us."

Yinmei says, "So you think I should depart your battleband?" She turns to Suki. "What do you think? Should I seek another alliance with you?"

Doi stabs a finger at Yinmei's chest and says, "Don't you dare threaten our captain."

Doi and Yinmei stare each other down.

At last, Yinmei bows her head and says, "What I have just done is demonstrated the turmoil that would be caused if we were to allow Suki in. Forgive me, captain. I only said those words to show you how dangerous a personality like Suki would be to the harmony of our battleband."

My mouth drops open. I hear Yinmei's point, but it disturbs me how well she's able to manipulate my emotions. Do I believe her?

"This should be a decision for our whole battleband," says Cricket. "You're the captain, and a good captain should honor fair process."

"All right, fine," I say. "Let's vote. Doi. Do you agree to let Suki into our battleband?"

Doi looks at Suki and says, "Make me die of laughing."

"Hisashi?" I say next.

"I'm with Wing Girl. If this girl hurt or insulted my sister, then trust me, she doesn't want to be around me." He throws his arm around Doi.

"Cricket?"

"We can use her skills, especially if two of us aren't great in wu liu. I vote to give her a chance, Peasprout. It's a luxury to work only with people we like." I'm not going to react to that.

"Yinmei?"

"My vote will be the same as our captain's," she says.

"Then it's settled. One vote in favor, lucky against. Now go!"

Suki grunts as if she were punched. She pulls her hood over her hair and clutches it close at her throat. As she skates from the circle of our lantern light into the darkness, she turns and says, "One day soon, Chen Peasprout, you will find that you're being dragged across the water by Shinian soldiers back to their ships. And you're going to be clutching a rope and begging me to haul you back up. On that day, I'm going to stamp my blade on that rope and send you back to Shin to burn."

CHAPTER
FIFTEEN

"**Nobody and the Fire-Chickens!**" announces Sensei Madame Yao through a hollering cone at the entrance into the Radial of Mighty Tranquility. I shut out the inane giggling over our name and lead my battleband onto the rail-gondola.

We pass the gondola filled with the previous battleband of students coming back from the other direction on the inbound rail. As they near, I see from their black veils, skullcaps, and smoked spectacles that it's Ten Thousand Secret Deadly.

Hisashi cries out to them, "How did it go?" They don't answer as they skate past us. They're all too busy crying, wiping their faces, and cradling wounded arms. One of them is clutching his amputated hair-tail to his chest.

Even though the entrance of the radial faces the Principal Island, this is Pearl, and the scenic route is always the only route. The wind from the sea makes us shiver in our academy robes, which are soaked in Cricket's pearlstarch mixture. The rail makes nearly a full loop around the islet before leading to its entrance. As we circle the radial on the rail, we see temporary platforms and netting stretched between the structure and the rail we are on. At the very least, if we fall, we won't be tumbling into the jaws of a coiling water dragon.

Our opponents are lined up on the temporary platform in a ring running around the entire radial. The entire third-year class is outfitted in nightmarish armor and helmets composed of red plates of carapace that sprout an array of horns, antlers, clubs, and claws. Each of them holds a round metallic shield. They're not wearing skates. They're wearing armored boots.

It looks as if the structure were surrounded by a sentry of monstrous lobsters.

"Why are they dressed like that?" I ask.

Doi seethes, "They're supposed to be *ahng-gwee*. Red demons. It's a slur to refer to Shinians."

Of course it is. Because this isn't some contest to see who's going to take the lead in the Drift Season Pageant. We're at a military academy now. And here we are, a battleband made up of mostly Shinians, inventing ways to fight our own country, for people who are insulting us.

"Forget it," I command. "The best way to answer their slur is to smash those ridiculous outfits off of them."

We near the entrance to the radial and see rows of skates lined neatly. We skate into the vast circular arena. Its floor is covered with sand, which is about as easy to walk across in skates as one would think.

Around us are tiers of stadium seating. A roof covers the rows of seats like a racing track, although the arena floor is open to the sky. Further, a temporary parapet wall as high as a person has been built around the radial's outer edge. We can skate on the track, or even on the parapet wall itself if we get enough speed, since it's circular and the outward force would keep us from falling.

As Doi, Hisashi, and I strap the forcedrums tightly to our waists, Sensei Madame Yao says, "Plant your banner in the sand in the center of the radial. The goal of this Annexation is to prevent the invaders from seizing your banner. Invaders that you are able to knock off their feet are counted as eliminated. You will be scored based on how many waves of invaders you are able to keep from taking your banner. The best score so far is eight waves." She hands us each an oval, metallic, mirrored shield, then makes her way across the sand and exits the arena.

She passes other senseis in the opening of the stadium wall leading out to the rails, who turn and exit with her.

Sensei Madame Liao. And the Chairman.

Fine, let them watch. I'm going to show them how a strange, extreme, and intensely lonely girl takes first place at this Annexation. I'm going to show them how a girl from Shin is the best person to keep Pearl safe.

We plant the banner for Nobody and the Fire-Chickens in the center of the sandy floor. Yinmei and Cricket position themselves back-to-back and array their central gong and eight bells on stands in a circle around themselves.

Doi, Hisashi, and I leap up the rows of stadium seating and stand atop the narrow track formed by the roof above the seats. Below, Cricket is holding two mirrored shields. He's examining the tether strung at the top of the arena that reaches from one edge of the radial to the other. It's not flexible rope, though, because it actually arches rather than sags in the middle.

Cricket unclasps the sash from the waist of his inner robe. He takes the two shields, ties their inner handles together, and whips the shields up at the tether. They catch, circle, and slam against each other. Their curved, mirrored surfaces now provide a view of the entire panorama *over* the edge of the radial's wall. My chest swells with pride at his ingenuity. Cricket and Yinmei will be able to see where the invaders are coming from before they climb over the wall!

The boom of a cannon splits the air. Something red comes shooting up over the wall toward us in an arc, a banner weighted on both ends. It catches on the tether and unfurls, reading WAVE NUMBER ONE.

On the floor below, Yinmei looks up at the mirrors and rings the bell for tone two at the same moment that Cricket rings the bell for tone seven. Invaders are coming at us from the northeast and the west.

I take the invader from the northeast. He or she scrabbles over the wall like some slow, crusted monster from the deep. The invader leads with the right leg, like most girls, so I assume she's a girl. The armor and the lack of skates make her about as nimble as a jumble of shells strung together. I spin at her in a double-toe quadruple scythe spin. In one fluid motion, she blocks my leap with the mirrored shield, immediately followed by whipping her other claw, which ends in a bouquet of horns, at me.

I raise my mirrored shield to block the heavy claw, but the force of the impact sends me sliding back on the circular track. This is not going to be as easy as I thought.

I hear a clatter below and see that Hisashi and Doi have sent the invader from the west crashing down to the sand below. They race along the track around the radial and come at my invader from her eastern side.

The bell indicating northeast is the only one that continues to sound, so we just have this one invader at present.

Hisashi leaps and executes a single-footed mantis cleaver jump at my invader, his extended skate blade jerking down like a mantis claw toward her feet. She blocks and sends Hisashi crashing down to the sand. His robe stiffens at the impact of his landing. He stands up to show that he is unharmed, thumping a fist on the cloth that has momentarily hardened into armor. "That's Cricket power!" he shouts as he clambers back up to the circular track.

I execute the identical move at the invader from the other direction. She blocks that, too, just in time, but then Doi executes the same move again. This time, Doi's skate slices under her boots, sending the invader plummeting to the sand with a satisfying crunch.

There is a boom, and another banner comes hurtling down and hangs itself on the tether, announcing WAVE NUMBER TWO.

Cricket and Yinmei gaze up at the mirrors tied to the tether above. Their fingers shoot out and five tones ring in the air, indicating north, northeast, southeast, south, and west. Doi and Hisashi deploy to the east, I deploy to the west.

I reach my invader just as he lifts his leg over the parapet wall and onto the track. He leads with his left leg like most boys, and he's less agile than the girl invader, especially wrapped in plate upon plate of armor. I skate toward him from his southward side, and he raises the horned ends of his arms preparing to smash them down on me.

However, at the last moment, I pound my fists down on the forcedrum strapped to my waist. I shoot far over in an arc and land behind him. He doesn't have time or room enough to pivot around to face me on this slender track. I press my legs tight together and perform a double-soled flying dolphin tail strike, slapping him down to the sand below so hard that he bounces and plates of armor go shooting off in different directions.

Of the bells that Cricket and Yinmei are still playing, the loudest and most urgent bell is indicating north. I turn in that direction and see Doi caught between two invaders. I drum my fists on the forcedrum, which shoots me forward so that I'm skating on the parapet wall itself. As I hurtle toward the back of the first invader, I fold a roundhouse loop into my path, swinging my skate hard into the side of the armored helmet and sending this one down to the sand.

Doi ducks, and I continue skating on the wall over her, straight at her second invader. He steps forward and holds his shield toward me, but he makes the mistake of looking at me around the shield so that his helmet is exposed. I change the aim of my extended skate and channel my gathered Chi into a twisting motion.

My skate blade flies at his face, but he seems unconcerned since the only part of his head that is vulnerable is a tiny slit in the helmet for his eyes. As I twist in the air toward him, I time my rotation so that when my skate impacts his helmet, it slots into the slit in his helmet. It doesn't go in nearly deep enough to touch his face but the skate blade locks like a coin twisting open a slot. The momentum of my twisting jump turns him enough to send him sliding off his feet and slipping off the track down to the sand below.

I land on the track and duck down as I hear Doi pound on her forcedrum and spring over me in a single-footed frog hop toward the southeast corner. She builds speed and skates on the parapet wall.

South of me, I see Hisashi mirroring her, skating on the wall as well. They hurl themselves toward the two invaders caught between them. At the last moment, they pound their forcedrums and explode in a twin flurry blade formation that I don't recognize. They easily knock both the invaders off the track and down onto the sand.

Before these invaders have time to even exit the arena, we hear another boom, and another banner comes shooting over, announcing WAVE NUMBER THREE.

Cricket and Yinmei strike the bells with their fingers. North, northeast, east, southeast, south, west, northwest.

Hisashi, Doi, and I spread out, equally distant from one another. The two invaders I meet at the west and northwest have armored limbs that each end in clusters like knobby, deformed mushrooms. They crowd me so that I don't have any room to take a leap at them. They coordinate their attacks, taking turns to hammer down on me with one blow after another so that I'm spending all my time blocking one or the other with my shield. I take a blow to the hip and another to the shoulder, but Cricket's pearlstarch snaps the cloth of my robe into a hard plate of armor at each strike.

Then they swing at me with all of their arms at once. I duck and leap down to the sand below and end in a roll, saved again by Cricket's pearlstarch. Above me, the two invaders can't stop the momentum of their swings. They clobber each other in the helmet, hard. They stagger a moment, then come crashing down toward me. I roll away just before they land and cover my head as sand and plates of armor blast over me.

Yinmei rings the central gong furiously, indicating that the banner itself is endangered. To the east, I see that one of the invaders has climbed down to the sand. He is wading across in labored steps made more difficult by the weight of the armor. Even so, he's only five steps from our banner. Brave Cricket has stationed himself in front of Yinmei and our banner, but he can't use any wu liu on this sand, and I'll never be able to make it to them in time.

Above us, Doi and Hisashi turn at the sound of the central gong. They simultaneously bang on their forcedrums and explode downward, blades aimed at the head of the invader advancing to our banner. Hisashi lands first from the northeast, but the invader pivots in time. She swipes a claw at Hisashi. The point catches his skate in the empty space between the boot and the blade, and she uses the force of his own leap to whip him into the side of the stadium. He crashes into the perimeter barrier, actually cracking the pearl.

An instant later, Doi's skate strikes the invader's chest, sending her sliding backward on her rear end with enough force that she plows a trough through the sand all the way down to the pearl surface of the radial underneath.

Doi and I look to Hisashi. He stands but holds up his skate. The blade is snapped in two. "I'm out," he calls to us. "I'll stay down here and protect the banner."

Doi and I each do three-pointed leaps up the stadium seating to the track above. Doi ascends on the north side; I ascend on the south. However, as I land on the track, the blade on my right skate snaps off. I reach out to catch the blade in time before it falls to the floor below. Thank the Heavenly August Personage of Jade, it's unbroken; it just came loose. Then I look up to see the three screws that had held it in place tumble through the air and bury themselves deep in the sand.

Bells ring out furiously, and I look to the directions indicated. Across the way, Doi is fighting an invader on either side of her, while two more invaders begin to make the difficult climb in armor down the covered stadium seating to the sand below.

"Peasprout!" hollers Cricket. "Use your shield!"

What does he mean, use my shield? No one's attacking me.

"The wall is a chute!" he cries.

The wall is a chute. The shield is a missile.

I take the mirrored shield, set it down on the track I'm standing on, and kick it as hard as I can along the track.

It slides on the track of the pearl, whipping along the curving wall. It speeds toward the two invaders holding on to the edge of the track as they start to make their slow, armored way down to the sand. The shield slices along the path, scraping them off the track one after the other, sending them bouncing onto their rear ends onto the sand.

My shield continues whipping along the path, barely slowed. One of the invaders flanking Doi blocks my shield with his own, sending my shield bouncing back along the circular track toward me. I stick my remaining skate blade out as it comes at me, popping up when it hits. I pluck it out of the air.

The two invaders then turn back to Doi and resume pounding at her as she cowers under her shield. The invader on the left brings both antlered arms down on Doi's shield so hard that it splits in two. Doi takes the remaining piece of shield, which is now a sharp, slender shard of mirrored metal, and begins lunging its point toward the viewing slit in the invader's helmet, curbing her strikes so as to distract but not injure.

Doi slips one skate blade under the invader's feet. As the invader plummets down, one of the antlered arms catches on Doi's blade. With two cracks, the antler snaps just as Doi's skate blade snaps. Doi and the invader go tumbling down together.

At this point, the exhilaration of being back at school and competing is starting to wear off and the fatigue is starting to take over. The final remaining invader looks at me. She begins clambering over from the east side of the radial. I sling my shield along the track at her, but she blocks it with her shield, sending it back to me again and again. She plows toward me in solitary tortoise formation. She has learned from the others not to peer over the shield. She stomps along the track toward me, blind but impenetrable. I can't use the forcedrum to leap above and behind her because I don't trust myself to land on the slim track on my one remaining skate blade.

I sling the shield down the circular track at her again and again, and all I get is my own shield bouncing back to me.

"Peasprout!" cries Cricket from below. "Use the architecture!"

Use the archi—

"It's a radial!" he continues. "It's circular!"

Then I realize it. Heavenly August Personage of Jade. My brother is a genius.

I stop kicking my shield along the track toward the invader's shielded frontside. Instead, I turn and whip my shield down the track in the other direction, toward the invader's unprotected backside.

The shield is traveling so quickly that the metal sings against the pearl.

Below, Cricket and Yinmei strike a riot of tones on the bells.

They're trying to mask the sound of the shield for me as it flies toward the invader's backside. It's working! The invader has no idea about the shield racing toward her back. She's continuing to advance in my direction with her shield facing me.

The shield sweeps the invader's feet out from under her, hard. She does a full backward somersault in the air. She bounces down on the track with a clatter, flops over the edge, and rolls down to the sand below.

I turn to Doi, down on the floor of the radial.

"It's no use!" she cries, holding up her broken skate. "I'm out!"

Another boom as a banner hurls into the air and lashes on to the tether. WAVE NUMBER LUCKY.

"My blade just came off," I cry down to my battleband. "Can anyone unscrew a blade and toss me up the screws?"

"There's nothing here to unscrew with!" says Cricket.

We're only on the luckieth wave, and I'm the last skater remaining on the track with one good skate. There's no way that we're going to top the current high score of eight waves. Not even close. And the Chairman and Sensei Madame Liao are watching all of this somewhere.

We needed more people in our battleband. I should have let Suki join. I should have considered—

What is happening below? Yinmei has stepped onto her swiftboard and taken up her poles. She's able to move on the sand using her swiftboard far better than we can on our skates. She's pushing her way across the radial, toward the entrance leading out of the arena.

"Where are you going?" I shout at her.

She twists around and yells back, "You said you were serious about winning."

"So you're going to just abandon us because we're not winning?" I cry out.

She doesn't bother answering, just continues through the exit of the radial leading out to the rails.

"Peasprout, look out!" Cricket glances at the mirrored shields strung above him. His fingers shoot out all at once to six directions, then seven, then eight.

"Cricket? What are you doing?"

"It's three groups coming up the walls one after another!"

The first six invaders crest the parapet wall. I ready to throw my shield.

Then, they all stop.

They're talking to their comrades below, over on the other side of the wall.

Through the entrance of the radial, Yinmei pushes back in on her swiftboard. She moves slowly because something is attached to the end of her board. It's her academy outer cloak tied into the form of a sack.

When she reaches the center of the radial, she unties the sack. Tens of skates tumble out onto the sand. She picks up one skate. She announces in a high clear voice like a Meijing opera singer, "Here is the skate signed by Little Ching-Ching, legend of Pearlian opera and winner of the Pearl Shining Sun Most Precious Skater Award."

"That's mine!" shouts someone atop the radial.

Yinmei calls up to the owner of the skate, "Come no closer, or this shall go into the sea."

Hisashi makes his way to Yinmei's side. Yinmei might not have the strength to fling the skate hard enough so that it goes into the sea, but no one can doubt that Hisashi does.

Yinmei continues, "And this one skate has an inscription on it. Two logograms intertwined. *Ong* and *Song*."

One of the invaders on the parapet climbs over and stands on the track. He takes off his helmet. It's that Ong Hong-Gee, the boy who, along with his boyfriend, were so kind to Doi, Cricket, and me last year.

"Disciple Wu Yinmei," he says. "Please don't do anything to

that skate. It belonged to my ancestor. She died fighting in the Bamboo Invasion. I gave it to my beloved Song Matsu when we declared our bond with each other."

"Then you must stand down, and all the other opponents with you," demands Yinmei. "And our battleband must be granted the first place in this Annexation. If not, this skate and all the others will go into the sea."

She hands the skate to Hisashi. He takes it and assumes the ibex bow position, readying to launch it over the wall of the radial into the sea at her command.

"What are you two doing?" I shout. "Hisashi, you drop that skate now! That's an order!"

"We are helping us to win," says Yinmei smoothly.

"This isn't winning! This is cheating!"

"This is not cheating," she replies. "This is besieging the cloister of Xie to rescue the kingdom of Wo. A time-honored battle strategy."

"No one's going to reward that kind of tactic here. This isn't Shin."

"It will be Shin if you do not employ this kind of tactic."

I feel the silence in the radial. Everyone must be thinking of the Empress Dowager's threats to invade Pearl.

"She's bluffing," says another of the invaders on the parapet.

Yinmei nods to Hisashi. He winces and says, "Really?"

She nods again.

He says to Ong Hong-Gee, "*Aiyah*, friend. I'm very sorry."

"Hisashi, don't—"

He sends the skate soaring in a high arc over the radial. Everyone holds their breath.

Someone cries, "The coiling water dragon!"

Far off, from the northwest, we hear the tiny splash. We wait.

No rising metallic hum, no approaching scream and roar. Only silence, broken by something that sounds like a whimper. We all look to the source. Ong Hong-Gee, that proud, kind, good young man, is covering his mouth, forcing back tears.

I turn to Yinmei and hiss, "You wicked, venomous, cowardly snake. How dare you do that to him? How dare you defy my order?"

At the entrance of the radial, Sensei Madame Yao appears. She announces, "After consulting with Sensei Master General Moon Tzu, we have made a decision."

I blurt, "Venerable Sensei Madame Yao, please, I'm the captain of this battleband and—"

"All the other battlebands," she continues over me, "shall proceed to be tested in the Annexation as planned. However, as for your battleband"—she looks not at me but at Yinmei—"that is enough already from you—"

"But I did *not* authorize—"

"—to take first place."

CHAPTER
SIXTEEN

We make our way back toward the baths at the dormitory compound. As soon as we have gotten away from any other students, I skid to a stop on the Bridge of Serene Harmony and turn on this Wu Yinmei.

"How dare you defy my order! You could have gotten us disqualified! You could have provoked a coiling water dragon with Ong Hong-Gee's skate!"

"My decision was the only thing that kept us from losing and kept you in Pearl," she says. "And dropping an unliving object into the sea would not provoke a coiling water dragon."

"How can you know that?"

"Because I dropped several objects into the sea first to test."

I'm so staggered by her response that I struggle to find words to express sufficient anger. "How dare you decide on your own to recklessly endanger the whole academy. We have no room for your treachery here."

"Peasprout—" begins Hisashi.

"And you, Hisashi. Why under heaven did you obey her over me? I'm your leader."

Cricket says, "Peasprout, calm down. We should discuss this as a battleband."

Yinmei says, "You are upset because you are afraid of seeing what a true leader must do to lead."

Doi says, "No, she's upset because we don't need a Suki in our battleband. Peasprout, her actions prove that your first instinct was right. She probably is a spy. She's going to sneak a letter orb to the Empress Dowager to tell her about the pearlstarch and the forcedrums and that *you* demonstrated to everyone how to use them against Shin!"

Yinmei turns and sings to me in perfect Shinian:

"Before you decide not to let me abide, may I try to provide explanation?

"Your prolonged hesitation and profound accusations over my motivations may subside."

Whatever she plans to say, it's clear she's been practicing for this moment. I shouldn't listen to another word she sings. But I admit that I want to hear what she has to say.

She finishes, "Let us meet in one hour without subterfuge or scheme . . .

"In the court where the power of the placid reigns supreme."

When Doi, Cricket, and I arrive at the Courtyard of Supreme Placidness an hour later, Yinmei and Hisashi await us. When I see them together, I remember what I forgot, what I wanted to forget: They spent a year together. They know each other in a way that I don't know either of them. There is a drum, an *erhu* fiddle, an Edaian *shamisen* that looks like a stretched lute, two seats, and scrolls displayed on stands. There is also, draped on a white plastered-straw mannequin, a complex headdress made of translucent gauze.

Hisashi motions for Cricket to take the seat in front of the drum, and Doi the seat in front of the *erhu* fiddle.

Hisashi bows and presents a scroll to me with both hands.

I unroll it. The title reads, THE BITTER TEA OF THE DYNASTY IN THE DYNASTY. It's a score written in Shinian for a scene in the Meijing opera style, a duet between two characters: Wu Yinmei and the Empress Dowager.

Hisashi lifts the headdress from the mannequin and holds it out to me. So I'm singing the part of the Empress Dowager. The idea of playing this vile woman repulses me.

I say, "So what, do you think that if I take her role, I'll understand her rather than fear her?"

Yinmei answers tonelessly, "I want you to understand me."

I place the headdress on my head, and Hisashi leads me to a spot in front of the exit out of the courtyard. The cloth of the headdress draws a haze over everything, as if we've been dropped into a cloud or a dream.

Across the courtyard's sixty-lucky squares filled with sand for meditating upon stands Yinmei, facing me like a counter on a chessboard.

Hisashi nods to Doi and Cricket. The three of them start to play the musical accompaniment from the score. Yinmei begins to sing in a voice of fear and doubt:

Why have you summoned me, great-great-grandmother?
The invitation called me to a feast.
But if this is a feast why aren't there any others
To join us but the honorable deceased?

I sing my lines from the score as the Empress Dowager:

I've summoned you to feast, great-great-granddaughter
On something that is precious beyond price.
So what I pour into your cup is more than water,
What I put in your bowl is more than rice.

Doi's *erhu* fiddle counter-melody rises, Cricket's drumming rumbles from below, and Hisashi's *shamisen* lute trills with poignancy as I sing the chorus in the role of the Empress Dowager:

Will you take the bitter tea
Of the dynasty in the dynasty?
For your sake, commit to me
And the dynasty in the dynasty.
Will you join us, will you Empress Yinmei be?

As the scene continues, Yinmei sings of her great-great-grandmother poisoning their family, one after another, as she decided that each one failed to make a good puppet, until only Yinmei remained.

Then the score has me sing the Empress Dowager's excuse for her ruthlessness.

They talk of vicious things that I have done to
Each person who's inheriting my throne.
It's only that I'm searching for the special one to
Convince me with some merit of her own.
A girl who has the courage to put finding
A way to change the law into her plan.
When she is Empress, Shin will have no more foot-binding.
Our girls will walk as far as any man.

Yinmei's singing becomes tense, punctuated by sharp, rhythmic claps as she recounts the Four-Day Feast. Her great-great-grandmother laid a great feast before her and ordered her to eat and drink. Did she do so to poison Yinmei or to test her loyalty? Yet, all of Yinmei's family swore their loyalty to the Empress Dowager, and they still ended up dead. So Yinmei made her decision:

So for four days and four nights I stay composed,
With my spirit steady, for my mouth is closed.
I refuse your poison, I will not comply!
I live unafraid until the day I die!

Yinmei throws her head back and her voice soars over us, intercut with my protests as the Empress Dowager.

*I won't take (*Why won't you break*) your bitter tea (*Come drink my tea*)!*
Of the dynasty in the dynasty,

*I won't break (*I tried to make*), so set me free (*you into me*)*
Of the dynasty in the dynasty!
I won't join you, I won't Empress Yinmei be!

The music of her singing and of the instruments ends at once, like a life cut short. The echo of her voice rings in the courtyard.

I sway slightly, fighting back emotion. I don't know if it's from the Chi expenditure of singing as my greatest enemy or from the enormity of what Wu Yinmei has shared.

At last, I ask her, "So you won the battle of wills? She let you out?"

"I walked out of the Four-Day Feast. She wasn't testing my loyalty. She was testing my courage to stand up to her. She wanted to know if I was a leader."

"But you defied her. What good is a successor who defies her?"

"A leader tests but then ensures. Afterward, she secretly fed me ivory yang salts to keep me from running away. I survived her test, but I am never going to walk more than five steps again in this lifetime."

This lonely young person did something few have ever done: She stood up to the Empress Dowager. And survived to recount it.

I say to her, "I'm not unmoved by your story, Yinmei. But all it tells me is that the Empress Dowager finds you worthy. I fear that's why she sent you here as a spy."

Yinmei says, "That is not what you fear. You fear that I am showing you what a leader has to do."

"I don't choose to be that kind of leader."

"You fear making bold decisions."

"No, I don't." I snap my head up. "Wu Yinmei, you are expelled from my battleband."

Hisashi says, "She helped us win!"

"I don't want to win that way," I say, shaking my head.

Doi reaches out and touches the edge of my sleeve. She says, "Peasprout, maybe you should listen to her. She's been through extraordinary circumstances."

I turn to Doi. "Wait, are you protecting her?"

"I'm just saying that you're not appreciating what she's been through. You have no idea what it is to have your own family, who should be protecting you—"

"Our parents abandoned us! Because of the Empress Dowager's law. So don't talk to me about how much she's suffered under the—"

"Being abandoned by your family is nothing like being attacked by them! Do you know how that feels?"

She's not talking about Yinmei. Or not *only* about Yinmei.

She's talking about herself.

Silence follows Doi's outburst. The sound of lowing wafts across the campus from the direction of the Conservatory of Music. It's Chingu, playing the same sequence of notes on the wave organ that she hummed to me.

Yinmei looks in the air as if reading the notes and says, "I shall depart this battleband if Peasprout orders it. If Peasprout decides she does not wish for my talents. If Peasprout decides to close her ears to my music. If Peasprout decides she does not wish to know the oracle hidden in the melody sung by Sensei Madame Chingu."

She knows exactly how to play on my emotions like a pearlflute.

And what I learned from last year is something that I don't like knowing: I'm easy to play.

I say, "No. I don't want to know what Chingu's oracle said or anything else from you. You are expelled from my battleband."

"I accept your decision, Chen Peasprout. The key does not fit the lock. I leave your battleband. I shall file a request for hearing over scoring."

"What do you mean?" I ask.

"To decide whether the points earned by Nobody and the Fire-Chickens at the First Annexation stay with you," she says carefully, "or leave with me."

CHAPTER
SEVENTEEN

The consequences of kicking Wu Yinmei out of our battleband make themselves felt immediately. The next day, after morning assembly, Sensei Madame Liao wordlessly hands me a scroll. I skate behind the knee of the statue of the Enlightened One and read it alone.

"To Disciple Chen Peasprout, Captain of Nobody and the Fire-Chickens: You are hereby notified that the senseis have received notice that your former battleband member Wu Yinmei has embarked on a solo career; that she has filed a petition arguing that your battleband was on the brink of defeat when she decided to take hostage the skates of your opponents; that such action won you the Annexation; and that all points earned should go with her and no points should stay with you. No reply to the petition from you is necessary as the facts were witnessed by all and are not in contention, and this is a matter to be solely decided by interpretation of law. We shall notify you of our decision."

It's signed, "On behalf of the senseis of Pearl Famous Academy of Skate and Sword, Sensei Chairman Niu Kazuhiro."

The Chairman will revoke my provisional sanctuary status if Yinmei takes away my first ranking at the First Annexation. He'd prance with glee at an excuse to send me back to the Empress Dowager, because he's just that petty.

And so is Yinmei. She doesn't need the points. She doesn't need to succeed at the Annexations. She's a political puppet. She could blunder at everything, fail in every discipline, fall in the water and bring coiling water dragons rampaging through Pearl Famous, and it wouldn't affect her at all. Must be nice to have no consequences.

By that afternoon, somehow the information has swept across the whole school. Probably through Yinmei.

During wu liu free training at the Conservatory of Wu Liu, Etsuko and her entire battleband Radiant Thousand-Story Very Tall Goddess keep skating by Yinmei. "Ah, your chair is so *kawaii*!" they squeal, petting her bladechair. As if a bladechair could be cute. Etsuko says, "Please accept this decoration I made to make your bladechair even more *kawaii*!" She bows and with both hands presents Yinmei a bright yellow pearlsilk kite in the shape of a happy-face butterfly.

When Suki sees this, she and the two other girls in the Last-Place Losers on Skates glide over to Cricket, hand him something, and leave. I race over. "What did they give you?" I ask.

He shows me a sweet red bean mochi.

"Don't eat that!" I say, knocking it out of his hand. "She probably blew her nose into the middle of it."

Cricket says, "I don't think so. They were eating them from a box."

So she's trying to woo my battleband members. By the end of the hour, it seems like every battleband's trying to pick off my members. Doi receives a bow and a smile every time the members of Fancy Pretty Princess World skate by. Doi bows back to them.

"Eh!" I holler at Doi.

Cricket says, "They're just being nice."

Doi says, "They did survive the eight waves in the First Annexation."

I shout at their backs, "Keep on skating. As if Doi would join a battleband with a name like Fancy Pretty Princess World."

Hisashi says, "I would have loved to see Suki's expression when she learned that they got to use the word *princess* in their name!"

Behind us, a boy's voice says, "How's it going, big brother?" It's Dappled Lion Dao and all the rest of the Battle-Kite Sparkle-Pilots. He places a hand busy with rings and bangles on Hisashi's shoulder. "We were just wondering if we could talk to you and ask you how you do that hip-roll thing when you come down on a scissor jump. It's got style!" And before I can think of a reason to stop him, off he goes with all the other handsomest boys at Pearl Famous. I have to admit: They look really good together.

From the snatches of conversations I hear, the consensus seems to be that

1. Peasprout's battleband has a talented lineup, but;
2. They have serious internal conflicts, and;
3. They're going to splinter apart before the Second Annexation because "Chen Peasprout has trash for leadership skills."

And throughout the whole of the session, Sensei Madame Chingu's wave organ moans the tones of that little melody that she hummed to me, like a key in sound that fills the very air around us. The answer to my own most desperate questions, the secret to my safety and my success, is ringing in my ears right now, in everyone's ears, but in a language that no one can understand. No one except this Wu Yinmei.

When White Hour is over, we line up to ride the gondola back to the Principal Island so we can bathe before evenmeal. Behind Doi and Hisashi is Yinmei.

I say, "I don't think Yinmei should come on the next gondola with us. We have things to discuss."

Hisashi says, "Peasprout, don't be like that."

Doi says, "I think that's a little petty, Peasprout."

"What?" I say, turning to Doi. "I can't believe what I'm hearing. She filed a petition to steal our points!"

"Peasprout, we're supposed to be nice this year," says Cricket.

"Well, I'm sitting as far from her as possible. And, Cricket, you're not to sit next to her. I don't want her putting ideas in your head."

Yinmei says, "I wish to sit next to Hisashi or Doi or both."

Hisashi says, "*Aiyah*, so much fuss. Peasprout, I'll sit between you and Yinmei."

Doi says, "No, I think I should sit on one side of Peasprout if you're going to sit on the other."

"Wing Girl! What does it matter?"

Doi continues, "And you got to sit next to Yinmei on the gondola ride over by yourselves. I should get a turn to sit next to her."

Why under heaven is Doi being so difficult? I'm irritated, but from her refusal to return my questioning look, I sense that she's struggling with deeper emotions that have nothing to do with the dispute over points. So I let the issue rest. For now.

I shuffle us so that it's me, then Cricket, then Hisashi, then Doi, then Yinmei boarding the gondola. Make me drink sand to death.

When we arrive at Eastern Heaven Dining Hall, we find that a special midmeal treat has been laid for us on tables outside in the middle of the southern quadrangle. It's vegetable-stew hotpot with glass noodles, served in a steaming vat over a live fire. Which is traditionally served on a rotating central dais. Which is why the tables are all round. Which means that the seating arrangement of me, then Cricket, then Hisashi, then Doi, then Yinmei around a circular table would leave me seated next to . . .

Ten thousand years of stomach gas.

In the days that follow, I assert my power over my battleband through tiny battle after tiny battle over Wu Yinmei. It's not fun. But I didn't expect leadership to be fun. However, Wu Yinmei never complains at my treatment. Never gives me a glance in resentment, never makes a snide remark.

One day, in wu-liu-combined-with-music class, Wu Yinmei watches me as I struggle with the drum exercises. We are supposed to lightly drum with our bare hands on an open-bottomed forcedrum in a regular rhythm to keep it floating slightly above the pearl. I make Wu Yinmei sit far away from my battleband in case we come up with something useful for the next Annexation. She doesn't protest.

I'm having trouble keeping the volume of the beats exactly the same as required to make the drum float in place. My drum keeps shooting out from under my hands at wild angles. I look over at Wu Yinmei. Her beats are as delicate and regular as beads on a necklace and her drum is floating slightly above the pearl. I can't see her hands, though. Then, as if she heard my thoughts, she switches position so that I can see that she's keeping the heel of one hand on the top of the drum, dampening its vibration. She keeps her gaze on the drum, but I know she knows I'm watching her.

Look at this girl from Shin turned out by the only other girl from Shin here. This girl who also suffered under the Empress Dowager's wrath, trying to find her way in this new place, dealing with suspicions because she's not from here, doing what she felt she needed to do to be safe, in a world where she is alone. I'm the only one who knows how she must be feeling.

Was I wrong about her? I want to be wrong about her. And it's not only because I need her points from the First Annexation. It's not only because this girl's talents would help me prevail at the next Annexations.

It's because I admire her. How could I not?

This is what I feel about her as I watch her, uncomplaining, helping me, even when I shunned her.

But I also know that this is exactly what she wants me to feel about her.

The Season of Spirits starts a little early this year, in the middle of the sixth month. Clouds come down from heaven and float above the pearl at waist level, tumbling slowly, changing from the shape of animal to animal, following us along the paths of the academy like fat, magical pets. It's a real hazard, because so much is shielded from view by them that near-collisions between students are a constant problem.

Why don't the senseis erect the fans that they use during the Season of Drifts and blow the vapors out to sea? Maybe because the clouds are so adorable and the effect is so picturesque, which matters to the senseis. And to me, too, actually. They can tell us that we're no longer an arts school—that we're a military academy now—but we are artists. Beauty matters to us. Joy matters. Even in a time of impending invasion.

Our first class of the Season of Spirits is being taught on the open courtyard of Divinity's Lap. Sensei Madame Yao is teaching, which makes everyone sneer, but then we learn that the lesson is devoted to learning about using forcedrums in wu liu, which makes everyone grin.

We spend the class working with the open-bottomed forcedrums that my battleband used in the First Annexation. What Yao teaches us goes beyond the simple dodges and escapes that my battleband demonstrated. Yao is combining her music and wu liu skills to teach us how to turn our jumps and spins into great bounds. You pound on the drums just as you are jumping and hit a certain resonant spot on the drumhead with the right volume, and boom! You greatly magnify the height of your jumps and go flying.

At first, we're cautious because it's hard to see due to the clouds and because of our proximity to the edge of the Principal Island. No one wants an uncontrolled jump to send us falling into the water. We're also afraid of losing grip on a drum and having it shoot out into the water. Throwing Ong Hong-Gee's skate into the water didn't rouse the coiling water dragons, so Yinmei was right about nonliving objects. However, everyone is still so frightened of them that no one wants to take a chance.

Soon the paths of our jumps have tunneled so many holes through the cloud layer that it's safe to go free-form. The entire court of Divinity's Lap becomes a joyful party, and everyone is bounding and flying in steps that are stories high, as if the world beneath us is harmless, safe, and fun.

Off to one edge of Divinity's Lap, I find Cricket. I tense when I see that he's alone with Yinmei. But then I notice what they're doing. They've each used the inner sash of their academy robe to strap a small forcedrum to their bellies. They're drumming their drumsticks on their forcedrums with unbelievably fast but soft little strikes that are so rapid, regular, and controlled, they blur like the wings of buzzing bees.

Then I look down at their feet. They aren't touching the pearl.

They're floating slightly above the pearl!

The stunning precision of their drumming channeled the energy of the forcedrum so that it was balanced between shooting up and being pulled down, causing them to hover!

When they see me, they look at each other, then each begin beating slightly harder with one hand than the other, causing themselves to pivot toward me as they hover. They lean forward, drive toward me, and touch their feet down. They shake their hands out in exhaustion and say to each other, "*Bwei bai*."

"Cricket, that was remarkable!" I say.

Cricket smiles. "It's fun! It was Yinmei's idea. I told you she was better than us at music."

I give Yinmei a cool look, then say to Cricket, "I can't see how that can have practical applications, though. It looks like it takes too much strain to control the rate of the drumming and just to lift a tiny bit off of the pearl."

"True. But that's not what I was thinking of mostly. Yinmei, I need your drum and sash."

Cricket skates to Yinmei's bladechair, parked at the edge of Divinity's Lap. He sits down on the pearl and lashes the forcedrums to the sides of the bladechair with the cloth, adjusting their angle so that they're balanced between pointing down and pointing to the back. He then gestures at it with an open palm.

Yinmei's face flutters with a sequence of emotions: She comprehends, she is astonished, then delighted, then grateful, then moved.

She unclamps her feet from the swiftboard and lays her poles on the pearl. She sits in the chair. She lifts the drumsticks and taps the drums strapped to her bladechair.

The bladechair nudges forward.

She taps three times on both drums, immediately followed by two taps on the right drum. The bladechair moves forward, then turns left.

She starts a moderate pounding rhythm, alternating between the two drums. The bladechair goes speeding forward. Yinmei begins to drum confidently, gaining speed. She quickly adds a roll of delicate taps to adjust her course and avoid a group of three boys fussing with their forcedrum straps in front of her.

A pair of students abruptly comes crashing down onto the pearl in front of her after a careless leap. She pounds hard on the right drum with the butt of her drumstick and makes a sharp turn to the left.

She speeds to a clear corner of the courtyard. She experiments with a series of drumbeats, alternating between two drums, in what I recognize as a mathematical progression that goes from slow to very fast. It sends her bladechair racing in the form of a spiral that circles tighter and tighter and tighter until it ends in a furious spin in place. Ten rotations, twenty rotations, thirty rotations.

She's doing rotations. She's transformed music into motion. This girl, who has been cursed never to take more than five steps again in her life, who has been imprisoned in her own body as if in a Dian Mai, is doing rotations like any practitioner of wu liu.

She finishes by striking the drums with a quick sequence of beats that stops her spin so abruptly, she's almost jolted out of the bladechair.

And she's laughing.

As is Cricket.

As am I.

With Cricket.

With her.

CHAPTER
EIGHTEEN

"**W**here have you been? What happened to your hair?"
I reach out to touch Cricket's hair, which is blown back so severely that it looks like he'd been tied to the prow of a ship.

"I was working on a . . . special project."

"What special project? Who were you with? Were you with Yinmei?"

"Maybe. Why can't I work on something with her?"

"Because she's not in our battleband."

"Peasprout, she didn't want to leave our battleband. You can't stop me from being friends with Yinmei. And anyway, we make a good team, like with the forcedrums. I would never have thought of applying music in that way."

That's true. I fold my arms across my chest and huff, "That's not true, you might have come up with the idea on your own if she didn't interfere."

"Let me work with her to come up with something for the Second Annexation."

I hadn't thought of it that way. Even if she's a spy, Cricket can, in his own way, spy on her. I want to relent, but I can't let him think he won this battle with me. It just wouldn't be good for our battleband to have members defying me.

I throw my hands up and skate away, saying, "If you're not going to listen to reasonable discussion, then I don't know how to talk to you."

Soon thereafter, I begin to hear strange drumming every afternoon, but I can't tell where it's coming from due to the mists. It must be Yinmei practicing on her new drumchair on the campus. I never see her at it, as she usually does it during White Hour, when I'm at the Conservatory of Wu Liu getting in extra training. It's impossible to see far in any direction during the Season of Spirits. However, I know she's out there, because I can hear the pounding of drums when there are no music classes scheduled, hear her turning sound into force, creating something that has never been before.

Then one day, something in the drumming changes.

There are two drummers hidden in the mist. I know because, sometimes, their sounds come from different points on the campus. And the music has become stranger. Faster but clearer. Wilder but more controlled. More complex and layered but more precise.

When he comes back to the dormitories to wash up for evenmeal, I say, "I need to know what you're doing out there."

"It's a surprise," says Cricket.

Doi says, "Let him do his work. I partnered with him last year during the boys' Third Motivation. He comes up with ideas no one else does if you just let him."

"But I'm the leader of this battleband."

"Oh, let him surprise you," says Hisashi. "It'll make him so happy. Plus, you look so cute when you're surprised. Do you know that?"

So I let him work.

One night, during evenmeal, the winds pick up. All the students are terrified of sitting near the windows after the coiling water dragon attack even though the shutters are kept latched now. The rattle as the wind plucks and paws at them is unnerving, but I see a strange gleam on Cricket's face.

Afterward, we skate out of Eastern Heaven Dining Hall toward the Hall of Six Excellences for tea anemone hour. The night sky above the garden between the two halls is clear. The winds have sent the clouds from the Season of Spirits tumbling away. Cricket says to Doi, Hisashi, and me, "Tonight is perfect! Please come in half an hour to the eastern edge of Divinity's Lap. I have something to show you."

"What is it?" I ask.

"Something that should be useful for the Second Annexation."

Doi, Hisashi, and I arrive at the eastern edge of Divinity's Lap. We stand under the great clarion in the shape of an orchid trumpet running up the tower on the eastern side of the Hall of Lilting Radiance. A thin veil of cloud has started to re-form on Divinity's Lap.

Then we hear the drumming. It's regular and low and emanating from the far side of Divinity's Lap. From across the dark square come Cricket and Yinmei. What they are seated on is unlike anything under heaven that I've ever seen.

They're each riding on a great blade, the sort that is attached to the bottoms of the gondola boats that take us to the conservatories, longer than a person is tall. The blades have been modified so that each one has a seat and pedals, like on a cycling apparatus, except pitched forward at an angle. But the strangest thing is that each vehicle has a complex set of six *taiko* drums strapped to it, three to a side, which are also tilted so that the bottoms of the drums are angled halfway between pointing down and pointing to the back.

Cricket and Yinmei drum in synchronized rhythm and then each pound with the heel of their left drumstick. The blades obey by skidding to the right in a sideways stop, carving a half-moon in the pearl below them. The two of them continue lightly tapping on their drums with both drumsticks, using the gently thrumming music to keep their blades upright.

Cricket moves forward on his seat to make room and says to me, "Get on! We're going to have a race!"

He gives Hisashi a lacquered fan and says, "You'll judge the winner. Please go to the entrance of the Garden of Whispering Arches." Hisashi bows majestically and skates off.

Yinmei slides forward on her seat and nods to Doi, who gets on behind her. Doi holds on by placing her hands on Yinmei's shoulder. Yinmei says over the purr of the drums, "That will not suffice. We shall go much, much faster than that." Doi's arms gently encircle Yinmei's waist, like vines wrapping themselves around the trunk of a tree.

Cricket says to me, "There's a set of drumsticks for you under the seat. When I yell 'strike,' pound on the two back drums as hard as you can."

He looks to Yinmei. Together, they chant, "Five! Lucky! Three! Two! One! Drum!"

Cricket and Yinmei bring their drumsticks down hard on their middle drums.

The speed is astonishing. We slice across the court of Divinity's Lap, cutting through the thin lingering mist so quickly that it flies apart in our wake, as two ribbons curling past our knees.

Beside us, Yinmei is pounding a furious rhythm, her drumsticks moving like a galloping horse.

Cricket alters his rhythm, and we veer into the path of Yinmei's blade.

Yinmei throws a roll into her drumming and swerves to the right.

Cricket changes the pattern of his drumming, causing our blade to shift back toward Yinmei's blade.

Then the two of them are weaving tightly back and forth, braiding their paths in a blinding show of virtuosity, bringing our two blades so close to crashing that my knee brushes Doi's twice.

As we whip past the statue of the Enlightened One, the western perimeter of Divinity's Lap comes into sight. The bridge spanning the canal in front of us leads to the edge of the Garden of Whispering Arches, where Hisashi stands.

Cricket and Yinmei both turn their drumming into a rampage of beats, as they each try to gain speed and overtake the other to cross the narrow bridge first. There isn't enough room for both blades to cross the bridge together, so whichever blade takes the bridge will crowd the other out, forcing it to cross after. There won't be enough time for the second blade to catch up before the first one crosses the perimeter of the Garden of Whispering Arches.

Yinmei unleashes a torrent of drumming, her hands blurring as she pounds with both ends of each drumstick, playing all the front and middle drums nearly at once. Her blade pulls ahead.

"Cricket, slow down or we're going to drive into the water!"

"Strike!" he shouts at the top of his voice.

I pound as hard as I can on the back set of drums as Cricket brings down his drumsticks on the middle set. Our blade jumps into the air, over the canal, landing next to Yinmei's blade.

Ahead of us, Hisashi waits to call out the winner. Our two blades fly past him as we cross the perimeter of the Garden of Whispering Arches. I crane my neck backward to see who won, but Hisashi doesn't snap open his fan to his left toward Cricket and me or to his right toward Yinmei and Doi. Instead, he sweeps the fan open and swipes right down the middle.

"Everybody wins!" he shouts. "It's a tie."

Grinning at each other, Cricket and Yinmei pound on their left middle drums in unison, bringing our two blades scraping to a side stop.

Heaving with exhaustion and pride, Cricket says, "See? As I said—something useful for the Second Annexation."

CHAPTER
NINETEEN

The very next morning, it becomes immediately clear how critical Cricket's drumblades are going to be when we learn about the nature of the next Annexation.

"The Second Annexation," says the Chairman in architecture class, "will test strategies for city defense. The Shinian forces shall number twenty to each Pearlian one. However, an invading army is especially weaker in a city, because those who call it home are familiar with its architecture and can use its layout to their advantage, even more so than on an open landscape. Further, wu liu practitioners are undefeatable on the pearl. Given this, which of you little birds can tell me why the Shinian army would attack the city of Pearl?"

"To besiege the cloister of Xie in order to rescue the kingdom of Wo," says a voice. We all turn to look at Yinmei.

"Correct, little bird of Shin," says the Chairman, smiling. "And what in the city of Pearl would they attack first?"

"They would try to capture the schools and take the children hostage," she replies.

I hear shocked whispers from the other students and blurt out, "Not all Shinians believe in such tactics! I had never even heard of that before."

The Chairman ignores me and continues, "Thus, the Second Annexation will test speed. Enhancing speed is critical in preventing an invasion of the schools. Increased speed will allow students who are less skilled in wu liu or otherwise vulnerable to successfully flee the enemy. It will also allow more skilled students to repel and even overtake the enemy."

The Chairman gives us an exercise to draw the quickest paths between every major landmark of Pearl Famous and certain critical entry points onto the campus. As we work, I say to Doi, Hisashi, and Cricket, "If speed is what matters, the drumblade is the key to winning the Second Annexation. And we're the only battleband that has it."

Cricket knits his brow and gets that new standing-up-to-Peasprout expression that I'm growing to hate.

"What is it now, Cricket?"

"Yinmei knows about the drumblade, too."

"Yes, but she can't use it. It's our idea."

"We can't stop her from using it. She helped me invent it."

"No, she didn't. You got the idea after you tied the drums to her drumchair."

"But she invented the music for it. I would never have figured out a way even to keep them upright, much less come up with all the musical passages needed to steer and thrust and jump."

"We can't let her use it. I saw Suki giving Yinmei a peony."

Doi snaps to attention. "What do you mean, Suki gave her a peony?"

"Remember? Suki gave me one last year to ask me to join the House of Flowering Blossoms."

"Oh, all right," says Doi, relaxing visibly.

"What do you mean, 'oh, all right'? She could join Suki's battleband!"

"Maybe you should have thought of that before deciding to kick her out," says Doi.

"What? You were as much against her as I was!"

"Maybe I was wrong." She mumbles it quietly, but then looks at me as if in defiance.

First Sensei Madame Liao. Now Doi. And I don't even know who Cricket is becoming.

It's all because of this Wu Yinmei. I have to deal with this before it becomes an issue. I skate over to her working alone at her desk, with Doi, Cricket, and Hisashi following close behind.

I say to her, "The drumblade is my battleband's idea."

"Yes," she says, looking at Cricket. "And mine, too."

"You have no right to use the drumblade."

"I have more right than you do, Chen Peasprout."

Other students are turning around to watch our argument. The girls of Fancy Pretty Princess World begin twittering behind their hands as they look at me.

Across the room, I see Suki with the other two girls of Last-Place Losers on Skates, watching not me but Yinmei.

I can't afford to look like a weak leader. I pound my fist on her desk and skate away.

I skip midmeal and go sit beneath the statue of the Enlightened One. Why did Yinmei have to come here? It's like she's deliberately trying to invade every part of my world and wedge herself between everyone that matters to me.

I quickly straighten when I see figures skating across Divinity's Lap toward me. It's Doi, Cricket, and Hisashi. Beside them is Yinmei, softly tapping her drumchair forward.

Then I see the stricken expressions on their faces.

"What's wrong?" I ask.

Yinmei places her drumsticks in her lap and unfurls a small scroll.

"Chen Peasprout," she says, "I have received the verdict of the senseis in response to my request for hearing over the results of the First Annexation. The senseis decide that I am awarded all points and place first at the First Annexation. You are awarded none and place last."

"Also, Peasprout," says Cricket softly, "the Chairman was looking for you."

"Let me come with you," says Hisashi. "I can talk to him."

I say, "I don't think he favors you anymore after you disobeyed him and brought us to the sanctuary hearing."

My stomach fills with stones. What have I done? I've jeopardized my own safety and the safety of Pearl. All because I was stubborn.

The sound of hasty skating makes us turn.

"Please, I can't stop to gossip with you. Very important work to do."

It's that girl with the honking voice who loves to spread gossip.

"The citizens of the city of Pearl need their news," she says, skating toward the rail leading to the Conservatory of Literature. "Of course, you heard about my apprenticeship with *Pearl Shining Sun*? Sensei Madame Phoenix recommended me for it before leaving Pearl Famous. She told them that I would be *perfect* for this kind of work."

Unfortunately, I'd have to agree with that.

"Oh, and, Chen Peasprout?" says Honking Girl. "I'm really sorry about this. It's nothing personal, but we at *Pearl Shining Sun* have a legal, moral, and spiritual obligation to report all the news, no matter how bad it is."

She hops on the gondola leading to the Conservatory of Literature. I watch across the water as she disappears into the Hall of Literary Glory. In a moment, she skates back out, followed by the swirling flock of green birds to write my doom on the sky.

"Two. Shinian. Ships. Arrive. Outside. Pearlian. Waters. As. Mayor. Demands. Pearl. Famous. Deport. Chen. Peasprout. Buy. Pearl. Shining. Sun. News. To. Get. Whole. Story."

Soon, the entire school is gathered at the edge of the Garden of Whispering Arches, squinting over the water through our smoked spectacles to the west. Two tiny specks anchor on the horizon, so small that they're almost invisible. It's especially hard to see them since it's the Season of Spirits and the rising mists constantly obscure them.

I use finger-geometry to calculate how far away they are. It would take probably two hours to row to them. I guess they're afraid to enter Pearlian waters because that would be an open act of war, and the Empress Dowager apparently isn't ready for that yet.

I whip around to Yinmei. "You conveyed a message to the Empress Dowager to send these ships."

She says, "I am not your enemy."

"You've been planning—"

A voice cuts through the air. "Where is Chen Peasprout?"

The Chairman.

"Little bird. You failed to take first ranking at the Annexations as you promised."

"My battleband came up with techniques for Pearl's defense!"

"Forcedrums and pearlstarch aren't going to stop any Shinian ships, little bird."

"They're not going to attack us. The water is filled with coiling water dragons. That's why they haven't come closer."

"You know nothing, little bird. You've put us in danger for long enough."

"You cannot send her back," says Yinmei. "You agreed to continue to grant her sanctuary status so long as she proves her value by taking first ranking at every Annexation."

"We granted your petition to take all the points for that performance with you."

"Yes, but I have rejoined Chen Peasprout's battleband."

I gape at her.

She smiles.

I skate to her side and cry, "Yes, she's ours again! Your

agreement was legally binding." I spot Sensei Madame Liao in the crowd. She nods. "So you can't send me back!"

The Chairman looks at all the faces staring at him and stuffs down his rage. He strokes the long nail on his little finger. "Very well. I'm looking forward to assigning you your opponents at the Second Annexation." With a dramatic toss of his head, he turns and sweeps away, like an opera diva exiting the stage.

I turn to Yinmei. She rises from her drumchair and stands.

"I told you, Peasprout," she whispers. "I am not your enemy. You are the lock, and I am the key."

Doi, Cricket, and Hisashi gather around us as the rest of the students and senseis begin to disperse.

We have prevailed for now. But it's even more critical than ever that we prevail at every Annexation and demonstrate ways to stop the Shinian invasion.

The sound of lowing fills the air. Mournful, watery tones, like the lament of whales, playing that same strange, wandering melody over and over.

I ask Yinmei, "Do you really know how to interpret Sensei Madame Chingu's wave organ–playing?"

"Yes. The oracle is hidden in the music."

"Show me."

That afternoon, all of us go to the Conservatory of Music. Sagacious Monk Goom is snoring with his head on a desk covered in musical-composition homework submissions. Sitting on a plinth is Sensei Madame Chingu, sucking on a bottle in long, irregular spasms, like a big, pink, twitching worm. I know she's a sensei, but she's the creepiest thing under heaven.

Still, I feel sorry for her. She didn't ask to be turned into this. Well, except that she was chasing innocent students on a rooftop with a metal cleaver during a lightning storm. But still.

Yinmei hums the melody that Sensei Madame Chingu originally hummed in response to both of my questions.

Sensei Madame Chingu removes the rubber nipple from her mouth and hums the melody back to Yinmei.

Yinmei says, "The oracle is hidden in the notation system. Ask her something personal."

I take Sensei Madame Chingu's hand. I ask in my mind, *What kind of battleband leader will I prove to be?*

She hums a little response.

"It's just notes," I say.

Yinmei says, "You're forgetting your Shinian. Each note corresponds with a word in the Shinian *gongche* notation system."

Cricket says, "Remember? The nuns taught us chants using *gongche*. It uses simple words instead of numbers for each note on the octave."

Yinmei continues, "Try singing out the word associated with each note instead of just humming it."

I dig into the refuse bin of my memory and say, "*Wu. Shang. Shang. Si.*"

Oh. *Wushang shangsi.* The Shinian term for "supreme boss." That's the kind of battleband leader I will prove to be.

So Sensei Madame Chingu *can* see the truth.

"How did you do that?" I say to Yinmei.

"I did nothing. This is not trickery. Now you know the answer to your questions."

Yinmei sings again the melody that Sensei Madame Chingu has been playing on the wave organ all year.

I say, "So you've known the answer to my questions all along."

"Yes," Yinmei says, "but only you knew the questions, Miss Lock."

I take Sensei Madame Chingu's hand again and say aloud the two questions: "What will be discovered to be the secret to winning the Annexations? What will be discovered to be the secret to stopping the Shinian invasion?"

She flings my hand away and goes bounding toward the pavilion of the wave organ, causing Sagacious Monk Goom to wake with a start.

She scrambles inside, and, once again, the notes boom out of the sea as she plays the massive instrument.

The notes are *gong, shi, liu, yi, shi* (or the alternate pronunciation, si), *shi, shi, yi, yi, gong, shi, si, yi, wu, wu.*

"It's just a string of random words," I say. "*Formula. Look. Four—*"

"Ooh, don't say that number," says Hisashi. "We don't need any bad luck."

Cricket says, "It's all right; it's Shinian notation, and we aren't as afraid of that number."

"Quiet," says Doi.

I continue, "*Spoons* or is it *keys? Show. One Wall. Palace. Follow.*

Willful. Zoom. Thing. Is this making sense to anyone? Is it some sort of list?"

"No," says Cricket, "it's telling you what it is. It's a formula. It's telling you how to read it."

Yinmei says, "If you remember, Shinian formulas omit all but the key words. I understand it to read as *Formula: Look for four spoon-keys to reveal a one-walled palace. Follow the willful, zooming thing.*"

"What are four spoon-keys?" I ask.

"It's an architectural riddle," says Cricket. "A one-walled palace."

"Do you think the willful, zooming thing is an animal?" asks Hisashi.

"What makes you think that?"

"Isn't *wu* the *wu* in *dongwu*, the Shinian word for *animal*?"

"There's only one thing I can think of that zooms, is willful, and is alive," I say. "If I want to keep winning the Annexations, if I want to stop the Shinian invasion, I have to follow the coiling water dragons."

CHAPTER
TWENTY

The coiling water dragons.

Just one of them nearly crushed or drowned Eastern Heaven Dining Hall and every student and sensei of Pearl Famous inside it.

The five of us slip into one of the larger practice rooms of the Conservatory of Music to discuss this. I close the shoji door, sealing out the sound of Sensei Madame Chingu's wave organ playing my destiny.

"How can the coiling water dragons be the answer to all my problems?" I ask.

Doi says, "Perhaps the oracle means that we have to negotiate with the coiling water dragons and persuade them to serve as a weapon?"

"I think you've got something by the tail there, Wing Girl!" says Hisashi, grabbing a nearby *shamisen* by the handle. He can't seem to ever talk without drawing attention. "We could ask the coiling water dragons to patrol the waters surrounding the island of Pearl and smash any Shinian ships!" He strums his fingers back and forth vigorously over the strings of the *shamisen*, then lifts it into the air as if hoisting a battle banner.

Cricket says, "Supreme Sensei Master Jio said that the senseis had signed a contract with the coiling water dragons. They're sentient, and normally they're reasonable and benevolent."

Yinmei says, "If you persuade the coiling water dragons to help you defend against invasion, you'll automatically win the Annexations and prove your value to Pearl."

I say, "I thought I was facing three problems: First, the coiling water dragons; second, how to prevail at the Annexations; and third, how to stop the Shinian invasion. I didn't see that one of the problems was the solution to the other two." I pause and make the words come out. "Thank you, Yinmei."

Yinmei says, "We work well as a battleband."

"And that's the new issue," I say. "I can't do this alone. I'm going to need your help to convince the coiling water dragons to defend Pearl from invasion, and to ask them to demonstrate their power at the Annexations. There's going to be a lot of risk. And not just physical risk. We're gambling that we can somehow survive long enough to get close to the dragon and negotiate with it. We're hoping that the senseis will agree that the coiling water dragons are so valuable, they'll forgive us for breaking all these rules. So, as your leader, I can only take us in this direction if our whole battleband agrees. Does anyone object to this new course of action?"

We all look at one another. No one says a thing. Cricket's

nodding. Doi rotates her fists as if stretching before a battle. Yinmei blinks slowly and smiles.

"Perfect answer!" cries Hisashi, throwing both hands in the air.

"How are we going to negotiate with them if we can't even get near them?" asks Cricket.

Hisashi says, "It's no problem to get near them. Just take a refreshing little dip in the water, and they'll come right to us, hahahah!"

Yinmei says, "We can go onto the water without going *into* it. The coiling water dragons seem only to rage when a person breaks below the surface of the water."

"Why would that make a difference?" I ask.

"It is a mystery," replies Yinmei. "But they have not attacked the ships from Shin. Perhaps because the people do not break the surface?"

"Maybe, but isn't it more likely that it's because the ships are too far away?" I guess. "They're not in Pearlian waters."

"But I also saw a ship of New Deitsu Pearlworks Company coming from around the Conservatory of Architecture," says Yinmei.

"When?"

"Last night."

"Why were you out past curfew?"

"To see if something would happen. I wanted our battleband to be prepared."

She's constantly vigilant. Constantly gathering information. Constantly preparing. I need to learn to do that.

I think aloud. "I don't think it's a coincidence that a Pearlian ship was coming from behind the Conservatory of Architecture. It's the one conservatory that we're forbidden from entering. And the senseis said the coiling water dragons built their nest beyond it. And now a New Deitsu ship has been sighted sailing from behind it. That's too much coincidence. Do you all feel how urgently the senseis want us to stay far from the Conservatory of Architecture?"

They all say softly as one, "Yes."

I continue, "We'll borrow one of the gondolas so that we can go on the water without touching it. We'll wait until after curfew and row out around the Conservatory of Architecture toward the coiling water dragon nest. Then I'll touch the water to summon them and try to negotiate with them."

Yinmei says, "I will help you prepare, but I should not accompany you on the water in case you need to flee or swim."

Doi says, "What are we going to do if it attacks us? It can fly a lot faster than we can row."

Hisashi says, "We can bring the pavilion trinket that I used to smuggle Yinmei back from Shin."

"When did you get that back?" asks Doi. I stifle a spasm in my Chi at the thought of the trinket.

"After Suki and her friends gave up trying to cut it open with their skates. It seems to still work all right. If the coiling water dragons start looking like they don't want to make new friends, we can throw the trinket into the water. It'll rehydrate and enlarge, and we can hide inside of it. It's sealed and really thick. You saw how the harpoon on Suki's barge couldn't penetrate."

"Excellent, Hisashi," I say. "Is there enough room in it for the three of us?"

"Yes, there's plenty of—"

"What do you mean the three of us?" asks Cricket.

"It's too dangerous for you. The coiling water dragon affects you differently."

"It was just a nosebleed. I'll live."

"No."

"Yes."

"Cricket, I said no!"

"And I said yes! Also, please don't call me Cricket anymore. That's a baby name. From now on, I'd like you please to call me Crick."

"I'm not calling you that, and you're not coming with us, and stop giving me that standing-up-to-Peasprout face."

"You need me. How are you even going to find the coiling water dragons if you're blindfolded?"

"What do you mean, blindfolded?"

"Remember? If you look at it, you'll be turned to salt."

I don't mention anything about accidentally seeing it when the main doors were ripped off during the attack on Eastern Heaven Dining Hall. Maybe it was because I didn't see its eyes—only its tails. But in any case, I say nothing, because I don't want Cricket using that as an argument that the coiling water dragons aren't that dangerous.

I say, "But if you came, you'd have to be blindfolded, too."

"Yes, but I know what direction it's coming from. I can guide us." Cricket taps his nose.

It's true. His sinus bone was so sensitive to the coiling water dragons that he could tell what direction the creature was coming from during the Eastern Heaven Dining Hall attack, even without seeing it.

"He's right, Peasprout," says Doi.

"I'm with Wing Girl," says Hisashi. "We need Crick."

Ten thousand years of stomach gas.

We're on the sea, rowing in the liquid darkness searching for coiling water dragons.

We decided it would be safest not to wear skates, in case we have to swim. It's a strange sensation to be blindfolded, sightless, with no pearl beneath our skates and no skates on our feet, led by nothing but sound.

An unexpected flurry of wind rises, and suddenly, I feel something slithering against my neck.

"What was that?" I cry.

"What happened?" says Doi.

"Something just flew past my neck!"

"What kind of something?"

"Long! Like a snake! But against my neck! And hairy!"

I hear Doi clambering over toward me. She pats my neck, my shoulders, my hair. She examines my hair with her fingers. And laughs.

"It's nothing to worry about. Your braid just came undone."

Why are all three of them laughing? I really don't see what's so funny.

Hisashi says, "Oh, I'm so glad that you did that and not I."

The prow of the gondola scrapes against something. I scramble to the front and reach my hand out. My fingers brush a hard surface. A wall rises out of the water. Its surface is uneven, as if covered in carvings.

The wall enclosing the Conservatory of Architecture.

We row to navigate around it as Cricket keeps one hand on the perimeter of the wall.

"I'll tell you when we reach the back of the Conservatory," Cricket says. "I can calculate from the curve of the wall."

We really did need Cricket to come with us. I still don't feel comfortable with it, though.

He says, "We're halfway to the back side of the Conservatory . . . ah—"

"Cricket, what is it?" I reach out and grip his shoulder.

"It's all right," he says, although I can sense from his Chi that he's feeling pain.

"I think the dragons are awake, but still far." He turns to Doi and Hisashi. "Keep rowing."

Somewhere to the front and the right, we hear a noise. Doi and Hisashi stop rowing.

"Do you hear that?" I ask.

"Yes," they both reply.

We listen to the sound again—a rhythm of little slaps hitting the surface of the water.

"It sounds like a giant spider scuttling across the sea," says Hisashi.

"It's going in a line straight behind the Conservatory of Architecture," says Cricket. "Follow it."

"Not too close!" I say to Doi and Hisashi.

We steer toward the sound as it grows fainter across the water. Something stirs in the water beneath us.

"There's something below us!" I say.

The sound continues moving, then whatever is making the noise is joined by another creature. And another. And another.

"I think they're circling us!" I cry.

"They're too small to be coiling water dragons," says Doi.

"Maybe it's the dragons' young," answers Hisashi.

"What do their young feed on?" asks Cricket.

"Hold on to something," I say. "I'm going to touch the water and try to—"

"No!" yells Cricket. "Don't touch their young! The adults are so protective of them!"

Something grazes the gondola as it passes underneath.

"It's touching us!" I gasp.

The thing surfaces on the other side and hisses a puff of exhalation and spray that dots my face. I hear a chattering noise. Almost playful.

I know that sound!

More blowholes puff air and water around us.

"It's just dolphins!" I say. "Ten thousand years of stomach gas. Oh, go away, dolphins! We need to concentrate."

When the dolphins see that we have no intention of playing with them, they swim off. We continue on toward the direction from which we heard the sound like a spider scuttling on water.

Something gently strikes the prow of the gondola.

"What was that?" I say.

I hear it continue to bump against the side of the gondola, thumping rhythmically.

I reach out and touch it.

A skate.

I wave my hand over it. Then under it. Then all around it.

Nothing suspending it, nothing lifting it.

It's just floating there, above the sea.

What under heaven is this?

I run my fingers over it and feel engraved into the boot some logograms. "It says *Ong* and *Song*." The skate that Hisashi threw into the sea during the First Annexation. Now it's floating here above the sea, defying natural law.

"It's Ong Hong-Gee's skate," I say slowly.

"Oh, please let me have it, Peasprout," says Hisashi. "I want to give it back to him."

I hand him the skate and hear him rustling and tying it under his inner robe.

Far ahead, we hear a hollow rush, as of water coursing.

"Do you hear that?" asks Doi. "It sounds like a river."

"Yes, but it has an echo," answers Cricket.

"How can something on the sea have an echo?" I say. "There's nothing for the sound to bounce off."

"Do you think it's the coiling water dragons?" asks Hisashi.

"Maybe they use echoes the way dolphins and whales use the echoes from clicks and whistles?"

"I hope not," says Cricket.

"Why?" I ask.

He replies, "Because dolphins and whales use those echoes to hunt their prey."

"Dragons don't eat people," I say. "They're benevolent. Usually. Don't they eat, I don't know, typhoons or things like—"

A slamming sound thunders from across the water.

"Something's moving toward us!" I cry.

A great rush of force sweeps over us, like something bursting across the dark sea, rocking our gondola so hard that my socks are planted in water.

Cricket lets out a sharp cry of pain and I hear him clap his hands to his nose.

Then the unforgettable whining roar of a coiling water dragon thunders in the air around us.

"Hisashi," I command. "Hydrate the pavilion!"

I hear a plop and a pop as Hisashi tosses the trinket onto the water and it expands to a full-size pavilion. I hear him tap the rhythm code into the side of the structure. The pavilion begins to shudder and hum. There is a sucking sound as its door spasms wide open.

"You three get in the pavilion," I order. "Keep it from rolling, and keep the entrance open above the water for me. I'm going to try to hail the coiling water dragon when it gets near."

I feel the weight shift as Doi, Hisashi, and Cricket clamber into the pavilion bobbing in the water.

The gondola begins to tremble with the bellow of the coiling water dragon. The metallic hum and the atmospheric change make my teeth sing with sourness. I crouch and grab on to the two sides of the gondola to brace myself. The rumble and scream quickly rise in pitch and force until it feels like my bones are shaking and—

"Peasprout!" cries Cricket. "Get inside! It's approaching too quickly!"

"I have to try to hail—"

"It's almost here! Get in!"

I scramble into the pavilion.

Hisashi taps out a complex rhythm code, then a wet, gelatinous slap sounds above us as the entrance to the pavilion puckers closed.

As we huddle inside, the sound of the coiling water dragon is muffled but quickly rises and rises.

"Ahh," moans Cricket.

"Cricket! Are you all right?"

"Peasprout, it hurts!"

I reach out in front of me. I touch Cricket's hands clamped on his face and my hand comes away wet.

I can't see it from under this blindfold in this lightless chamber, but I know that my fingers are covered in blood.

"Cricket!"

But he can't hear over the screeching thunder of the coiling water dragon as it collides into us.

We are thrown together to one side of the pavilion as the coiling water dragon flings our pavilion through the air.

Then we go weightless as the pavilion begins to plummet.

We hit hard on something solid, and we hear the sound dwindle as the coiling water dragon retreats.

"Open the portal!" I say to Hisashi.

He drums the rhythm code into the structure, but nothing happens.

"It's damaged!" he says. "It won't open!"

"All right," I say. "Everybody stay calm. We're safe for now. First, Cricket, how is your nose?"

"The bleeding's stopped."

"Where's the coiling water dragon?"

"It's not here."

"Are we on the Conservatory of Architecture?"

"I don't think so. It didn't throw us back that far."

"Then what are we on?"

"Something else."

"Out in the middle of the sea?"

"We must be on top of the one-walled palace."

"Peasprout," says Cricket, "we have to get out of this pavilion, or we have to get the pavilion off of this structure. Immediately."

"Why?"

"We're not touching water."

The pavilion around us moans like great timbers creaking against one another.

It's not touching water, which means the pavilion is drying out again. It's already beginning to shrink around us.

"Hisashi! Get us out of here!"

Hisashi furiously pounds the rhythm code again and again. I

hear the space where the portal should be. It's spasming and trying to open, but it stays closed.

"Peasprout, it's really stuck," he says.

The roof above gives a squeal, then pops as it buckles close enough to touch with my outstretched hand.

"It's going to crush us!" says Doi. "We have to cut the door open!"

"We don't have skates!" I say.

"Wing Girl, mirror flying iron fist triple jump?"

"There's not enough room in here to gather sufficient momentum. Especially without our skates."

"Let's try anyway."

Cricket and I press against the side of the pavilion. I hear Doi and Hisashi move to one side of the structure, then launch forward in a synchronized move that lands in two blows on the portal surface.

"Ahh!" cries Doi.

"Holy venerable mother of . . ." cries Hisashi as I hear him whipping his hand about in the dark.

The pavilion groans and, with a snap, collapses farther, shoving us toward the center.

"Peasprout," says Cricket. "There's only one thing we can do."

"What?"

"We have to rock the pavilion into the water to stop it from shrinking."

"Then how are we going to get out? What if the pavilion sinks?"

"I don't know."

I'm the captain of this battleband. I have to decide quickly.

"It should float because it's sealed," I reason. "And we can then try to roll it back to the academy. Let's do it."

Cricket says, "The pavilion is round and as tall as it is wide across."

Doi says, "Yes, so if we all do standing leaps—"

Hisashi cuts in. "And strike the side at the top at the same time—"

Cricket finishes, "We'll tip it over onto its side and rock it into the sea!"

"All right. Ready? Lucky, three, two, one, leap!"

We leap at the same time and punch the top of the circular wall of the pavilion.

The impact sends the structure toppling onto its side.

We are suddenly falling.

We hit the surface of the sea.

The pavilion pops back out to its full size.

Water immediately begins to spray in at us from all sides.

"The pavilion's cracked!" I cry. "We have to roll it to the academy before we sink below the surface."

"Peasprout," says Cricket. "We've already sunk below the surface. We were too heavy for the air in here to keep us afloat with the leaks."

How am I going to get us out of here?

I'm their captain.

Everyone waits for me to come up with something in silence and darkness. The water continues trickling in around us, pooling at our feet.

At last, the pavilion thuds.

We've hit the bottom of the sea.

"Ahh," says Cricket. "Peasprout, it really hurts down here. It really . . . it really . . ." His words trail off as he tries to stifle the sob bubbling up in them.

I can't fail him. It's up to me to keep him safe. I'm his sister and his battleband leader.

"We have to get this portal open!" says Doi.

"No," says Cricket. "We're so far below the surface, we wouldn't be able to swim up in time before our breath ran out. Plus, as soon as we opened the portal, the sudden change in pressure from the weight of the water this far down would kill us."

"Which way is the academy?" I ask. "Can we roll it back to campus and then try to cry for help?"

"We're too far," he says. "We'll never make it there before the water in here drowns us."

The water streaming in from the leaks is up to our shins now.

Cricket suddenly exhales as if punched in the belly.

A great moan surrounds us, lower than before due to the muffling of the water above, but unmistakable as the roar of the coiling water dragon.

"It's down here with us!" says Doi.

"We've angered it," says Hisashi. "Brace yourself."

"Ahh, it hurts!" cries Cricket, and I hear him slap his hands to his nose again. "It's coming! It's coming back for us!"

"We need to roll out of its path!" yells Doi over the growling rumble.

"It's going to fling us again!" says Hisashi.

"No," says Cricket. "It's all right, its path is veering away."

Then it comes to me.

I yell over the roar around us, "Cricket, which direction is it in?"

"It's swimming back and forth to the left of us."

"Everybody!" I order. "Roll the pavilion to the left!"

"What do you mean—"

"That's an order! Do it!"

We all stride on the round wall of the pavilion. It begins to wheel to the left.

After just eight steps, we feel a stunning rush of motion as the coiling water dragon seizes us.

We're pressed to the wall beneath our feet as we're ripped through story upon story of water.

Then, once we break the surface of the water, we shoot even faster as we whip through the air.

We toss over and over one another as the pavilion is flung through empty space.

I send up prayers to the Enlightened One and hope that we are flying in the right—

Suddenly we're bouncing over a surface. A hard surface. We rattle and spin as the pavilion rolls. Its speed causes it to tip upright, and we are no longer rolling but skidding until we collide into something.

We break apart in a spray of pieces of pavilion.

I slide across the pearl until my back slams into something.

I tear off my blindfold. It's the statue of the Enlightened One soaring into the night sky above me.

We're back on the campus. On Divinity's Lap.

I stand up and scream, "Cricket!" I don't care if prefect patrols hear us.

Across the court, a figure stands up in the moonlight and lifts a hand.

"I'm unharmed," shouts Cricket.

"Doi! Hisashi!"

To the left, two figures silvered by the night stand and call back, "We're all right. Not so loud!"

I listen to hear if the coiling water dragon followed to continue punishing us for entering the sea. But the only sound I discern is the gentle slap of waves against the edge of the Principal Island.

I look around us at the sweet, sweet sight of Divinity's Lap, made of solid pearl. I fall to my knees, bow down, and kiss it.

CHAPTER
TWENTY-ONE

I glide across Divinity's Lap to Cricket and cup his chin in my hand. I try to wipe the blood from his nose and mouth, but I just smear it more.

"It's all right, Peasprout. It's stopped."

Doi and Hisashi join us.

"Look at him!" I say to them. "Look what I did to him!"

"Peasprout, it's not your fault," Cricket whispers.

"Of course it is!" I cry. "I take you blindfolded onto the sea against clear orders from the senseis, who had very good reasons. I make us chase after a monster and get us mauled and nearly crushed, then drowned, then whipped through the air. We could have died!"

I turn to Hisashi and Doi. "What am I doing, leading you? I took Cricket right back to the thing that's most dangerous to him, something that makes him bleed just by coming near. I have no idea what I'm doing. I have no right to be your leader. Make Doi your captain. Make anyone—"

I stop speaking as I see Cricket's eyes flutter. He staggers, then slumps into my arms.

The first thing that Doctor Dio asks me after she revives Cricket at the Hall of Benevolent Healing is "Has this boy been exposed to ivory yin salts?"

Why is she asking about ivory yin salts? Cricket took them because they were the only way to keep his body lithe and limber enough to do girls' wu liu moves, which were the only moves taught in Shin. I don't know if I should answer. I wish Doi and Hisashi didn't have to wait outside. At last I say, "Yes."

"Well, there we have it. It interferes with the development of the heart and lungs, which manifests in sensitivity of the sinus bone. Was your village in Shin near an ore mine?"

"No," I say.

"Then how under heaven did he get exposed to ivory yin salts? Don't the authorities in your country know how toxic they are?"

I don't answer. I've never heard this before. Why would the nuns at the temple allow Cricket to take them if this were true? Didn't they know? I'm frightened by Doctor Dio's words, sickened at the thought of Cricket voluntarily taking this substance for all those years, a substance that this healer talks about as if it were poison.

Cricket shakes his head and says, "But I haven't been exposed to them since we arrived a year and a half ago."

"Oh, well done, little one!" Doctor Dio pats Cricket's head. But then she draws me close and says, "I'm afraid it's too late. His heart is much too small. It's the size of a three-year-old child's. I'm surprised he's still alive."

She whispers in a showy gesture of mock discretion, "I wouldn't get too attached to this one, if I were you."

I whirl away from her. What does this ludicrous quack know? I grab Cricket by the arm and shuffle out.

Doi and Hisashi follow us out the hall, asking, "What happened?"

"Nothing," I snap. "Cricket, don't you listen to a word of what she says. She's a fool."

"Am I going to die?"

"Of course not!"

"I haven't even built anything important yet."

What a fool I was to think I was his protector. I brought him, the most precious person under heaven to me, right into the jaws of a dragon.

"She knows nothing," I say. "I'm not going to let anything happen to you, Cricket. You're going to grow up to be a great man who does great things. And when we're old, you're going to remember when you were growing up and your sister kept you safe, because you didn't have parents to do that for you and because she would die rather than ever let anything harm you, because if anything ever happened to you, her world would drown in darkness forever."

A sob erupts out of my throat. I press my face into my hands and weep with shame and fear for how I failed him, how I failed all of them. I know they shouldn't see their leader like this, but I'm no leader.

Cricket throws his arms around me. He says, "It's not your fault. If you don't mind, maybe I shouldn't go with you near the coiling water dragons again. But it's not your fault."

My sobs shudder through both of us, embraced.

With Cricket in my arms, my fear and shame recede, and in their place, anger fills my being.

I dry my face and say, "You are correct, this is not my fault. It's this Wu Yinmei's fault. She's the one who lured us into the mouth of the coiling water dragon."

"You!" I cry when we find Yinmei. "Do you know how much danger you put Cricket in?"

"Cricket's in danger?"

Doi tries to interrupt, but I cut her off. My voice shakes with rage as I recount the coiling water dragon mauling and its effect on Cricket. Yinmei's face exhibits lots of showy emotion and the first thing she says is, "The imperial court has better healers. Maybe they can help him?"

"The last thing Cricket needs is help from you!" I point at her and say, "What did you think would happen when you sent us out there chasing after the coiling water dragon?"

"What do you mean?" she asks with such innocence. "Sensei Madame Chingu's oracle—"

"You manipulated that. Lots of words sound the same in the *gongche* notation system when it's sung. You took some meaningless notes that Chingu obsessively played and you chose words to assign to them and called it an oracle that gave me all the answers I wanted so that I would fling myself right into the mouth of danger and get myself killed. Just like your great-great-grandmother ordered you to do. And you wouldn't even have to dirty your hands or blow your cover as her spy."

Yinmei says solemnly, "Chen Peasprout. I swear that is not true. Chingu's oracular powers are real. She tells the truth."

Doi says gently, "Peasprout. Her oracle was true last year."

"This isn't last year!" I snap at her.

I turn back to Yinmei and say, "All right then. Even if Chingu's powers are real, you willfully misinterpreted the notes. And if Chingu tells the truth, then we're going to pay a visit and ask her what your real purpose was for coming here."

Sagacious Monk Goom rarely leaves Sensei Madame Chingu's side, so we have to wait until that night when the whole school gathers in the Hall of the Eight Precious Virtues for Pose Battle. It's a silly exercise that signifies nothing. Each battleband skates down a runway in the middle of the hall's central stadium, stopping to strike legendary wu liu poses, like stargazer and last warrior skating, while the third-year Conservatory of Music students drum out thunderous beats. The winner is chosen by audience applause, and it's almost always Wu Wu Wu Liu Liu Liu. One side of the stadium chants "Wu Wu Wu!" and the other responds with "Liu Liu Liu!" faster and faster until it devolves into riotous roars and stamps.

It provides a perfect opportunity for what I want to do, because the noise of the stamping is too similar to the sound of thunder, and Sagacious Monk Goom leaves Sensei Madame Chingu at home so as not to drive her into hysterics. Thus, while the rest of the students are busy numbing their minds with Pose Battle, I lead Doi, Cricket, Hisashi, and Yinmei to the little temple in which Sensei Madame Chingu lives.

Her eyes look up softly at me as I take her scarred hand in both of mine. I ask her, *Will we discover that this girl Wu Yinmei has come here seeking sanctuary from the Empress Dowager, or is it for some other reason?*

Sensei Madame Chingu sings back notes six and upper one. *Gongwu.* The Shinian word for "official business."

I turn to Yinmei. "So you're not here because you fled the Empress Dowager. You're here on her 'official business.'"

Yinmei's face twists in all sorts of expressions of shock and fear but it's all so false. I take Sensei Madame Chingu's hand again and ask, "What will I discover that this boy Niu Hisashi is to this Wu Yinmei?"

Sensei Madame Chingu sings back notes six and seven. *Gongfan.* The Shinian word for "accomplice."

Hisashi says nothing. I don't want to look at him because I don't know what I'm going to see in his face. I don't want to be betrayed by him all over again like last year.

Instead, I take Sensei Madame Chingu's hand and ask her a final question: "What will I discover this Wu Yinmei's plans to be with regard to me?"

Sensei Madame Chingu sings back the same notes, meaning "accomplice."

What can she mean by accomplice? How can *I* be—

Sensei Madame Chingu shudders and then sings out two more notes—note two and note lucky. *Sishang.* My Chi freezes down my back as I recognize it as the Shinian word for "casualty."

Then Sensei Madame Chingu spasms and sings the notes for "accomplice," then "casualty," then "accomplice," then "casualty," as if being tugged apart by two competing destinies.

So am I going to be Yinmei's accomplice?

Or her casualty?

Sensei Madame Chingu can't seem to decide.

So who's going to decide that? This Wu Yinmei? Or me?

I say, "Wu Yinmei, Niu Hisashi, I'm going to the senseis now. And I'm going to tell them about this evidence of your treason against Pearl."

CHAPTER
TWENTY-TWO

I **ignore Cricket's cries in defense of these two traitors** and throw off Doi's hand when she tries to grab my arm. I skate out of the little temple. I have to get to Sensei Madame Liao or maybe Sensei Master Ram to report Yinmei's treachery before my battle-band tries to stop me. I hop over the gondola and skate directly on the rail back to the Principal Island. Behind me, Doi, Cricket, Hisashi, and this traitor Yinmei clamber into the rail-gondola. They row furiously after me with the oarfans, calling my name. I could easily outskate them, but I'm terrified of falling off the rail into the jaws of a coiling water dragon in the water below. However, I skate faster than I want to because Yinmei poses a greater danger—a danger to all of Pearl.

I reach the Principal Island and hop off. I begin to skate toward the—

From around the corners of the Courtyard of Supreme Placidness come figures pouring forth in silent lines.

They wear boots, not skates.

I know these uniforms. They're the same red as those of the soldiers who burst through the doors of the temple searching for our parents.

Shinian soldiers. Perhaps fifty of them.

They begin to surround me.

Their faces are painted so that their features are obscured, but their vision is unimpeded. Their face paint is done in the style of the actors in the Meijing opera that Nun Hou took Cricket and me to once. It had been the best day of our lives.

How did I ever think that those painted faces looked festive?

Doi, Cricket, Hisashi, and Yinmei disembark the gondola behind me.

I turn to Yinmei and say, "You called them here! You told them we would be here alone."

Her face of serenity is gone. She's as shocked to see the invading soldiers as I am. "I had nothing to do with this," she says.

Each of the soldiers holds in his hand a loop of rope, encircling us just ten strides away.

"Seize the target!" one of the soldiers cries.

As they tighten their ring around us, I try to shove Cricket behind me.

"No, Peasprout!" he cries. "It's you that the Empress Dowager wants!"

Cricket, Doi, and Hisashi form a line of defense in front of me. Behind us is the edge of the Principal Island, and beyond is dark water.

We're trapped.

Yinmei shouts, "Pull out the hairs from the mole of the one in the center!"

I see that in the center of the line of soldiers is one with a mole as fat as a tick poking out of the face paint, right in the middle of his forehead. Three disgusting wiry hairs grow out of it as long as my forearm.

"Wha—" cries Doi.

"Just do it!" commands Yinmei.

"Seize the target—or kill her." The soldiers descend on us in a tide of flowing red.

Doi and Hisashi instantly pivot and face away from each other. They begin to chop and slice at the soldiers.

Five soldiers throw loops of rope at me, but Cricket and I sever them in midair with roundhouse kicks.

One of the soldiers breaks in, shoves Yinmei off her swiftboard, and kicks it into the sea. Then he ignores her.

They don't want to seize her. Is it because she told them to come here? Because they don't know she's the heir? Because she's not who she says she is?

Doi and Hisashi each furiously fend off half the soldiers, dividing their ranks and cleaving a path between them for me.

"Peasprout, get out of here!" yells Hisashi.

"I'm not going to leave you! I'm the captain!"

"They only want you," shouts Doi. "Go!"

Doi and Hisashi both leap away from the soldiers and slam against each other, back-to-back. They intertwine their legs and form a coupled yin-yang formation. The soldiers pour in, but Doi and Hisashi spin and burst apart, sweeping the soldiers down onto their rear ends in a tide of air and released Chi.

"Go, Peasprout, go!" screams Cricket.

I'm their leader. But a leader has to make difficult decisions. I can't keep Cricket or Pearl or myself safe if I'm stretched on a rack in the Empress Dowager's dungeon.

I nod my thanks and skate hard on the path Doi and Hisashi have cleared for me between the scrambling soldiers.

I skate toward the dormitories, but five Shinian soldiers block my escape to the north. I scrape to a stop and change direction, skating hard to the west on the path beside the front wall of the Palace of the Eighteen Outstanding Pieties.

Shinian soldiers pour silently out of the great entrance of the palace, their red capes fluttering like jellyfish tentacles. They've cut off my path.

Across the Central Canal to my left, I hear a sound that freezes my Chi: the creak of bows being pulled taut.

Ten bows are pointed at me across the canal. And here I am, pressed against the spanning side of the Palace of the Eighteen Outstanding Pieties, waiting for them to nail me to the wall.

A sound like cupped palms gently slapping on the pearl approaches.

Through the mists comes a figure.

This Wu Yinmei.

Without her swiftboard. Hobbling on her unskated feet.

She took more than five steps.

She crossed half the length of the campus on those feet to get to me. She's clutching her chest, heaving with pain. Her heart and lungs are growing as much as they would in a year. I cover my mouth in shock. If she keeps walking, they could burst.

She stretches her arms out, palms facing the soldiers around us, and stands between me and the archers, shielding me.

"Halt!" she shouts. "You shall not harm this girl."

She turns to me and says, "Peasprout, do not return to the dormitories. The way is blocked. We have to get to the clarion formed by the tower on the eastern side of the Hall of Lilting Radiance and sound the alarm."

"If we just get to Divinity's Lap, we can shout for help."

"They'll never hear us over the noise of Pose Battle."

"Then we should pull one of the alarm cords that send the metal balls clattering—"

"I tried," she says between pants. "They cut all the cords. We have to get to the clarion. It's the only thing loud enough."

"But that's a li and a half away! How are you going to get there?"

"It will be done, for it must be done."

We retreat in the direction from which we came, moving slowly eastward, Yinmei protecting me from the archers with her body.

When we near the corner of the palace, she clutches her chest and stumbles. As she falls, I instantly drop to the pearl behind her just as two arrows bury themselves in the wall of the palace above us.

She rises slowly, and I rise behind her, matching each lift of her leg, each step of her foot, each limb of her body keeping each limb of my body safe.

We round the corner and proceed along the eastern wall of the palace.

"Faster, Peasprout," she says.

Above the sound of the fighting to the south of us, I hear the beat of boots stamping around the palace. They're trying to head us off and block our path to the Hall of Lilting Radiance.

"Flee, Peasprout!"

I skate hard across Divinity's Lap, toward the great orchid-shaped clarion grafted along the side of the Hall of Lilting Radiance.

Behind me, I hear the little slaps of Yinmei's steps on the pearl as she runs after me, each soft pad of her feet like fists pounding on my chest as I imagine her heart and lungs growing monstrously in her chest.

As we near the Hall of Lilting Radiance, I hear her slip and tumble onto the pearl.

"Go, Peasprout!" she cries. "Go!"

I launch forward, slam into the side of the hall, and wrench the clarion's pearlsilk cord. A great siren trumpets out of the orchid shape high above, and I fall to the pearl as a volley of arrows pierces into the side of the hall above me.

I scramble around the corner of the hall, but there's no need.

The soldiers are already retreating, scurrying in their boots back toward their skiffs to the south as senseis and students come pouring out of the Hall of the Eight Precious Virtues.

I skate back to Yinmei, who is lying curled on the court of Divinity's Lap. I slide to my knees and take her hand.

"Are you harmed?" I ask her.

Her chest heaves under her hand. She gulps air through her grimacing mouth. Her teeth are stained red.

"You fool!" I say through tears. "You could've died!"

"I had to help you."

"Why?"

"Because you are my . . ." She pauses.

"Don't say I'm your captain. I don't deserve to be your captain."

". . . friend," she says softly.

CHAPTER
TWENTY-THREE

As Sensei Madame Liao and Sensei Master Ram carry Yinmei to the Hall of Benevolent Healing, Yinmei looks around frantically.

"Where's Doi?" she cries.

In a flurry of lunging steps that end in a hard skid, Doi is beside her.

"I'm here, Yinmei," pants Doi. "What happened to you?"

"Did you get the mole hairs off the soldier?"

"Yes, but why—"

Yinmei says to all the senseis gathered around, "Send a letter orb to the Shinian ships immediately. Say these words exactly: 'Come ashore again and we shall chop your fortune into forty-four pieces and burn them.'"

With that, her eyes fade and she goes limp.

Doctor Dio is useless as usual. When she comes out of Yinmei's patient room in the Hall of Benevolent Healing, all that this supposed healer says to us is, "Ivory yang salts. Very bad. Very bad. How many steps did she take? I can't believe her heart and lungs haven't splattered in her chest cavity already."

"But what can you do for her?" I say.

"*Do?* Well, of course, there's nothing you can *do*. It's ivory yang salts!"

"But won't her body eventually grow large enough to accommodate the enlargement in her heart and lungs?"

"That's not the issue. It's the rate at which they grew. It fills the tissues of the heart and lungs with all sorts of rips and tears, like the stretch marks on skin that form when muscles grow too quickly underneath them. The organs never function properly after that, even if they shrink back down some. The damage is irreparable." She pauses and then says, slowly, "Although . . . of course, perhaps I could investigate other therapies, but it'd require removing her nose for study."

Yinmei falls in and out of consciousness. Doi, Cricket, Hisashi, and I take turns sitting by her futon. Especially Doi.

When Yinmei awakens, she is delirious and desperately asks only one question: "Did they send the letter orb?"

They did.

And the Shinian soldiers do not come again.

The whole academy, the whole of the city, waits and waits for the soldiers to return.

Honking Girl's birds get a lot of exercise. There are two, sometimes three headlines a day. About the endless bureaucratic arguments among the Pearlian senators over whether to consider this an act of war. About how Pearl Famous's harboring me is risking the safety of the entire island. About the increased calls by the mayor of the city of Pearl to hand me over to appease the Empress Dowager.

But still, the Shinian soldiers do not come again.

No formal statement comes from the senseis that the danger has passed. However, eventually, when no new threats appear, we move on. The headlines start reporting about other things, talk on campus starts to center on our studies and the upcoming Annexation, and academy life returns to normal.

It appears that whatever Yinmei did, we are safe because of it. For now.

What did Yinmei do?

At last, she recovers enough to be moved back to her own dormitory. She declines care from the Shinian serving girls in her recovery. Instead, she asks for me.

Me. The girl who accused her. The girl she almost died for.

When I arrive, she rises slightly from her futon and asks, "Who has the mole hairs?"

"Doi gave them to me to hold on to. I mean, not literally hold on to. I don't want to actually touch—"

"Did you hide them somewhere no one will find them?"

"No, but I had Cricket use sewing needles to weave them into the shape of a ring. They look like metal wires. No one would recognize them for what they are."

She sinks back down onto her futon with relief.

"You hold the safety of Pearl in your hands for now," she says.

"What did you do, Yinmei?"

"I besieged the cloister of Xie to rescue the kingdom of Wo."

"What do you mean?"

"Captain Cao. One of the Empress Dowager's favorites. I recognized him despite the face paint because of the mole hairs. He's brave but very superstitious—the only Shinian I know who says *lucky* instead of *four*."

"I don't understand."

"Did you never read a mole atlas?"

"Ah . . . yes, of course."

Why's she smirking at me? She says, "Then you would know that a mole located in the center of the forehead indicates peaceful and happy later years. The longer the hairs are that grow out of it, the longer is one's good fortune. Cut the hairs and you shorten the good luck. Burn them and you destroy the owner's fortune. You hold the destiny of a very superstitious man in your hand. A very superstitious captain of the Shinian ships."

"Oh, I know. That's what I was going to—"

A laugh bubbles out of her throat. She props herself up on an elbow to look at me. "You don't even remember if you've seen a mole atlas or not, do you? You've only been here in Pearl a year and a half. How quickly this place can make one forget one's homeland."

My Chi rises, but I calm it down because I don't want her to see that she's bothered me.

"I'm not insulting you," she says. "I understand. This place has that power. But don't forget where you come from. You sneer at Shinian tactics, yet Shinian tactics saved Pearl today."

"I don't understand . . . why do you risk your life for me and then challenge me? I mean . . . Look, I'm going to have Doi take over your care. I wanted to look after you to thank you for, well, saving my life but if it's upsetting to you . . ."

"No," she says. "Please."

And then, for the first time, I see Yinmei be . . . what is the word . . . *insecure*. I never thought I would see that. How brave she is. I would never let someone see that.

As I help with the duties of feeding her, keeping her clean, and all sorts of things I've never done for anyone, her recovery continues steadily but with labor. Doi asks again and again to help take care of Yinmei, but Yinmei won't even let Doi see her.

At first, I'm perplexed. However, I come to understand. And it has nothing to do with me and everything to do with a complicated relationship that has been blooming right in front of me this entire time.

One day, Doi meets me as I exit Yinmei's dormitory chamber with a bowl of water and used garments. I cover the dirty washing with a towel so that Doi won't see it. She notices my gesture and says, "Why won't she let me tend to her?" Her tone is neutral, but her Chi pulses with emotion.

She's jealous.

I say, "Doi. Don't you understand anything?"

"Just because she saved you doesn't mean that you're the only person who cares about her now. Or that you're the only person she should care—"

"Yinmei is permitting me to tend to her because she doesn't care if I see her in so unattractive a state, but she—"

"I don't care if it's unattractive! It's not unattractive! Her courage, her—"

"—but she does care if you see her."

"Why does she care? That's silly, there's no—"

"Because she cares about what you think of her appearance."

She's still confounded, but slowly, I feel a tide reverse in her Chi, and her spirit begins to float as the revelation finally sweeps over her face.

"Doi," I say as I skate past her, "you can be so oblivious sometimes."

Yinmei proves to be an obedient patient, as she does not wish to push her recovery too quickly. When she thinks she is finally able to stand, she asks me to help her up from her futon. She stands for several moments. It goes well until, suddenly, a pain stabs through her Chi.

"Help me sit, *dajie*," she says to me between sharp breaths. *Dajie.* The Shinian term of affection for "big sister."

"I tried to do too much too quickly," she continues in Shinian.

Since we've arrived in Pearl, I haven't allowed Cricket to speak

Shinian; he needs all the practice with Pearlian that he can get. Having Yinmei speak Shinian to me day after day, when I'd not heard it for so long, stirs something in me, like the aroma of a favorite dish from childhood. I turn to hide the emotion in my face and wring a fresh facecloth in the bowl of water.

Between her whistling gulps of air, she says, "I wish I hadn't heard what Doctor Dio said."

"Never listen to that quack!"

"It's too late. I know she's right. Every time I inhale, I can actually count the individual rips in my heart and—"

"She's never right. Ever!"

She turns her big, dark eyes to me. "Did she say something about Cricket?"

"Of course not."

"Perhaps it is better to know. So that you can be prepared."

"She makes up diagnoses so she can seem valuable enough to keep her job. She's never right. I mean, look: You're already so much better."

"Because of your care."

"No, because you're strong. And you're going to be all better soon," I say. "Because we need you for the Second Annexation."

"So you didn't report what Sensei Madame Chingu said as evidence that I'm plotting against Pearl?"

I'd completely forgotten about that. All my doubts about her evaporated after she saved my life.

"Oracles can be misinterpreted," I say simply.

"So it sounds like you still want me in your battleband."

"Of course. I would be honored if you w—"

"I follow nobody . . ." she says coolly.

"I am so sorry that I doubted—"

". . . and her fire-chickens."

She smiles. It's the first joke I've ever heard her tell. But she winces with pain again and struggles to control her breathing. "Please tell me a story," she says. "To direct my attention until the pain subsides."

"What do you want to hear?" I reply in Shinian.

"Tell me how it feels to skate."

I don't know what to say. Should I speak honestly or—

"Why do you hesitate?" she asks.

She always seem to speak what everyone else leaves unspoken.

Yinmei continues, "Ah, I see. You fear it would be cruel to speak with passion about something that I will never be able to do. You are kind, Peasprout. I shall ask a less uncomfortable question. When did you first start learning wu liu?"

"Near my fifth birthday."

"Tell me of the first day."

As I gently dab the moisture from Yinmei's brow, I think of that day. A day of firsts and a day of lasts.

"My parents brought Cricket and me to the door of a temple. They told us that it was a school where we would learn wu liu."

"Why does this memory make your voice turn sad?"

I answer, "Because they'd dressed me in the only fine suit of clothes that any of our family owned. And when I learned that this was a school and there would be proper teachers here, I was ashamed of my parents' patched clothes. I was afraid they would smile and show their missing teeth. I told them I didn't want the teachers to see Cricket and me with them, and I told them not to wait with us. I told them to go away."

"You were little more than a baby," Yinmei says. "You were blameless."

"Perhaps. But when I arrived here last year, all of the Shinian servant girls must have been so excited, because I was the first Shinian student at the academy. And I was the Peony-Level Brightstar. They must have felt so proud to have one of their own attend Pearl Famous as a skater and not as a servant. And I shunned them and wanted to undo my braids so I wouldn't resemble them. I wouldn't even look at them. How hurt they must have been. I've learned nothing since that day my parents took me to the wu liu temple."

"There's anger hidden under your voice when you mention that day."

I finally say what I've never spoken aloud to anyone. "Because it was the last day that I ever saw my parents. I didn't learn until years later. The reason my parents had to abandon us at the wu liu temple was because they, by accident, broke one of the Empress Dowager's laws and had to flee."

"Which law?"

"It doesn't matter. But they couldn't pay the fine. They used the last of their money to visit a fortune-teller. The fortune-teller said that my family's destiny lay in my feet. My parents thought it meant that they should bind my feet so that I could be sold to a wealthy household. However, they didn't have the heart to do it. So they left

Cricket and me at the temple where we would learn wu liu. The last time I saw them, I was ashamed of their appearance, and I told them to go away. And they did. Forever."

Yinmei gently waves me aside when I try to continue dabbing at her forehead. She pushes herself up into a sitting position and peers at me with soft, intense eyes. She says, "Permit me to rebraid your hair in the Empress Dowager's favorite hairstyle, the staircase royal phoenix crown." I turn so that I am sitting on her futon with my back to her. I'm grateful for an excuse to turn away from her penetrating gaze. She begins loosening my braids and combing out my hair.

"That is a painful memory, Peasprout. But the fortune-teller was correct. Your family's destiny does lie in your feet. But you were meant to be a champion, not to be bought by a household of strangers."

"Yes."

She separates a section of my hair and gathers the rest to the side. She says, "Do you know how old girls in Shin are when they start to get their feet bound? Five years old. Just like you were that day that you were left at the wu liu temple. They are told that they must do so to keep their feet small and delicate or they will never find a husband. They are told that when they grow up, the bound feet will force them to take mincing steps in order to reduce pain, which will make their hips sway in a way that is attractive to men. Attractive to *men*. These girls are five years old and they're already taught to think about husbands."

As Yinmei works my hair, I can feel her Chi rippling off her hands with rage.

Her anger surprises me. I grew up in Shin never questioning foot-binding, because it was everywhere. Both among noble women like Yinmei but also poor women, who I watched struggle through their work in kitchens and fields on feet folded in half. Here in Pearl, every part of a girl is valued, including her feet. I think of what has been done to, what has been stolen from, tens of millions of Shinian girls. How many of those girls could have become legends of wu liu?

They could have had my destiny.

And I could have had theirs.

Yinmei loops a section of my hair around the rest to create a knot, saying, "The Empress Dowager might do things that are brutal; I have suffered her ruthlessness more than anyone under heaven. However, I cannot condemn her completely because I know that she is working to change the laws of Shin concerning girls and women. If she is able to bring Shin an unprecedented treasure, the Great Council must allow her to change the laws to allow females to inherit and to ban further foot-binding. As the proverb teaches, *A precious thing is defined by being costly.*"

"Yinmei," I say carefully. "May I ask you . . . how did you avoid having your feet bound? I thought all ladies of the imperial court were subjected to foot-binding?"

"The Empress Dowager abhors the practice," she says, her hands shaking in my hair. "It is ignorant, barbaric, repulsive, maddening, and heartbreaking—the practice of a backward, decaying, mindless culture."

Her ferociousness startles me.

Yinmei collects herself and continues, "The Empress Dowager spared all of her female descendants from foot-binding and had us raised in secret, away from view, so that no one would protest. That's why you never heard about me."

She gathers another section of my hair and combines it with the end of the knot. She repeats the process again and again while I work up the courage to ask her a question I fear to ask. Perhaps because I fear the answer.

At last, I speak, "But if she deplores foot-binding so much, how could she bear to bind Zan Kenji's feet? Even if he was her hostage."

Silence stretches between us. Yinmei gathers the braid around my head and pins it in place, forming a ring around my head.

At last, she says, calmly, "Little girls have had their feet bound for a thousand years to please men. Eighty million girls living in Shin today have had their feet bound."

She hands me a mirror. I look at myself. My braid encircles my head in a staircase royal phoenix crown.

Just like the Empress Dowager.

She says, "Perhaps the Empress Dowager thought that if binding the feet of one man could save the next generation of eighty million girls, it was worth it." I'm chilled by the logic of her calculation.

She adds softly, "And perhaps she is right."

CHAPTER
TWENTY-LUCKY

Yinmei's sympathy for the Empress Dowager, and for ruthless tactics in general, sits in my belly as well as a stone would. However, I know I need her. If it weren't for her, my corpse would be pierced against the side of the Palace of the Eighteen Outstanding Pieties by Shinian arrows. If it weren't for her, the Shinian soldiers would have probably tried to invade Pearl Famous again. If it weren't for her, we wouldn't have someone to write the songs that we need to drive the drumblades.

It becomes clear that the drumblades are how we're going to maintain first ranking at the Second Annexation and continue proving my value to Pearl, because the Annexation will be all about speed.

Each battleband will be tasked with defending one designated member, whose feet will be unskated, from being captured by the opposing battleband. Any opponent who we are able to make fall on the pearl is eliminated. We'll be scored based on how long we can keep them from capturing our unskated battleband member and reaching the edge of the Principal Island with that captive. Thus, the speed that the drumblades grant us to respond to a threat will be a critical advantage.

Cricket sources the discarded gondola blades, laboriously files away the chips in them, and makes six customized drums for each of them from raw kelp leather. From the enthusiasm that he shows for his work, I can tell that there's nothing really wrong with him. He just gets a little sick when he gets near a dragon that's trying to drown or crush or eat him. Who wouldn't? His heart's not too small, what nonsense. Dr. Dio is a fool.

The drumsongs that Yinmei writes to control the drumblades are astonishing in their precision and power to turn music into motion. Cricket, Doi, Hisashi, and I practice every White Hour together in the Garden of Whispering Arches, where the games played on sound shield the drumming of our practice from the ears of others. Yinmei joins in when she feels strong enough, which is more and more often. We rehearse each song that Yinmei wrote to make the drumblades accelerate, turn, skid-stop, drift-swipe, leap, rear, and even execute an instant course reversal using a flip and half-roll.

I think I know every battleband on sight by now, even the lowest-ranked ones. But then, shortly before the Second Annexation, a small new band appears at the morning assembly that I've never seen before. They carry a banner with their name: the Pink Army.

They are three girls, or at least I think they're girls. It's hard to tell from their combat armor and severe haircuts, which are perfectly chopped above the shoulder and feature blunt bangs that look like someone placed a bowl over their heads and cut whatever stuck out beneath the edge. They seem to be evaluating the appearance of every other battleband. The girl in the middle looks familiar . . . at least, that sneering express—

Heavenly August Personage of Jade, it's Suki! But she and the two other girls in her battleband have been made over to look like nightmarish soldiers.

Hisashi winces as if he just smelled something rancid. "Uuukk, it looks like Sensei Madame Yao grew little copies of herself."

Suki barks at the members of Forever Action Beauty Girls, "I said form a line, citizens!"

The girls and boys of this battleband have today braided their hair into one another's so that they are arrayed in a double loop. The leader of their battleband, Pearblossom something or other, says, "We can't. We braided our hair today in a defensive formation—"

"Unauthorized hairstyle!" barks Suki at her. "There are only three authorized hairstyles now! Small bowl, medium bowl, and large bowl!" She turns to the two other Sensei Madame Yao copies and says, "Liberate their hair!"

Her girls approach Forever Action Beauty Girls. They perform flying saw forward flips and slash down in spirals of steel, severing the braids binding the battleband together. The battleband members all scream and then stand around, doing nothing to fight back!

They were never about the wu liu; they were always all about the hair.

I don't particularly like Forever Action Beauty Girls, but I like what Suki just did to them even less. "What do you think you're doing, you scorpion?" I shout at Suki. "Just because you can't pretend to be a princess anymore, you dress up as some sort of nightmare soldier with a hair helmet? You're pathetic."

She skates over to me.

"I," she says, placing a fist across the heart, "as captain of the Pink Army, am authorized to correct all evidence of insufficient zeal for the national defense and of uselessness in the counter-offensive to liberate the mainland!"

"Authorized by whom?"

"New Deitsu Pearlworks Company."

"What right do they have to—"

"New Deitsu is the Savior of the State! The only protector of the beautiful nation of Pearl! And we are its Pink Army, for we shall mix the white of the pearl with the red of the blood of all enemies of Pearl. And you are an enemy of Pearl."

"And you are the captain of a battleband called Last-Place Losers on Skates!" I shout back.

"Beloved Chairman authorized our name change when we joined the Great Cause."

"Changing your name's not going to make your performance any better."

"No," says Suki, dropping the proclamation tone and falling back into that purr that I know so well. She whispers to me, "We've got something *else* lined up for that. You'd better start packing now for your voyage home to Shin." She turns from me so fast that her severe hair spins out like a skirt.

I say to her back, "I suppose you think you got in some chilling last word."

She skates back to me and says, "I suppose you think that's some sort of spirited retort to keep me from having the last word. Well, *I'm* going to have the last word, Chen Peasprout."

She turns in a huff again and skates away.

"No, you're not," I say.

She skates back to me and says, "Yes, I am!" And she whips away from me and skates off.

"No, you're not."

She spins back and hisses, "Yes. I. Am!" She turns again from me and skates away.

"No, you're—"

"Peasprout, stop," says Hisashi, laughing. "It's cruel to tease babies."

E ight days before the Second Annexation, my battleband and I are still arguing about everything, including:

1. Whether we should create custom matching uniforms (of course we should, every good army understands the importance of presentation);

2. Whether the uniforms' theme should reflect the name of

our battleband (nobody is going to want to dress as a nobody or a fire-chicken);

3. Whether we should wear face paint to look like ogres (I can't believe we're even discussing this, does Hisashi take *anything* seriously?); and

4. Whether Cricket should be allowed to frost his bangs with kelp vinegar (he says it's to defy Suki's haircut protocol, but that's a lie. He hasn't stopped talking about frosting his bangs since Dappled Lion Dao of the Battle-Kite Sparkle-Pilots with his silly bleached hair said "*bwei bai*" to him one day after an architecture exercise).

We finally put it to a vote of all five battleband members. The votes come out thus:

1. No to custom uniforms;

2. No to theme;

3. No to face paint (thank the Heavenly August Personage of Jade); and

4. Yes to Cricket frosting bangs (ten thousand years of stomach gas).

What we argue about the most in the final few days before the Annexation is Yinmei's role.

"I'm sorry, Yinmei, this is completely unacceptable," says Doi. "Your injury was too serious for you to be ready to participate. You wrote the drumsongs for us. That's contribution enough. You're not strong enough to take part in the Annexation itself."

Doi turns to me. "You can't allow this, Peasprout."

Yinmei opens her mouth to speak, but Hisashi cuts her off.

"Don't worry, Wing Girl. Yinmei knows how to make an accurate assessment of whether she's up to it."

I say, "Yinmei, what's your decision? And no heroics."

"I am strong enough to play a drumblade," she answers. "And I should be the unskated battleband member whom our opponents will have to try to capture. I cannot use skates anyway, so it is logical that I take this role."

"I don't like this," says Doi.

"I think she'll be safe," says Cricket. "The drumblades aren't about strength; they're about musical precision. No one's better at that than Yinmei."

"I still don't like this," says Doi, crossing her arms. "I'm going to be sick with worry."

A smile spreads over Yinmei's face at hearing this. Why is she smiling? Then I understand. She's smiling because she's never had someone care about her enough to worry. I'm starting to think now that I've been misreading her smiles all year long.

I look over at Hisashi. Would he worry about me in the same way? Nothing seems to worry him. He's warm to me. But he's warm to everyone. Who cares? I don't want to be hurt again like last year. I don't want to open my heart again only to have—

"Peasprout, what's wrong?" asks Hisashi.

"Nothing," I answer. "Why?"

"You just looked so sad for a moment. I was worried."

I look at him. Then I look at Yinmei, smiling a little, and seeing everything.

And I smile.

The night before the Second Annexation, the five of us gather after evenmeal to meditate together at the Courtyard of Supreme Placidness. Our Chi harmonization exercises are interrupted by a voice.

"Good luck at the Second Annexation tomorrow, little bird."

We all snap our attention to see the Chairman at the gate to the courtyard, softly slapping a folded fan in his palm. Even Hisashi tenses. Whatever special status Hisashi had in their father's eyes disappeared when he defied him and brought Doi to the sanctuary hearing to accuse him of treason.

"I've got friends," I say, looking at my battleband. "I don't need luck."

"You'll be singing a different song when you see the three battlebands I've selected as your opponents tomorrow."

"Three?" cries Doi. "You can't do that. It's supposed to be one-on—"

"Quiet, you ungrateful girl. Accusing your own father of treason. I don't want to hear another word from you."

"Father," jumps in Hisashi, "please don't—"

The Chairman turns on Hisashi and points the folded fan at him.

"And you brought them to the sanctuary hearing! When I specifically told you not to. What did I do to deserve such children?"

I snap at the Chairman. "We're not afraid of three battlebands. Make it even more. It's just more points for us."

"Peep peep peep," he says, reaching into the pocket of his robe and pulling out a small object. "What is this, little bird?" We all squint in the lantern light at it.

Heavenly August Personage of Jade. It's the ring woven from Captain Cao's mole hairs.

"Give that to me!" I say, skating toward him.

"Back!" he warns, lifting it to his mouth. "Or I'll swallow it. I swear I will."

I skid to a stop. What a childish, petty man!

"What is this little ring?" he says, picking at it with the long nail of his little finger. "Some shiny thing this bird managed to pluck from a Shinian soldier? I don't know exactly what this is, but I think from your reaction that it's what's keeping the Shinian soldiers from making another attempt, isn't it? That's why Wu Yinmei implored us after the attempted abduction to send a letter orb to the Shinian ships. That's why you kept this little ring under your pillow. You've never kept anything under your pillow before."

Before. So this is not the first time he's gone into my room.

"That's the only thing keeping Pearl safe!" I plead.

"Oh, no, I think it's the only thing keeping *you* safe. I think they made it very clear that all they want is you."

"You don't understand what you're—"

And then several things happen at once. Doi is lunging for the ring, and Hisashi is holding her back, and the Chairman is popping the ring into his mouth.

I watch in disgust and see the Chairman's throat working as he swallows the ring of Captain Cao's mole hairs.

He lets out a small belch. "I wish you a pleasant voyage home, little bird."

He turns to depart and sees Cricket gaping up at him with wide eyes.

"And you," he says to Cricket, "I never liked your face. Hopefully you'll join your traitorous sister."

As he leaves, he snaps his fan open in our direction for emphasis, like an actor from a bad street opera.

When he's gone, all lucky of my battleband members begin talking at once. Words like "Don't worry—" and "They'll never find out—" and "We'll find other mole hairs—" but I hold up my hands for silence.

"Thank you, but I don't need your comfort," I say to them. "I need your performance. We have to win the Second Annexation tomorrow. Not just to prove my value to Pearl. Not just to keep me from being deported. But to make that man choke on his words."

CHAPTER
TWENTY-FIVE

Something's wrong.

It's been nearly five minutes since Sensei Madame Yao called out "Nobody and the Fire-Chickens" to begin the Second Annexation.

We've been keeping our drumblades upright and humming in place by tapping out a gentle rhythm on the small front drums, ready to burst forward at the first sight of an enemy.

However, scanning to the southwest from my station at one corner of the Palace of the Eighteen Outstanding Pieties, I still see no opponents. The mists have all risen from the pearl since it's the end of the ninth month, so I can see all the way to the edge of the Principal Island.

The thirteen senseis peer down at us from their viewing dais atop the Palace of the Eighteen Outstanding Pieties. The Chairman is smirking.

"Nothing from the southwest!" I yell.

"Nothing from the northwest!" replies Cricket.

"Falling asleep from boredom here in the northeast!" calls out Hisashi.

"Southeast quadrant still clear," responds Doi.

Yinmei is stationed before the entrance of the Palace of the Eighteen Outstanding Pieties. She calls out, "Look! They do not come from those directions; they come from above!"

Nine bats glint in the sky. No, not bats. Boys.

"It's the Battle-Kite Sparkle-Pilots!" cries Cricket.

Dressed in black kelp leather and strapped into kites of pearlsilk stretched on struts, the nine boys glide toward us in an arrowhead formation.

At their vanguard is Dappled Lion Dao, unmistakable even from this distance with his bleached-gold bangs whipping in the wind and the glinting silver studs in his outfit. He commands, "Deploy sparklebombs!"

The boys together launch their hand-cannons of bamboo trunk.

Nine balls as large as winter melons whistle toward us, trailing tails of shimmering flakes.

They explode all along the south face of the Palace of the Eighteen Outstanding Pieties, turning the air into a dazzle of fine pearl-scales that flash sea-foam green with blushes of pink, distracting us with their shimmer and completely obscuring Yinmei.

"Yinmei, execute evasive short melody number three!" I yell, but I know from hearing the burst of beats that she has already drummed on the back drums and sped out of the cloud of sparkles.

I follow the sound of her powerful beats in lucky meter, which go round and round like an enraged ferret trying to bound its way out of a cage.

I dart out of the cloud of scales and catch sight of Yinmei racing ahead, in front of Eastern Heaven Dining Hall.

Above us, five battle-kites turn in unison and fly toward Yinmei. As they pass over the quadrangle, their pilots release a catch on their battle-kites and descend on lines to the pearl below. Their harnesses haul their kites on tethers in the air above them as they skate.

They chase hard after Yinmei's drumblade, around and around in the quadrangle, attempting to yank her off. She executes a deft drumroll on the left set of drums, causing her drumblade to skid and take a sideswipe at the boys. However, each time she tries to knock one of the boys off his skates, he simply punches a plate on the chest of his harness to activate his tether. The tether spools in, and he's hoisted up out of harm's way by his battle-kite, only to drop back down to pursue Yinmei again when it's safe.

Doi and I reach the quadrangle, and together, we pound a three-layer rhythm on the middle drums. Then we thunder down together on the back drums.

Our drumblades leap into the courtyard above the boys' heads, with the bottom of our blades slicing sideways toward the tethers connecting them to their battle-kites, like a pair of great scissors.

"Retract!" shouts Dappled Lion Dao. The boys punch their fists against the plates in their harnesses and fly up along the tethers to their battle-kites with a high singing zip just in time to miss our shearing blades.

"Yinmei, go!" cry Doi and I together.

Yinmei pounds out a rhythm of power and delicacy and goes whipping around the southeast corner of Eastern Heaven Dining Hall tightly.

We take the northern route around the hall and meet her at the seaward side of the Courtyard of Supreme Placidness.

The three of us speed toward the canal separating us from the dormitories. We punch our back drums and leap over the canal like three dolphins breaching in unison.

We tear through the central path dividing the girls' dormitory from the boys', come out the other side, and pop over the canal leading to the Hall of the Eight Precious Virtues, where Cricket and Hisashi await us.

We scrape to a hard stop at the base of the hall to discuss our next plan of attack. The central waterfall cascading down its surface meets the canal in a roar of churning that masks the sound of our voices.

We are all heaving and sweating from the exertion and welcome this moment to catch our breaths. It feels like someone poured vinegar into the muscles of my arms and shoulders, and we've only just started.

"We have to separate them from their battle-kites," I say.

"Let's lure them into the Garden of Whispering Arches," says Cricket. "They can't follow us under the arches with their kites, because the strings will get tangled."

"Yes!" I beam at Cricket. "Full speed across Divinity's Lap to the garden."

I pound on the back drums to kick my drumblade over the canal. I bounce twice and then my driving double rhythm on the middle and back drums sends me racing across Divinity's Lap with the rest of my battleband in formation behind me, like mist trailing behind a flying spear.

As I reach the towering statue of the Enlightened One, I see something grotesque has happened to her. It looks like she's standing, not sitting, and that she's covered in human bodies.

I quickly play a sharp roll of beats to stop myself from sliding forward, but I mistime them and my drumblade spins in two full circles before I'm able to come to a full halt.

My battleband mates execute better skids to stop behind me. We take a longer look at the transformed figure of the statue of the Enlightened One.

It moves.

I realize we aren't looking at the statue, but something in front of it.

Before us is a complex formation of maybe fifty girls, girls standing upon girls, rising five stories high.

They're locked together and stacked on top of one another to form the legs, arms, and body of a giant figure. The enormous figure's skate blades are composed of two giant gondola blades.

Atop the formation stands one girl holding reins, limning the shape of a head.

Etsuko.

So this is her battleband, Radiant Thousand-Story Very Tall Goddess.

"Advance!" commands Etsuko.

The twelve girls composing the right leg curl and contract to operate the armature around them. The leg lifts and sets down one great skate.

All five of us speed our drumblades in different directions, frantically attempting to escape the rampaging goddess.

A shadow crosses my path, and I bang hard on my left drums to swerve just in time as the goddess's right skate comes stamping beside me.

Two of her arms swipe down at me, the girls at each end stretching their arms out to talons. I slam down on my right drums so I slide sideways under their grasp.

I pull up my drumblade short, just in time to miss a third goddess arm slamming down. The girl forming the talons lands upside down on the pearl in front of me, close enough for me to hear the breath of her exertion.

"Where's Yinmei?" I cry out, but I'm the only one of my battleband left on Divinity's Lap.

I deploy the six-drum martial power anthem that Yinmei wrote for quick escape. It's extremely forceful but difficult to steer and shuts down all jumping ability until its last vibration clears from the drums. I explode toward the western edge of Divinity's Lap in a wild wobble.

The speed is so great that my sweat is sheared right off my face. I try to aim for the bridge, since I won't be able to leap over the canal. My drumblade is veering too hard to the left, but I'm so tired that I don't have the strength to do the course-correction drumroll song that Yinmei taught us. In order to urge my drumblade to the right in time, so that I don't miss the bridge and go diving into the canal, I stand up on top of my seat, crawl to the edge of my drum kit on the right, and hang out one arm and one leg, so far that my braids brush against the pearl below.

My drumblade barely makes it onto the bridge, but I miscalculate the vibrations and the right front and middle drums are smashed off by the balustrade. Ten thousand years of stomach gas. Now I can't turn left! And I need to turn left to get to the Garden of Whispering Arches to the south. How am I going to—

Radiant Thousand-Story Very Tall Goddess comes crashing down in front of me. The sharp, daggerlike points of her two giant skates are aimed at me. Above me, the goddess is flexing her torso and readying to slam down all six arms on me.

I don't think; I just react. I pound down on my drums and head straight over the northwest edge of the Principal Island toward the sea.

I'm able to regain control of my drumblade in time to layer a triple-meter scale up and down my left drums to guide me around the narrow strip separating the Pagoda of Filial Sacrifice from the water. I can't turn left, but if I keep circling right around the pagoda, I'll eventually head toward the Garden of Whispering Arches. And the perimeter around the pagoda is too narrow for the goddess to follow me.

She totters over to the pagoda and wraps her six arms around it, as if she were going to crush it, but she isn't tall enough for Etsuko to see over the top of the pagoda. I shoot past her and race toward the Garden of Whispering Arches. As I coast, I give my throbbing muscles a rest.

No one's at the Garden of Whispering Arches.

To the east, I hear the thundering of drumblades.

But there's something in the sound that's impossible:

The drumming is coming from *seven* drumblades.

I make another arcing loop to the right until I'm facing east. I shoot out of the Garden of Whispering Arches, leap over the canal, and plant down hard on the great straightaway in front of the Palace of the Eighteen Outstanding Pieties, as long as half the campus. In front of me, I find Yinmei and Doi speeding away from me, down the straightaway.

And close behind them, I see Suki. On her own drumblade.

Make me drink sand to death! So that's the "something else" she had lined up. Where did she get it? She must have spied on us while we practiced, after we refused to let her join our battleband.

To their right, across the Central Canal, Cricket and Hisashi race the other two girls of Suki's the Pink Army, who are on drumblades of their own. Cricket and Hisashi are ducking and jumping their drumblades again and again, and I think how silly it looks until I see the flashes of metal and realize that they're doing so because the two girls are swiping at them with swords. Real steel swords. How can this be legal?

What am I saying? This is Suki's battleband. Of course she's playing dirty.

Ahead of me, Suki lifts a lacquered, banded handle in the air in one fist. She depresses a button. Two blades shoot out from either end of the handle, which Yinmei and Doi duck just in time to miss.

I beat my back drums to blast forward and catch them.

They pass the Bridge of Serene Harmony halfway down the length of the straightaway.

Suki is using one hand to alternate beats on her left and right drums while spinning the double-bladed staff in the other hand like a twirl of knives.

Doi blocks the rotating blades with skate and drumstick, until one of them slices her drumstick in half. Her drumblade threatens to unbalance. As she struggles to regain control, Suki attempts to stab holes in Yinmei's drums. However, Yinmei anticipates Suki's jabs and dodges them by adding subtle trills and grace notes on her front drums that cause her to prance forward and lurch aside every time Suki stabs down.

With a burst of furious thundering on my back drums, my drumblade explodes forward, veering to the right. As it goes sliding toward the water of the Central Canal, I extend my arms, leap off my drumblade, and execute a backward flip into the air.

Time slows as Suki glares at me from under her severe bangs in hatred and I soar high above and land right on the seat of her drumblade behind her so that we're riding together. Suki screams in frustration as she jerks her drumblade from side to side to try and unseat me.

I reach around Suki, grab her double-bladed staff, and before she can let go of it, I heave backward hard while kicking her rear end. I send her flipping back over my head to land on the pearl behind me, crunching on her plates of armor. Without her staff. I drive forth on Suki's drumblade.

To my right, Doi raises a drumstick in my honor, and to the left, Yinmei gives me the same salute. We twirl our drumsticks in our fingers and strike them against one another.

This is fun.

Behind us, I see the two other girls of the Pink Army have stopped battling Cricket and Hisashi. They drive up beside their stranded captain, seething on the pearl.

Suki shoves one of the girls hard, sending her flying off her drumblade, then snatches her drumsticks. As the girl splashes into the Central Canal, Suki brings her drumsticks down hard and comes shooting after us.

Doi, Yinmei, Cricket, Hisashi, and I meet at the southeast corner of the Palace of the Eighteen Outstanding Pieties. Without having to speak, we turn at once, like a team of horses that have worked together since they were colts. We speed along the perimeter of the Principal Island. We race past Eastern Heaven Dining Hall, leaping over the little waterfall where the runoff from the canal flows. All five of us are completely soaked in sweat from our tremendous effort, and the wind from our racing gives us some much needed cooling.

We need to cross back to the Garden of Whispering Arches. The Battle-Kite Sparkle-Pilots can't keep up with us when we are at full velocity on our drumblades, but we can't defeat them unless we bring them down to the pearl in the garden. Further, Radiant

Thousand-Story Very Tall Goddess will have trouble stomping on us amid the knolls and curved paths there.

We shoot into the southern quadrangle only to find the goddess is standing in its center, blocking our path to the garden.

We swerve hard on our five drumblades and arc to the right around the goddess. She slams down fist after fist behind us, but she can't pivot as quickly as we can turn.

We gain speed to try to shoot past her, but then several Sparkle-Pilots drop out of the sky on lines, blocking our path. We'll have to turn around and go back the long way, along the perimeter of the Principal Island. None of them will be fast enough to catch us.

I point back toward where we came from, only to see Suki and her remaining battleband mate come jumping over the canal runoff toward us, their bangs flapping up with the impact.

We slam our drumsticks and veer hard right to continue circling the quadrangle.

More and more Sparkle-Pilots shoot down on lines from the sky above, and we have to swerve to dodge them as they slam down on the pearl in front of us.

Behind us, the goddess pounds down again and again, barely missing us and making the pearl beneath our drumblades tremble in a way that interferes with our playing and precise navigation.

As we race in loops around the quadrangle, every exit is cut off by the Sparkle-Pilots or by goddess fists and feet pummeling down on us from the sky.

Suki and her battleband mate surge forward toward Yinmei, blades drawn to puncture her drums and seize her. They pursue us hard around the courtyard as we take repeated tight right turns, churning around the figure of the furious goddess like a water funnel, with the Sparkle-Pilots moving more slowly at the outer rim of our orbit, zipping up into the sky every time we try to knock one of them down.

There's no way out. We're trapped here against these three formidable battlebands. Each of them with unique powers.

We can't defeat them. Not all three at the same time.

But we don't have to.

We can make them defeat one another.

I motion for my battleband to drive in tight formation around me.

I command them, "Yinmei, when I give the signal, slide your drumblade sideways so that you are no higher than chest level. Doi, Cricket, Hisashi, when I leap, leap up off your drumblade and grab the tether of a battle-kite, tug down, then dig your skates into the pearl! Now!"

At that, Yinmei unleashes a storm of beats on her front left drum, causing her drumblade to dip down and the blade to almost slip out entirely from under her, until she is sliding so low that her knee is nearly touching the pearl.

Doi, Cricket, Hisashi, and I shoot up. Our drumblades go flying out from under us, burying their front points in the wall of the Gallery of Paragons of Honor. The lucky of us each grab a tether connecting a Sparkle-Pilot to his battle-kite above.

We tug down hard, and lucky battle-kites come plummeting down to the pearl.

The falling tethers tangle in the other tethers, bringing the rest of the battle-kites crashing down to the pearl, lashed together at chest level by the net of lines.

We dig our skates in and brake hard on the pearl before we run into the tethers while Yinmei's skid-drifting drumblade dips easily under the net.

Suki and her battleband mate, however, drive right into them. Their drumblades go shooting out from under them as they are yanked off, slung backward, and shot onto the pearl on their rear ends.

Some of the Sparkle-Pilots remain upright and try to skate after us to haul us off our drumblades. However, the tangle of tethers has caught around the legs of the goddess, and the Sparkle-Pilots' skating just wraps them tighter.

The knot of battle-kite tethers unbalances the giant figure, and Etsuko shouts, "Left foot adjust!" It's too late, though. The lines have bound the goddess's legs into one huge stem.

We watch as Radiant Thousand-Story Very Tall Goddess comes tipping over so slowly, so gracefully, and smashes down at our feet, sending pieces of armature and girls sprawling across the pearl.

Etsuko pops up from the wreckage and screams, "Infuriate me to death!"

Yinmei reverses her drumsong and drives over to us.

We look around us at the quadrangle filled with the moaning figures of our downed foes.

We prevailed! We defeated them! We didn't just defeat them, we knocked them on their rear ends! We covered the floor with them! If I'm correct, that means we'll be awarded the equivalent of holding off our opponents for an infinite amount of time, which means we'll have taken first place at this Annexation.

We worked together as one. This cluster of five people.

We were a battleband.

The five of us turn to look up at the thirteen senseis on their dais atop the Palace of the Eighteen Outstanding Pieties. We bow deeply to them.

I look at the Chairman. It's impossible to read his emotion, but I see him swallow.

As if he were choking on his words.

And then Yinmei and Doi throw their arms around each other. With a great smile, Hisashi rushes over to me and for a second, I think it's going to happen to—no, he hesitates, or I hesitate, or he hesitates because he thinks I hesitate or something, then, suddenly, we're doing that awkward triangle-shaped lean-to embrace that some boys give each other because they're afraid of standing too close, and it's so clumsy that I almost want to laugh.

Yinmei and Doi eventually disentangle but remain holding hands. Hisashi puts his hand on my shoulder. It's warm, but it's friend-like. Was I hoping for more than that? Maybe? But for now, it feels good to have this boy as my friend.

Then, as if we all think it at once, we look for the only one left out of our quadrangle of warmth, Cricket.

He's standing off to one side with a sour look on his face. He's tugging down his bangs, which are blown up so straight that it looks like he was struck by lightning.

"Uhhk. Too sugary. You're making my teeth hurt," he says, then breaks into a smile. "At least there wasn't kissing."

He squeals and tries to skate away when he sees us puckering our lips and coming for him, but it's too late. We're on him, and we're kissing him all over his head with his silly bangs frosted like a pony's mane as he squirms and laughs and says, "Don't mess up my hair!"

CHAPTER
TWENTY-SIX

Nobody and the Fire-Chickens is soundly in first place after the Second Annexation, followed by Radiant Thousand-Story Very Tall Goddess, then the Battle-Kite Sparkle-Pilots, then the Pink Army. After the Annexation, other battlebands immediately start trying to create drumblades as well, but none of them seem to be able to get both the mechanical and musical aspects correct.

Subtle changes appear between Yinmei and Doi. I see it when I pass Doi on her way to visit Yinmei, watching as my best friend hurriedly hides something in her pocket. Once, I caught a glimpse of one of these objects. It was an Edaian paper sculpture folded in the shape of a crane. Doi, making sentimental presents. I see it in how Yinmei pulls a chair out for Doi at meals. I see it in the ways that they both struggle to accept every nurturing gesture from each other, as if swallowing a large pill without water.

Doi has definitely started to avoid being alone with me. I wonder if it's because I remind her of the complicated history between us last year. Does she want to put me behind her as much as she can, now that she's found someone?

Though I try to put it out of mind, every time I see Hisashi, all I can think of is that awkward, triangle-shaped lean-to friend embrace that we gave each other. Am I disappointed? Am I relieved? Perhaps it was for the best, because perhaps he's *too* much like the false Hisashi from last year, except even more so in every way. And I must never forget that that person doesn't exist. That person skated right over my heart.

Even though I successfully led our battleband to victory, Sensei Madame Liao keeps requiring me to attend remedial leadership class with Gou Gee-Hong. I don't understand the point of memorizing all these gibberish Zendoshi koans, like "If you wish to hear a whisper from halfway across the world, make the world into an ear." Why is she teaching us ancient philosophy when we have far more urgent things to worry about, like Shinian invasion? And why do I, who led the battleband that fought off the abduction attempt, have to sit in a remedial leadership class? However, I don't complain. I want to show her that I have the self-control required of a leader.

One day, I arrive at leadership class to find Sensei Madame Liao standing before only one desk.

"Where's Gou Gee-Hong?" I ask.

Sensei Madame Liao says, "She graduated from leadership class."

I don't think; it just explodes out of me: "How do I get a fair shot with you? My battleband is ranked first. Gee-Hong's battleband is in second-to-last place. We fought off Shinian soldiers! I would have thought that my successes would make a difference, but apparently nothing is ever good enough for you. At least not if *I* do it."

"Sit down, Peasprout."

I sit. I don't want them to, but hot tears flow down.

"Peasprout, your use of drumblades to win the Second Annexation was very significant. You do not realize just how sig—"

"Is this supposed to make me feel better? You grudgingly toss me a little crumb of praise only after I have to make a fool of myself begging for it." I don't look at her. I look off to the side and blink away tears.

"Are you finished? You have not listened to what I am trying to tell—"

"Oh, so now you're saying that I'm also a terrible listener. That I never let people finish. Well, I guess that makes it complete then. I'm the worst, most horrible person under heaven, the absolute most—"

"Peasprout, silence!" says Sensei Madame Liao. "Please. I want you to listen to what I am going to say. A leader finds a way forward when no one else can. A leader does not just make decisions between two unbearable choices; a leader finds a new third way. You have more natural leadership in you than any student I have ever met. It radiates from you."

I don't believe what I'm hearing. "So why did you place me in a remedial leadership class?"

"Who said this was a remedial leadership class?"

"But Gou Gee-Hong . . ."

"There are many things you still need to learn. For example, as I was saying: the drumblades. I do not think you understand the danger they place you in."

"What do you mean?"

"With them, you proved to the Chairman that you *are* valuable. You do not want the Chairman's attention, good or bad. Now, he is going to want to use you for his plans. If you refuse to do what he wants, he will never let you go. You are too dangerous to let go."

She's right. How did I not see that?

"So what am I supposed to do? If I don't keep coming up with ways to defend Pearl, he's going to revoke my sanctuary status. If I do come up with ways, he's going to want to keep me for his own."

"A leader finds a new third way."

Oh, that's a lot of help.

Sensei Madame Liao says softly, "Peasprout, this class was for the students who needed it most. Gou Gee-Hong needed it because she has never taken on any form of leadership. You needed it because you are facing just about more than any leader has ever had to face. You are a leader, Peasprout. If you would only allow yourself to be."

She can't help me. She can only give me this affirmation.

But after all this time having to do without her affirmation, I think I'm just fine without it.

I'm in more danger now than ever before. So what? I found

hidden doorways out of inescapable situations last year. I can do it again. I just need to pay attention and learn how to use everything around me.

The curriculum is no help, though. For reasons unexplained to us, all the disciplines begin focusing on magnets after the Second Annexation. In wu liu class, Sensei Master General Moon Tzu, through Sensei Madame Yao, teaches us about fighting with magnetized skate blades as a way to alter the flight of incoming arrows and deflect the thrusts of swords. We learn how to whip and strike our blades so that the yin and yang in the metal separate to turn them into temporary magnets. Some attract metal and some repel it, depending on the orientation of the yin and the yang in them.

In wu-liu-combined-with-music class, Sagacious Monk Goom and Sensei Madame Chingu teach us how to greatly amplify sound by changing the strings of fiddles and zithers from kelp-gut strings to metal ones that we then magnetize with rods. Doing so creates sounds of monstrous volume. When aimed properly, the blast from the magnetized strings can send someone's legs shooting out from under them, causing them to land on their rear ends. The possibilities for application to combat are obvious. The Battle-Kite Sparkle-Pilots immediately discover that playing chords rather than single notes on the magnetized strings sends a punch of sound that can rock an entire structure.

In wu-liu-combined-with-literature class, we study what magnets can teach us about the power of ideas. Sensei Master Ram says,

"There is a form of literature called propaganda. It is all about controlling another entity. Please take the block of tenderized kelp trunk on the desk before you. Now, push nails into it. Deep. Just pretend it's Sensei Madame Yao's face."

We all laugh.

"Now come to the front of the class. This gelatinous array is filled with disks of magnetized metal. Each of you take two and *no more than two*. To keep track of how many are checked out, you'll need to trade one skate for each disk. You won't get your skates back unless you return both disks."

When we have all exchanged skates for magnetized disks, we return to our desks.

"Now use the disks to guide the block. The metal you embedded in it allows you to control it."

The students gesture about with their disks clutched clumsily in their fingers, as if trying to coax a mouse out of a hole with a rice cake. They're able to make the blocks of kelp trunk move about because of the magnets pulling the metal inside them.

"Thus it is with ideas. It is possible to plant ideas in people's heads that allow them to be controlled. For example, I could tell you that Sensei Madame Yao hates it any time she hears a student giggle like this." He covers his teeth and emits a "tihihihi!" in a high tone. We all twitter. "And I could tell you that she hates it enough when girls do it, but when boys do it, it makes her face turn plum purple with fury. But if I told you that, I could get the whole student body baiting her on my behalf. And that would not be responsible behavior for a sensei. It would, however, be an illustration of how propaganda embeds an idea and gets people to do things you want, just like a magnet."

Most of the students in the class begin practicing "tihihihi" while covering their mouths.

Meanwhile, Cricket is doing something else. He's waving his hands cupped over the disks as if running them over the contours of a form that we can't see but he can feel. Suddenly, he jerks the disks in his hands with a flick of his wrists. The nails come flying out of the block of tenderized kelp trunk and stick to his magnets.

Doi, Hisashi, Yinmei, and I gather around him.

He whispers to us, "If we could get close enough to Shinian ships, we could use magnets to pull the nails out of them and make them fall apart. We could sink their whole navy."

Heavenly August Personage of Jade.

"Cricket, you've saved Pearl!"

"Not yet." He smiles, but doesn't deflect the compliment. My Cricket, accepting his due praise. "These magnets wouldn't be nearly strong enough to pull the nails out of the Shinian ships. And even if they were, the bigger problem is that we would have to get very close to the ships, close enough for the archers to hit us. Our boats wouldn't be fast enough to dodge the archers. Our drumblades would be, but drumblades can't go on the water, so there wouldn't—"

Cricket's face winces with pain.

"Cricket, what's wrong?" I ask.

"My nose."

He slips the magnets into his pockets and cups both hands to his face.

"Sensei Master Ram," he says. "May I please be excused? I'm feeling ill. I need to go see Doctor Dio."

With Sensei Master Ram's permission, Doi and I carry Cricket in a lucky-fisted palanquin formation to the Hall of Benevolent Healing.

"I told you," says the always-unhelpful healer, "human sinus bones are magnetized. That's why all this schoolwork with magnets is affecting him. If he isn't careful, the magnetization will interrupt the pulses from his heart, which can only shorten the little time he has left in this world. He really shouldn't be going to school, anyway. What's the point in educating him when by next year he'll—"

Doi and I shut the door of the hall on the loathsome, lying healer and carry Cricket back to his dormitory chamber.

As he sleeps, I skate to the northeast shore of the Principal Island to be alone. I don't believe Doctor Dio. I don't believe that the ivory yin salts did any permanent damage to Cricket. I do believe that the coiling water dragon is lethal to him. But I'm never going to let it get close to him again.

He's the only family I have. I can't let anything happen to him. I don't allow myself to wish that Father and Mother were here to tell me what to do. What use is there wishing for something that cannot be?

Then I hear tones. They're drum tones, faint but carrying far across the water, like the open-bottomed martial drums that Dappled Lion Dao talked about in music class. They're coming from the direction where I know the Shinian ships are stationed.

They repeat a sequence over and over.

I realize that, like Sensei Madame Chingu's wave organ, the drums carry notes.

In the *gongche* notation system.

Yi. Wu. Yi. Wu. Yi. Fan. He. Shang. Si.

It means, *Barter. Barter. Yi-Fan. And. Shang. Die.*

Yi-Fan is the personal name of my mother, and Shang is the personal name of my father.

It's telling me, "Barter, barter, or your parents die."

Can it be true? Have the Shinian authorities really located them? But if they have, it only means that they're being used as hostages. They can't help me, and I'm being threatened with losing them just as soon as I've gotten them back.

I can't stop myself. I bury my face in my hands and burst into tears.

CHAPTER
TWENTY-SEVEN

"**T**he message means that the Shinian ships are demanding to trade Captain Cao's mole hairs in exchange for my parents' safety," I say to Doi, Hisashi, and Yinmei under the Arch of Crossed Destinies immediately after I heard the message in drum tones.

"Don't believe them, Peasprout," says Doi. "If they had your parents on board, or even imprisoned back in Shin, why didn't they say anything before? They could have threatened to harm your parents if you didn't turn yourself over. They don't know where your parents are any more than you do."

Hisashi adds, "And there's nothing we could do even if they did, since Father decided to *swallow* Captain Cao's mole hairs. Who knew we had such a mature and dignified father, Wing Girl?"

"I am sorry to say this," speaks Yinmei, "but there is a much greater problem."

"What?" I ask.

"The Shinian soldiers used the *gongche* notation system to send you a message encoded in drum music. That means they almost certainly know the answer to your questions that Sensei Madame Chingu has been playing on the wave organ."

Heavenly August Personage of Jade.

I moan, "So they probably figured out that the answer is the coiling water dragon."

"Yes," answers Yinmei, "but they do not know what the question was."

"It hardly even matters," I say. "They're going to figure it out. And they're going to try to capture a coiling water dragon to use as a weapon against us!"

"We must negotiate with the coiling water dragons first," says Doi.

"Wing Girl, in case you didn't notice, they're not exactly friendly. Further, Peasprout would have to leave the campus again. She could have been seized out there on the sea, not just by the Shinian soldiers but by the Pearlian city police to be deported."

I'm touched that he doesn't just care about our safety. He cares about *my* safety. Not that I ever really doubted that. So why do I need constant reminders of it from him?

I nod at Hisashi and say, "The problem is that we can't even get near them. We can't navigate quickly enough on the sea to dodge them in case they don't want to negotiate. Like last time. They're too fast to escape by rowing or swimming."

"We could probably maneuver around them on skates," says Doi.

"But skates cannot go on the sea," says Yinmei.

"We could fall into the water near the academy and bring them back on campus again," says Hisashi, slapping his palms together like a belly flop onto water.

"No way! I'm not bringing them *anywhere* near Cricket ever again."

"So how are we going to negotiate with them before the Shinian soldiers capture one?" asks Doi.

"I don't know," I say.

I look down at the sea beyond the edge of the Garden of Whispering Arches. It moves with suggestions of shapes. They're not coiling water dragons, though. It's the Season of Glimmers, but the senseis decided not to turn the academy to a nocturnal schedule this year, because they didn't want us to be asleep in the daytime, when the Shinian soldiers would be able to see better and might be more tempted to attack. I know that below the calm surface of the water, the sea is filled with luminous octopuses. The depths churn with life. Life, not death.

When Cricket wakes, I don't tell him about the message regarding our parents. He doesn't need the stress while he's recovering from whatever the magnets did to his sinus bone. And I have to get him well quickly. Even if I have to deal with the Shinians knowing about the coiling water dragon, even if they really are holding our parents hostage, I can't focus on anything if Cricket is in any sort of danger.

Doi and I take turns bringing Cricket meals and anything else he asks for. One evening, I skate to his dormitory chamber to check on him. I pass Doi in the corridor. She left earlier to bring him some pan-fried pot stickers stuffed with chopped leeks and simmered vinegar-tofu chunks, which is Cricket's favorite of her recipes.

"How is he?" I ask.

"His appetite is healthy, and his Chi is strong. However, I still feel some throbbing from his third-eye Chi point."

"Maybe the magnets in class really do affect his sinus bone. But it's been days since he was exposed to them."

"He seems happy, though. He made a strange request this morning. He asked me to bring him two bowls, one with drinking water and one with seawater, and a spoon but to make sure that it was a metal spoon rather than a porcelain one."

I catch Doi's gaze as she says metal, and we both realize it at the same time.

He's still doing something with magnets. That's why his third-eye Chi point is still throbbing.

We skate to his dormitory chamber and slide open the shoji door.

"*Aiyah!*" he shrieks. "I could've been naked!"

He's kneeling, dressed in his sleeping robe and socks, in front of two bowls of water.

"What are you doing?" I cry.

"I'll show you if you shut the door!" he says, irritated. "Please."

We slide the shoji door closed behind us and kneel down next to him.

He cups in his hands the two magnetic disks from wu-liu-combined-with-literature class. I completely forgot that he snuck them in his pockets before we carried him to the healer.

"Watch this," he says. "The left one is drinking water."

He drops the little metal spoon into the water. He then touches one of the magnetic disks to the water. The spoon slides and sticks to the disk just as it would with no water. He pries the spoon from the disk, then drops the spoon in the other bowl.

"The right one is seawater. Now watch . . . this!" he says with the equivalent of one of my legendary hand flourishes in his voice.

He touches the magnetic disk to the seawater. The spoon leaps from the bottom of the bowl and floats above the water!

"Heavenly August Personage of Jade!" I cry. "How did you do that?"

"The magnet activates something in the water that repels metal. But it's only something in seawater, not in fresh water. There's something in the seawater here in Pearl."

"How under heaven did you discover that?"

"The way that my sinus bone hurt in class with the magnets was like how it hurt when we were on the sea with the dragon."

"Yes, we know that its presence makes your nose hurt."

"No, it's not the dragon's presence, but the sea itself. It got worse when the dragon got close, but the pain started before. And it was at its worst not when the dragon mauled us, but when we were under the sea."

"But that doesn't make any sense. We've been surrounded by sea all this time."

"Which means the sea was different that night, Peasprout. *It was magnetized*. Do you remember how we found Ong Hong-Gee's skate suspended in the air? It had been pushed up from the bottom of the sea and was floating above the water because the magnetized sea repelled the metal skate blade."

"But why didn't you feel this all the other times you were near the sea?"

"Because someone hadn't turned on the magnetization then," Cricket says with triumph. "My nose only hurt that night when we were looking for the dragon. And maybe when the dragon attacked Eastern Heaven Dining Hall."

"But why would someone want to magnetize the sea?"

"So that they," says Doi with a look of shock and delight spreading on her face, "could skate on it."

CHAPTER
TWENTY-EIGHT

So this is how we can approach the coiling water dragons safely. By skating on the magnetized sea around them. Just like whoever we heard out on the sea the night that the dragon mauled us. This is how we are going to maneuver close enough to negotiate with them and beg them to help us before the Shinian ships capture one.

At first, I wonder if magnetizing the sea could hoist the ships into the air by their nails, and I feel like a prodigy for it! However, Cricket does the calculations and says that the metal in the nails is far too negligible to lift the whole ship.

Cricket recovers from his magnet sickness as soon as we return his magnets to Sensei Master Ram in exchange for his skates. We've lost time with Cricket being sick. The Third Annexation is just two months away, which is not much time at all to figure out how to apply what Cricket learned about magnetizing the sea to our advantage.

The first meal that Cricket's well enough to join us in Eastern Heaven Dining Hall for is a special banquet. To make up for the disappointment of not having a Festival of Lanterns since the academy is no longer nocturnal, the senseis have been scheduling weekly banquets during the Season of Glimmers, taken from ancient Edaian traditions. I have no reason to believe that the histories of these banquets are any more authentic than the supposed two-hundredth anniversary of the Festival of Lanterns last year was, but all five of us are happy that no octopuses will be burned alive this year.

The Shinian servant girls bow to Yinmei when they serve us. She is their princess, after all. They place in front of each of us a bowl that looks like a letter orb. This banquet is all about Zendoshi koans interpreted in food. We open the lids covering the bowls.

"It's empty," says Hisashi.

Cricket holds the bowl to his nose and says, "No, it's not! It's a scent course. Mine smells like plum porridge."

"Mine smells like lotus-root soup," says Doi.

"Which Zendoshi koan does it interpret?" I say.

Hisashi replies, "I know! The parable of the fools who found profundity in sniffing unwashed dishes! Hahahah!"

Once the Shinian serving girls move on to tables far from us, we continue our debate in hushed tones. Thankfully, the ribbing of the beams in Eastern Heaven Dining Hall helps to isolate sound. If we whisper, it's impossible to hear from even a table away.

"Someone deliberately magnetized the sea," says Cricket.

I reason, "But how do we know it wasn't some effect of the coiling water dragon on the water around it?"

Doi replies, "Remember? We all heard people skate onto the water right after Crick said his nose was hurting."

"I'm with Crick, too," says Hisashi. "We heard eight feet like a giant spider running across the surface of the water. That was lucky people wearing eight skates. They turned on the magnetization of the sea so they could skate on it."

Yinmei speaks as if reasoning aloud. "The appearance of the coiling water dragons; the purported location of the nest behind the Conservatory of Architecture, which they forbid us to enter; the magnetization of the sea . . . As you yourself said, Peasprout, it is all too much to be coincidence. I believe Crick is correct that someone magnetized the sea in order to chase after the dragons."

So it seems the nickname Crick is catching on.

They're all coming together as a battleband. They're ready to help me skate on the magnetized sea and negotiate with the coiling water dragons.

If I solve this problem, I solve all my problems. At last—at long last—I'll be safe.

I want that so badly, it aches.

But I'm their leader. And as their leader, I need to consider their safety at least as much as my own.

I announce, "I'm not going to let any of us go searching for the coiling water dragon again unless we have a lot more information about how to deal with it."

"The third-year architecture students would know," says Cricket.

"The three of them along with their sensei were probably the people we heard on the water that night," reasons Doi.

All five of us look at the three third-year architecture students, two girls and a boy, seated at a table alone at the far end of Eastern Heaven Dining Hall. They catch us watching them and give us a good, long look in return. They huddle closer together over their bowls and resume whispering. However, because of the ribbing of the beams, we can't hear them any more than they can hear us.

"They'll never reveal anything to us," I say. "They're not just honoring an academy rule or New Deitsu Pearlworks Company secrets anymore; they're part of this whole plot. They would never say anything within our hearing."

I look at the little empty bowl like a letter orb before me.

I think of the Zendoshi koan hidden in it.

I think of the architecture students whispering everything we want to know just out of earshot. Their entire final year at Pearl Famous has been turned upside down. They weren't expecting to be conscripted into this plot to magnetize the sea and skate on it and wrangle coiling water dragons. This all started after Yinmei arrived, and the Thousand Flowers Campaign was launched, and we all started being used as weapons for Pearl's defense. The three architecture students are probably overwhelmed with their new duties and talk of little else.

If I could just hear a few moments of their conversation, I would learn so much.

I think of another Zendoshi koan from leadership class: *If you wish to hear a whisper from halfway across the world, make the world into an ear.*

"I know how to learn what they're talking about," I say, picking up the bowl. "We get the Shinian servant girls to substitute letter orbs for the bowls that they serve to the architecture students. The orbs will record whatever they're whispering. Then when the servant girls clear the bowls, they will clamp the lids on the orbs to capture the words and give them to us."

I stop speaking as the Shinian servant girls come to take away the bowls for this course. I smile at one girl and say to her in Shinian, "Thank you, sister. What is your name?"

She doesn't even look at me, just turns away without answering. I don't blame her. I've never talked to any of them. She probably thinks I'm only talking to her now because I want something from her. And she's right.

"Let me try," says Yinmei. She taps on the drums of her drum-chair and follows the Shinian serving girls out of the hall.

The next course resembles an experimental opera production more than a meal. We get three tiny, flavorless courses in a row. The first comes with a placard reading, THINGS THAT ARE NOT VERY RED. The next comes with a placard reading, THINGS THAT ARE LESS RED. When the third course arrives, bearing a placard that says, THINGS THAT ARE EVEN LESS RED and looking like a melted candle in turnip broth, Yinmei returns.

"What happened?" I ask.

She smiles and nods her head in the direction of the three third-year architecture students at the far end of Eastern Heaven Dining

Hall. They're speaking to one another with intensity. On the table between them lie three empty letter orb halves.

"How under heaven did you convince the servant girls to do this?" I ask.

"Soon after my arrival here, I went to the kitchen to meet them."

"Why?"

"Because we are Shinians."

Their princess went to visit them in the kitchen. No wonder they would risk getting in trouble for her.

"I knew you could do it," says Doi, radiating pride and adoration as she places her hand over Yinmei's.

Yinmei's expression doesn't reveal much. However, I can imagine what she's feeling under that mask. *I knew you could do it*. I know what it's like to have someone say those words to you. Doi said them to me last year at the far end of the Arch of the Sixteenth Whisper, when I still thought she was Hisashi.

Then the Shinian servant girls swoop in and we watch as they carry off the three precious orbs from the architecture students. I hope they screwed the lids tightly.

Yinmei drums away on her chair again. When she returns, she sweeps her sleeve across the table.

Three letter orbs roll out, sealed tight and intact.

We quickly excuse ourselves from the banquet, and the five of us gather in the Garden of Whispering Arches to open the orbs. We crouch together under an arch that amplifies sound. We'll have only one chance to hear what the orbs say, so we decide to open them all at once. The recordings will be of poor quality. Playing all three at once will allow them to supplement gaps in one another.

Doi, Hisashi, and I each hold a letter orb. Cricket and Yinmei each hold a brush and a scroll to take notes. We lean in close enough to touch foreheads, then twist open the orbs and hold their halves upward. Thin scraps of whispered conversation rise from them.

". . . need to magnetize the sea earlier to regularize the . . . told you the salt soldiers would . . . actually do have to stir the water faster then, or the coiling water dragon refuses to birth . . . when we unstick the Repellers and slap down together, we might not get enough lift for it to clear the wall of the nest . . ."

The orbs abruptly fall silent. They've reached the end of their recording capacity.

"Cricket, Yinmei, did you get all that?"

The two of them compare what they wrote. "Our two transcriptions are identical."

We look over the words Cricket and Yinmei each wrote. What can it all mean?

Magnetizing the sea.

Salt soldiers.

Stirring the water faster.

Repellers.

Slapping down together.

The nest.

"Is this starting to mean anything to anyone?" I ask.

Hisashi juggles the six orb halves and replies, "I'm sure it'll all make utter sense ... after we've already stumbled across what they're talking about."

"The only thing," I say, "that I have some idea about is the salt soldiers. I don't believe they were actually people turned to salt after looking at the coiling water dragon."

"Why not?" asks Doi.

"Because I accidentally looked at the dragon during the attack."

Cricket gasps. "What did you see?"

"Whipping tails and tentacles that looked like they were made out of black water."

"That's what I saw, too," says Doi. "Tails and tentacles spinning in the sky."

"You looked, too, Wing Girl!" laughs Hisashi. "And I thought I was the only one!"

"What did you see?" I ask him.

"Same thing. Tails and tentacles. Black fluid squirting everywhere. Like an octopus spinning on a potter's wheel in a storm."

Yinmei says, "The senseis lied to us about the salt soldiers because they did not want us to look at the dragons."

"Just like they lied to us about the contract and the supposed nest behind the Conservatory of Architecture," I say. "This is part of some plan the senseis came up with to keep us from being meddling little monkeys."

We all take a moment to let our minds absorb this.

All the warnings they gave us, perhaps even the attack on Eastern Heaven Dining Hall itself. All of it staged for the purpose of keeping us away from the information that is out there across the sea, the truth that the senseis wanted intensely to hide. Except for maybe Sensei Madame Liao.

But I also remember what she said to me as the coiling water dragon was flying toward Eastern Heaven Dining Hall: "This is real."

"So," says Hisashi, clapping his hands together and stacking the orb halves he was juggling into a perfect tower. "Who's ready to be a meddling little monkey?"

CHAPTER
TWENTY-NINE

Coiling water dragons.

Shinian ships.

Pearlian police.

Peasprout, what are you doing out here on the water again?

But I can't think about those things now. I need to focus as Doi, Hisashi, and I row on the skiff toward the back side of the Conservatory of Architecture.

"Do you think we should be looking for a nest built of kelp?" I ask.

Hisashi replies, "Maybe kelp trunks, given the size of coiling water dragons?"

"I wonder if it'll be floating on the water or below its surface," Doi says. She turns to me and asks, "So you've prepared what you're going to say or do if the coiling water dragon appears?"

I say, "Yes. Well, I mean . . . sure."

Even though the academy is sleeping, I'm anxious that we could easily be spotted from the Principal Island because this night is not dark. The sea is filled with luminous octopuses and unlike last year, they aren't all amber-colored. There are streams of pink and sea-foam green and sky-blue octopuses as well. Perhaps the fact that they aren't being fished out has allowed different strains to emerge. It looks like we're rowing through an aquatic garden of blooms of light.

Their radiance shimmers against the wall of the Conservatory of Architecture as we approach. The structure appears like a flat, smooth wall from the Principal Island. However, it isn't flat; it's a curved wall that encircles the conservatory within. It appears flat only because it's enormous, far wider than the rest of Pearl Famous put together. And what we didn't appreciate when we first encountered it blindfolded is the riot of carved forms covering its surface in the shape of dragon faces, tail fins, blossoms, scales, fronds, prows, halberds, trumpets, and paws.

After perhaps half an hour, we reach what must be the back side of the conservatory since the entire academy is now blocked from our view.

A sole, slender pier protrudes out of the back. We perform pear blossom single-footed spins to leap softly as petals from the skiff onto the pier. It connects with the wall of the conservatory at a vast arch in the form of a scallop shell, but the door leading in is sealed closed.

We skate toward the end of the pier. I squint at several objects sticking up where the pier ends. A strange thing begins to occur. The closer we skate to the objects, the harder it is to push onward.

We reach the end of the pier. There are lucky instruments made of metal sticking up. The top of each instrument is a sort of ring, like a handle. The bottom is slotted into the pier itself, but the part that is visible is flattened into a bowl, like a spoon.

Chingu's oracle comes flooding back to me. *Formula: Look for four spoon-keys to reveal a one-walled palace.*

These must be the spoon-keys. If these are keys, how big are the doors?

Big enough to hold in a coiling water dragon.

The strange resistance is even stronger now that our skates are so close to the objects. It feels as if they're repelling our skates. Like reverse magnets.

These must be the Repellers that the architecture students mentioned in the letter orbs. The Repellers are the spoon-keys in Chingu's oracle.

I grasp one by the handle and lift it out of its slot. It goes shooting out of my hand toward the water.

It hits the surface of the sea with a crackle like streaks of lightning and embeds itself there, vibrating lightly.

There is a metallic hum in the air and the quality of the atmosphere changes. Doi, Hisashi, and I look at one another and nod.

So this is how they magnetize the sea. These Repellers are reverse magnets of tremendous power.

Something in the seawater can be magnetized. Instead of attracting the metal in our blades, it repels.

The Repeller stands in the water like a spoon stabbed into a bowl of rice, buzzing quietly, little licks and coils of blue sparks crawling up its length intermittently.

We grab the remaining three Repellers and leap onto the water.

When we hit, our skates dip down but then bob back up. We're floating above the water at about the span of a hand, but we're rising and falling with the rhythms of the sea.

We brace and listen for any indication that we have disturbed the coiling water dragon. However, we hear only the lap of tide against the pier and the crackle and buzz of the Repeller in the water.

So Yinmei was right. As long as we don't break the surface of the water, the coiling water dragon doesn't attack.

Skating on water is the strangest thing I've experienced. It's like skating on the belly of some giant creature as it snores beneath us, shifting in its sleep. I feel every rumble of its stomach as it digests its meal, shuddering under our skates.

We haven't touched the other three Repellers to the water yet. It seems that as long as one of these Repellers is in contact with the water, we can skate on the sea, so it's not clear what purpose the other three hold. Perhaps as keys to open a one-walled palace, whatever that means.

We skate holding our Repellers by the ring handles and dragging the spoon ends in the water behind us, because they soon get too heavy to hold aloft. The instruments trail a train of leaping sparks in the water. The pushing force of the Repeller behind me feels like it's urging me forward or that it has thought and will. After a luckieth of an hour thus, we must have skated ten, fifteen li out to sea. We're so far out that there are no more octopuses, and the water below is a sea of ink.

Obviously, there's something special in the seawater here in Pearl that the Repeller is interacting with, but where does that something end? It can't extend all the way to Shin. Does the magnetization of the Repellers run out and have to be recharged?

It's an unnerving thought as I look down at the black water below our skates, slapping little waves with each of our steps. Are there Pearlian sharks? Could we swim all the way back if the magnetization gave out? I had practice swimming in skates last year after Doi demolished the Temple of Heroes of Superlative Character with me in it, but what about Doi and Hisashi?

Ahead of us, clouds like bouquets of smoke peonies part to reveal the brilliance of the moon against the dark sky. I am glad for the light, because otherwise, we could skate right onto or over the nest of the coiling water dragon and not realize it.

Before us, the ocean stretches to the horizon with fluffs of cloud cover tumbling above them. Then, my Chi chills as I see that there's something wrong with the sky ahead of us. The clouds in the top half of the sky don't match the clouds near the horizon. As if someone had sliced a painting of a sky and slid apart the halves.

"Do you see that?" I say to Doi and Hisashi.

"Yes," they answer.

We skate faster toward the anomaly in the sky. The cleanness of the seam is deeply wrong. Nothing in the natural world exhibits so perfect a line.

This sky is unnatural. This sky was made.

"Look!" cries Doi. "There are people on the water!"

I squint out and see the forms skating toward us.

"Defensive positions!" I command to Doi and Hisashi.

We begin skating forward in tight half crouches, readying for combat, and we see the people ahead of us do the same.

"They're readying to fight us!" I say.

We're not prepared for this. I never thought to train Doi and Hisashi for combat on the sea, and I wouldn't know where to start. Skating on water is so different that it must change everything in wu liu. All balances are off, all resistances reconfigured.

Then I see that the people skating toward us are holding something in their hands. They're attempting to drag them behind their backs to conceal them, but I can make out that they're long and metal.

Weapons.

I've brought us into danger. Again. Then something leaps behind the figures.

A light.

Sparks.

They're not carrying weapons but Repellers.

"Stop!" I command.

The three of us stop.

Just like the three of them.

"It's our reflection!" I cry.

CHAPTER
THIRTY

We skate toward our reflection.

Rising out of the sea is a great mirrored wall three stories high.

The seam that we saw in the sky was the top edge of a mirror. The mirror reflected the water and sky in front of it, but where the mirror ended, there was a clean edge, and we saw the real water and sky. Of course.

This must be some special form of the pearl, polished to a reflective finish.

We follow the wall to see where it ends.

"It's curved, too, like the Conservatory of Architecture," says Doi, running her hand along it as we skate.

"And it's probably mirrored to hide it from view," I say. "Look how hard it was for us to understand what we were seeing until we came right up to it."

"It looks like some kind of silo or storehouse," Hisashi says.

"Maybe they keep the pearl in there?" I say. "Anyway, let's keep skating. We're supposed to be looking for a nest."

"Or a one-sided palace," says Doi, her hand still running along the curved wall.

"I'm sure that's a metaphor," I say. "How can any structure be built with only one—"

I look at her hand running along the curved surface of the round structure. Then I figure it out. I must have drunk sand to death, because my head is as thick as mud.

A structure can be built with only one wall if the wall is circular.

"Takes you a while," says Doi, "but you get there eventually."

"Oh!" says Hisashi, rapping his knuckles on his skull a moment after me. "I'm so dense. I'm lucky that I'm good-looking. Crick would've figured that out before we even set skate on the water."

"But if this is the palace in Chingu's oracle, how do we get inside?" I ask.

We continue skating around the curved mirror wall. Ahead of us, something breaks the smoothness of its surface. We skate closer and see several pedestals rising from the sea lining the wall.

On each pedestal, at our chest level, stands a figure of white.

A salt soldier. It's wearing a metal breastplate.

When I skate closer to it, the breastplate begins to rattle.

"It's your Repeller," says Hisashi.

I hand my Repeller to Doi and skate closer. I put my hand on the boot of the soldier. It's coarse and grainy. I touch my finger to my mouth.

"Peasprout!" shouts Doi. "What did you learn last year about putting weird things in your mouth?"

"It's definitely salt," I say.

I run my hand over it and notice a raised line on the ankle. It goes all the way up the side of the figure and down the other.

It's a seam.

Seams don't occur in nature.

They occur in made things.

"This came from a mold!" I say to Doi and Hisashi. "That's why all their faces looked the same!"

Doi asks, "Do you think they're here as a last warning in case any students make it out here?"

"That seems a bit weak as a final warning. They must be here for another purpose."

A salt soldier. Wearing a metal breastplate.

Metal. The Repeller. Salt. The pearl.

"I think I know how we can get inside!" I say.

I take my Repeller from Doi and swing it around hard and point the spoon end straight at the metal breastplate. The metal flies back, taking the salt soldier with it. The figure smashes against the wall behind it in a spray of grains and powder. The wall begins to sizzle and curl up vapor as the salt eats through it.

A hole forms in the wall with uneven edges. It yawns to twice the height of a person above the water.

Doi and I look at each other. We found out last year that salt eats through the pearl. I say to Hisashi, "Don't tell Cricket about what salt does to pearl. New Deitsu wants to keep it a secret and it'll endanger him to know this."

"All right," he says. "Eh, what about endangering me?"

"You're Pearlian," says Doi. "You can't get deported."

"Look!" I shout. The hole in the pearl slowly begins to shrink. The pearl is healing itself. This isn't like any pearl that we've seen before.

"Hurry!" I bark.

We skate through the hole and it seals shut behind us. The wall shows no visible scar or discoloration. There's nothing else in here, no pedestals with salt soldiers. So we're trapped.

We're inside a circular structure as wide across as Divinity's Lap. We skate to the middle of it and look around. Nothing. Just a smooth round wall, with water below, open to the sky above us. Like a great tank.

Black water undulates below my skate blades. It's so deep that it swallows all the light of the moon. What's down there beneath our skates? It has to be the coiling water dragons.

This has to be their nest.

"What do we do next?" asks Hisashi.

"The architecture students said something about the Repellers sticking together," I say.

The three of us look at our Repellers. Together, we lift them toward one another. The flat little bowls at the end of them leap at one another and stack, pulled together by magnetic force, like spoons cuddling spoons.

The water below the point where the Repellers meet begins to bubble. We watch, but nothing further occurs. Just bubbling.

"Didn't they say something about stirring the water quickly?" I ask.

"Yes," replies Doi, "and something about unsticking and slapping the Repellers down on the water."

"So," I say, "let's join the Repellers and hold on to them while skating quickly in a circle. That must be what the handles must be for. Then we disconnect them and slap them down on the water. That's how we summon the coiling water dragon."

Now that the nest is here, lying below us, I hesitate.

We saw what it could do. The first time, it ripped Eastern Heaven Dining Hall off its foundation and flipped the entire structure on its side, along with every student and sensei at Pearl Famous within.

The second time, it grabbed the pavilion that the lucky of us were in and flung us who knows how many li or tens of li through the air, as if we were a pebble.

And that was just one of them. Who knows how many of them are below us, here in this nest?

The senseis said that coiling water dragons are normally rational and benevolent, but when they have eggs to protect, they turn vicious, vengeful, and devastating. I don't know if we should believe that, but if it's true, we've trespassed right into their nest.

When I find an enemy, why can't I ever just turn and skate away? I could be safe. I could learn to live with unanswered questions, like everyone else does. I could come to accept that knowing the truth is often a luxury, that most people live lives shrouded in parts by mist. That most people learn to breathe mist.

But I am Chen Peasprout. And I need to know the truth like I need to breathe air.

I must face the coiling water dragon, even if it's the most dangerous enemy I've ever faced, if I want us to be safe. I see in Doi's and Hisashi's expressions that there's no turning back for them, either.

Holding on to the handles of our Repellers, we start skating in a circle. The bubbling in the middle of the tank begins to complain and intensify. The water within the great structure starts turning under our skates in a circular motion as well but in the opposite direction of our skating.

Doi's grasp on her handle falters, and as she readjusts, she twists the ring of her Repeller. All three of us feel the Repellers start to come apart. She immediately levels it. The other two Repellers seal tightly again above and below Doi's. So that's how we disconnect. If we twist the handles, they pry apart.

We skate faster and faster, and soon the water is boiling. The speed of our skating is mirrored by the speed of the water churning in the opposite direction beneath our skates. The curve of the wall funnels the water along, intensifying the churn.

The water of the entire structure is soon rolling and leaping like breaching dolphins. The waves buck and toss the three of us, but we anticipate one another's tumults and hop with them in time.

Something's happening. A clear, light-colored disk appears below the surface of the churning water under our Repellers, surrounded by a larger, darker disk whose edges ripple and waver like the skirt of a jellyfish. It looks like nothing so much as a giant eye fluttering into being.

"Skate faster!" I holler at Doi and Hisashi over the thunder of the water.

We explode forward, with all of our collected Chi channeling into the churn.

The eye responds to our burst of energy by spiraling out in a pattern of light- and dark-colored bands like tails or tentacles on the surface of the water below our skates.

"It's coming!" I scream at Doi and Hisashi. "The coiling water dragon is coming! Strike the water with your Repellers!"

We twist the ring handles of our Repellers. We fly apart from one another toward the wall of the nest. The three of us whip our Repellers over our heads and slam them down with the last of our strength onto the water.

A column of spiraling water explodes up in the form of an inverted cone. Before I crash into the wall of the nest, I am lifted up and whipped into the sky, along with the sea itself.

CHAPTER
THIRTY-ONE

I'm tumbling through water, through air, through water in air. There's nothing below my skates. I'm slinging through emptiness, then hit in the face by a wall of water that I can't find my way out of.

I'm going to drown. But how can one drown in the sky?

I'm shot through a great pocket of air, and I suck in breath. I squeeze the salt water out of my eyes and see that I'm in a column of air. Its walls pulsate around me in black and gray, alive with tails and tentacles.

Then I'm flipped toward the moving wall of water, and suddenly, I'm flying through open sky.

I'm free of the coiling water dragon! I survived it!

I orient myself as I fall. Dark ocean spreads below me, tens of stories down. From this high up, I'm going to hit the water as if it were stone. There's no way I can survive such a fall. I open my mouth to scream, but the air whips the sound away.

As I plummet toward the water, I feel something happening.

I'm not accelerating.

I'm slowing down.

The magnetization of the sea! It's repelling my skates. The magnetized sea is pushing back at them.

I come down on the water with a muffled impact. I bounce up and come back down again steadily. The repelling force of the magnetization perfectly balanced against the force of my fall. The faster I fell, the more it pushed back.

I turn to look behind me in the direction of the howling roar, at the coiling water dragon.

What I see, twisting in the sky before me, astonishes me.

The coiling water dragon is no dragon.

It's a water cyclone.

It's like the little water cyclones that infest Pearl during the Season of Spouts and chased us into the teahouse where we had the infinity noodle. I hopped into one of them to win the First Motivation last year. But this one is forty, maybe fifty stories high.

Chingu's oracle finally clicks into place. The architecture students and the senseis are able to summon the coiling water dragons, I mean, the water cyclones, using the Repellers, the magnetized sea, and the circular structure that they call the nest. They orchestrated the attack on Eastern Heaven Dining Hall to frighten us from coming onto the sea. So that we wouldn't learn things they didn't want us to know. But it must have gone out of control.

I look for Hisashi and Doi, wondering if they were also picked up by the coiling—I mean the water cyclone. I realize I can't even see anything that looks like the nest anymore. It must have lifted us out of the nest and zoomed us far across the water.

Unlike on campus, which is filled with structures, out here, the water cyclone can't hurt us, because it can't throw us into anything since there's nothing here but water. Even falling from a terrible height is harmless, because the magnetization of the sea softens the fall.

Two hands slap on my shoulders. I turn to see Doi's and Hisashi's faces. They're pointing at the water cyclone with their Repellers in disbelief. I can't hear them over the roar in our ears, but the three of us skate after the water cyclone as it churns in the distance ahead, weaving in the moonlight like a slender skater as it drives through the water.

I laugh at the unlikeliness of this all. Three children, skating on a magnetized sea, chasing a dragon into the night—a dragon that turned out to be a cyclone. If a scene so strange can be real, then anything is possible. And for some reason, the thought fills me with joy.

Before us, dolphins dive deliberately into the twisting column of water. They go spiraling up inside its center and come shooting out the top. They fly through the air until they spear back nosefirst into the sea.

The coiling water dragon—it's going to be hard to stop calling it that—churns into a river of wayward luminous octopuses. Suddenly, its entire height, fifty stories high, blazes with light, shimmering gold and pink and sea-foam green and blue.

When the octopuses are flung out of the top, they spread their arms by some instinct, stretching the webs between them. They catch the buffeting gusts and sweep in patterns like petal-fall stirred in a spring wind. When they get distance from the water cyclone, their luminous forms float gently down around us, as if the stars were blanketing down to sleep the night in a welcoming sea.

Why am I crying?

I know.

Because it is not my enemy. It is not my enemy.

The most frightening thing I have ever faced turns out to wish me no harm.

It is just powerful. It is just doing what it needs to do.

Its power might be fearsome.

But it does not wish me harm.

It is not my enemy.

I wish Cricket were here to see it.

I look over at Doi. I know she's thinking the same thing, wishing that a person she cares about were here to see this remarkable thing.

I wish she were here with us, too, Doi, I think. *We wouldn't have seen this without her contribution.*

Within half an hour, we see the coiling water dragon dwindle and die out in an elegant flourish of silver vapor.

But it leaves something behind.

We skate toward it.

It's difficult to make it out because it's the same color as the seawater. We can only identify its contours by the sheen of moonlight against it.

Where its center had been, the coiling water dragon has left behind a dark object shaped like an egg, as large as the Pagoda of Filial Sacrifice.

I reach out to touch its side. It's neither liquid nor solid. It's like a jelly or a preserved thousand-year-old duck egg.

It begins to sink back down into the sea.

Some instinct tells me that we can't let it slip out of our hands. The coiling water dragon turned out not to be a dragon but that doesn't mean we can't harness it. In fact, it's probably going to be even easier to harness it since it's just a phenomenon of water and wind and not a thing with a mind and will of its own. And maybe we can find a use for this "egg" that it has birthed. Something tells me that this is the mystery we've been seeking, even more than the coiling water dragon itself.

"Quick, grab on to it!" I order Doi and Hisashi.

We try to grab on to it, but it's like trying to hold on to a whale.

As it dips down between us, Hisashi stabs his Repeller into it. The spoon end bites in deeply. He twists the ring handle and a section of the egg pops off while the rest sinks below the water.

He wraps it under one arm and says, "Let's set Crick on figuring out what this is."

It's hard to tell how long it takes us to skate back to the pier. An hour? More? The night has seemed so unreal, and the Chi of all three of us is seriously depleted, so it's impossible to tell.

We leap up from the water onto the pier and replace the three Repellers in their slots at the end of the pier. We skate down to our skiff, which is tied to the ladder leading down to the water. We row out to the final Repeller, still impaled in the water and keeping the sea magnetized.

I pull it out of the sea.

Out across the dark water, we hear a noise.

"What was that?" I say.

We listen.

It's the sound of splashing and a struggle.

Then a voice coughs out, "Help me!"

CHAPTER
THIRTY-TWO

I stab the final Repeller back into the water.

We leap out of the skiff and onto the sea and skate in the direction from which we heard the struggle and the cry.

A boxy shape like a kite floats above the water, twisting in place. Near it, a figure frantically treads water.

As we rush toward the person, we see it's not a kite—it's a drumchair tipped onto its side, the magnetization of the sea pushing at its blades and making it spin.

And in the water is Yinmei.

She's sinking into the sea even though it's magnetized, because she's not wearing skates. Hisashi rights the chair. Doi and I haul Yinmei out of the water and onto the seat of her chair. When we reach the Principal Island, Yinmei says, "Don't take me to the Hall of Benevolent Healing. Doctor Dio is useless."

Doi says, "But we need to know if treading water made your heart and lungs grow. The exertion could be like taking five steps."

"I can already tell that it did, butterfly. I am sorry."

I still would have taken her if Doi insisted, but she nods and her face crumples.

We carry Yinmei quietly to her dormitory chamber, change her out of her wet clothes, and wrap her in blankets. Doi enters into a healing meditative state to try to drive the chill out of the core of Yinmei's body and to her extremities. She stifles a cry when Yinmei drifts into unconsciousness.

"It's not enough," says Doi. "My Chi's helping, and I think that the heart and lung growth wasn't as bad as when she took steps on the pearl, but I can feel from the shudders in her Chi that the cold has entered into her whole circulatory system."

"But she wasn't in the water that long," I say, "and it wasn't that cold."

"The circulatory system can be susceptible to radical changes in temperature with profound exhaustion."

"She needs healing through Chi entanglement," says Hisashi.

Doi says, "But she needs a twin or a sibling or someone she's very close to for Chi entanglement."

"What about you, Wing Girl? You're closer to her than anyone."

Doi says softly, "I tried. The connection between us is apparently . . . not strong enough."

I feel her disappointment, and I'm hurt for her, but I know she doesn't want my sympathy.

"Let me keep trying," says Doi.

I step outside the dormitory chamber to give her privacy.

A moment later, the shoji door slides open. Hisashi skates to me.

I ask him, "Have you and Doi ever healed each other through Chi entanglement?"

He laughs and says, "Yes. Once, when we were very young, she healed a blade slash on my arm."

"A wu liu injury?"

"No. Someone threw a pair of scissors at me."

"Who?"

"She did. It was my fault."

"What happened?"

"I came into her room when she told me not to. She hadn't come out of it in three days. I was worried. Her eyes were nearly swollen shut with crying. She screamed at me to get out, then she threw the scissors at my arm."

"What did you do?"

"I skated to her, put my arms around her, and embraced her."

"Why would you do that?"

"Because I knew she must be in terrible pain to act like that. And then I saw the dead baby bird in the basket. When she was ready, Doi told me that she found it outside her window. It was so small and underformed that she guessed its parents had shoved it out of the nest so as not to waste food on it, knowing it would never survive. She nursed it for weeks. When it died, she cried for three days."

"But you didn't know that when you embraced her."

"I didn't, and I did."

"What do you mean?"

"I knew that that baby bird wasn't the only one who knew what it felt like to be shoved out of a nest. That's why I never assume that someone truly means me harm."

"Even when they actually do harm you?"

"They get one free shot at me," he says, smiling.

I don't know what world he lives in. But I want to live in that world. Perhaps he's a fool and that world doesn't exist.

But it should.

I want to throw my arms around him and press my cheek against his and hold him tightly. But should I start with a lean-to-friend embrace and then see if he wants to turn it into a more-than-friend embrace? How can I tell if that's what he wants? *The Imperial Anthology of Pearlian Courting, Romance, and Flirtation Protocols* stated that there is a transitional embrace between lean-to-friend embrace and more-than-friend embrace but there wasn't a diagram to display how it is performed. How I can recognize if he's initiating it? Should I ask him? Or will that kill the moment with thinking while he's waiting for me to do something?

And then Hisashi smiles in a friendly way and says, "Well, I suppose we should go back in and see how Yinmei's doing."

I've killed the moment with thinking. Ten thousand years of stomach gas.

Hisashi and I return to Yinmei's futon-side.

Doi is sitting beside her, no longer doing Chi work on her. It's no use.

I cup my hands and begin to channel my Chi into Yinmei's energy points. I don't know how much time passes, but I must fall into a deep meditative state because I feel the jolt associated only with coming out of such a state abruptly.

I look around. Hisashi peers at me with bafflement.

Doi regards me with a stew of emotions: gratitude, relief, but also hurt, jealousy.

In the center, propped on the futon, Yinmei blinks her long lashes at me.

"Thank you, Peasprout," she says hoarsely.

I realize my Chi entangled with hers.

But how can I be the closest person to her here? I'm the one who's been the most distrustful of her.

"Are you injured?" I ask.

"Not as seriously. Treading water apparently does not harm my heart and lungs like walking does. But may I have salt and cloth for my hands?"

Doi takes Yinmei's clenched hands and uncurls her fingers.

A great strip on each palm has been rubbed bare of skin.

"What happened?" asks Doi.

Yinmei replies, "I did not use the drums to follow you because I did not want you to hear me and try to stop me. I did not think how poorly poles would serve as oars, even with my arm strength."

Doi cries, "You could've died! Don't you ever, ever do this to me again!"

"I am sorry, butterfly."

"How far on the sea did you go?" I ask. "Please tell the truth."

Yinmei hesitates, then says, "To the structure in the sea behind the Conservatory of Architecture. The one that you entered with salt."

My Chi freezes as she says this.

"Did you see what we did inside?" I ask.

"No. When I arrived there, you were gone already. I heard the coiling water dragon's roar, but it was many tens of li away."

"Then how did you know how we entered the structure?"

"I scratched a handful of salt out of one of the soldiers and burned a hole through the pearl with it. But I did not go inside it."

So she doesn't know what the coiling water dragon is.

But now she knows that salt destroys the pearl.

Heavenly August Personage of Jade, if this girl isn't who she says she is, if she isn't here fleeing the Empress Dowager's wrath, then we're all in greater danger than ever. She could take this back to the Empress Dowager, who could threaten to melt our city with salt if we don't share the secret of the pearl with her.

I look at Doi's silent tears as she plucks splinters out of Yinmei's scraped palm. Yinmei bears the pain without showing any of it on her face, but I can feel her Chi toss every time Doi's fingers run over another splinter.

"Why did you follow us?" I ask.

"I wanted to see the coiling water dragon."

"So badly that you would put yourself in danger?"

"Yes. Because I am like you, Chen Peasprout."

I look at this girl before me, and quietly, I kneel and take Yinmei's other palm.

"I don't always understand why you do what you do, but you are Wu Yinmei, and no one is going to stop you from doing what you do. You're just doing what you have to do," I say as I gingerly begin taking out splinters.

You are not my enemy. Not any more than the coiling water dragon is.

And I am not yours.

And we are stronger together.

CHAPTER
THIRTY-THREE

Cricket is busy with all that we learned after our discovery about the dragon. It changes everything. Now that we know it's not actually a dragon, we abandon the idea of negotiating with it but we begin to consider how we can harness the power of a water cyclone. We also don't have to worry about the Shinian soldiers capturing one. We don't have to be afraid of going on the sea. Now that we can go on the sea, we can use the magnetization to turn our drumblades into the navy that Pearl doesn't have.

But we still don't know why the senseis were so intent on keeping us off the water in the first place. Clearly, they didn't want us finding out that the coiling water dragon isn't a dragon, but why did they install the coiling water dragons to keep us off the water in the first place? It's obvious that the coiling water dragons are meant to prevent us from discovering something else in the water. Cricket thinks that it has everything to do with the "egg" that we saw it "lay."

"Peasprout, close the door, please," says Cricket as I squeeze into his dormitory chamber, which is littered with equipment on an afternoon after wu liu class.

"What have you got for us?" It's only a little over six weeks left until the Third Annexation and we need all of that time to figure out what we have and how we can use it.

He whispers, "I think you need to see this first to decide what we share with anyone else. Because the terrible secret I've just discovered could destroy our world, whose fate now lies in our hands."

"You sound like a promoter of a bad children's opera, Cricket."

His face sours with irritation. He lifts a hand wrapped in a fingerless kelp-leather glove and wipes the frosted bangs out of his eyes, one of which has a line of kohl stage makeup painted under it. He says, "My name's Crick now, please."

"So what did you find out about that slab of jelly egg we brought back?"

"Remember how I suspected that there's something different about the seawater around Pearl that allows it to be magnetized? Well, that's what the coiling water dragon is for!"

"What do you mean?"

Cricket hands me some sort of toy: a little disk of bark wood or thick paper with two holes near the center and twisted strings running through them, ending in finger loops. I know this game.

"Do you remember curly-whirly?" he says.

"Of course I do. I was champion of curly-whirly for all of Shui Shan Province twice by the age—"

"That's what the coiling water dragon is! It's a giant curly-whirly!"

He holds up a glass vial containing liquid. He says, "The curly-whirly acts as a centrifuge. When it spins, the heavier stuff goes out to the edges, and the lighter stuff is gathered in the middle. They're using it to separate the seawater from the thing in the seawater."

Cricket brushes glue onto the wooden disk and presses the vial against it. As it dries, he says, "The seawater is heavier than the thing in the seawater."

He strings the curly-whirly onto my fingers and says, "Play it." I tug the loops apart and then let the strings contract. The disk begins to turn with each pull and contraction. The wheel spins faster and faster until it's a blur.

Cricket indicates for me to stop. He uncaps both ends of the vial. What I presume is seawater pours out one end. At the other end is a plug of something that looks like seawater, but Cricket has to puff into the vial to blow it out onto his palm. It stands there quivering. I touch it. The little clear cylinder is neither liquid nor solid. It's just like the jelly egg that we cut the slice from.

He says, "This is a smaller sample of the substance that the dragon left behind. I think it's some sort of sea mold that can be magnetized. They're summoning the coiling water dragons to harvest it out of the sea."

"But why do they want it?"

"Because of what happens when the substance dries and loses its magnetization. Look."

Cricket places a little white sculpture in the shape of a sea turtle on my palm. I almost drop it, as it's far heavier than it looks.

"Put it in that bowl of seawater," he says.

I drop the sculpture into the bowl. As soon as it touches the water, it explodes out larger than an actual sea turtle with such speed that it sends the bowl clattering across the floor. Just like the dragon-phoenix boat Doi gave me last year. Just like the trinket with the criminal inside. Just like the pavilion that Hisashi hid us in.

Heavenly August Personage of Jade.

"So this is where the pearl comes from!" I cry. "This jelly substance becomes the pearl when it dries!"

"Yes."

"And they use the coiling water dragons to harvest it from the sea, by separating it from the seawater."

"I wish I could have seen it doing that," sighs Cricket.

"So New Deitsu must have been summoning coiling water dragons all this time out at sea to harvest the pearl," I say. "And they staged the coiling water dragon attack to keep students and everyone else from going out on the water."

"Yes. The coiling water dragon is both the method they use to harvest the pearl and the threat they used to keep us from learning that! It's a self-protecting secret!"

"But why now?" I ask.

"I think it's because of Yinmei," answers Cricket. "All this started after she arrived. They must be even more afraid of the secret of the pearl leaking out now that we have the Empress Dowager's heir and there is the real threat of Shin invading."

"I still don't understand what role the magnetization plays," I say.

"They need to magnetize the sea to form a coiling water dragon in the first place. From what you described to me, the Repellers stimulate some natural motion between the yin particles and the yang in either the seawater or the pearl, which assists the churning motion. I also suspect that the nest is made of some specially treated pearl that further amplifies this effect."

"So why can't the city be magnetized? Does the pearl die after it dries?"

"No, it's still alive, in some way. That's why it can be destroyed by salt that is a higher concentration than the saltiness of the sea. I think there are three forms of the pearl. The raw state, which is the jelly that you saw pulled out of the ocean. Then the dry state, which is the little trinket. You can carve the dry pearl into any shape, such as a building. Then you strike it all over, very hard, like we did with the pearlstarch in architecture class. After that, it will lose its susceptibility to magnetization but will retain the shape of the carving and the hardness, even when it's rehydrated back to full size by seawater, which is the third and finished state."

So this is what the senseis and New Deitsu have been trying so hard to keep us from learning all year, even as they encouraged us to invent strategies for defense of Pearl against Shinian invasion.

I understand now their unease about this information getting out. Anyone who learns this would know how to steal the pearl from us. It's just lying there in the water.

Anyone who wants it would understand why there's no point in negotiating for Pearl to share it. We don't make it; we harvest it. And like with any natural thing, there's probably only so much of it in the sea at any one time.

We can't let Shin know about this. They'll invade and steal it all, like they tried to do with our bamboo during the Bamboo Invasion after they used up their own.

The Empress Dowager would do anything for this information. And the senseis were even more frightened of the secret getting back to the Empress Dowager after Yinmei fled to Pearl. That's why they frightened the students into staying off the water.

Now that I know the secret of the pearl, I understand just how vulnerable we've been all this time. Pearl is like a wealthy lord whose gold grows inside magical peaches in his orchard. And the only thing stopping thieves and murderers from stripping him of his riches is the fact that they don't know the gold is there for the plucking. No wonder New Deitsu and the senseis and all the authorities in Pearl are so nervous. However, knowing this doesn't give me any comfort. It only makes me realize how likely they are to take extreme measures to keep the secret.

Unless we can find a way to use it to prove our value and loyalty, knowing the secret of the pearl only puts Cricket and me in even more danger. I say to Cricket quietly, "Don't share with anyone what you've discovered yet. This is dangerous to know."

Cricket says, "I'm not telling anyone until you instruct me to.

You know when it's the right time to share information. You're the captain."

I might be the captain, but I'd be a better one if I had even half the tact and kindness he has.

"Thank you," I say, "Crick."

What the senseis share with us about the Third Annexation confirms everything that Cricket—I mean Crick . . . it's going be hard to remember to call him that—figured out. We are told that the Third Annexation will test our strategies for defense against bombardment. If the Shinian forces fail at breaching our perimeter or invading our cities, they can retreat to the sea and bomb us from afar. Why are they telling us this five weeks before the Third Annexation? We've already lost seven weeks since the Second Annexation, time we could have spent working on this. Are they just making this up as they go along?

Third-year students will have skiffs on the water, firing projectiles at all the battlebands on the Principal Island, who will demonstrate ways to both defend against and neutralize the bombardiers. There is a timer, though.

There's no wind during the Season of Drifts, which is why we need the great propelling fans to suck the flakes floating up from the pearl out to sea so that they don't impede visibility and get into everyone's clothes, food, and eyes. However, the Third Annexation is scheduled on a special day. At sunset on one day each year during the twelfth month, wind comes blowing out furiously to the west for three hours. They call it the Western Belch. We will all be unbalanced by the wind, and worse, all projectiles shot at us from the east will travel with extreme speed, making them nearly impossible to dodge. So we must plan on scoring as many points as possible against the bombardiers before the edge of the sun touches the sea and chaos reigns.

I try to hide the contempt from my face when the senseis tell us that they have signed an addendum to the contract with the coiling water dragons that allows the students to enter the water on the day of the Third Annexation. As long as nobody goes beyond the Conservatory of Architecture, of course.

How convenient.

The inability of other students to see through their ruse baffles me. I guess that the senseis achieved their goal of frightening the students with the attack on Eastern Heaven Dining Hall.

It makes our task easy, though. We don't say anything to the senseis about what we have learned. For one thing, we were violating curfew and I was stepping beyond the borders of the campus of Pearl Famous, jeopardizing my sanctuary status. Further, we want to save up this information to use to our advantage at the Third Annexation. While all the other battlebands will struggle on the shore to shield against the bombardiers, we can magnetize the sea and go after them directly on our drumblades. One swipe unleashed by Crick's and Yinmei's drumsongs will flip a skiff over. Further, the magnets we used in class might not be strong enough to pull the nails out of a Shinian ship, but Crick said that they might work on the skiffs.

I know I'm skating dangerously close to revealing what we know by magnetizing the sea. But if we use it, we'll take first place at all three Annexations and I'll secure my safety. Further, our use of the drumblade on a magnetized sea and possibly pulling the nails out of ships are undeniably powerful tactics that Pearl can employ against Shinian invasion. *It gives Pearl the navy it needs but doesn't have.* Nobody will be able to argue that I'm not valuable to Pearl when they see my battleband drumming across the sea and using music to take down a fleet of bombardiers.

The day before the Third Annexation, after morningmeal, Sensei Madame Liao skates to me. She takes me by the arm, which alarms me.

"Peasprout," she whispers, "please come to the Hall of the Eight Precious Virtues at White Hour."

"What is this about, Sensei?" I'm still angry at her for being no help at all this entire year. For not telling me the truth about the coiling water dragon.

She pours her Chi into me through that hand on my arm and says softly, desperately, "Peasprout, this is *important*. Please come, and tell no one."

That afternoon, I arrive at the Hall of the Eight Precious Virtues. I slide the doors closed behind me. All thirteen senseis stand in the central atrium in a crescent formation except for Sensei Master General Moon Tzu, who snores softly in his bladechair, the tails of his mustache curled like kittens in his lap.

"What's going on?" I ask. I look at Sensei Madame Liao but she avoids my gaze.

Supreme Sensei Master Jio stands before me, a letter orb in one hand, the other wielding a sword. He bellows in a strangely resonant tone, "Chen Peasprout! We have received a letter orb from the Empress Dowager. She has offered immunity to you and to Pearl Famous if we serve as a base for her soldiers to lead a secret coup to overthrow the government of Pearl. We have accepted.

"Are you with us, or are you against us?"

CHAPTER
THIRTY-LUCKY

I am so stunned that I just gape at them silently.

If this is true, then he might dispose of me if I refuse so that I can't report their treasonous plot to help Shin.

But what if this isn't true, and they're just testing my loyalty to Pearl?

Without thinking, I blurt out, "I'm not helping you."

Supreme Sensei Master Jio nods sternly and raises the sword. I back away as he points it at me. "Then you shall die, wretched girl, so that you cannot betray our treacherous plot to the—oh, ahihahaha, I cannot do this! This is such silly dialogue, Sensei Madame Yao. I told you I would not be able to keep a straight face. You should have let Sensei Master Ram write it."

"You can't even complete a simple loyalty test!" Sensei Madame Yao spits back. "I'll club her in the knee and we'll see how loyal—"

Sensei Madame Liao snaps, "Enough! If you so much as touch

that girl with a blade of grass, I swear by the Enlightened One that—"

Sensei Madame Chingu begins to whimper piteously. Sagacious Monk Goom says, "Be very nice! Chingu hates fighting. She is a lover of peace now."

Sensei Madame Liao says, "I told you that this was a ludicrous idea. And I told you that we need no further assurance of loyalty from Chen Peasprout."

The Chairman says, "That's correct. No need for a test, because we already know that we can't trust anything she says. The little bird always sings whatever song will get someone to open her cage door."

"Is this a review hearing regarding my sanctuary status?" I demand. "I haven't had a chance to compete in the Third Annexation yet."

Sensei Master Ram says, "No, Chen Peasprout. We need your help in interpreting something. We received a letter orb from Zan Aki. He had it smuggled out of the Empress Dowager's palace wrapped in the peel of an orange. Or so we are told by the merchant who delivered it to us. It could be a feint planted by the Empress Dowager herself. That's why you need to confirm some things Zan Aki said in it."

"Can't the Chiologists tell if he was saying the words against his will?"

"The Chiologists listened to his tone and unanimously decided that he was not speaking against his will. But the Empress Dowager is cunning. That's why we need your help. Because you've met her."

"So have Yinmei and Hisashi. They spent a whole year in the palace."

Sensei Madame Liao answers, "But we do not know them as we know you, Peasprout."

I say to her, "So you want me to help you figure out the truth. Truth suddenly matters so much to you now?" Sensei Madame Liao returns my gaze with meaning.

"Truth is a luxury . . ." With a flick of a glance in the direction of the Chairman and Sensei Madame Yao, she adds, ". . . for those in power."

What is she saying? That she was threatened into silence? That the Chairman and Sensei Madame Yao staged some sort of quiet overthrow of the powers at Pearl Famous?

"That's never a good excuse," I say. "*I* always found a way to tell the truth. And I'm only a fifteen-year-old girl."

"You're not *only* anything, Chen Peasprout," she says softly. "You never were."

My Chi pounds with emotion. So Sensei Madame Liao does appreciate me. She just wasn't in a position to save me. She couldn't be what I wanted her to be for me. But it's not because she didn't care. It's not because she didn't see me. I still want to be hurt and angry at her. But, ah, make me drink sand to death, I'm not.

"All right," I say. "What do you need me to confirm?"

Sensei Master Ram says, "Zan Aki said in his letter orb that the Empress Dowager always sat behind a curtain when she appeared in public. Is he speaking in metaphor or was this actually so?"

"Yes. Every time."

"Did you hear talk in the palace about this?"

"I was only there for a month during the Brightstar competition."

"Please think. Did you hear any talk about why she hid behind a curtain?"

"Yes, but it was silly."

"Please let us decide what is silly."

"I heard rumors that the Empress Dowager had resorted to sorcery to unnaturally extend her life. She had been on the throne as dowager for eighty-eight years since the Emperor died. She was one hundred and six years old and yet still refused to name an heir. They said that the elixirs had extended her life but made her appearance monstrous. And that's why she hid behind the curtain."

"Who did you hear say this?"

"The other girls who were competing. A few servants, I think. And once, after a performance, I heard some conversation among the Great Council of Holy Men, who were speaking in classical Shinian and didn't think that a girl from Shui Shan Province would understand them."

The senseis all trade glances filled with import.

"What have I said?" I ask.

"What we needed to know. Thank you, Chen Peasprout."

"May I ask why you asked me these things?"

Sensei Madame Yao says, "That girl is in no position to be—"

Sensei Master Ram cuts her off. "Oh, I think we've had enough words out of you today, Madame. And if we need any more, we still have the rest of this speech that you wrote for Supreme Sensei.

What was that part you wrote about 'our love for peace, which is as strong as Sensei Madame Yao's magnificent physique'?"

All the senseis burst into laughter. Sensei Madame Yao's head jerks around the room, like she's looking for a gong to batter.

Sensei Master Ram continues, "You are entitled to an explanation, Chen Peasprout. We needed you to confirm how widespread these rumors about the Empress Dowager's purported use of sorcery are within the palace. We are considering sending an expedition of exorcists disguised as diplomatic emissaries to the Empress Dowager's court."

"But sorcery isn't real," I say.

"No more real than dragons," he answers.

I don't make any reply to this, but watch him carefully. His skills of communication are so powerful and his control of his Chi so advanced, I can't read anything from his tone. Could he be indicating that he knows that I know more than I'm supposed to know?

Before I can decide, he says, "It doesn't matter what is and isn't real. What matters is that there are already rumors of sorcery. We're sending the exorcists to fan these embers."

"For what purpose?"

"To encourage the Great Council of Holy Men to rise up, declare her a sorceress . . . and burn her."

So here it is. I swallow thickly. I have again helped draw back the bow aimed at my enemy's head. Have I sealed the Empress Dowager's death decree?

May our arrow strike before hers does.

Sensei Master Ram continues, "You doubtless understand that many lives would be endangered if this information were shared."

"Yes, of course," I say.

"Thank you for your assistance in the effort to keep Pearl safe, Chen Peasprout. I know that you have involved yourself in our defense in ways that should be asked of no child. We would not have asked it of you if we did not know you to be equal to the burden. If it were up to me, I would say that you have already more than proven your loyalty and value to Pearl."

I bow deeply and say, "Thank you, Sensei."

"Oh, and, Peasprout," he adds. "Blast them out of the water tomorrow at the Third Annexation."

CHAPTER
THIRTY-FIVE

One winter in Shui Shan Province, when I was eight, while out early searching for winter nuts for Nun Hou, I encountered a bright sunrise during a snowfall. The sky was thick with clouds except for a layer on the horizon, where the wind had swept the cover away. The dawn tinted the snow around me orange like blessings from a goddess, and I shouted, "Do you see that?" But of course, there was no one to look at it with me. Because I was all alone.

This is what it's like now, here in the Garden of Whispering Arches, with the afternoon sun of the Season of Drifts piercing through.

Except that the flakes around me are floating up, not down.

And they're glowing with the gold of a sun heading toward setting, not rising.

And most important of all, I'm not alone.

Cricket, Doi, Hisashi, Yinmei.

My battleband.

It's almost time for us to join the rest of the second-years in Divinity's Lap for the Third Annexation. There are two hours left before sunset and the winds of the Western Belch pick up. But I wanted to gather them here. It's not just that I want Nobody and the Fire-Chickens to enter together with style. It's that I want to tell them how much they mean to me.

As my battleband waits for me to speak, I flip through the pages of the moving speech that I have prepared to deliver to them. I look at the stirring and eloquent words of inspiration before battle and my touching recitation of all the unique qualities that each of them brings to our battleband, which perfectly supplement the qualities of every other battleband member, as incisively laid out in the table on page fifteen of my speech.

I turn to Doi and open my mouth, but pause when I notice that the second button on her academy jacket is undone. I begin to tell her to do her button, but then I notice that Hisashi's second button is also undone.

I look closer. The second buttons aren't undone.

They're missing.

Doi and Hisashi each have a hand thrust in the pocket, each undoubtedly clutching a button. Cricket and Yinmei look at me, then look at the empty buttonholes I'm squinting at. They don't understand the significance, but they see from my face that I do.

As stated in *The Imperial Anthology of Exotic and Inscrutable Pearlian Customs and Behaviors*, Pearlian students often remove the second button from their school uniforms and offer them to an object of adoration in order to propose formal status as a couple. They use the second button because it's believed to be located closest to the heart.

It's clear that after this Annexation is over, Yinmei and I are each going to be offered a button.

Yinmei watches me as a tumult of emotions fans through my Chi and probably my face as well: joy, tenderness, a desire to flee, an impulse to stand here for eternity, a sudden awareness that I didn't clean my teeth after eating onions at midmeal. I don't know if either of us is ready for this, but I know that whatever we decide, we decide it in safety with one another. I stuff the pages of my speech back into the pocket of my jacket.

I clear my throat and say simply, "You are all very, very important to me."

There is warm silence. Then it's punctuated by a choked hiccupping sound.

It comes out of Yinmei's throat.

She purses her lips, trying to clamp the tremble from them.

She reins in her emotions and says, "I had no idea when I came here that this would be the happiest year of my life. Whatever destiny brings and whatever destiny takes, we will always have this year. Thank you for that. I had no idea. No idea."

Yinmei takes Doi's hand, and Doi's eyes shimmer with tears.

We hear the orchid clarion at the Hall of Lilting Radiance sound. It's time.

We turn our drumblades in unison toward Divinity's Lap. We

begin to beat on the drums as we drive slowly forth, singing together in chorus "The Pearlian Battlesong":

" 'Sisters of the skate,

" 'Brothers of the blade,

" 'Come and lend your hands and stand up for your motherland.

" 'Answer the command,

" 'Come and join our band!' "

We bring our drumsticks down hard on the back set of drums, leaping over the moat onto Divinity's Lap as all heads turn toward us. We pound furiously as we shout:

" 'Come and join, come and join our band!

" 'Come and join, come and join our band!

" 'Come and join, come and join our band!

" '"Come and join our band!"' "

A great sequence of cracks resounds from the cannonskiffs, and everyone looks to the east.

Twenty yellowish balls as big as summer melons come slinging across the water at us. When they hit, they burst apart into soft chunks like pieces of firm tofu.

A sound that is something between a chord being strum and a scrape of metal blasts over us. We can actually see the sound's flight across the campus by the ripples it makes through the floating drifts in the air and across the water. It slams into one of the skiffs, sending it flipping end over end.

We turn back to look at the source of the sound. Dappled Lion Dao blows the frosted bangs out of his eyes. He and the rest of the Battle-Kite Sparkle-Pilots stand next to giant Edaian *shamisens* taller than they are, glistening with magnetized metallic strings. Their instrument picks are the size of oars, large enough to scrape crusted creatures off the bottom of a whale.

Sensei Madame Yao's voice booms from the orchid clarion of the Hall of Lilting Radiance. "One point to the Battle-Kite Sparkle-Pilots!"

The pearl beneath our drumblades shudders, and we turn to see Radiant Thousand-Story Very Tall Goddess striding in bounding steps across the campus. She lifts one huge foot off the edge of the Principal Island and onto a raft in the water below, then the other foot. She slowly moves forward on the two rafts as if skating on the water, holding what looks like a giant Edaian origami blossom in her hands.

The twenty cannonskiffs crack, and cannonballs fly toward Radiant Thousand. She tugs apart two tabs on the folded paper flower, and it snaps out into a giant geometric parasol shield. The balls smash into bits against the shield, except for one ball, which rebounds and smashes into the water in front of a cannonskiff, capsizing it.

"One point to Radiant Thousand-Story Very Tall Goddess!" announces Sensei Madame Yao.

"Let's get some of these points," I shout. "Crick, commence confounding strategy overture number three. Doi, throw it!"

Crick patters on his front-left drum and back-right drum to skid his drumblade in a half circle. With another pound of the back drums, he flies off toward the Battle-Kite Sparkle-Pilots to start his interfering maneuvers.

Doi flings the Repeller that she plucked off the pier this morning. It flies in a tumbling arc and spears into the sea with a crack, sending a storm of blue sparks scurrying around it.

Doi, Hisashi, Yinmei, and I continue to thunder on our drumblades harder and harder as we speed toward the edge of the Principal Island. As we approach the cliff overhanging the sea, our drumsticks beat out a trill that ends in a rumbling *pop*, and we leap off the edge and onto the sea.

We speed over the water and swerve around the legs of Radiant Thousand-Story Very Tall Goddess. With the roar of our drums and the snap of our cloaks as we sweep across the ocean, we sing:

" 'Come to summon some

" 'Of what you would become.

" 'Come to understand the grandeur of the greater plan.

" 'Answer the command,

" '"Come and join our band!

" 'Come and join, come and join our band!

" 'Come and join, come and join our band!

" 'Come and join, come and join our band!

" '"Come and join our band!" ' "

We approach the first cannonskiff. Its cannon turret swivels to track us.

"Separate!" I order. "Then execute plunging dolphin bob song!"

Doi and Yinmei veer off to the left, then split up, Hisashi and I peel off to the right, then divide.

The turret jerks back and forth as it tries to decide which of us to aim at.

We take lucky paths that weave around it. Then, as we approach it from all sides, we each execute a trill that sends the noses of our drumblades rising up. At the peak of the arc, we hammer down on the back drums, driving our drumblades plunging into the water.

Our metal blades repel off the sea's magnetization with great force and we come popping out of the water under the cannonskiff, sending it flying into the sky and toppling over.

"One point to Nobody and the Fire-Chickens!" announces Sensei Madame Yao from across the water.

We regroup and, with rattles and beats, align like a team of raging mares toward the next cluster of cannonskiffs. There are three of them grouped tightly, side by side. We position ourselves so that only the one closest to us can get good aim.

The front cannon shoots ball after ball at us. We slam down on our drums to shift and dodge around them. The missiles hurtle past us harmlessly into the water, but they keep us from taking a clean shot at the cannonskiffs.

The third-year students finally figure out that they should realign their cannonskiffs to have better access. They circle around to form a wall of cannons facing us.

As I see the cannons jerk back, I holler, "Rearing-mare fanfare!" We thunder down on our front drums, causing our blades to rise and fly forward with only the back tips trailing in the water. We present only blades to the line of cannonballs flying at us.

Our raised blades slice the cannonballs as they hit, and the halves fly past us on either side.

As we drive toward the line of three cannonskiffs, I call out,

"Deploy magnets!" We each pull out one of the magnets we secreted from Sensei Master Ram's classroom. We snap our arms out and aim the magnetized disks at the cannonskiffs as we pound on alternating drums. We weave in and out between the cannonskiffs, flicking our wrists as Crick taught us. The air is filled with the sound of wood creaking and nails singing as they fly out of the planks and ping against our metal disks. With a crumple and a moan, the cannonskiffs collapse all at once into a pile of wooden boards.

We drive away, leaving the wood and the stunned students bobbing in the sea.

Sensei Madame Yao announces, "Three points to Nobody and the Fire-Chickens!"

Doi, Yinmei, Hisashi, and I lift our drumsticks in the air, twirl them in our fingers, and bang all eight of them together.

We scream with all the air in our chests:

" 'No one can deny

" 'Someday we will die!

" 'How we live and what we give will be determinative!

" 'Answer the command,

" '"Come and join our band!

" 'Come and join, come and join our band!

" 'Come and join, come and join our band!

" 'Come and join, come and join our band!

" '"Come and join our band!" ' "

Overhead, several of the Battle-Kite Sparkle-Pilots are careening on their battle-kites toward a trio of cannonskiffs. As the sparkle-pilots prepare to dive down, a blast from a magnetized giant metal *shamisen* punches into them, sending them and their crumpled kites crashing into the face of Radiant Thousand-Story Very Tall Goddess. The pilots spiral into the water as Etsuko tries to disentangle herself from pieces of kite and moaning sparkle-pilots.

Crick is doing his job out there on the Principal Island to disrupt the other battlebands. He must have gotten control of one of their magnetized metal-stringed *shamisens*.

A riot of drumming sweeps toward us. It's Suki and her two other little bowl-haircutted copies, pounding on their drumblades. The Pink Army. They finally figured out what we did to the sea. So our advantage is ended, but we have lucky points over them right now.

The Pink Army drives straight toward the feet of Radiant Thousand-Story Very Tall Goddess on the rafts floating on the water. The girls that form the feet are clamoring and screaming at Suki and her battleband to stop. They should know Suki better than that. When they realize that she has no intention of being reasonable, they abandon the armature and dive off to the side into the water.

The Pink Army shouts, "Long live Pearl!" and drive right into the armature struts of the goddess's feet, severing them with the speed of their angled drumblades. Radiant Thousand-Story Very Tall Goddess sways on its amputated stumps. More and more girls abandon the armature and leap into the water, dropping from the collapsing goddess until there is only the tiny figure of Etsuko left at the top.

We hear a shrill shriek of "Infuriate me to death!" as the armature of the goddess comes toppling down and slams into the water.

The force of the impact sends waves rollicking around it, flipping three of the cannonskiffs onto their sides.

"Three points to the Pink Army!" yells Sensei Madame Yao.

The Pink Army rides the crest of the first great wave emanating from the fall of the goddess and speeds southeast toward another cluster of cannonskiffs.

I thrum on my right drums lightly to sweep my drumblade in a circle. I scan the bobbing sea around me, filled with debris and students swimming back to shore. I catch sight of Doi and Hisashi. They, too, are turning their drumblades, looking around.

"Yinmei!" we all call out.

She's nowhere to be seen.

I drive my drumblade over to Doi and Hisashi.

"Did you see what happened to Yinmei?" asks Doi.

"No, did you?"

"Last I saw her was before Radiant Thousand fell," says Hisashi.

"She must have been pulled under the surface of the water!" cries Doi.

"No," I say. "Her blade would have popped back up because of the magnetization."

"Then where is she?" asks Doi with rising panic.

"Be quiet," I order. "I need to focus. We'll find her."

There's so much noise around us: the sloshing of the sea. The moaning of bruised students. The bang of the cannonskiffs firing in the distance. The drumsong of the Pink Army across the water to the southeast.

And far off to the northeast, so soft that it must be fifteen li away, and getting fainter with every beat, we hear the pounding of a drumblade as it races away.

In unison, we whip our heads around.

Yinmei.

Fleeing from us.

Toward the Shinian ships.

CHAPTER
THIRTY-SIX

Yinmei doesn't know where the pearl comes from.

But she knows how to destroy it.

Yinmei's been waiting all year for this moment to tell the Empress Dowager the secret of the salt. Trying to learn as much information as she could. Waiting until the sea was magnetized and the noise and tumult of seven other drumblades pounding at the same time would mask the sound of her escape.

My sanctuary status depends on my battleband. And now one of my battleband is racing across the sea to tell Pearl's greatest enemy about our greatest weakness. I'm sure she'll also tell the Empress Dowager of the ingenious weapons I developed.

Everything she'd done all year was to gain my trust, to peer over my shoulder at the secrets I was learning. I'll be seized and deported back to Shin, to face the Empress Dowager's fury. Even if I'm not sent back, the Empress Dowager will send her navy to demand the secret of the pearl. We can't give it to her, because there's only enough of it to build and maintain one city. But then her navy will bombard Pearl with salt balls to melt our whole city into the sea and watch us drown.

So whether we obey her or not, we face the end of the city of Pearl.

All because I trusted Yinmei.

She could be fifteen, twenty li away by now.

And on a drumblade, she's as fast as I am. Faster. I'll never catch her before she makes it to the Shinian ships.

I scan around me. Out here at sea, there are no rising drifts, and I have to squint through my smoked lenses against the glare of sun on water.

Hard to the south, by the outward curve of the rail leading to the little temple where Sagacious Monk Goom and Sensei Madame Chingu live, I catch a glint of metal surrounded by a skirt of blue sparks on the water. The Repeller holding the magnetization of the sea under our drumblades.

Yinmei wouldn't have taken one of the other Repellers. She'd have to take more than five steps to get up the ladder leading to the pier. She wouldn't risk damaging her heart and lungs again, especially not before having to drum so far to get to safety.

So that means that there's only one way to stop Yinmei from getting to the Shinian ships.

I execute a roll of beats on my drumblade in a hard spin and head south.

"Where are you going?" asks Doi, drumming along beside me.

I say firmly, "We can't let her get to the ships."

"What are you going to do?"

I beat on my back drums to burst forward away from Doi. She follows with a burst of beats of her own.

"Peasprout, what are you planning to do?"

"Yinmei's going to tell the Empress Dowager about the salt!"

"You can't just unmagnetize the sea under her. She'll drown."

"She can tread water just fine until we get to her."

"Her heart and lungs will burst! They're already damaged from treading water and from when she walked to protect you from the Shinian soldiers!"

"Those soldiers wouldn't be here if it weren't for her!" I yell. "They've been waiting all year to speed her back to Shin as soon as she discovered what the Empress Dowager needed!"

"You don't know that!"

"Yes I do, and so do you!" My drumblade leaps ahead, leaving Doi behind.

As I near the Repeller, I drum with my left hand while I reach for the Repeller with my right hand.

A flurry of syncopated beats erupts beside me. Doi's drumblade comes slicing hard toward mine, ramming me far aside of the Repeller.

"What under heaven are you doing, Doi?" I shout across the water at her.

"She'll die."

"She won't. We'll get to her in time."

Doi executes a martial drumming sequence that ends in a crescendoing spiral of beats round and round on all six drums. Her drumblade leaps into the air and comes spinning toward me, blade pointed outward like a lethal iron fan.

I execute a double-knee forward chrysanthemum spin off my drumblade. I flip into the air like a flower slapped off its stem by a gust. As Doi's drumblade slashes into mine below me, I aim my legs so that I land on Doi's shoulders. I hook my legs under her arms and sling her overhead off her drumblade, slamming her hard onto the surface of the sea.

She hits with a splash and dips below the water, but then rights herself with her skates beneath her.

"You can't just drown her!" Doi shouts.

"Better her than our whole city!" I cry.

Doi pumps her skates hard and hurtles toward me. She pounds her right skate down with her full Chi. It slices into the water, but the magnetization responds by sending her bounding up in an arc, shooting toward me with a blade pointed at my chest.

I execute a lunar rabbit diagonal jump, using the repelling force of the magnetization to quicken the three reversals of direction. Right, left, right. I spin toward Doi and knee her hard in the chest, sending her sliding across the water. She tumbles backward but executes a scissor sweep and roll, popping up to face me again.

Then she sees my hand. I'm beside the Repeller, grasping its ringed handle. "Peasprout, you can't! We'll never get to her in time."

"Yes, we will."

"She could be forty li from here."

Doi is circling me as I speak to her. Heavenly August Personage of Jade, she's preparing to execute an unblockable flying dragon grasping the clouds spin on me! But she'll have to give up fifteen of her lifetime's six hundred and eight riven crane split jumps to do it. She'd give that away to attack her best friend to protect this girl? I stand in the circle and pivot in place to watch her progress, my anger growing.

"How dare you!" I shout at her. "You're responsible for this, too! You convinced me to trust her."

Doi speeds up her skating around me.

"After all you and I have been through. You'd betray your best friend, endanger your best friend. And your brother. And Crick. For that girl."

Doi skates harder and harder, ignoring my words.

"You'd destroy our home," I say, pointing at her. "You'd drown the whole city of Pearl. You'd condemn three million people. For that one girl."

Doi's velocity is already past the point necessary to arm the spin, but she keeps skating, the magnetization pushing her to unprecedented force. She's going to make the manuever not just unblockable; she's going to make it devastating.

There's not the least bit of fatigue in her Chi. Her desire to protect Yinmei is stronger.

I can't stop her with my wu liu. I have to stop her with my words. I need to think of the most hurtful words I can say to her. I have to make my words not just unblockable; I have to make them devastating.

Forgive me, Doi.

I hiss at her, "You'd throw all that away for a girl who threw you away!"

"You threw me away, too!" she hurls back.

"You brought that on yourself by lying to me for a whole year! You're good at pretending to be someone you're not. That's why the two of you get along so well. You're perfect for each other."

"At least I have someone," Doi cries. "You're so hurtful and mean. No wonder you have such weak relationships. Just like Sensei Madame Liao said."

"Better to be alone than chase after some girl who just used you because she could sense your desperation."

"Stop it! You don't know what's true."

"And you'll never know the truth because you're never going to see Yinmei again. But you'd—"

"Peasprout, stop! How could you say such things?"

"—sacrifice everything you love for her. You really have that little respect for yourself? Butterfly, indeed. You're the only butterfly under heaven to crawl back into the cocoon and turn back into a worm. You're the only . . ."

But I can't get any more words out because I'm crying too hard.

Doi's standing still on the water, doubled over, her face pressed in her hands, sobbing quietly.

It sickens me that I have to do this.

It sickens me that I can do this.

That even if I don't mean the words, they're always there when I reach for them, always ready for me to use.

And I'll always use them.

Because I'll always have to.

I'm learning how to be a leader.

And I'm unlearning how to be the person I want to be.

I look at the Repeller under my hand. How long has it been now? Half an hour? How far out is she? In what direction? Doi's right. Maybe we had a chance to reach Yinmei in time when we first discovered she was missing.

We'll never find her in time now.

"Please don't do it!" pleads Doi.

"Don't make this harder for me."

"Peasprout, please don't take this away from me!"

Through tears, I look at my friend, heaving with pain over my words, with the doubt and hurt that I shot at close distance straight into her heart.

A quotation from leadership class comes back to me: *A leader doesn't just make decisions between two unbearable choices. A leader finds a new third way.*

I take a deep breath and release the Repeller.

"I think there's another way," I say to Doi as her expression deflates with relief.

"Thank you, Peasprout."

"But I need your help."

"Anything."

"We have to summon a coiling water dragon."

CHAPTER
THIRTY-SEVEN

We won't be able to overtake Yinmei before she reaches the Shinian ships. However, even if she boards one of the ships, they're stranded until the sun sets, when the winds of the Western Belch will pick up. This is Pearlian sunset, though, which means sunset is when the bottom edge of the sun touches the horizon of the sea, not when the sun sinks entirely. I measure the distance between the sun and the sea using finger geometry and calculate that we still have one hour left before the two meet.

The pearl in the water repels and is repelled by metal. If we launch the metal of our drumblades at it with the right force, we should be able to nudge it in the direction that we want. Thus, we have only one hour left to summon the coiling water dragon and try to herd it with our drumblades to smash into the Shinian ships while they're stranded, waiting for the winds.

Doi and I find Hisashi out on the water. Together, we drive to the Principal Island and hail Sensei Madame Liao at the Hall of Lilting Radiance. I don't tell her that Yinmei knows about the secret of the salt or what we know about the coiling water dragons. I just tell her that we need to halt the Annexations because Yinmei is missing.

She and the other senseis confer. Sensei Madame Yao is sent immediately to the city. She'll alert the Pearlian authorities to send police boats to find Yinmei before the winds of the Western Belch rise.

When we find Crick, he has one of the Battle-Kite Sparkle-Pilots' giant *shamisens* with the metal strings strapped to his back. I lead the three of them to the northwest edge of campus. We park our drumblades on the seaward side of the Arch of the Sixteenth Whisper. I explain my plan to Crick, and his eyes light up. He looks out across the sea, past the Conservatory of Wu Liu, toward where the Shinian ships are anchored. He asks, "How high did you say the wall of the nest was?"

"About three stories," I say.

"And the coiling water dragon that you summoned last time?"

I look to Doi and Hisashi. They answer together, "About fifty stories."

"But almost all of it remained below the water until we slapped our Repellers down," Hisashi says.

"And how many full rotations in the water did you make to summon it?"

I turn to Doi. She's been a master of counted spins since she was Baby Swan Doi. She says, "About three hundred and seventy, I think."

Crick begins doing calculations on the palm of his hand. He shakes his head. "You're going to have to make the coiling water dragon much, much smaller. About five stories tall. To summon it, you'll—"

"Is that big enough to destroy a ship?" I ask.

"We're not going to destroy the ships."

"Nobody will drown; they can grab on to the debris and float until the police boats get to them."

"No, Peasprout. We're just going to damage them so that they can't go anywhere. We're going to have to aim it at the exact middle point between the two ships. According to Shinian naval formation, they'll be no farther than three ships' lengths apart so that the crew of one can board the other with rope bridges in case of an emergency."

"Why do we have to drive it between the two ships?"

"When you deliver the final frequency force shot, the coiling water dragon will pass between the ships so quickly that its wake will pull the two ships together and slam them into each other. That should damage them enough that they can't set sail."

"Can't we just use the magnets to pull the nails out?"

"Those magnets aren't nearly big enough."

"I don't like your plan. It sounds too imprecise. We should just drive the coiling water dragon directly into one ship and then the other."

"I told you, we're not going to hurt anyone. Remember, we're supposed to be *nice* this year. And anyway, you only get one chance, because you'll never be able to control the coiling water dragon after you've delivered the final frequency force shot. Now, can we get back to how to summon the coiling water dragon?"

I sigh and wave my hand. "Go on, Crick."

"You'll need to skate eighty rotations in the nest before slamming the Repellers down on the water. That should summon a five-story-tall coiling water dragon."

I say, "That doesn't make sense. Three-hundred-seventy rotations to summon a fifty-story-tall one, but eighty to—"

"It's not a direct ratio; it's a receding progression. I'm sorry to cut you off, Peasprout. It's like the proportions of a seashell's spiraling chambers if you— Oh, please just trust me! I'm good at calculations!"

"All right."

"But even if you make it only five stories tall," he continues, "three drumblades won't be enough to herd it. This coiling water dragon is going to be much, much faster than what you saw last time. You're going to need at least six drumblades."

"We don't have six drumblades," I say.

"And how would six drumblades be any faster than three drumblades?" asks Hisashi.

"It's not that they're faster," answers Crick. "If we make the coiling water dragon small enough to respond to the metal of your drumblades, it's going to be so agile and able to switch direction so quickly that it'll slip right between three drumblades. You'll need at least six of them following tightly in the form of a semicircle to herd it and keep it on course."

"Well, we only have three drumblades," I say. "So figure something else out."

"But, Peasprout, what if—"

"No, Crick, you are *not* coming with us onto the sea! The magnetization is too dangerous for you."

"That's my decision to make," Crick says, "but anyway, that's not what I was going to say. Suki. Suki has three drumblades."

"**M**ake me die of laughing!" As soon as Suki realizes that the words coming out of my mouth are a plea, her face lights up as bright as a Festival of Lanterns. She fingers a curtain of perfectly straight bangs. "I told you, Chen Peasprout, that someday you would come begging me for help and that on that day, nothing would be sweeter to me under heaven than to laugh in your face! Well, I hope you're satisfied now. You did this to yourself."

"This is not about me or you, Suki. This is about the safety of Pearl."

"Of course it is. Everything Chen Peasprout does is so important. So urgent. Is that why you always look like you're dying to go to the bathroom?"

"Suki, it's only three-luckieths of an hour until sunset. We don't have time for this."

"Excuse me, but I get to decide what we have time for. And I think we have time for me to savor every delicious moment of your agony right now. And when your Empress Dowager finally gets her hands on you, the first thing she's going to do is bind your feet. You know that, right?"

Crick skates forward. "Please forgive us, Gang Suki. We were wrong to deny your request to join our battleband. We don't deserve your forgiveness, yet we beg you to join our endeavor. If we're able to stop Yinmei, we will all be considered heroes and certainly be awarded first ranking at this Annexation. Please join our endeavor."

"There's no way I'm joining your stupid, stupid battleband."

"Then we beg you to allow us to join yours."

"Crick!" Doi and I cry together. Hisashi places his hands on our shoulders, and we let Crick continue.

He says to Suki, "We took first ranking at the last two Annexations. Together, we will take first ranking if we succeed in stopping Yinmei. All of that will go under your name if you allow us to join your battleband."

No, no, no, infuriate me to death! I watch Suki weighing the arguments. She glares at Doi and me.

Crick says, "Let them all see you save Pearl. Let them all owe you."

Suki's fury begins to subside as she stares at Crick.

Crick, whom she battled alongside on the Bridge of Serene Harmony during the first demonstration of battleband fighting.

Crick, who urged us to pity her and value her and use her talents rather than stew over past feuds.

Suki nods at Crick and says, "Deal."

"**I** need to come along to deliver the final frequency force shot!" argues Crick as we prepare to launch our drumblades off the western edge of the Principal Island toward the Shinian ships.

"No means no," I say. "I'll deliver the shot."

"You can't."

"Yes, I can. My forceful frequency final shots are legendary."

"It's called a final frequency force shot and you don't even know what it is!"

"Then hurry up and tell me! Crick, we only have half an hour until sunset!"

"It's not enough just to steer the coiling water dragon toward the ships. A coiling water dragon that's small enough to steer won't have enough force to damage a ship, much less drive between two ships fast enough to pull them into each other with its wake. You need to give the coiling water dragon a last shove. That's the final frequency force shot."

"We'll all leap at it at the same time."

"Not nearly fast enough. You need something that travels at the speed of sound."

"That's impossible. Nothing travels at the speed of sound."

Crick slaps his forehead and says, "Sound travels at the speed of sound!" He lifts the giant metal-stringed *shamisen* strapped over his back. I remember how their magnetized strings made sound of such force that they rocked the cannonskiffs right out of the water.

He continues, "I need to hit the coiling water dragon at the last moment with a certain power chord to send it shooting between the two ships."

"I can play the *shamisen*!"

"But you won't know what chord to play! The notes in the chord will depend on the proportions among the height, the width, and the velocity of the coiling water dragon that is summoned. Then you have to select a chord composed of notes that naturally harmonize with the frequencies of these three values, or else the blast of sound will be swatted away by the coiling water dragon's wind. I'm the only who can do that, and I have to see it to do so!"

"I'll just try every chord."

"You won't have time! You have to deliver it right when the coiling water dragon lines up between the two ships!"

"Crick, I am not permitting you to go on the magnetized sea again."

"This is to save Pearl!"

"I'm not going to risk losing you to save Pearl!"

"That's my decision to m—"

I claw the *shamisen* from his hands.

"Peasprout!" he shrieks.

"Go ahead and hate me," I say. "Everybody else does."

I jump on my drumblade, strap the *shamisen* on my back, and blast away.

On the eighty-first rotation, Doi, Hisashi, and I slam our Repellers down on the spiraling water in the nest.

A twisting spear of water punches up from the center, sucking us up with it over the wall of the nest.

It hurls my drumblade back onto the water hard. I bounce on the water and spin twice before I right myself and drum vigorously to surge back toward the dragon.

Crick was right. This new, smaller coiling water dragon is so fast, so breathlessly nimble. It shrieks and whistles as it streaks across the water.

I join Doi and Hisashi. We charge forward and meet up with Suki and her two battleband mates. *Our* battleband mates, now. Together, our six drumblades flank the coiling water dragon in a half circle behind it.

One quarter hour before sunset.

We beat more fiercely on our drumblades than we ever have just to keep up with the coiling water dragon. All six of us bank and swoop together to anticipate its sways and lurches as it charges across the water.

It tips to the left and then suddenly lunges hard to the right.

Doi and Hisashi immediately veer with it, executing a synchronized fanfare on their back drums that slaps the coiling water dragon with their blades, sending it back on its course.

The water under our blades tosses as the coiling water dragon plows ahead of us. Our drumblades buck and plunge over the heaving water until our teeth feel like they're going to rattle out of our mouths.

Wave upon churning wave of drumbeats tumble and cascade over one another. Above our music, the coiling water dragon screams and whines as it tries again and again to dart away from our circle. Every time, we pound and leap up and fling our drumblades at it in coordinated launches and bring it back, like dogs nipping at the tails of their quarry.

Ten minutes before sunset.

We're halfway to the Shinian ships. The coiling water dragon begins to do something different. Tendrils of water sprout from the column of its body, sweeping around it like black tentacles. They whip down on the water at us. We careen and dodge to keep from being struck by them.

Three tentacles of water come swiping around toward us.

"Look out!" I cry.

Suki's two girls take the first tendril right in the face, flipping backward off their drumblades. The rest of us crouch down on our drumblades as the tail of water passes over us.

The second tendril swings at us low. We all pound down hard on our back drumblades and leap over it.

We are immediately met by the third tendril coming at us at chest level. The tendril takes Suki hard, slinging her clear away from the coiling water dragon, and shooting her rolling drumblade straight at us.

Doi, Hisashi, and I leap up off our drumblades to avoid being hit by the tendril and sliced by Suki's drumblade. Doi and I sail over them and come down on our drumblades on the other side. However, the silly ornamental tail-fan of Suki's drumblade clips the seat of Hisashi's drumblade, sending it spinning straight at me.

I beat hard on my drums to pivot out of the way, but I'm not swift enough. Hisashi's drumblade hits my two front-left drums and slices clean through the kelp-leather skin atop them.

As Hisashi, Suki, and Suki's battleband mates swim back to their drumblades bobbing on the water, Doi begins to drum toward me. I shout, "No, keep going! I'm all right! Don't let it go off course!"

I lift the flaps where the blade ripped through my drum skins. So all I have now on the left side is the back drum. I'll have speed, but not precision. How am I going to be able to line up the final frequency force shot so that it goes directly between the two Shinian ships?

Someone else should take the shot.

But we only get one try. One try, on which the fate of three million people depends.

It's too great a failure to ask someone else to risk. As captain, it's my responsibility to bear.

The dislodged battleband mates get back on their drumblades and the six of us speed forth, catching up with the coiling water dragon, and with coordinated leap after leap like rolls on a drum, we prod and thrust it back on course.

Seven minutes before sunset.

We explode forth in a storm of drumming and blast toward the ships.

Six minutes before sunset. The ships are twenty li away.

The thunder of drumming sends us charging forth like a stampede of enraged horses.

Five minutes before sunset.

We're going to get there in time. With time to spare to find the right chord to play.

Lucky minutes.

With a final burst of speed, we strike and hammer with all our might on our back drums and hurtle toward the Shinian ships.

Five li away, the ships loom before us, their masts as tall as the coiling water dragon, sails ready to receive the wind.

I unsling the giant *shamisen* from my back. I place my fingers on the metal strings for the notes *he*, *yi*, and *che*, the most basic chord, and strum as hard as I can with the pick. A blast of sound shoots forward into the coiling water dragon before us.

Nothing.

The impact of playing the chord destabilizes my damaged drumblade, and I wobble dangerously.

Lucky li away from the ships.

I place my fingers on the strings to play the notes for *shang*, *gong*, and *liu* and rake the pick over them.

The sound bursts forth and strikes the coiling water dragon. It wobbles, then regains its center of gravity.

Three li away.

I play chord after chord.

Two li away.

Nothing.

Three minutes left before sunset.

Peasprout, you brought this on yourself.

As leader, you made decisions that no one wanted to make.

But you also made decisions that no one wanted you to make for them.

You should not have decided for Crick whether this endeavor was worth the risk to his safety.

You should have—

Something careens in front of my view, then steers alongside me.

Crick. On his drumblade.

Half his face is smeared with the blood pouring from his nose, the red swept back in streaks along his cheeks, ears, and neck by the wind from his pursuit of us.

He looks as if he's going to faint.

I make to toss the *shamisen* toward him, but he weakly shakes his head.

Crick looks at the form and motion of the coiling water dragon before us as it races toward the Shinian ships. He lifts one hand in the air and gestures with his fingers in a tortured position.

A five-fingered chord. Formed of the notes *he, yi, che, fan, wu.*

One li away.

Two minutes before sunset.

I stretch my fingers out to form the strange, unprecedented chord. I slash the pick down across the metal strings of the *shamisen.*

A ferocious wave of sound roars from the instrument in my hands.

It flies over the water and blasts into the coiling water dragon.

The coiling water dragon shoots forward between the two Shinian ships with such speed that the vacuum makes my ears pop.

As it passes between the two ships, it veers closer to the ship on the right, stripping planks off it as it goes, shredding its sails, and snapping its mast.

It sends the ship on the left spinning in place, then drags it along, filling its sails, serving as the wind it was waiting for.

Sending it westward.

Back toward Shin.

I turn away from watching the coiling water dragon driving far off into the distance. I frantically scan the sea behind me and spot Crick in time to see him close his eyes, sway, and slide off his drum-blade into the water.

The bottom lip of the amber sun touches the line of the water on the horizon.

With what sounds like a sigh and then a howl, the winds of the Western Belch rise and sweep us into the churning water.

CHAPTER
THIRTY-EIGHT

I wake to find that I am lying on a futon that is not my own. When did I lose consciousness? Did the Western Belch drag me under and nearly drown me? I slip on my skates and burst out of this room into the corridor.

I'm in the Hall of Benevolent Healing. Down the corridor, sitting on a bench, I find Doi and Hisashi looking completely unharmed.

"Where's Crick?" I snap at them.

"Doctor Dio won't let anyone in to see him yet," says Doi.

"I have to see him," I demand.

"She said you'll be the first to see him as soon as she's done," she answers.

"Where's this Wu Yinmei?" I seethe, looking at Hisashi.

He says, "In the suite at the northern end of the hall." He avoids my gaze. His face is the color of bones. He was the one who vouched for Yinmei's character.

"What did you know about her plan?" I bark at him. "Because you knew something. And by knowing something, you played some part in harming Crick."

When Hisashi says nothing, I turn to Doi.

"And you," I say. "You made me spare her. You made me doubt my own instincts as much as your brother did. You, too, played some part in bringing the harm that has come to Crick."

Doi also says nothing, only reaches into her pocket. She takes something out and flings it all the way across the hall so that it bounces among the walls.

The second button. That she was going to give to the girl she loved.

"Peasprout," says Hisashi. "I don't blame you for being furious with me. But before you go in there, there's something that you have a right to know. The coiling water dragon disabled the ship with Yinmei on it. However, Doi and I caught Yinmei and forced her to tell us the truth. The truth is that she gave a letter orb to the other Shinian ship that got away. In it, she told the secret of the salt and how to use it to destroy the pearl."

Doi adds, "But the senseis don't know that. They think the Shinian soldiers abducted Yinmei. Captain Cao and all the other captured soldiers confirmed that. The senseis think Yinmei was a victim. They know nothing about the leaking of the secret of the salt."

So we're in as much danger now as ever. More so. The Empress Dowager will be coming for us.

"Peasprout," says Doi in a hush. "We have to warn the senseis that Shin has the secret to destroy our city. But if we tell the senseis that Yinmei sent back the secret of the salt, she will almost certainly be killed as a foreign spy and threat to Pearl."

Hisashi says, "We don't know what to do."

They both look at me with round, pleading eyes.

I'm so tired of difficult decisions. I never asked for them.

I say, "Leave me alone. I need to go see Crick."

I sit alone outside the chamber where I am told he is being held. I wait and I wait, and at last, Doctor Dio comes out of the chamber in which Crick rests.

I bolt up from my seat.

"Can I see him?"

Instead of promising gloom and death, she says softly, "Hush. He's asleep. Go to your dormitory. I'll send for you when he awakes."

"Is he going to be all right?"

"You are the sister?"

"Yes."

Doctor Dio says, with a new gentleness that chills me, "His heart is too small. You might want to send for your parents immediately."

As she skates away, I silently repeat to the closed door behind which lies my brother, *Your heart is not too small, Crick. Your heart is not too small.*

This is all Yinmei's fault. And I'm going to make her pay. I skate to the suite of chambers where Yinmei is recovering.

When she sees me enter, Yinmei pushes up from her drumchair and stands. She asks in Shinian, "How is Crick?"

"Don't you dare ask after him!" I hiss at her. "He trusted you. He stood up for you. He was your friend. We all were. We let you into our battleband. We let you into our hearts. And you broke our battleband, and you broke our hearts!"

"What I did broke my own heart, too."

"Oh, enough of your startling mystic viewpoints. I protected you, even when you knew about the forcedrums and the pearlstarch and the drumblades and the magnetizing of the sea and the coiling water dragons. But now, you've harmed my little brother.

"I'm going to tell the senseis that you know about the secret of the salt and that you sent that back on the ship to the Empress Dowager. You've put all of Pearl in danger. But you've put yourself in even more danger. Because you betrayed us, but you failed to get away. And now you're going to pay."

I turn to race out of her chambers.

"Wait!" she calls out. "You deserve some answers, Chen Peasprout."

I know I shouldn't, but I stop. "Yes, I do deserve answers."

"You are the lock, and I am the key," she says.

"You're admitting you're the spy of the Empress Dowager?" I ask.

"No, I am not."

I turn to leave.

"Peasprout, I'm telling you the truth."

I turn back to her and say, "Then who are you? Are you even really the great-great-granddaughter of the Empress Dowager?"

"No, I am not."

I don't want them to, but the tears finally come. In all the change and uncertainty and fear of the past year, the thing that has perhaps wounded me most was how everyone made me doubt myself.

My instincts were true. I was right all along. I didn't imagine an enemy. I wasn't an untrusting person. I wasn't becoming Suki.

"Who are you?" I ask.

"I am not the spy of the Empress Dowager," she says.

She lowers her chin but keeps her eyes on mine.

"I am not the great-great-granddaughter of the Empress Dowager."

She sits down on her drumchair.

"I *am* the Empress Dowager."

CHAPTER

"**S**orcery!" I cry, scrambling back. "So the rumors were true! You're one hundred and six years old. You can't die—you can't even age!"

"Sorcery is as real as dragons are," Yinmei sighs.

"Tell me the truth. How old are you?"

"Fifteen. The same as you."

"Then how can you be the Empress Dowager? The Emperor died eighty-eight years ago."

Yinmei replies, "After the Emperor died, his first wife ruled as Empress Dowager. She perpetually delayed the appointing of a male heir. She worked to change the laws governing girls and women, to outlaw foot-binding, to allow for female inheritance, to gain approval from the Great Council of Holy Men to appoint a female heir. The Empress Dowager failed."

"I thought you said you're the Empress Dowager." Is this some imperial custom for the Empress Dowager to refer to her royal person as if talking about someone else?

"I am," she replies. "Listen, Chen Peasprout. When the Empress Dowager herself finally died, a secret council of court women hid her death. They installed one of their own to imposture as the Empress Dowager and continue to rule in her place. For all these years, a succession of women has impostured as the Empress Dowager, one after another, while trying to change the laws governing girls' and women's rights, forming a secret female dynasty within the dynasty. I am simply the latest female to continue this invisible chain."

The dynasty in the dynasty.

I look at this delicate fifteen-year-old girl sitting here before me. She is not just a girl. She is simply the girl at the end of a line that has stretched before her for eighty-eight years.

I say, "So the prior Empress Dowager offered you the bitter tea to invite you to join her secret female dynasty, during the Four-Day Feast. And you refused her and she was so impressed that she appointed you anyway. So you truly *are* her great-great-granddaughter."

"No. There was a great-great-granddaughter. But I am somebody else."

"What happened to her?"

Yinmei pauses, and I can feel her suppress a toss of emotion in her Chi. At last, she says, "She refused the bitter tea."

"So the Empress Dowager killed her."

"Our work on behalf of the girls and women of Shin . . . has been costly."

"So who are you? Are you even related to the original Empress Dowager?"

"Yes but of more remote lineage. And raised in secret in the inner chambers of the palace, like all the potential candidates to join the dynasty in the dynasty. Unlike the great-great-granddaughter, I did take the bitter tea."

"And it wasn't poisoned."

"No."

"Why did the Empress Dowager secretly feed you ivory yang salts even after you obeyed her?"

"She wanted to make sure that I would never lose courage and try to run away. Her great-great-granddaughter's refusal to obey affected her deeply."

"So she made sure you'd never walk again. That's almost as bad as binding your feet."

"As I said, our work has been costly."

My Chi shudders with revulsion at her acceptance of this. "You are ruthless. All of you. You wouldn't hesitate to sacrifice Pearl."

I turn to skate out. I have to tell the senseis that she shared the secret of the salt with Shin.

"Peasprout, wait!" I hear a rustle and turn to see her rising from her drumchair. She takes a step onto the pearl.

"What are you doing?"

"Don't go. Or I will follow you."

"You can't just make threats like that."

I start to turn from her but hear her shoe set down as she takes another step.

I shout, "What are you doing?"

"I am besieging the cloister of Xie to rescue the kingdom of Wo."

"I'm not going to play that g—"

Before I can finish, she has taken two more steps.

"Have you lost your sense?" I cry. "Why are you doing this?"

"I'm rescuing eighty million women and girls."

"Don't move." If she takes one more step today, her heart and lungs will grow as much as they would in a full year. I push her drumchair behind her.

"Sit!" I say.

"Only if you stay and listen to me."

"You are so extreme. All right. Talk."

She takes a shaky breath, sits in her drumchair, and continues, "We have done all of this in order to maintain this imposture for eighty-eight years."

"How did you hide the truth from the Great Council of Holy Men?"

"It is an offense punishable by death for anyone to gaze upon the face of the Empress Dowager after she takes the veil of a widow. The Great Council of Holy Men declared that the next person to see the face of the widow of an Emperor must be the Emperor himself in heaven. They say it will bring misfortune on the realm if anyone else sees her face. I believe it is simply that powerful men do not like the idea of anyone looking at their wives after they die."

"So you used the Great Council of Holy Men's own prejudices against them."

"Yes. However, we cannot continue the imposture. The rumors of my using sorcery to extend my life have caused the Great Council of Holy Men to issue an edict that they will no longer await for me to appoint a male heir, and they are going to identify the Emperor's reincarnated self as the heir. If I want to change the law so that it permits female succession, I have to bring Shin an unprecedented treasure. That is why I need to discover the secret of the pearl, to build Shin a Pearl City of its own."

My head is reeling with this information. I don't know how to tell her that because of my testimony to the senseis, Pearl is going to send an expedition of exorcists to incite the Great Council of Holy Men to declare her a sorceress and burn her.

Yinmei says, "And then you entered my story." My Chi freezes down my backbone. Can she read minds?

"How did I enter your story?"

"Last year, I received a letter orb from my Peony-Level Brightstar, whom I sent to Pearl as a cultural emissary in a goodwill exchange for the New Deitsu skaters that I wanted as hostages. She urged me to step inside this pavilion that this third skater brought from Pearl. She told me that sleeping inside it would produce a Bai Lou Meng, an oracle that would reveal any secret I wished. I had no idea that my own Brightstar would betray me."

So Hisashi's plan did work after all. My letter orb in fact did exactly what it was intended to do.

"When I stepped inside it, Hisashi sealed the door. He threatened to let the pavilion shrink until I was crushed into a trinket unless I granted him and the remaining New Deitsu skater safe passage back to Pearl. When I realized that I had been tricked by my own Brightstar, I wanted to learn more about this Chen Peasprout. If the Pearlian authorities and New Deitsu refused to share the secret of the pearl, perhaps this girl who tricked an Empress Dowager would have the cleverness to discover it for me."

I feel as if a hand has reached out toward me from behind a curtain deep in the imperial palace.

"You see, Peasprout? *You* are why I came to Pearl."

The import of her words staggers me.

Two girls from Shin. Playing with the destinies of tens of millions.

And despite all my honorable intentions, circumstances conspired like in a cautionary fable, and my attempts to protect Pearl from its greatest enemy brought that enemy here.

I say, "So Hisashi has known all this time that you weren't the Empress Dowager's great-great-granddaughter."

"I told him that I was forced to join this secret female dynasty. That once the role of Empress Dowager was offered to me, I could not refuse it or I would be killed. I told him that if I were discovered by the Great Council of Holy Men, I would be killed for defrauding the realm. All of this was true. I begged him to help me escape to Pearl and plead for sanctuary here."

"But you didn't tell him that the real reason you came here was to find the secret of the pearl."

"Of course not."

"Did you tell him that you ordered Zan Kenji's feet to be bound when we wouldn't give you the secret of the pearl?"

"That was the idea of the other women in the dynasty in the dynasty who advised me."

"But you approved the order."

"A leader makes decisions that no one wants to make. I know that you understand that, Peasprout."

I gaze at this girl who willingly let herself be injured and willingly let this innocent, talented skater be injured. Who probably would sacrifice me, too, if necessary.

Rage erupts out of me and I shout at her, "Did you also send the Shinian soldiers to try to abduct me and shoot me full of arrows? Was that whole incident just a stunt to make me trust you?" I don't know which part of that I'm more upset by: that she tried to have me abducted or that her friendship was a lie.

"No. I arranged to have the Shinian ships come and wait offshore. I did not order that attack. Something is happening back in Shin. The other women who advised me in the dynasty in the dynasty approved of my mission to come here. But now, they are making movements without me. Which is why it is urgent that I complete my mission."

So Chingu's oracle was correct. Yinmei came here on "official business."

Pearl's greatest enemy came here to steal our most precious secret.

But she failed.

And now Pearl holds its greatest enemy in its hands.

I say to her, "Your ship might be racing back to Shin with the secret of the salt. The other women of the dynasty in the dynasty might mount an invasion and threaten to end the city of Pearl." I lean my face to hers.

"But we've got their Empress Dowager. And we've got the secret of all their Empresses Dowager. They can make our city melt into the sea. But we can make them *burn*."

I turn and skate from her.

"Peasprout, wait!"

I ignore her and begin to slide open the shoji door to exit.

I hear the pad of a shoe behind me.

She's taken a fifth step in one day! I listen for the cries of pain but hear nothing. I can't let her win this way. I refuse to turn around. I continue to slide open the shoji door.

Pad, pad, pad.

Heavenly August Personage of Jade, she's going to make her heart and lungs burst in her chest! She must be wracked with pain, yet still she makes no noise. I want to turn to her but I can't submit to her ruthlessness, even when that ruthlessness is directed at herself.

Pad, pad, pad, pad, pad, pad—

"Stop it, you fool!" I say, whipping around to face her.

Her fists clutch her chest, her eyes are squeezed shut, her trembling lips press against each other, her face is wrenched in a silent grimace of pain. Her whole body spasms with each step that tears new rips in her heart and lungs.

I race to her. She crumples in my arms and collapses onto the pearl beneath us. I bring her drumchair to her, and haul her up onto it.

"I'm going to get Dr. Dio!"

"No!" she commands with more force than I thought she could summon in her state. "Close the door."

I slide the shoji door closed.

"You fool, you fool," I hiss at her as I crouch down to place my hand on her forehead. Throbs of pain pulse in her Chi under my hand. Tears of hurt, rage, and frustration fill my eyes against my will.

I watch her face contort in pain as she gulps for air. Every time I think she's beginning to settle down, her body shudders again with new spasms of pain.

At last, she seems to drift into a fevered sleep. I feel her Chi begin to quiet at last. How much damage has she done to herself? How many rips has she made in her heart, to prevent me from telling her secret?

Who is this fearsome, fearless, frightening girl? Is this what leadership looks like?

I cup my face with my hands, close my eyes, and hide in the darkness there. *If this is leadership, I don't want it. I never asked for this.*

When I lower my hands from my face and lift my eyes, she's awake and looking at me.

Yinmei says, "And this is where you take over the lead role in my story."

"What do you mean?"

"Chen Peasprout. I, Wu Yinmei, Empress Dowager of the Imperium of Shin, offer to adopt you as my heir if you will keep my secret, help me escape back to Shin, and help bring to Shin the secret of the pearl. With your help, we can build Shin its own pearl city, satisfying the Great Council of Holy Men's quest. We will change the laws. We will change the destinies of the next eighty million girls in Shin."

"I love Pearl. I'm not going to help end it."

"I love Pearl, too. More than you know. But the place we love is going to end, either way. Let it be in peaceful cooperation rather than with loss and destruction."

"No."

"You have a big heart, Peasprout. But consider other things. Your parents. You were abandoned due to the harsh justice of a law that I enacted."

"What do you know about that?"

"If you are Empress Dowager, you will be able to locate them and grant them an imperial pardon. You can at long last apologize to them for telling them to go away. You can thank them for not binding your feet and for giving you all of this."

She gestures with her hand in a full circle, taking in the whole of the academy and the city of Pearl beyond it.

"Or," she continues, "you can drown with everyone else in futile defiance. But we must decide now. Before the other powers in the dynasty in the dynasty make decisions for us. We do not let others make our decisions for us, Chen Peasprout. Not you. Not I."

And so here it is. Chingu's last oracle.

What will I discover this Wu Yinmei's plans to be with regard to me?

When Chingu sang out her oracle, she said "accomplice," then "casualty." Then she flipped back and forth between the two.

Which destiny will I choose?

Yinmei rises from her drumchair. She stands before me, lifts her head, and sings,

" 'Will you take the bitter tea

" 'Of the dynasty in the dynasty?

" 'For your sake, commit to me

" 'And the dynasty in the dynasty.

" 'Will you join us? Will you Empress Peasprout be?' "

THE PEARLIAN BOOKSONG

(to the tune of "The Pearlian Battlesong")

Thank you to Tiff Liao,
Carol Ly, Tom Nau,
Hayley Jozwiak, Robert Allen, Laura Wilson,
Rich Green, Afu Chan.
Thank you to my band!

Thank you, Jean Feiwel,
Idina Menzel,
Roxane Edouard, Lauren Festa, Mark Podesta,
Kayla Overbey.
Thanks for backing me!

Erica Ferguson,
Samantha Edelson,
Patrick Collins, Mark von Bargen, Brisa Robinson.
Tom Mis, Nancy Wu.
Thank you, all of you!

Elisabeth Alba,
Pier Nirandara,
Christian Trimmer, Jennifers Gonzales and Edwards,
Mary Beth Roche, Brittany Pearlman, Jessica Brigman,
Tamara Kawar, and Queen of Awe Tina Dubois,
Skate by skate we stand.
Thank you to my band!

Thank you to, thank you to my band!
Thank you to, thank you to my band!
Thank you to, thank you to my band!
Thank you to my band!